THE
NANNY
MURDERS

MERRY JONES

THOMAS DUNNE BOOKS
ST. MARTIN'S PRESS
NEW YORK

The Nanny Murders *is a work of fiction; any resemblance between its characters and real people, living or dead, is purely coincidental.*

THOMAS DUNNE BOOKS.
An imprint of St. Martin's Press.

www.stmartins.com

ISBN 0-312-33038-3
EAN 978-0312-33038-5

First Edition: May 2005

10 9 8 7 6 5 4 3 2 1

To Robin

ACKNOWLEDGMENTS

Deep and lasting gratitude to Liza Dawson, my agent, and to Thomas Dunne, Marcia Markland, and Diana Szu at Thomas Dunne Books. They are my heroes, and I have been lucky to work with them.

Thanks also to Emily Heckman for her invaluable insights and guidance; my mom, Judy Bloch, for her consistent and avid support; my sister Janet Martin for her sound advice; Larry Stains for steering me to Liza; Lanie Zera for her in-depth analyses and spiritual vitamins; Nancy Delman, Jane Braun, Susie Francke, Gina Joseph, Leslie Mogul, and Jan and Michael Molinaro for their years-long encouragement; Bob Sexton for the pencils; Patty and Michael Glick for the pen; Ileana Stevens for that long-ago conversation on the beach; our Corgi, Sam, for his uncritical calming companionship while I wrote.

Boundless appreciation to my daughters, Baille and Neely, for their unfailing confidence and cooperation.

Thanks to my husband, Robin, for his repeated readings, honest input, enduring patience, persevering faith, and unflagging determination, even when he was so severely ill.

Thanks to a few who are dearly missed: my friend Susan Stone; my brother, Aaron Bloch, and my dad, Herman S. Bloch, who remain close by despite death and the passage of time.

ONE

SMALL FOOTPRINTS LED DOWN THE STEPS TO THE SIDEWALK where Molly played in the snow.

I sat on the front porch, absorbing a stray beam of late afternoon sun while my almost six-year-old daughter delighted in two inches of what would soon become puddles of sodden gray slush. I was tired from a daylong monthly staff meeting and craved some peace. A few houses down, a workman started up his chain saw.

Our neighborhood, Queen Village, was caught in an endless process of renovation and gentrification. We were sandwiched between South Philadelphia with its traditional ethnic households and Society Hill with its fancy colonial landmarks. Dowdy old row houses sagged beside gleaming restorations. The neighborhood was home to both rich and poor, the upwardly mobile and the newly disenfranchised. The area was struggling for respectability, but despite the disruption of continuous construction, it was unclear whether it would get there.

Watching Molly play beside parked cars and grimy gutters, I imagined living in some shiny suburb on the Main Line— Gladwyne, maybe, or Rosemont or Bryn Mawr. Someplace where trees, not trash, lined the streets; where kids played on grass, not asphalt.

I often thought of moving. But I still hadn't left. Despite my complaints, I thrived on the city's energy, its sounds and faces, its moving parts. I wasn't sure how long I'd hold out, but I'd worked hard to make us a home here, and so far I'd refused to give it up.

"Mom," Molly called, "what if my tooth comes out and falls in the snow?"

"It's not ready to come out yet."

"Are you sure?"

"Positive."

"Because we'd never find it. Everything's white."

"It won't come out today."

She was quiet again, working the snow.

"Mom," she called moments later, "it's not enough. I need more."

She knelt near the curb, gathering handfuls of snow in her mittens, packing them into a lump.

I came down the steps and stooped beside her. "What's the problem?"

"I need more snow." She stared hopelessly at the tiny mound.

I reached into my pockets and found an old phone bill. "Try this." I scraped snow with the envelope, making it a paper snowplow.

"Okay." She grabbed the envelope and plowed away. I wandered back up to the wrought-iron chair on the porch, leaned my head back against the wall, and closed my eyes.

"Mom, guess what I'm making?"

"What?"

"Guess."

She wasn't going to let me rest. "A snowman?"

"Nope."

"I give up."

"No, guess again."

She won't always be five years old, I told myself. You can rest when she's in college. "Hmm. A sneaker."

"Uh-uh."

"The letter Q?"

"No."

"W?"

"Nope. Don't be silly. It's not any letter."

"Then it must be a washing machine."

"Stop being silly, Mom."

I opened my eyes. Dozing wasn't going to happen. Molly kept plowing, patting, building. "Well?"

"Give me time. I'm thinking." I stretched the pause, savoring it. Across the street, the blinds went up in Victor's second-floor window. I watched, hoping to catch a glimpse of him. Victor was phobic. To my knowledge, he hadn't left his house in years. I didn't know why, although local lore was rife with explanations. One rumor held that Victor's mother had died in the house and he hadn't left since; another that a fortune-teller had warned him he'd meet a violent end next time he stepped onto the street. Despite the stories, I suspected that Victor's real problems were locked inside the house with him, in his own head. Apparently, he had money to live on; groceries, laundry, pizza, and parcels arrived at his door regularly. Once in a while, Molly and I left him baskets of muffins or cookies; the food disappeared, but we rarely saw Victor. Now, pale hands taped a cardboard snowman to the glass. The blinds went down again. Hands, but no face. This wouldn't count, then, as an actual Victor sighting.

Even unseen, Victor was one of the only neighbors I knew. Victor and old Charlie, Victor's next-door neighbor. Charlie was the handyman for the remodeled townhouses across the street. Somebody new had moved into the house on the other side of Charlie. I hadn't met him yet, but I'd become well acquainted with the huge electric Santa and reindeer that flashed on and off, day and night, from his first-floor window like the sign at an all-night diner. Every blink announced that Christmas was coming and that I wasn't ready, hadn't gotten organized, didn't even have our tree. Or presents or baking ingredients or decorations.

"Mom?"

Oh. Molly was still waiting for my guess. "Okay—I bet I have it. It's a song."

"A song?" She turned to look at me. "You're teasing. You can't make a song out of snow."

"You mean it's not a song? Then I give up."

"Okay. I'll tell you. She's a snowbaby. A little iddy biddy one." She busied herself gathering and shaping snow, narrating her process. "And her name's going to be Kelly. No. Emma . . ." She jabbered on, accompanied by the chain saw. I let my head rest against the bricks, my eyelids float down, my mind drift.

"Eww. Yuck."

Eww, yuck? I didn't want to get up again. I didn't even want to open my eyes. The sun felt so gentle and soothing. A warm caress. "Molly. Remember, don't touch stuff you find in the street. Leave it alone. Okay?"

Silence. Damn. What relic of city life had she found now? I always worried about debris she might encounter on the sidewalk. Broken Budweiser bottles, used needles. Discarded underwear. Used condoms. "Molly? What are you doing?"

She was fixated on it, whatever it was; her monologue had stopped. I opened an eye and watched her dig, retrieving something from the snow.

"Molly, don't pick up stuff from the street." How many times a day did I have to repeat that? Ignoring me, she closed her hand around it and lifted the thing.

"You're not listening to me. Okay. Time to go in."

She didn't move. She held on to whatever it was and stared.

The gravel eyes of a snowbaby followed me as I came down the front steps.

"Molly. Drop it."

Silently, she let it go, and it landed on the snowy sidewalk with a tiny frozen thud. I looked down. At first, I thought it was a stick. Then I saw the red part. Damn. What had she picked up? A hunk of rotting meat? A half-eaten hot dog?

"Molly. Answer me. Are you allowed to touch stuff from the street?"

She looked up with wide, baffled eyes. "No."

Taking her by the wrist, I glanced once more at the thing on the ground. It lay at our feet, filthy, bright red at one end, its form gradually taking definition. I blinked at it a few times. Then, holding on to Molly, I fled with knees of jelly, in slow motion, up the steps.

Under the grime, there was no mistaking what it was, even though the nail was broken and the crimson polish chipped.

TWO

"ZOE, WHAT DO YOU EXPECT? THAT'S WHAT HAPPENS WHEN kids play on the street."

Susan set the measuring cup on the counter and pushed a lock of hair out of her eyes. Susan Cummings was my best friend. As soon as the police left, Molly and I had rushed to her house, and I'd just finished telling her what had happened.

Susan's house felt safe. Located about ten blocks from us on Pine Street, it was a solid 150-year-old brick building with twelve-foot-high ceilings, framed arched doorways, cut glass windows, and polished hardwood floors. It was full of fireplaces, cushioned furnishings, and cinnamon smells. Susan's neighborhood, near Rittenhouse Square, was a picture of prosperity and stability. Neighbors with Gucci shoes popped over for a glass of pinot noir or homemade biscotti. In summers, they organized block parties; in winters, they gathered for eggnog and Christmas gifts. The street was pristine, wreathed for the holidays and safe to walk, even at night.

My neighborhood, on the other hand, managed to remain rough-edged and unruly. In the mornings, nannies pushed lace-lined prams down sidewalks where drunks had relieved themselves hours before. Crime was common; cars and homes were broken into, muggings were not unheard of, and recently a couple of young women had simply disappeared. Susan and I lived in homes just a mile apart but somehow on different planets, and I ran to Susan's whenever I needed to escape mine.

While we talked, Susan was busy baking, gathering ingredients for crust. "Which detective did you talk to?"

I saw him again, standing on our front stoop. Behind him, two uniformed men crawled on the curb, sifting through street soot and gutter slush. "Ms. Hayes?" he'd asked. "Detective Nick Stiles." He'd flashed his badge.

"Stiles?" Susan repeated. "Young guy?"

At the time, I hadn't considered his age. Now, trying to estimate, I recalled my first impression of the detective at my door. He'd checked the spelling of my name, Z-O-E, H-as-in-Harry-A-Y-E-S, assessing me quickly, up and down. I'd felt his eyes register each inch of a taller than average, still slender woman with strands of gray streaking her long hair, lingering a bit too long on the full lips and smallish but nice breasts. I bristled at the memory but stayed with it long enough to pull out the image of his face. Yes, there it was, with pale blue eyes that were a tad too intense. A well-defined jaw. A scar near the cheekbone. Sandy hair flecked with gray. A strong face that wasn't quite symmetrical.

"Not really. Forty. Forty-five at most. Our age."

"Hmmm. I don't know him. I'll ask around." She gulped some tea. "What did he ask you? What did you tell him?"

What did I tell him? What did he ask me? Why was the telling of this afternoon's events so difficult? Why was I so flustered and incoherent? Susan waited, wanting to hear what happened. But she was acting as my friend, not interrogating me as a criminal attorney; she was measuring shortening for a pie, not weighing evidence for a case. I wasn't under oath. I could relax.

So my mind plowed through the detective's visit, scanning for highlights. I heard myself tell him that I was forty-one years old, had lived in the house for thirteen years. That, no, I wasn't married; Michael and I had divorced about five years ago. That I lived alone with my daughter, Molly, who was five and a half. I could skip all that. And I could skip the expression on Stiles's face as he did the math. And the part when I'd blurted out that I'd adopted Molly after Michael had gone.

"Well?" she looked up without breaking her pace. The events of my day didn't slow her down. Susan mixed flour and shortening, pounded out the dough. She was, as usual, spinning in her kitchen, spilling this and that, slapping ingredients together, creating chaos that would transform, magically, into something delectable.

I reached for my coffee mug, and my arm brought to mind another arm. Stiles's. His large hand had emerged from a dark woolen sleeve, his arm lifting gingerly, picking up the thing with a tweezer-like appliance and dropping it into a Baggie. Again I heard the small, plastic thud and saw Stiles's brow wrinkle. Yes, this was it, the answer Susan wanted. The part where Stiles talked about the missing women.

"He asked about the nannies? What did he say?" She straightened and looked at me, shaking her hair out of her eyes.

"He asked if I knew them. What I'd heard about them."

"And?"

"And nothing. I guess he thinks it might belong to one of them." I squeezed the mug, inhaled steam, and concentrated on the kitchen, the smell of cinnamon, the energy pulsing around me.

Susan's kitchen, unlike mine, was huge and alive. Mine was closet-sized, a detail off the entranceway, usually littered with takeout cartons and pizza boxes. I couldn't stand the messy monotony of preparing meals and never made anything that took more than fifteen minutes. For Molly, I fixed eggs, grilled cheese, an occasional lamb chop, a hundred variations of pasta. But Susan actually cooked. Thoughtlessly, effortlessly, as a way of life, a technique for stress reduction, a ritual of being. Even now, while we discussed dismemberment, she rolled out piecrust on her thick butcher-block island. I sat close, huddling under flour clouds.

From time to time, Susan's children wandered in with Molly, circling, swiping sugared apple slices, and scooting into the next room to plop in front of the blaring large-screen TV. Spigots turned on and off. The refrigerator hummed.

I watched Susan stretch piecrust and splash flour, performing her dizzying domestic dance. I envied her ability to bake biscuits while dictating legal briefs, change diapers while phoning an opposing counsel, interview caterers and murderers within the same hour. Susan's moods fluctuated, and she never completely focused on one thing or settled in one place, but meals made it to her table on time, and her hair always shone. Whenever an aspect of life overwhelmed me, I found myself drawn to her. Today, I needed her. I needed to feel her energy build, erupt, and settle onto dinner plates.

But at that moment, Susan seemed removed, even annoyed. I waited. She said nothing, threw more flour at the dough.

"Well," I finally said. "Don't you have anything else to say?"

"What's to say, Zoe? What should I say?"

"What do you mean, what's to say? I've just had a completely horrible, bizarre day."

"Oh, Zoe," she snapped. "For godsakes. Your day was not all that bizarre. From where I sit, finding a finger on your front porch is pretty standard stuff."

"Right, Susan. It happens every day. Comes with the daily paper."

She didn't answer.

"How can you say that?" I kept at her. "Your idea of 'standard stuff' is pretty warped."

She squinted, still silent, still rolling.

"Well, it is," I persisted. "Not that it's your fault. You spend every day with the scum of the earth, with crime and criminals. Your work's affected your thinking."

She shrugged. "On the other hand, maybe my work shows me how normal this is. I see stuff like this all the time. And worse."

"Really? Well, if it's so normal, how would you feel if it was your child?" My voice was rising. "What if Emily brought home some detached body part?"

She looked up at me and blinked condescendingly. "I'm not saying it's normal. But it happens. It wouldn't faze me."

"It wouldn't faze you? If Emily walked in holding somebody's finger?"

"I don't think it—"

"—or nose—"

"—would. No."

"—or an ear? Or penis? How about a nipple? Would a nipple faze you?"

"Okay, I'd be upset. But I wouldn't be fazed."

I sipped some tea. "You've been in your job too long."

"Maybe so." She put down her rolling pin, set her jaw, and brushed her forehead with the back of her hand, leaving a trail of flour. We faced each other in charged silence, each wanting validation from the other, each unable or unwilling at the moment to validate.

My eyes burned, head ached. I stared at her folded hands, the emerald rings crusted with dough, the floured manicure.

"Look, Zoe." She pushed flour-streaked hair behind her ear.

"You know I love you. But for all your brilliance and creativity, you can be really clueless."

"Meaning?"

"Meaning that you completely deny the parts of reality that you don't like. For years—since your divorce, you've lived in your little bubble where everything is just as you want it to be. Gentle and fluffy and nurturing. And now, when reality shatters your illusion, you get upset. The truth is that people do cruel and horrible things. There are six homicides in Philadelphia every single week. Not to mention the rapes, robberies, and assaults. But that's not new. What's new is that you've noticed it. You've finally looked beyond your bubble and seen what's been there all along. Welcome to the world." She pressed dough into the tin, punctuating her words.

I closed my eyes. What could I say? I had no defense. There was a lot of truth in what she'd said. I did try to protect myself and my daughter from the ugly parts of life. Was that so wrong? Once again, I saw Detective Stiles pick up the finger and drop it into the Baggie. Thwap. I opened my eyes. Susan dumped the bowl of apples into the tin and slapped the rest of the dough on top.

"Sorry," she barked. "I don't mean to sound harsh, but that's how I see it."

I watched her cut off the extra crust and squeeze the excess into her fist. She moved abruptly, without tenderness. Susan was ferocious. Not her usual self.

"So," I asked, "what's wrong?"

"Who said anything was wrong?" she snapped. Then she relaxed, lowering her shoulders. "I'm sorry, Zoe. Everything's wrong. Tim's traveling again, so I'm the only parent again this month. Bonita's got final exams, so she's not sitting regular hours. I'm up to my ears in lunches and laundry and homework and car pools and baths. And a huge caseload—three felony cases. That means three people will go to jail if I mess up." She threw the pie into the oven and slammed the door. I felt a familiar rush of fondness for her.

She sighed, leaning against the stove. "You know, except for Tim, you're the only one who ever does that."

Uh-oh. What had I done? "Does what?"

"Pins me down. Makes me say what's bothering me. Always knows when something's bothering me."

"Well, you're not exactly subtle about it."

"What? I've been completely calm and composed." She yanked a dish towel off the rack.

"Right, Completely. A moment ago, if I'd said another word—another syllable—I'd have been wearing that pie."

She grinned. "No, I never waste my pies. Maybe a bowl of flour, but not a pie." She sighed and sat on a stool. "But you're right. I'm on overload. I'm nuts. Completely bananas." Her eyes wandered to the wall clock. "Speaking of nuts and bananas, it's time for dinner. Staying?"

"As long as it's not finger food," I smiled. "Or hand and cheese."

Susan winced. "No. Today's special is knuckle sandwiches." She handed me a cutting board. "Here, give me a hand."

"Hey, I'm the guest. Guests don't have to lift a finger."

"Yes they do, just not the middle one."

"Oh, cut it out."

"Just chop the damn carrots. Watch your aim."

"Quartered or sliced?"

"And skinned." She threw a tomato at me. "Heads up." Lettuce flew into my arms. Something green—a cucumber?—whizzed past me onto the counter. Scallions and then a green pepper bounced off my shoulder. I dodged, laughing, and caught the endive midair.

"Shut up and cut up." She dropped a knife onto the cutting

board, raised her index fingers, and, waving them, shimmied to
the stove. Manic again.

So I chopped. Being busy felt good. The carrots were not
body parts. Susan and I were making salad and frying flounder,
easing back into the steady rhythm of our friendship.

Susan poured us each a glass of wine. We sipped and talked.
I felt the tension ease out of me. My shoulders felt lighter and
my neck looser. I'd almost completely relaxed by the time Lisa
and Julie thundered in, flushed, shouting, tripping over the dog.

"Mom!"

"Mom! Guess what—"

"Guess who was on the news!"

"Remember Claudia? She sat for us? She's—"

"She's the third one—"

"—missing!"

Susan and I got to the television just as the picture switched
from a young woman's snapshot to the anchor.

". . . five-month-old girl," he said, "was found unharmed at
home, asleep in a laundry basket. Like the other two missing
childcare workers, Claudia Rusk disappeared in broad daylight,
while working. We'll keep you posted as police release further
information. In other news, an Amtrak train—"

Susan snapped off the television. Her face was dark, drained.
"No more TV," she announced.

"But Mom, what happened to Claudia?"

"I don't know. Set the table," Susan breathed. "Zoe and Molly
are staying for dinner."

"She's the third one missing. What's going on? Do you think
she was kidnapped?" Lisa squealed.

"No, stupid," Julie replied. "Why would they kidnap the
babysitter and not the baby?"

"Because of sex, stupid," Lisa shook her head. "You're too
young to understand."

"I am not—"

"That's enough," Susan yelled. "Stop it, both of you. We don't know what happened. There's nothing we can do about it, and it's not our business, so let's just have our dinner in peace. Go set the table."

Muttering, the girls stomped into the kitchen. Susan stared vacantly after them. White knuckled, she held on to her ring finger, twisting her wedding band.

"Susan?" I asked. "Who's Claudia?"

THREE

CLAUDIA RUSK WORKED FOR SUSAN'S NEIGHBOR. SHE WAS A friend of Susan's nanny, Bonita, and had helped Susan on many occasions when Bonita couldn't. Like Bonita, Claudia was a college student at night, earning tuition as a nanny by day. Now, Claudia had disappeared, leaving the neighbor's baby in the laundry room, stuffed in a basket among dirty towels and undershirts. It made no sense. Why would she do that? Where had she gone? Why?

I thought about Claudia as I tucked Molly in. I thought about her as I went downstairs, made myself a cup of tea, and snuggled under an afghan on my overstuffed crimson chair. I thought about her as I laid my head back and closed my eyes. Stop worrying, I told myself. Worrying won't help. There's nothing you can do about Claudia or her disappearance. Still, I couldn't help wondering if, on the day she disappeared, Claudia had been wearing red nail polish.

I took deep breaths. I told myself to center my energy, not to think of the finger, Claudia, or the other missing women. Our doors were locked; Molly and I were secure inside our brownstone. My bubble. It was a good bubble. I'd worked hard to put it together, and it was cozy. I looked around my tiny, cluttered living room. The built-in shelves filled with books and small treasures. My great-grandmother Bella's heavy brass mortar and pestle for grinding flour, and her porcelain soup tureen, now stuffed with dried flowers. On the walls, paintings by people I knew, aspiring artists like I used to be. A huge abstract oil, bold strokes of umber, yellow, and beige. A fat nude. An etching of a farm beneath a crescent moon.

The furniture was sparse and strewn with stuff: one of Molly's many half-finished art projects with her jars of beads and bottles of Elmer's glue, a half-dressed baby doll, a lone red knee sock, a well-worn teddy bear. In the far corner, the Stair-Master gathered dust, sulking and nagging at me. Last year, my New Year's resolution had been to work out. I knew I should, but I hadn't gotten around to it; the machine served primarily to take up space and tug at my conscience.

I adored my heavy purple sofa, the handwoven blankets draping its back, the cabinet I'd painted with funky designs, the chair I'd found at a flea market. Nothing matched. Colors, textures, and shapes had nothing in common except that I liked them. Yet, gathered together, all the pieces seemed to fit. Like odd members of a family, a collection of strays, they made this a home. I sipped my tea, feeling it warm my blood. Gradually, I let myself relax and felt the tension lift and went up to bed.

But I couldn't sleep. I thought about Claudia; then I began to think about our sitter, Angela. She wasn't a college student, not even trained as a professional nanny, but I trusted Angela and relied on her. She was almost a member of the family. She had her own house key. She'd once snaked our toilet. She scolded me about the way I loaded the dishwasher, tried to teach me how to organize my cabinets. Angela knew what went on behind our closed doors, our private stuff.

She stood maybe five feet tall, wore lots of large gold accessories, and blue eye makeup, had long sculpted fingernails, and dyed her hair purplish black. She had a throaty voice and a loud, hoarse laugh. She'd been with her boyfriend, Joe, since high school and planned to marry him. Born and raised in South Philly, second youngest of five kids, she didn't like to leave her neighborhood; Queen Village, a few blocks north, was about as far away as she'd venture. Except for the mall.

I usually smiled when I thought of Angela, the twang of her vowels, her street-smart, in-your-face attitude. Except now, I didn't smile; I worried. Claudia and two other local nannies were missing, and someone had lost a finger. Angela could be in danger. I couldn't bear to think about that; the idea was too awful. Besides, Angela was a babysitter, not, technically, a nanny. I wondered if the kidnapper would make the distinction.

I lay back and watched the darkness, listening to night sounds: wailing sirens, revving engines, screeching brakes, and, whenever I'd begin to doze, the patient flapping of black wings.

I puffed up the pillow. I tossed. I flipped. I looked at the empty pillow next to mine. My ex-husband's ex-pillow. I frowned at it and turned my back. I already had too many scary images in my head; I didn't need to stir up more by revisiting my former marriage. Desperate for diversion, I reached for the remote. Colors flickered. Animated candy bars sang Christmas carols and flew in reindeer-driven sleighs. I changed channels. A green convertible careened around a corner, pursued by police. Click. A talking head with a necktie and an authoritative voice updated the news. I turned him off before he could mention the missing nannies.

Finally, giving up, I got out of bed. Go downstairs and exercise, I told myself. Go work out. You'll get tired. You'll sleep better. You'll feel better about yourself. I thought about it. I imagined turning on the StairMaster and climbing to exhaustion long into the night.

Instead, I went to the window. Occasional cars passed, even

at this bleak hour. Across the street, the electric Santa blinked on and off, bathing the street with alternating beams of light and darkness, darkness and light. Victor's upstairs light was on, a solitary silhouette behind his shades. Apparently, he couldn't sleep, either. Old Charlie was up, too. He was out on his porch, sitting alone in the cold shadows, smoking a pipe.

FOUR

I OVERSLEPT. MISSED THE TRAIN—I'D HAVE TO FIND A CAB. I'D
already kissed Molly good-bye and headed for the door. I was almost gone, and would have been if I hadn't stopped to answer
the phone. Who knows why I did it—Angela would have picked
it up. Maybe it was habit, a trained reaction. Maybe I was like
those lab animals and had a conditioned response. Hear the bell
ring; get the phone. For whatever reason, though, I answered it.

"Hi, Zoe."

Damn. Why hadn't I just kept going?

"Zoe? You there?"

No, I told myself. I'm not. In fact, I'm not even me—I'm the
wrong number. I'm the maid.

"Hi, Michael," I finally said. "What's up?"

Why? I asked myself. Why had I answered the phone? And
why had he called? What did he want now? I had no patience, no
time, no energy for Michael. Not that I was bitter or anything.
Michael and I had parted "amicably"—wasn't that how people
described divorces that didn't involve actual hit men? Our divorce had been that kind of "amicable." In fact, we still spoke
regularly; Michael called every few weeks to ask for something—
a favor, a recipe, a book or CD. Our living room furniture. Our
silver. Of course, maybe this time it would be different. Maybe
he just wanted to hear my voice. Or ask my opinion. Or maybe
he had to tell me something—like that someone had died. But I

doubted it; there weren't many people we both still knew. When we'd divorced, along with the bath towels, we'd split up the friends. We hadn't shared anyone in over five years. So what did he want?

"How are you, Zoe?" His voice was chatty, casual. He talked as if we spoke every day. He droned on, telling me news of his work, his parents, his sister, his new car, and for a moment it seemed as if the corpse of our ten-year marriage had stirred to life. As if Michael were just at the office, calling to see what was for dinner. I fought the dreadful impulse to ask what time he'd be home. What was going on? What did he want? Upstairs, Molly and Angela argued about what Molly would wear. Angela was losing.

"Michael? Look, I'm on my way out. What's up?"

"Oh. Okay, then. I'll call back when you're not busy."

He sounded disappointed. Actually, he sounded desolate. A very unlike-Michael way to sound. And it wasn't like him to back off. Michael never hesitated to ask for anything; he seemed to think I owed him whatever he wanted. So why was he offering to call later? Something was wrong. Did he need money? Or—oh God—was he sick? Dying? Lord. Maybe he needed bone marrow. Or a kidney.

Or a finger.

There it was again. The damned finger kept poking its way into my thoughts. I looked out the kitchen window. Jake, a local contractor, hurried by carrying a large sack and a toolbox, wearing a sleeveless sweatshirt and cutoff jeans. Jake dressed for summer no matter what the weather, and his beefy shoulders and biceps rippled in the morning light. Across the street, Charlie stepped out onto his front stoop, carrying his trash. He looked around, squinting into the frosty sunshine.

"It's just that this is real important, Zoe. I need to ask a big favor."

I swallowed. I wasn't willing to part with an organ. I'd give blood, but that was it.

"Well, not a favor, actually. I've told you about Margaret."

Margaret? Phew. I was off the hook. He didn't need a donor. This was about Margaret, the woman he'd been seeing off and on for a year. Had she dumped him?

"Well, we're going ahead with it. We're tying the knot."

The knot? Marriage? Oh. He was getting married. Well. That explained why he'd been afraid to say what was on his mind. But did I care? No. Of course not. I'd thrown him out. I wasn't in love with him, didn't want him back. Michael's life was his own business. So why was I having trouble following what he was saying? Why was my stomach upside down?

". . . since you don't ever wear it anymore. Besides, it was intended for the woman who is my wife."

"Sorry?"

"That ring's been in my family for two generations, and I want to keep it there. I want it back, Zoe. What do you say?"

What did I say? A reflexive, absolute, irrefutable "Gosh, Michael. I don't know."

"Come on, Zoe. What would you want with it?"

Truth was, nothing. It sat in a velvet box at the back of my sock drawer. I never even looked at it. But Michael had called to get it back. Not to ask for a kidney. Not even to tell me about his upcoming marriage. No, he'd only wanted the ring. Maybe I should give it to him—wait, whoa, I told myself. Just a second. Whether I wore the ring or not wasn't the point. The point was that Michael had to stop asking me for stuff. I always gave in to him, had already given him enough. Too much. Our leather sofa. The Oriental carpet. The dinnerware. The camcorder. The hutch. Now he wanted the ring. Next time it would be—what? My electric toothbrush? The trash compactor? How about my pearl earrings? They'd been his mother's, too. As had my roasting pot. And my eggbeater. Would he want them, too? No, this had to stop. Michael had to detach. He seemed unable to accept that we were divorced and that whatever was mine wasn't necessarily his as well.

I stared at the cement mixer down the street, parked where Michael used to park. Five years ago, I'd asked him to leave. I'd stood at this same kitchen window, watching him load his car and drive off, his taillights fading into the night. When they were out of sight I'd exhaled, finally alone with a half-empty medicine cabinet, a half-empty closet, and my freedom. But I'd kept the engagement ring. Why?

"Mom!" Molly ran into the kitchen. "Look—do you think it'll come out today?" She wiggled her tooth. It clung pretty tightly in place.

I covered the mouthpiece. "Don't think so."

She ran out, then back in. "Do you know where my red sweatpants are?"

Amazingly, I did. "The dryer."

She headed to the laundry, with Angela trying to catch up.

Michael was still talking. "Look, it's not like you'd miss it. You don't wear it anymore, but Margaret would, and she loves antique jewelry. Besides, it belongs with my bride."

So Margaret wanted my ring. Why would someone want her husband's ex-wife's ring? I picked up Molly's cereal bowl and plopped it into the sink, picturing gems hopping from woman to woman, finger to finger.

"What do you say, Zoe?"

"I don't know, Michael—"

"Why?" He was annoyed. "What don't you know? What could you possibly want with that ring? It was my grandmother's, for godsakes."

"Try to understand this: It isn't about the ring. It's about you wanting things all the time. Why I do or don't want the ring—or anything else in my possession—isn't your business." Damn. How had he managed to twist it so that I sounded wrong for not automatically giving him back something he'd given me years ago? Oh Lord. Why had I picked up the phone?

"Zoe, I thought you'd be more reasonable. Please do this for me." He was beginning to whine, a grating sound, like a cat in heat.

"Look, okay. I'll think about it."

He pounced on that as encouragement. "When? I need to know."

His voice was pathetic. It was too easy to be mean to him. And what was the point? There was nothing to win; we were finished.

"I'll let you know."

"Great. I'll call you tonight."

"No, not tonight."

"Zoe. The wedding's on New Year's Day. I'm planning to give it to her for Christmas."

How touching. My ring would make a lovely Christmas gift. Technically, of course, it was not Michael's to give, but a detail like that wouldn't faze him; he just assumed he could have whatever he wanted. My property was his stash, there to dig into anytime.

"Gotta go, Michael." I hung up, fuming.

Michael was so—so Michael. How had I married that man? Had I ever loved him? I wondered. He'd been smart, charming. Cute, in a soft, preppy sort of way. A great kisser. Ambitious, hardworking. But had I loved him? I wasn't sure. More likely, back then, I'd had no sense of who I was. I'd tried to define my-self through him, wrapping myself in his life and career as if they were a snug bathrobe. I'd married not so much to be with Michael as to be married. To be a wife. And the ring was a sym-bol of that marriage, of being Michael's wife, someone I wasn't anymore, didn't want to be. I stood lost in thought, images and questions darting through my mind, until Molly zoomed downstairs, wearing her red sweatsuit.

"Found 'em, Mom."

"Good work." I grabbed her for a hug.

She looked pensive. "Mom? How does the Tooth Fairy get in the house?"

"I guess she flies."

She frowned. "She isn't real, is she? You made her up."

What should I tell her? I was late for work, had no time for a discussion. Molly at times revealed insight beyond her years; at others, she clung to childlike fantasies. I wasn't sure which way to go on the Tooth Fairy. "I didn't make her up. But can we save this for tonight when we have more time?"

Still frowning, she nodded, and I was temporarily off the hook. Angela approached, carrying socks. A block away, the church bell began ringing the hour. Oh Lord—I was late. It was nine. I grabbed my coat, said good-bye to Angela, kissed Molly, and ran out the door.

Jake stood at the bottom of our front steps, biceps bulging, sandy hair tied back in a ponytail, the dimple in his chin shadowed by three days of beard. "Morning, Ms. Hayes."

"Hi," I nodded.

"Watch yourself—your steps are icy," he said. "I'll have my guys sprinkle some salt."

"Thanks, Jake, that's great."

"No trouble." His teeth twinkled when he smiled. Almost handsome, he would have been irresistible if his eyes were just a tiny bit farther apart. Jake's contracting company had done most of the renovations on our street. He was always around, always helpful. When Molly was a baby, he'd helped me lift her stroller up the steps at least a hundred times. "Be careful," he warned. "Sidewalk's slippery."

"Thanks, Jake."

I rushed on down the street, passing curbside trash bags, realizing it was trash day. Michael had distracted me, so I hadn't put our bag out; maybe Angela would remember. Damn Michael, anyway. He'd made me later than I'd already been. I should have told him flat out, no, forget it. No way was I going to give him another thing. But then, the ring had been his grandmother's. Maybe I should give in one more time. Cursing, I stared at the sidewalk, resisting the debate, refusing thoughts of ex-husbands, rings, and fingers. I plowed ahead, watching only the squares of pavement ahead of my feet, not where I was going. At the corner of Fifth, I almost ran smack into old Charlie.

"Oops, sorry," I called, whizzing by. Damn, that was close.

"Whoa, Miss Zoe," Charlie wheezed. "You'll get a speeding ticket, you don't slow down."

"Sorry." I kept moving, trying to get around him, but Charlie stepped sideways, blocking me, apparently determined to have a neighborly chat.

"I'm late for work," I explained.

"You can't be late, miss; you haven't even got there yet," Charlie replied. "Besides, you have to meet someone. We have a new neighbor."

The new neighbor stood beside Charlie. He wore a camel cashmere overcoat and tortoise shell glasses. He was slight in build, pale in complexion, sparse in hair. Refined, probably in his late thirties. Removing a leather glove, he extended his hand. "Woods is my name. Phillip Woods."

His hand was larger than I'd have expected, his grip softer.

"I'm Zoe Hayes," I panted. "I live right across from Charlie."

He nodded. "Yes, of course. The house with the wrought-iron chairs. I've seen you out and about." He blinked rapidly, almost twitching. A nervous person.

I tried to calm him down with a compliment. "My daughter

likes your Santa Claus." I smiled, trying to conceal how I felt about the thing.

"Does she? Well, that's the idea, isn't it? 'Tis the season. It's all for the children, right?" His eyes flitted from point to point, settling nowhere.

I nodded, backing away. "I really do have to run—late for work. See you, Charlie. Nice to meet you, Mr. Woods." I stepped around Charlie to the curb.

"Yes. Likewise, Ms. Hayes."

Charlie took my arm and walked with me for a few steps. Lowering his voice, he said, "Miss Zoe? Watch your step. Mind yourself and your little girl. It's a bad world we live in. You hear?"

I nodded and kept walking. "Don't you worry, Charlie. I will."

I hurried off to find a taxi, but I felt Charlie's eyes on me, the weight of his gaze, until I turned the corner at Sixth. He seemed kind—even grandfatherly—but he said the oddest things.

FIVE

THE INSTITUTE WAS SEPARATED FROM WEST PHILADELPHIA BY high wrought-iron fences and expansive sculpted gardens. A rambling configuration of dark brick and stone, for almost a hundred years it had housed patients with disabling diseases of the mind. Today, it hunkered moody and brooding under the stark winter sky.

The taxi dropped me off at the far end of the circular drive. I hurried past manicured hedges through the arched double doors. Inside, they'd decorated since last week. A massive blue spruce towered overhead, heavily laden with tinsel and metallic balls of green, red, and silver, an open-winged angel precariously perched at the top. The tree was colossal; even so, it struggled to bring cheer and festivity into the Institute's somber halls. A huge brass and crystal chandelier dangled above it in the domed foyer, glittering like a huge tiara. The floor was marble laid with Orientals; the walls were inlaid with mosaic cherubs and figures depicting biblical tales. The one nearest the door showed the Garden of Eden. Eve and the serpent engaged in eternal conversation while chubby-winged infants peeked disappointedly at them from the skies. Across the foyer, the receptionist's desk sat alone where three wide corridors met, each holding echoes of lost voices, forlorn whispers that would never be heard.

Agnes and I knew each other, but neither was particularly happy about it. Agnes used her position to shield staff and patients from any and all visitors, and she considered herself, with her thirty-odd years on the job, superior to relative new-comers like me. With only three years at the Institute, I was in her view still an outsider, possibly more suspect even than visi-tors. I'd learned that I would never win her approval; it was bet-ter to avoid her when I could.

I rushed past her desk across the expansive foyer toward the wing where I worked; Agnes flashed a professional smile, expos-ing a polished overbite.

"Oh, Ms. Hayes. You have a message." She held up a yellow piece of paper. Agnes color-coded her messages. Yellow meant that the message had originated "out of house." When I reached the desk and took the paper, she flashed her teeth again and turned away.

"Nick Stiles" was scrawled at the top of the paper. Nick Stiles? It took a second to place the name; he was that police detective who'd come about the finger. The one with those piercing eyes. Why had he called? And why here? Why not at home? Agnes had checked the box marked "please call." Beneath that, she'd written his number and "at your convenience."

At my convenience. Then it wasn't an emergency. My curios-ity would have to wait until after the morning session. I shoved the note into my coat pocket and rushed to the art therapy room. The room, formerly an employee lounge, was where I had my small office. With only two small windows, greenish fluores-cent lights, and tan linoleum floors, it wasn't the optimal setting for an art studio, but here the art itself was secondary to the artists' creative expression. Their easels and worktables clus-tered around a wooden riser beneath the windows; I headed for the storage closet to lay out supplies.

Art therapy hadn't been my dream. My dream had been to be the next Georgia O'Keeffe. But as my marriage had soured and my need for an income had grown, I'd recognized the need for a

Plan B, so I'd gone back to school and prepared for a career that, unlike painting, could actually pay some bills. My studio had become an office, and the art I worked with was no longer my own. For now, at least, being Georgia O'Keeffe was on hold.

The session that day began well. Patients seemed energized and ready to work. One by one, I greeted them and led them to their easels. As usual, I planned to spend a few minutes with each of them, hearing whatever they wanted to tell me, directing their energy to their artwork. Before I could, though, Kimberly Gilbert, plump, thirty-one years old, and schizophrenic, began to wander, splashing asymmetrical shapes onto the walls, furniture, even other patients—any surface except the one provided for her. I gave chase and repositioned her at her canvas, but as soon as my back was turned, she floated away again.

Then Sal Stephano and Hank Dennis began bickering. Hank, sleekly handsome and forty, suffered a compulsive disorder and insisted that his every brushstroke be perfect. In a typical session, he'd begin and destroy a picture twenty times; nothing was exact enough for him. Given his fixation on perfection and order, he became unsettled when Kimberly applied paint where it didn't belong—especially on his own shirtsleeve. Hank became flustered and furious, cursing, then verbally swiping at Kimberly. I separated them, reassuring him that the paint would wash out of his sleeve, directing his attention back to his own project, but he remained agitated, pacing and talking incessantly, narrating Kimberly's every move.

"Look—My God. She's not going to—yes, she is—My God, she did it. My God—she painted the curtain!"

I went after Kimberly, but she skittered out of my arms as I promised Hank again and again that the paint was water soluble. Meantime, Sal, a heavyset twenty-seven-year-old diagnosed with bipolar disorder, had had enough of Hank's nerves and began mimicking him in annoying falsetto.

"Oh God oh God! Oh no!" he wailed. "She's going to, no she isn't, yes she is, no she isn't, oh my God, yes she is—OhmyGOD, the curtains!" Sal pulled Amanda DeMarco's arm to get her attention. Amanda, working on her self-portrait, ignored him.

Amanda, twenty-two, had worked on this painting for weeks. She'd painted herself with long, flowing chestnut-colored tresses, arm in arm with a smiling older woman who resembled her mother. In reality, Amanda had pulled out most of her hair and eyelashes; there were no flowing tresses, not anymore. All that remained on her head were a few hard-to-reach clumps. And her real mom was ice cold and much removed. But the world in Amanda's picture was perfect, ideal, and completely false. Amanda's bubble.

Or it was until that morning. Even with the help of Gus, the orderly on duty, I couldn't calm everyone. The group was out of control, skittish. Hank got fed up with Sal for mocking him and shoved Sal. Before Gus or I could intervene, Sal stumbled against Amanda, knocking her brush into her perfect world, leaving a stripe of cadmium across her mother's throat. I ran in, fending off pandemonium, separating Sal from Amanda, Hank from Sal. Amanda frantically wiped at her painting with an acetone-drenched rag, effectively erasing her mother's head and neck, wailing inconsolably as I soothed her with useless phrases.

All this time, Sydney Ellis stood at his easel, at attention. He didn't paint, didn't touch a brush, didn't blink when Kimberly Gilbert painted circles on his pants. Sydney was a new patient, a schizophrenic still adjusting to his medications. Last session, he'd walked in circles around the room, too agitated to stay still. Sydney needed a calm, nonthreatening environment to ease himself into treatment. Art therapy was supposed to provide it. Who knew how poor Sydney was affected that day by our chaotic little group?

Progress was not linear, I reminded myself. People took back-steps, sidesteps, and sometimes they stumbled. Still, I was angry with myself. I was responsible for the group's focus or loss of it. I scolded myself, analyzing how I might have taken control and protected them, reviewing could-haves and should-haves. Finally, escorts arrived; the session ended. As everyone left, I noticed that Amanda had pulled out the remainder of her eyelashes. I was exhausted, felt defeated. And it wasn't even noon.

When I had a minute, I called Detective Stiles. He was out; I left the message that I'd returned his call.

My next session was with Evie Kraus, at the Institute as a guest of the Commonwealth; a few years ago, she'd filleted her lover with a kitchen knife and hadn't spoken a word since then. Evie's doctors, hopeful that she'd begin to speak, had reduced her regimen of medications. So far, she remained silent, but she'd begun to draw prolifically. Hunched over a sketch pad, working her tongue, she concentrated on her picture so completely that, despite her formidable size and multiple serpent tattoos, she seemed more like a girl Molly's age than a twenty-eight-year-old psychotic killer. Evie's drawings always showed what was literally in front of her. The chairs in the corner. A potted plant, a pair of slippers. The view of the train tracks out the window. I wondered if her mind ever traveled outside these walls to other times or places. Her drawings hadn't let on.

Her session went peacefully. I began to relax. Then, near the end of the session, a new, overeager orderly barged in to take her back to Section 5. Maybe Evie thought he wasn't going to let her finish her drawing. Maybe his energy level startled her. Whatever her reason, though, she moved quickly. Six feet tall and 190 pounds, she bounced up and grabbed a chair and swung it at the orderly's head. He ducked, avoiding the blow, then grabbed the chair legs. I came up behind her and, while the two of them danced around the chair, tried to hold on to her, telling her in a calm, soothing voice to put down the chair. But the orderly sounded an alarm, and suddenly nurses, aides, orderlies, and the janitor ran in. I was certain that, given a moment, I could have calmed her. Instead, half a dozen frantic screaming people in pastels rushed her from all sides and tackled her and slammed her to the floor.

Afterward, I lost it with the orderly and his cohorts. As the therapist in charge, I and only I should have determined what happened in the session. But the damage had already been done, and all afternoon I kept hearing the crunch of Evie's jaw landing on linoleum.

The day that had begun with Michael's call did not improve with age. Each of my patients and even the staff members were off kilter, unsettled. Like me. Maybe there was a full moon. Or maybe emotions were contagious, spreading like the flu.

Finally, just before four, I closed the art room for the day. It was Thursday, the night Susan and I took Emily and Molly to gymnastics class—our weekly night out—and I wanted to get home early enough that Angela could get home before dark. I hurried to Market Street to catch a train and, reaching into my pocket for my SEPTA TransPass, found the message from Detective Stiles. Damn. I wondered if he'd gotten my message. I tried him again on cell, but there was no phone service in the subway, so for the entire train ride it nagged me. Why had he called? What could he want?

SIX

THE WALK HOME FROM THE TRAIN, AT LEAST, WAS PEACEFUL. Crisp December air, late afternoon sun. The sounds of traffic and my own shoes on solid pavement. Finally, I thought, my day was settling down. But when I got to my house, old Charlie was sitting on the front steps. I hoped he was just resting, that he'd get up and let me pass. He didn't. No, as I approached, Charlie didn't move at all, other than to stretch his mouth into one of his wide, open grins.

"Hi, Charlie." I tried to step around him to follow.

"Hello, Miss Zoe." He nodded my way. "Not too cold today." Still smiling, he slid over slightly to the center of the steps, blocking my way. "Sit awhile?"

"Sorry." I tried to sound friendly. "I can't. The sitter has to get home, and we have someplace to go."

Charlie looked up the steps. "Give it a minute. All that can wait."

What? He didn't budge. "Charlie, I've got a million things to do before we go."

"Sit a minute." It was a command. "Just for a minute." He didn't look at me. "Go on. Sit."

It wasn't like Charlie to order people around. Something must be on his mind; as reluctant as I was to linger, I was also curious. Besides, I was tired. It wouldn't hurt to sit for a minute. One.

So I sat. The cement was hard and cold, and Charlie's aroma

was strong. It wasn't quite offensive, just stale. Musky. I leaned back against the railing and looked at him. Charlie's jacket was frayed at the collar, worn at the cuffs. His shoes were scuffed, his pants stained with paint and oily patches. A handyman's uniform. For a while, he was silent. I watched his breath clouds swell and fade as he stared into the street. Finally, quietly, he said, "Miss, how many years now have we lived across the street from each other?"

It was an unexpected question. How many years had it been? I remembered moving in, Michael carrying me over the threshold, my arms around his neck. I didn't want to remember that, didn't want to count the years. "I don't know. Thirteen? Thirteen years, I guess."

"Thirteen years. That's a pretty long time, right?"

"I don't know. You've lived around here a lot longer than I have, Charlie."

"Well, that's true. I've lived here since before they came in and fixed up everything. Gentrified it. I was here way before your house was even built. This used to be a vacant lot with poor folks' homes all around it. They're all gone now, of course. Torn down. And the poor folks have mostly gone."

I nodded, wondering what visions Charlie saw when he looked up and down the street.

He turned to face me. "Miss, who do you think you can trust?"

"Trust?"

"In the world, I mean."

The question was oddly personal, and Charlie's stare made me uncomfortable. I looked up at the door, wondering if Angela would be in a hurry. Then I searched a pocket for my keys.

"Seriously, think about it. Who do you trust? These days, anybody can be anybody, for all you know. Even a neighbor."

"True enough." I might as well agree with him.

"The police were here yesterday, miss. You called them?"

Oh, so that was it. He was curious about the police. "Yes, Charlie, I called them."

"Why? What happened?"

I didn't want to tell him about the finger. Lord, if I did, we'd be out here for hours, discussing it. "I had a problem."

"There was trouble, so you called the police."

"Yep."

"Well, that's natural. That's what they're there for, to help people. You trust them, don't you? You trust the police, Miss Zoe?"

I thought of Detective Stiles. His steady pale eyes. "Yes, Charlie. I trust them. Look, I really have to go in."

"But you didn't tell me what the trouble was. Even though you've known me for thirteen years. Even though we share the same street."

"Charlie. It's not that I don't trust you. I just don't want to discuss it."

"Miss, you trust the police, but not old Charlie. I understand that. You know me, but you don't know if you can trust me. Right?"

I started to get up. "It's not that I don't trust you, Charlie, but really, I've got to—"

He put his hand up. "Don't be in a hurry. Settle down and listen. Because you can trust me, Miss Zoe. I want you to know that. Even with your life. Or your child's."

Trust him with my life? With Molly's? Why would he say that? Did Charlie think we were in danger? Actually, I didn't want to know. I wanted to end the conversation. "Thank you, Charlie. That's nice to know. You can trust me, too."

He didn't look at me; he scanned the street, the rooftops, the sky. I followed his glance. Alongside an empty house, Jake's dump truck backed up, beeping, parking for the night. In Victor's window, a curtain snapped shut. On Phillip Woods's porch, Santa beamed red and green. I wanted to go inside.

"But except for me, miss, don't trust anybody. Not around here." His tone had changed. It was suddenly blunt, gruff. Disturbing.

"Charlie—"

"I mean it. Keep an eye on your back all the time."

Probably Charlie was worried because women were disappearing. He was concerned about the single mother and child who lived across the street. He was being protective, that was all. And, in his way, sweet.

"You don't have to worry about us, Charlie. We're fine."

"No, listen. I tried to tell you before. There's lots of depravity these days. Swelling appetites for evil. It's all around." His eyes rested briefly on the Santa flickering across the street.

I fidgeted. The cold cement step was freezing my behind. There was no point in arguing with him. "Thanks, Charlie. I'll be real careful." Again, I started to stand; again, Charlie put his hand on my arm.

"Miss, wait. Don't look alarmed or run away. Somebody may be watching us, even now. Listen, I know things. I'm taking a big risk, telling you."

Oh dear. Maybe it was worse than I'd thought. Charlie thought people were watching him? Poor Charlie. He might be losing it. How old was he, I wondered. Seventy-five? Older?

"You don't want to listen to me, but you must." His whisper was urgent. "I'm just a handyman. But I see things. In the alleys, the basements. I have the tools to work under the floorboards, inside closets. In old houses or new. In basements of every house on this street. People don't think much about me, but I know things. Houses have secrets. There's evil here, miss. Close by. Serious evil. And it's gone too far—into the bricks, the drywall, the wood."

Apparently, Charlie had gone too far, too. He'd crossed a line, entered a place where perceptions got twisted and played tricks on the mind. Where truth became fragmented and jumbled, patched with imaginings. Still, with all his ramblings, he wasn't scary. Old Charlie seemed damaged, not dangerous. Like a worn-out teddy bear.

". . . so you can't tell," he went on. "Anybody can wear anything. Disguise themselves as police or doctors, judges. Businessmen. It's their clothes, their costumes that tell you who they are. If you see somebody driving a fire engine, you assume he's okay, right? He's a fireman. You trust him. Or the mailman. Certainly you can trust the mailman! But how do you know that the mailman's really a mailman? That the fireman's really a fireman? Because of the uniform, right? But how do you know that he's not really a madman—a murderer dressed in a uniform? With a disguise, could somebody fool you? Sure they could."

I leaned away, wondering how long he'd go on, how long I'd have to stay there. Charlie tilted toward me, whispering dank words. "Somebody might wear a uniform. Like a policeman. Or a dentist. Or he might dress normal, in a business suit, so you wouldn't even notice him. That would be the best disguise of all. He'd blend in and trap you—miss, please, just smile, act as if we're shooting the breeze here. Please. In case we're being watched."

He looked straight ahead again, watching cars drive by, smiling casually and nodding his head. I wondered how long he'd had these thoughts, whether he'd forgotten to take some kind of medication.

". . . that you and your child are in danger."

Wait. What was that? "Oh, come on, Charlie—what are you saying? That the mailman's a murderer? Or some fireman's planning to hurt me? Because that's what it sounds like."

Charlie folded his massive, calloused hands, nodding, relieved. "Not necessarily the mailman. Or a fireman. Evil can take on any form. Any disguise. A taxi driver. A cop. So trust no one. Be on guard. Hear me, miss. Evil is nearby. Watching, lurking, planning. Listen to what I'm saying."

Charlie's face was an inch away. His eyes bulged, and a cloud of fermenting breath engulfed my face. It was all I could take. I got to my feet. "Charlie, I've got to go in." I started up the steps.

"Don't be afraid, miss," Charlie spoke over his shoulder without moving. "I've been protecting you, and I'll keep on. I'll protect you both. You can count on me. You and your little one can count on old Charlie. That's all I have to say."

"I've got to go in."

When I opened the door, I looked back. Charlie was watching, frowning with concern. The man was disturbed, but he couldn't be dangerous, not with a face so sincere and troubled. Shutting the door on him would be rude, maybe even cruel. Still, I wanted to discourage his behavior.

"Charlie, don't worry about us," I assured him. "Really. We're fine." Then, without giving him a chance to reply, I went inside and shut the door. Molly's jacket and bookbag had landed in the hall.

Angela's voice floated down the stairs. "Yo, Zoe—that you? We're upstairs."

"I'm getting in my gym stuff, Mom."

"Great. We've got about ten minutes," I called.

Unbuttoning my coat, I went to the window. Victor's shades hung at an odd, twisted angle. Construction trucks blocked my view of Santa. Charlie, having gotten up off my front steps, hobbled back to his side of the street on crooked, unsteady legs.

SEVEN

THURSDAY NIGHT. MOLLY'S GYMNASTICS CLASS. MOST EVENINGS
Molly and I stayed home, unwinding after busy days. Usually,
she'd work on art projects, each of which seemed to require
thousands of beads, miles of string, tons of buttons, carloads of
markers. Oh—and glue. Gallons of glue. Oceans of it. While
she created, I generally got organized. Paid bills. Prepared paperwork. Pretended to clean the house. Thursdays were different. Thursday was our one evening a week of structured
out-of-the-house activity. First we went to class, then Molly,
Emily, Susan, and I went out to eat.

During class, while kids worked on balance beams and trampolines, their mothers visited in the observation room. Even
now I didn't know all the women's names, but I knew which kid
each belonged to, and I'm sure I was simply Molly's mom to
most of them. We were, to the outside eye, despite our varying
ages and body types, indistinguishable, almost interchangeable.
A mass of chipped manicures and imperfect hair. A throng, a
gaggle of moms, all chattering. Davinder, who had a doctorate
in chemical engineering, had finally found a foolproof way to
get little Hari to eat vegetables. Karen, an ICU nurse, had found
a bargain on pajamas for Nicholas. Gretchen, an amateur tennis
champ, couldn't comprehend how fast her Hannah had out-
grown her shoes.

To me, the chitchat was soothing, almost musical. Connecting with other women reassured me. It made me confident that divorce hadn't made me less capable or adoption less maternal than other women. Given the events of the week, that night I especially craved the comfort of normal conversation, the gentle company of women.

Molly and I walked to the Community Center in the fading light. Only five o'clock but already dark. As soon as we got there, Molly peeled off her coat, shoes, and socks, everything but her leotard and leggings, eager to get started.

"Wait till you see me on the unevens."

"I can't wait."

"You never watch me. You're always talking."

"I watch you and talk at the same time."

"No, you don't. I see you through the window. You talk to Susan or Billy's mom or the other ladies. You don't watch."

"I'll watch this time."

She looked doubtful. "Promise."

"I promise."

"I'll know if you're lying, Mom. I'll look to see."

"Fine. Look. You'll see me watching."

Her face was still skeptical as she tossed me her socks and ran into the gym to begin the warm-up. Two seconds later, she was back. "Mom, what if my tooth comes out in class?"

"I don't think it will. But if it does, we'll wrap it up and take it home in a tissue."

She frowned. "But what if it falls in the pit? What if I lose it?" Her eyes filled with terror at the thought.

"Mollybear," I said, "don't worry. The Tooth Fairy will accept a note from your mother."

"Are you sure?" Again, that doubtful look.

"Positive."

"There is no Tooth Fairy, is there? She's fake like Santa Claus."

"Who said Santa Claus is fake?"

"Everyone knows that. He's just make-believe. It's really the parents."

I sighed. Was this the time and place for this discussion? "Molly, hurry. They're in there warming up. You'll be late."

I stood at the window, wondering what to tell her. Truth was important to me; I wanted never to lie to her or shatter her trust. Maybe I'd fudge it, tell her that if she believed in Santa or the Tooth Fairy, they'd exist, at least in a way. Oh, who knew.

I watched her confidently take her spot in the circle of five- and six-year-olds who prepared to stretch, kick, leap, flip, jump, and tumble. Equipment was strategically arranged throughout the gym—trampolines, vaulting horses, balance beams, bars, parallel bars, rings, and floor mats, and, at the far wall, the kids' favorite: the pit, an in-ground swimming pool filled with odd-shaped chunks of foam rubber. After each class, children leaped, lunged, flipped, cartwheeled, or got pitched into the pit, then worked their way out screaming and laughing.

Molly was adept at gymnastics. She flipped fearlessly, cart-wheeled artfully. Gravity did not intimidate her. To me, her skill was a clear reminder that we had no genetic ties. I was not and had never been light on my feet. "Graceful" and "agile" were not adjectives used to describe me. I'd been a swimmer, a water per-son, never completely comfortable on land, but Molly was. For the zillionth time I wondered what else she'd inherited, what other surprising traits or talents would emerge over time. She knew she'd been adopted but hadn't seemed too interested in that fact. Not yet. I wondered when she would be, what she'd want to know, what I would tell her. What I could.

Mothers clustered on folding chairs in the observation room, heads bent together, buzzing. I knew better than to look for Susan—she and Emily were always late—so I found an empty chair and joined the group. Nobody greeted me. Not a single person as much as looked my way. I swallowed. I waited. Still nothing. I began to feel awkward, as if I were intruding. But that was nonsense. I belonged here as much as anyone; these women were my friends.

Something was wrong. Normally, Karen greeted me with a hug, dark eyes smiling. Now, Karen didn't even blink at me. In fact, Karen and Davinder were staring at—what was her name? Chubby little Serena's mom—the spunky woman with the curls—Ileana? That was it, Ileana. Why? Oh. Because Ileana was crying.

Then I noticed Leslie. Her long red hair hung limp and dull; her skin was so ashen that even her freckles seemed washed out. Her eyes were glazed, focused inward. Even though she was staring my way, she didn't seem to see me. Finally, Karen motioned for me to come take the seat beside her. Quietly, with a sense of dread, I edged my way around the chairs and squeezed in.

"But why'd she leave Billy there?" Ileana dabbed her nose as she asked. "Didn't she say anything about where she was going?"

"No. Nothing," Karen shook her head. "We don't know why. She just ran up to the woman, told Billy to stay with her, and ran out of the park."

"And the woman—she just sat there? Why didn't she do something?"

"How could she? She had her own two kids. She couldn't just leave them there to chase a stranger."

"Maybe not. But she could have stopped her. She could have done something."

"Stopped who? What happened?" I broke in.

Wordlessly, without glancing at me, Ileana handed me the morning *Inquirer*. With all that had happened at work, I hadn't had a chance to see it.

"No, probably she couldn't," Davinder insisted, her dark eyes swollen with sorrow. "We shouldn't blame her. She had no idea what was going to happen. We've got hindsight."

I glanced at the paper. The faces of four women stared at me from the front page. One of them was Tamara, Leslie's nanny. I looked at Leslie, then closed my eyes. This couldn't be true.

But the newspaper insisted that it was, in glaring boldface above a three-column spread. Another young woman was missing, the fourth in three weeks. This one, also a nanny, was from Society Hill. I looked at Tamara's picture, then at the one beside it. The caption identified it as Claudia Rusk, the third nanny to disappear. I thought of Susan's children, running into the kitchen after they'd heard the news. I put the paper down.

Leslie spoke flatly. "What does it matter, anyway? Tamara's gone."

"What happened?" I kept asking the same question.

"They were in the park—he was riding his bike—"

"What park?"

"Three Bears."

Three Bears was a local playground named for its cement sculptures of a mother bear with two cubs. We all took our kids there. It was a place we'd all considered safe.

"When?"

"Wednesday." This was Thursday evening, gymnastics day. Suddenly, it was difficult to remember how far it was from Wednesday to Thursday. The names of days sounded meaningless. Tamara with wavy golden hair, long legs, and a contagious laugh had been gone, missing, since yesterday morning. Nothing was making sense. A finger on the doorstep. Nannies missing. Tamara gone. Tamara? She was one of us. Family. I was having trouble absorbing it.

"Somebody tell Zoe what happened," Leslie said. "I can't right now."

Davinder pushed a lock of shiny black hair behind her ear and began in a monotone. "Yesterday, Tamara and Billy weren't home when Leslie came back from shopping. She went to the park to look for them." I looked at Leslie. Her chin wobbled slightly. Her freckles were striped with mascara. Karen reached over and touched her shoulder.

"They weren't there," Davinder went on. "Leslie found Billy's bike near the statue. But nobody was at the park, and there was no sign of Billy or Tamara."

"It's so unlike Tamara to be late." Leslie managed to pick up the story. "I went looking. Up and down the block, knocking on doors, asking strangers if they'd seen them. I was afraid—what with what's been going on—that they'd both . . . vanished."

Karen took her hand. "It's all right, Leslie. Billy's fine. Look at him. He's doing jumping jacks with Coach Gene."

Indeed, Billy was smiling and red-faced, his blond curls bouncing while he jumped with the others. "Billy's fine. And Tamara will show up. You'll see." Karen held onto Leslie's hand and looked at me with eyes that said she'd talk to me later.

I picked up the article again and read. Tamara had apparently vanished in broad daylight, but not before thrusting Billy at a complete stranger. "Stay here," she'd told Billy, and she commanded the woman, "Take care of him until I get back."

The woman had waited at the park for over an hour, then left a note on Billy's bike with her address. She'd taken the boy home with her own children and called the police. Before police could locate the child's family, however, Billy's mother, Leslie Baumann, had found the note, called the woman, who wished to remain anonymous, and retrieved her son. The whereabouts of the nanny, the paper reported, were still unknown.

The article pointed out that Tamara was the fourth childcare worker in a month to disappear from the area. It mentioned the others: Vanessa Ramsey, Claire Garnet, and Claudia Rusk.

Their smiling faces lined up neatly across the page, beneath the headline.

I put the article down and looked at Leslie. I'd known her and Tamara both for years—we'd pushed baby swings together at the park. Now, Tamara's absence surrounded Leslie, emanated from her. She adored Tamara, relied on her, treated her like a younger sister. They even looked alike. With Tamara gone, Leslie seemed to have faded. I closed my eyes and imagined finding Molly's bike abandoned in the park, the relentless panic of not knowing where my child was. But I didn't want to imagine that, couldn't bear to. Besides, what was the point? Billy was here, not missing anymore. Tamara was unaccounted for, but at least the children were safe. Even so, I had to check.

I edged around the chairs and went to the window, searching the small groups of children at each piece of equipment. I found Leslie's wiry Billy, Karen's stocky Nicholas, Gretchen's petite Hannah, Ileana's substantial Serena. Finally, I saw Molly. She waited in line at the trampoline. Yes, she was fine. Attentive. Having fun. They all were.

But Tamara's spirited face floated through the gym, laughing, singing, chasing after Billy. Showing him how to ride his bike. How to Rollerblade. How to make a peanut-butter bird feeder. Talking about growing up in Nebraska, the five younger siblings she'd had to watch. All the kids loved her, took to her naturally. Where was she? What had happened to her? What could make her abandon Billy? I had to believe she'd merely run off somewhere, that she was safe. Maybe she'd been threatened. Stalked. Or blackmailed. No, that made no sense, She wasn't rich enough to be blackmailed. Probably it was something else— maybe a romance.

Of course. That had to be it. Odd behavior in women was usually caused by men. Tamara must have gotten involved with some guy and run off with him. She was all right, just too embarrassed now, after all the publicity, to call or come back. Or maybe he wouldn't let her come back. Maybe the guy was abusive. Or maybe it was something entirely harmless. Like, maybe she knew the other missing girls and they'd all gone off somewhere together. It wasn't beyond possibility. Nannies tended to socialize with each other, and no evidence had been found indicating that anything serious had happened to any of them.

Except the finger.

I caught my breath. Stop it, I told myself. Probably Tamara's absence had nothing to do with the finger. Hundreds of young women wore red nail polish. Tamara wasn't the only one.

No, Claudia probably wore it, too.

Charlie's voice echoed, "Evil is all around . . . You and your child are in danger." Molly jumped and spun around, bounced from her knees to her feet, her feet to her seat. Six other children ringed the trampoline, waiting their turns. When Molly's turn was finished, she turned to the window, saw me watching, and waved. I gave her a thumbs-up and smiled. But my chest was so tight, I almost couldn't inhale.

I did inhale, though. I exhaled, too. Then I repeated the process. After a few more rounds, I looked back at the women in their huddle. I would rejoin them, but for a while I lingered, gazing out the window at the children, trying to insulate myself from the quiet hysteria in the room. In the gym, the world seemed normal. Children laughed; holiday music played; tinsel decorated the posts set at intervals into the floor.

But this side of the window reverberated with the shock of the headlines.

Davinder came and stood beside me. "Coach Gene looks all right, doesn't he?" She stared at him. Eyed him up and down.

I was confused. Gene was hardly Davinder's type, at least four inches shorter and twice as wide. And Davinder had a doctorate, while Gene had maybe finished high school. Not to mention that she was married. "Really?" I tried to sound nonjudgmental. "You think?"

"Yeah. I expected he'd be devastated, the way he felt about Tamara. He asked her out only about forty times."

"No, that wasn't Tamara," Ileana interjected, overhearing. "Gene liked the other one—Claudia Rusk. You know, she worked for Susan's friend."

"No, uh-uh, it's Tamara. Gene's been hounding her to go out with him for months, but she keeps shooting him down. Poor guy."

"That's Claudia. Ask Susan. Coach Gene kept asking Claudia out until finally she gave in. But she dumped him after one date. It's Claudia, not Tamara."

Davinder and Ileana continued to bicker. It was Claudia; no, Tamara. No, Claudia.

"You know," Leslie interrupted, "maybe he liked them both. Tamara told me Gene kept bugging her. But he still might have had a thing for Claudia. You're both probably right."

I watched Coach Gene through the window as he guided the children, one by one, over the horse. A compact little man, built of solid muscle, Gene radiated grins and tireless enthusiasm. He offered each child individual encouragement, motivating even the clumsiest to run, leap, bounce, swing, and flip. As a coach, he seemed ideal. But how would he seem as a romantic partner, as a man? Now that I thought about it, his perpetual smile was unnatural. Even creepy. What lay behind it? His eyes were flat, giving no information. Maybe there was more to Coach Gene than anyone imagined. Apparently, he'd been involved with two of the missing women. Was that mere coincidence? Could this squat, cheerful man know something about the disappearances? As I watched, Coach Gene's smile distorted into sinister sneer, a clown's face, a mask.

Stop it, I told myself. You're being ridiculous. Gene was a

healthy young man; it was only natural for him to be attracted to striking young women like Tamara and Claudia. Still, if Gene was fond of either or both, his peppy demeanor was unsettling. He didn't seem the least bit bothered that the women were missing.

Stumpy little Serena performed a cartwheel; Coach Gene beamed and gave her a high five. He must be hiding his feelings for the sake of the children. The children were Gene's priority; he'd never let his personal problems touch them. Satisfied with that explanation, I left the window and rejoined the group, taking a seat beside Leslie.

"It's been a hell of a day," Karen sighed. Darkness ringed her eyes. "We're all upset. But even so, we've got to think of the kids. They love Tamara, and they're going to wonder where she is. And they're going to sense that we're upset, so they'll know something's happened and worry."

"So what are you saying?" Gretchen asked. "That we should tell them what happened?"

"No. I don't think we should—"

"So we should pretend nothing's happened?"

"I didn't say that, either, Gretchen. All I'm saying is that we should do what's best for the kids and keep—"

"Leslie!" Susan burst in shouting, dragging Emily by the wrist. "I saw the paper this morning and called, but you didn't pick up—and then I had to be in court—my God, are you okay?"

Leslie gaped, not replying.

"Listen, I talked to the precinct. It's definitely the same MO as the others. Same guy who took Claudia and the others." Emily was whining for Susan to let her go, but Susan seemed to have forgotten all about the wrist in her fist. "I tried to find out what the cops know, but nobody's saying anything yet. Too soon." Emily finally broke away, shed her coat, and took off for the gym. "I'll let you know the minute I hear anything at all," Susan went on. "Meantime, what are we going to do?"

"What?" Leslie blinked at her, confused.

"Do?" Davinder asked.

"There isn't much we can do, is there? It's up to the cops." Ileana sat up straight.

"You're kidding, right? We're not going to just sit around waiting for our babysitters to disappear one by one—that's crazy."

Leslie let out an audible sob. I took her hand; Karen hugged her.

"Susan," I whispered. "Everyone's kind of upset here. Give it a break."

I knew she wouldn't. She gaped at me, then the others. Susan didn't understand breaks or inaction of any kind. To Susan, passivity was poison.

"Well, as I was saying," Karen said, "what I think we should do is stick to routine. Familiar structure might feel good right now."

"Routine and structure," Leslie echoed. "Keeping our lives going. That won't be easy."

"No, but it might be the best thing. For the kids and for us."

Davinder spoke. "I agree. Even if we feel miserable, we should keep the kids' lives normal."

Susan was speechless, almost sputtering. I lowered my head, awaiting the inevitable explosion, counting down. Three, two . . .

"Shit—I can't believe what I'm hearing." Boom. Susan was shouting. "This isn't about us or our kids—it's about our sitters. Our nannies. These are young, vital women whom all of us rely on. Who's home right now with your newborn, Gretchen? And while you play tennis every morning, who takes care of the kids? Karen, when you're on duty, who's with Nicholas? Ileana—who watches your kids when you show houses? Davinder, you have a job now, too, right?"

"Only part-time—"

"Fine. Who watches your Hari 'part-time'? Do you expect your sitters to risk their lives just so you can keep your kids' routines normal and undisturbed?"

"Susan—" I started, knowing she was spouting without thinking, and probably just getting started. "I don't think that's what anyone meant—"

"I, for one, am giving Bonita a gun. I want her to keep it on her person at all times. I'm getting her a license and paying for her to take shooting lessons."

Karen's eyes widened. Leslie seemed to sway in her seat. Someone moaned a soft "Oy."

"Susan, is that smart? A loaded gun? Around the kids?" I asked.

"You bet, a loaded gun around the kids," she said. "Guess what—I want them to learn to shoot, too. Nobody at my house is going to wait around to be a goddamned victim. Someone messes with us, they're dead."

The other women exchanged meaningful glances, silently agreeing that Susan had lost it. But she'd gotten them out of their funk. Now they were debating issues of self-defense, the benefits of Mace versus stun guns, karate versus tai chi. I stood and went to the window, needing another break.

Molly stood beside the pit, by the uneven parallel bars. She stepped up and, with Coach Gene's help, lifted herself to the lower bar. My heart stopped. I watched her little body swing, gather momentum, and somehow fly itself up to the high bar, defying gravity. Molly fearlessly held her position, her back arched and toes pointed, then leaned forward and spun back down to the lower bar. She flipped and flew back and forth between the bars, until finally she swung into her dismount, a cannonball from the high bar into the pit. When my heart began to beat again, I stifled the urge to burst into applause.

It was true; familiar activities, routine, and structure were therapeutic. They soothed us, kept us in the here and now. There we were, the gymnastics moms, the same as every week. Even with the disappearance of Tamara, we were following our routine, sticking together. A bunch of women, a mini-community bound by little besides the age of our children and hectic schedules that, by chance, had led us to sign our kids up for the same class. But now, aroused by Susan's spirit, we were organizing ourselves to take action—any action—against the paralysis of grief and fear.

"We'll need a buddy system," Gretchen suggested. "Nannies go nowhere if they don't go in pairs."

"And cell phones—programmed with emergency numbers."

"And we should hire that self-defense teacher, that guy who teaches women to poke out attackers' eyes—"

"Yeah, and knee 'em in the balls—"

"Mom?" Molly's head poked through the doorway. She looked puzzled.

The conversation stopped dead.

"Hi, honey."

She was glowing from exertion, damp with sweat. "Mom, did you see me? Were you watching?"

I crossed the room to hug her, wondering what she'd heard, and my chin quivered unexpectedly. "Yes, I did, Molly—I watched. I saw you, and you were amazing."

She beamed proudly, escaping the hug to run to the water fountain. The other children swarmed in, finding their mothers, pulling on their coats. Plans for moms organizing against crime were, at least for the time being, abruptly suspended.

EIGHT

AT FIFTH STREET DELI, EMILY AND MOLLY IMMEDIATELY GOT busy with the puzzles and games on the kids' place mats. Susan and I sat looking nowhere, saying nothing. I told myself to relax; still, a sooty finger beckoned from behind the salt shaker, Tamara's eyes peered over the cold-cuts counter, and old Charlie's cryptic warnings echoed under the buzz of conversation. Stop it, I ordered myself. Focus on the here and now. The familiar and routine. But even as I scolded myself, I fantasized about running out of the place, just grabbing Molly's hand and fleeing with Susan and the girls down the street back to our house where we could bolt the door and be safe. I even planned our escape route. I'd grab my purse and pull Molly out of the booth, lead Susan past the chair in the aisle, dodge that guy in the herringbone coat, veer past the cash register, and then—

What was happening to me? Couldn't I just sit quietly and have a meal with my friend? Couldn't I take even a brief break from the craziness around me? I should be able to; I was a therapist, a mental health professional, trained to deal with emotional problems.

But the fact was that I wasn't dealing. I was tense, tired, and stressed. And Susan looked like I felt. Maybe even worse. She sat across the table, at once wired and haggard.

"Mom, can you find any forks in this picture?" Molly pointed to a puzzle on her place mat. Arthur the Squirrel couldn't eat his dinner without dishes and utensils, and they were all hidden in the drawing.

"I found it," Emily bragged. She pointed to a tiny fork hidden in a tree branch. Molly leaned across the table to see, and the girls chattered, weaving a nonstop conversation.

Susan and I, though, were quiet. Susan's mood pendulum seemed to have swung. After her impassioned rabble-rousing at gymnastics, she'd suddenly deflated. Her black hair hung limp, framing bloodshot eyes. Her skin had a grayish tone.

"Susan," I asked, "you okay?"

She sighed. "As okay as any of us."

"You look awful."

"Thanks. I love you, too."

"If I didn't love you, I wouldn't tell you."

"So who asked you to love me?" Her shoulders caved, and she let go of her menu. "You're right, though. I've been a mess since Claudia. And now—Tamara? I adore those girls, Zoe." Her eyes filled. "It's just too much. I haven't slept—I stay up thinking all night. About who took them. If they suffered. You know."

I knew. We sat, silent and hurting.

"I didn't know that Coach Gene asked Tamara out," I finally said.

"Oh, please, Zoe. He asks them all out. Coach Gene likes anything that wiggles."

"Coach Gene likes what, Mom?" Molly's ears had perked up.

"He likes wiggles," Emily explained. "You know." She began, of course, to wiggle. Molly joined her, erupting into squirming giggles.

"Girls," I rubbed my temples. "You're shaking the booth."

"Emily," Susan barked. "Sit still."

The girls quieted, stifling laughter, and Susan and I settled back into our glumness.

"Last time I saw Tamara, she talked about you," Susan said.

"About me?"

"She said she admired you. Called you a survivor."

Now I was the one blinking away tears. "A lot of single people adopt—"

"Why do you assume it's about that? We were talking about strong women. She used you as an example of an old soul, strong because of—I don't know—something about knowing how to flow with life instead of fighting it. Anyhow, she thought you must have lived many lives."

What was she talking about? "Tamara's always been a flake."

"She said I should learn from you. That I waste energy by fighting battles that can't be won."

Then again, maybe not such a flake.

"Mom—I can't find the cup." Molly shoved the place mat in front of me.

"I'll show you," Emily offered. "Here's a hint. Look near his tail."

Molly continued to search. "How come you can find everything?"

"Cuz I'm older than you."

"When's your birthday?"

Their conversation went on, traveling its separate path, occasionally crossing ours. Molly opened her mouth to display her loose baby tooth, Emily to introduce two emerging permanent ones.

"By the way, I asked Ed about your detective." Ed was a cop, one of Susan's pals in Homicide.

My detective? "Stiles?" I saw him at my door, his eyes sizing me up. I still hadn't found out why he'd called. He hadn't called back. Maybe he hadn't gotten my message. I should try to call again.

"He's new in town. A hotshot from Baltimore. Has degrees in criminology and psychology and every other ology Ed could think of, and he's heading the nanny investigation, which has all the guys who are senior to him, which is basically everybody, pretty pissed off. Apparently, he does things his own way or no way, isn't exactly a cop's cop. But he's supposed to be smart."

"So what did Ed say about the finger?"

Susan's voice was flat. Listless. "They haven't matched the print yet, but Ed said it's gotta be one of the nannies'. I didn't say this to the others, but the cops figure those girls are dead."

Tamara blinked from behind the sugar bowl. I looked away, at Emily and Molly. They were engrossed in their games, holding their parallel conversation, cheerful. Oblivious.

"No wonder you haven't slept."

"It's not only the nannies. I'm stressed out. I scream at the girls. Lisa asks me to help with her homework and I scream. Julie wants a ride somewhere and I scream. I haven't even started my Christmas shopping. The plumbing leaks upstairs so we've got to redo the master bath and the ceiling under it, and we need a new roof. I've got those three felony cases, more coming up. My caseload's staggering. Tim's out of town again, has to be in L.A. off and on, commuting back and forth, probably through March. Bonita won't be back until next week, and the sitter who's filling in has to leave early every day but Thursday, the one day a week I don't need her to stay. I want to scream."

I sat with my hands clasped, holding on. As long as I'd known her, Susan had been on overload, managing the many and complicated levels of her life tirelessly, with grace and aplomb. She could be passionate and scathingly articulate, but never frazzled. She could multitask, multitalk, and multithink. She'd been my support during my divorce, the adoption, the millions of times I'd needed a shoulder or a friend. To me, she defined stability, capability, dependability. She was my rock.

But now, she was imploding. Coming apart.

Susan looked at her hand and studied her wedding ring, her

brow furrowed. I knew, by her expression, that there was more. She was deciding how much to reveal.

"Go on," I said. "What?"

She looked up, all innocence. "What do you mean, 'what'?"

"What else?"

"Nothing else. So," she dodged, changing the subject, "how's work?"

"Work's fine. Don't change the subject."

"What subject. We weren't talking about anything.."

I didn't know whether to press the topic or let it go, wasn't sure what she wanted me to do. This was a new situation for us. Suddenly, I smelled flowers.

"Ready?"

No, not flowers. I smelled Gladys, the waitress. Her lily of the valley toilet water.

Gladys didn't like waiting and punctuated passing seconds by batting her false lashes. She had large hands with long, silver sculpted nails, silver rings on every finger.

"Can I have a milk shake, Mom?"

"Can we get onion rings?"

Normally, it was Susan who ordered. She naturally assumed the alpha position. Top dog, head hen, queen bee. But now, even menu items were beyond her; she had no capacity for making choices. Gladys tapped her nails on the order pad, shifted her pen, rolled her eyes, and glowered until, finally, I managed to spit out the names of enough dishes and drinks to feed the four of us and probably half the people in the place.

Gladys scribbled on her pad and snorted off.

"I'm starving." Molly whined. "How long till the food comes?"

"Don't whine," I said. "You're not starving. You don't even know what starving is."

"Yes, I do. It's dying of hunger. And I am."

I didn't want to get into it with her. "Hang on. It'll be here soon." She complained some more but gave up after a while, when I didn't respond. She and Emily began a hidden-word place-mat game.

"I see one. P-I-G. That spells pig."

Molly had sounded it out. I kissed her as Emily, ever competitive, declared that she'd found D-O-G first. I returned my attention to Susan.

"It's really nothing." It took a second to figure out what she was talking about. She'd picked up our conversation exactly where we'd left it.

"What's nothing?"

She fidgeted with her silverware. "It's no big deal, Zoe. I just don't want to talk about it."

"Why not?" Obviously, she did.

"Talking won't do any good."

"Susan, please don't say that to a therapist. It's like telling a lawyer that suing won't do any good."

"You're an art therapist, not a talk therapist. I didn't knock making pottery or mosaics."

"Okay. Don't tell me."

"I've had some nightmares, that's all."

"Nightmares?" Susan had my attention. I was, after all, an expert on nightmares, having had my share. I knew what it was to wake up sweating, caught in the talons of a bad dream.

"All week. Since Claudia. I've just been rattled."

Except that Susan didn't rattle. She dealt with murders and murderers every day. Reality, even brutality, didn't shake her.

"Dreams can seem more real than reality," I said.

She nodded. "I don't sleep. That's the main thing. I'm so tired."

I couldn't help playing therapist. "Do the nightmares come only when Tim's out of town?"

"No. It's not like that."

"Well, do you know what sets them off? PMS, maybe? Or the moon? Your diet? Trial dates?"

"No, no. They just began the other night. After Claudia." She stopped, irritated, wanting the topic to go away. "I really don't want to talk about this."

"But if they're so bad that you're not functioning—"

"It's no big deal. It's just temporary. Stress. I'll manage. Let's forget I brought it up? And, please, don't repeat this—"

"Repeat it? Why would I—"

"I know you wouldn't. It's stupid to say that. But I have trouble enough being taken seriously around the Justice Center—I'd be finished if anyone knew about this. Not even Tim knows."

"Susan. There's nothing shameful about having nightmares."

"Yes, there is. For a criminal lawyer, there is."

She glanced at the girls, making sure they were absorbed in their own banter. "See, they're about the crimes. The victims." Susan looked at her hands, studied her manicure. "They, uh, come back in the night. Every night, since Claudia disappeared. They're after me, as if it's my fault they're dead. They blame me."

"Blame you? For what?"

She looked at me as if I were addled. "For what. For defending their killers. For getting their killers off so they can go free."

"Oh," I nodded. "That's scary." A macabre chortle slipped out my mouth.

The girls, finished with the puzzles, began discussing what colors to make Arthur and his shirt and pants.

Susan went on. "Zoe, they stalk me. They're broken, cut, shot, slashed—however they were when they were found. That black kid who was beaten to death? He follows me—he just walks into my dreams with his head bashed in, leaking brains."

Okay. That was scary. "Jeez, Susan."

"This has never happened to me before, not in thirteen years of criminal defense work. Dealing with crime and grit is my job.

I defend the accused, no matter how sleazy—guilty or innocent, violent or benign. I've seen it all, defended it all. But suddenly it's coming back to haunt me. I see death, victims, corpses every time I doze off."

Susan's voice was getting louder and higher as she talked. Emily and Molly stopped talking and watched her, and the two men in the booth behind her cocked their heads, listening.

"See, in our country everybody has the right—and I believe that they should have the right, guilty or innocent—to be represented by counsel who present their best possible defense. That's how our legal system works. But lately—"

"*Shhh*—Mom, you're shouting," Emily shouted.

Susan leaned across the table, whispering now. The men in the booth behind her leaned back, straining to hear. "Lately—Zoe—don't tell anyone, but I want to see my own clients fry. I see what they've done to their victims and I can barely sit in a room to interview them. How am I supposed to argue for their defense?"

I didn't know. I reached over and squeezed her arm.

"Zoe, you realize you're the only one I can talk to about this."

Molly and Emily stared at her, twin wide-eyed expressions. One of the men behind Susan took our lull in conversation as an opportunity to turn around and gape. I met his eyes; he turned back and hunkered into his seat.

"Susan," I said softly, "maybe you're burned out. Maybe you need a break. A sabbatical. Look at all the pressure on you. I mean, forget about the nanny situation. In normal circumstances, you've got three kids, a house, a traveling husband, unreliable child care, a job that people's lives depend on. One minute you're helping a kid with long division and the next you're trying to save a guy from lethal injection. Most people make mistakes at work and so what? They have to retype a page or they lose a sale. But if you make a mistake, somebody goes to jail for years—or gets the needle. That's pressure."

"It is, isn't it?" Her voice was a subdued wail.

"Maybe the dreams are your mind's way of telling you to take a break and think about your own needs for a change." I sounded confident and assured. It was easy to give advice, but my advice was pure fluff. Susan's crisis had not been brought on by overwork or pressure; it had started specifically with Claudia's disappearance. And it wasn't going to stop just because she took some time off work or got a weekly massage.

"Lisa wants to quit piano. And Julie's begun to lie. About the stupidest things, like whether or not she's been to Disney World. Does she think I don't know the truth?"

"Yeah, Julie lies to me, too," Emily chimed in, suddenly part of our conversation. Molly looked up attentively.

"She does?" Susan's voice was unimpressed.

"Yesterday, she said there was a dead bird in the backyard, but there wasn't. And she ate the last pudding pop and said she didn't." Emily continued coloring while listing offenses. "And know what? She said somebody's stealing all the babysitters. Julie's such a liar."

Susan became even more gray.

"How can someone steal a babysitter?" Emily shook her head, as if the concept were ridiculous.

"What, Mom? What did Emily say?" Molly tugged at my arm. "What did she mean, 'somebody's stealing babysitters'?"

"It's just a lie," Emily declared.

Susan fumbled for an answer.

"Mom? Billy said Tamara went away. Did she get stealed?"

"Stolen," I said.

"Did she? Will the stealer steal Angela?"

"No, of course not—"

Plates slammed the table. Gladys had saved me. "Tuna on rye, onion rings, hot tea, one diet, two vanilla shakes, two barley soups, BLT with, veggie burger with, two kids' grilled cheese, two minestrones, half cantaloupe, side of slaw, side house salad, extra pickles. Anything else?" The check landed in a puddle of coleslaw dressing, and Gladys wheeled the cart away.

Gladys didn't believe in courses. Food was food. Soups, desserts, salads, entrées—they were all served in a simultaneous jumble. Molly grabbed the ketchup and a fistful of onion rings and attacked her dinner. The girls ate and chattered, distracted and happy again in their world and leaving us to ours. Despite what we'd ordered, neither Susan nor I had much appetite. Susan sat playing with her soupspoon and I fiddled with some pickle slices, and we yammered on about the Christmas Pollyannas at the Institute, the futility of New Year's resolutions, the madness of pre-Christmas sales, and the drudgery of gift-wrapping— anything except what was really on our minds.

NINE

WHEN WE GOT HOME, MOLLY GOT INTO HER PAJAMAS AND snuggled under her covers. We read *Amelia Bedelia,* her favorite book, until she fell asleep. Exhausted, I got into bed and sank immediately into a deep, healing sleep. In the morning, I awoke refreshed. I'd slept so soundly that it took a while to remember that Tamara was missing, that Susan was a mess, that, as Charlie had warned, evil lurked close by. I had the sense that somehow dreams and reality had traded places, that daylight carried nightmares from which, by sleeping, I had temporarily escaped.

But Angela arrived carrying warm fresh scones from the Pink Rose, complaining that some construction worker had gawked at her all the way up the street. It had to be a guy from Jake's crew. Or Jake himself. I reminded her that those guys gawked at every woman; they considered it part of the job.

"Yeah? Well, he wouldn't look that way at anyone on my street," she declared. "He did, somebody'd make sure he didn't look at nobody else for a long time."

"Anybody else." I buttoned my coat. "He wouldn't look at anybody else for a long time."

Angela poured Molly's milk, ignoring me. "The guy pissed me off, Zoe, you'll pardon my expression. Don't you listen," she wagged a finger at Molly.

"What's wrong about somebody looking at you, Angela?" Molly smeared raspberry jam on her scone. "I look at you all the time."

"It was how he looked at me."

Molly blinked at her. "How?"

"Like he shouldn't have."

"Like this?" Molly scowled at her. "Or this?" She tugged her lips and eyes diagonally with her forefingers. "Or this?"

I left them to their discussion and hurried to work. Given the disaster of the previous session, I decided to assign a new project. I asked the group to close their eyes and picture a place that made them feel safe and peaceful. Then, distributing oil sticks, I asked them to draw these places. They responded well; apparently whatever had been plaguing them in our last meeting had been purged. At any rate, they quickly became absorbed in their work. Nobody bickered or wandered. I moved from easel to easel, discussing each work in progress, encouraging each effort.

Amanda was drawing a castle on a steep hill by the sea. Eyelids raw without lashes, bald spots hiding under a kerchief, she explained that she visited this place sometimes in her mind. I felt a pang, realizing that the place Amanda felt safest and most peaceful was imaginary. But she seemed content forming moats and turrets, her hands for the moment too busy to pluck her remaining wisps of hair.

Kimberly's work was, as usual, a scramble of splotches and jagged lines, but so far she'd managed to keep her work within the confines of her paper. I asked her to tell me about the place she was drawing. Laboring on a purple zigzag, she replied without looking up. "Wails pills healing pillows mellow yellow marshmallows." As always, I encouraged her and made a note of her comments. Sometimes meaning could be deciphered, sometimes not. Kimberly continued mumbling, drawing random markings apparently without effort or affect; not for the first time, I wished I could interpret the ideas she intended to articulate, see the images she intended to create.

As I approached Hank's easel, I caught a glimpse of a

sun-drenched greenhouse, blossoms and green everywhere. But before I could look closely, he ripped the page off the drawing pad and crumpled it up. "It's not right," he repeated, tearing it. "It's just not right."

I looked at the clock. Hank had spent a record twenty-three minutes working on a drawing before destroying it. I congratulated him on that, but, panting, Hank broke into tears. The flaws weren't in the picture, he sobbed. They were in his compulsive need for perfection. He knew what it was. He recognized it but couldn't control it. He sat on his stool, broad shoulders hunched, raw with emotion. I wanted to hug him and promise him he'd be okay. Instead, I handed him a tissue, and when he'd dried his tears, I took his hand, reminding him that journeys were made of small steps taken one at a time. I congratulated him on his progress; a few weeks ago, he hadn't been able to describe his problems so clearly, hadn't had the insight. He'd come a long way in a short time and deserved credit for that. We sat together hand in hand, and I felt his struggle pulsing through his body. Gradually, his breathing slowed, his muscles relaxed. I offered him another oil stick, and when he was ready, he took it. Pressing on, facing another blank page.

Meantime, Sydney Ellis was also making a leap. Sydney was standing beside his easel, an oil stick clutched in his fist. He'd stood that way for the entire session. Although he hadn't made a mark on his paper, he'd managed to join the group. In the last session, he hadn't even noticed that there was a class, much less that he could become part of it. Now, he'd claimed a spot among the others. Small steps, I reminded myself, taken one at a time.

When the session ended, I felt gratified. The group finally seemed to be responding to art therapy. I ran around the studio, humming "Standing in the Shadows of Love," an old Four Tops song, as I stored supplies and unfinished pictures in the closet. Then, files in hand, I rushed out, and somehow slammed full force into a wall—or no—not a wall. Something soft, woollier—something charcoal gray? Rebounding, stunned and off balance, I let out a screech and tried to regain my footing. Arms reached out, grabbing at me. Reflexively, I swatted, slapped at them, letting papers, files, patient notes, everything fly from my hands as I backed away, tripping over an easel leg, arms flailing, falling flat on my back into the storage closet. Oh my God.

Nick Stiles gawked in alarm. Panting, flustered, I tried to collect myself, rearranging my skirt so it would cover at least part of my thighs.

"Jesus," he said. "Are you all right?"

My face got hot. My elbow felt broken. Not to mention my ego. "What were you doing, sneaking up on me like that?"

"I didn't sneak up on you." Large hands grabbed mine and pulled me to my feet.

"You should have said something." I'd regained my balance if not my composure.

"I thought you saw me come in."

"How could I see you? I was in the closet—"

"You're right." He cut me off. "I should have said something. Sorry. I didn't mean to startle you."

I blinked at him, sputtering but unable to go on. He'd admitted being wrong, agreed that he was at fault, even apologized. He'd escaped unscathed. How infuriating was that? His eyes twinkled. How high up had my skirt gone?

"Are you sure you're all right?"

I nodded, still flushed, and began picking up my papers. What was he doing here? He knelt beside me, helping. His knee brushed my arm, just barely. He smelled fresh. Showered. A man in the morning.

"I am sorry. Really." He handed me a stack of files.

"I guess I'm a little jumpy." I managed a smile.

We stood. There wasn't much space between us, but he didn't move away. If I did, I'd be back in the storage closet. My eyes came up to his lapel. I stared at it, didn't look up. The moment was too long. People didn't stand this close together unless they were going to kiss. This was absurd; women were disappearing and I was thinking about kissing the police detective? My face was hot again. I was embarrassed by my own thoughts. I didn't know what to look at, where to point my face. If I looked up, my mouth would point right at his chin, kissing posture. Awkwardly, I turned my head, tilted it, and glanced at him sideways. He smiled. The smile was crooked. Not symmetrical. More like a half smile. A smirk.

"Well, you saved me a phone call," I said, my head still cocked. "I was about to try you again. You were out yesterday when I returned your call."

His eyes were ice blue. Very pale, outlined in navy. I hadn't known eyes came in that color.

"I got your message, but actually, I decided it would be better to talk to you in person, Ms. Hayes. Is there somewhere we can talk in private?"

In private? About what? It had to be the finger. The missing women. Something too important for the phone. My mind raced, trying to figure out what.

Stiles stepped back, making room for me to lead the way. I took a deep breath and adopted a professional mode. But I wasn't quite successful. Something was off. As we walked, I became increasingly aware of the blond hairs on the back of his hands. And I had the strangest desire to reach out and run my fingers along the woolly sleeve of his charcoal coat.

TEN

"HAVE YOU EVER WORKED WITH A FORENSIC PSYCHOLOGIST, Ms. Hayes?" Eighteen empty chairs had offered themselves, but after removing his coat and tossing it onto the conference room table, Detective Stiles had chosen to sit on the one directly beside me. Crowding me again. Was it deliberate? He watched me closely, as if studying my reactions, and his voice was muted, as if what he was saying were to be held in the utmost confidence.

"You mean a profiler? No. I haven't."

"But you know what they do, right?"

I nodded. "I watch TV like everybody else."

There was that crooked smile again. As if half his face were happy, the other half grim. There was a shadow on the grim half, some kind of scar.

"These days, everybody's an expert, with all the crime shows on the tube." The smile faded. His eyes moved quickly, taking in details of the room, returning to me. "Reality's a little different, though. The department works with various profilers, experts who analyze crime data and come up with a set of characteristics belonging to the perpetrator. They get pretty good results, too. Profilers described the character and lifestyles of serial killers like Ted Bundy and the Boston Strangler and locally, if you remember, Troy Graves, the Center City rapist."

I recalled the name. Graves had raped several women and murdered one, terrorizing the city in the late nineties.

"Police profilers nailed Graves's race, age, sexual history, social tendencies, physical build, and personality traits and the general location of his residence at the time of the crimes."

"But, as I recall, he wasn't caught here. Wasn't he arrested out in Colorado?"

"He was. But the profilers had the information just right. You've got a woman on staff here at the Institute who does profiling for the department. Beverly Gardener? You know her?"

Everyone knew Beverly Gardener. She was a celebrity, a tall, ambitious, confident, self-possessed brunette with legs to die for and a list of academic credentials as long as my arm. She hosted a call-in radio show, testified at trials as an expert witness, and wrote mass-market books on topics like the sex drives of mass murderers, the childhoods of serial killers, and the spiritual lives of death row prisoners. At the Institute, she was on staff as much for public relations as for her research. The board of directors was in awe of her. She was handled like a superstar, and, aloof and self-absorbed, she carried herself like one. As many times as I'd attended meetings with her or passed her in the hall, she'd never acknowledged me. Never as much as nodded hello.

"The department tends to consult Dr. Gardener, but since I've usually worked with the FBI, this is my first case with her. So far, I'm impressed."

I nodded, having no idea why we were having a conversation about Beverly Gardener. I waited for him to explain. The pause was heavy as he continued to study me. Why was he staring? We sat in adjacent chairs, knee almost to knee. Again, too close. I fidgeted, shifted in my chair, wished I'd tweezed my eyebrows. My knees tingled. I was aware of the muscles in my thighs. And in his.

Finally, I cleared my throat. "So. What does Beverly Gardener have to do with the finger?" I assumed that the finger was what he wanted to talk about.

"The finger?"

"The finger on my doorstep? Isn't that what you're here about?"

"Oh, of course. Well, yes and no. If not for the finger, I wouldn't be here, but actually I'm here to talk about you."

About me? Again, my face warmed. His eyes were riveted onto mine. Lord. What was he staring at? Was my hair messed up? Was my mascara clumped?

"Let me explain, Ms. Hayes. It's not a sure thing, but you might be able to help us."

I wasn't following. "Help you? How?"

"First, you're a psychotherapist."

"No, I'm not—I'm just an art therapist."

"Okay, then. An art therapist—"

"Well, it's an important distinction. I don't work alone—I'm part of a team of therapists, psychologists, and psychiatrists who work together. I work specifically with creative expression using visual media."

"So you do what? Analyze your patients' artwork? Try to figure out what it means?"

"Sometimes. Mostly, I help patients find ways to express themselves—"

His cell phone rang, but he nodded, apparently not interested in a description of my profession. "Anyhow, you're trained, an expert in human behavior." He took the call, and I remembered that Stiles had a degree in psychology. Shouldn't he know what an art therapist did? Why was he playing dumb? On the phone, he gave gruff instructions in words of one syllable, then continued as if there had been no interruption.

"Not only are you trained, but you're also in a unique position. You live smack in the middle of the area where serial crimes are being committed. Women are being abducted within a five-block radius. Experience and two profilers tell me that the perp most likely lives or works within that radius."

I swallowed. What was he saying? That the person taking the nannies was one of my neighbors?

"What I'm about to say is between you and me, okay?" He leaned closer. I smelled aftershave. "I want to enlist your help. Unofficially, of course. You know the neighborhood, the people, as no outsider can. You're also a mom, right? Presumably, you know at least some of the victims and potential victims—local babysitters and nannies."

I closed my eyes. Yes, indeed. I did.

"And you know people who've been in contact with those women. We want to find out who has links to the victims. Especially men who're connected somehow to all of them."

I blinked, remembering gymnastics. The conversation about Coach Gene asking out Tamara and Claudia, getting rejected by both. Did he know the other missing women, too? I thought about him while Detective Stiles kept talking. Everyone liked and trusted Gene; kids loved him. No one would suspect a peppy, friendly guy like him. And, working with young children, he had daily contact with lots of nannies.

"Think about it," Detective Stiles was saying. "As you come up with names, make me a list. Also, I'd like you to study Dr. Gardener's perp profile. See if you recognize anyone who fits the picture. Anything that rings a bell. Even if nothing does, I'd like you to be on the lookout, keep your eyes and ears open."

I was confused. I pictured Charlie on his porch, alert, standing guard. Was I supposed to join him? "You want me to spy on my neighbors?"

Half his mouth rose in its lopsided smile. "That's pretty cold, Ms. Hayes." The smile disappeared. "But no. It's nothing that extreme. Just read the profile, look around you, and communicate any relevant thoughts directly to me. What do you say?" His eyes waited, alert and intense.

What did I say? I pictured myself leaping a fence, chasing

suspects around the corner like a damn Charlie's Angel. He couldn't be asking for that. More likely, he wanted me to be his local informer. A snitch. How did I feel about that? Did I want to sleuth around the neighborhood, hunting a dangerous psychopath? I had a child, a home. A bubble to protect. But that was the whole point, wasn't it? I wanted to protect my home and child and Angela and Bonita and the whole neighborhood. Yes, I'd help. You bet I would.

"Of course, I'll do whatever I can."

Stiles gave me a hearty half grin. "Good. Let me get you a copy—" His cell phone rang again and he picked it up. His free hand rubbed his eyes, then brushed through his hair. What had happened? What was wrong? His gaze returned to me and stayed there. What was he looking at so hard? Was there paint on my nose? His eyes were disturbing, intense. Something awful had happened. "Mother of God," he blinked. "Give me five minutes."

He stood there, watching me. "Sorry, I have to cut this short." He stood, reached for his coat.

Again, I saw the finger drop into the Baggie, felt a dizzy spin.

Stiles's coat was on, the doorknob in his hand. "You all right, Ms. Hayes?"

No. I was cold as ice. "Yes. Fine."

"We'll need to go over the profile some other time. To talk, uninterrupted." Detective Stiles glanced at his watch. "How's dinner?"

Dinner?

"You know Ristorante La Buca? Near Washington Square? I can have a car pick you up—"

Wait. Detective Stiles was asking me to dinner? "No, that's okay—thanks."

He winced. Why was he wincing? "Oh, well. Then, maybe we can meet in the—"

"Oh—I mean, La Buca is close to my house. I can walk."

He brightened and I understood; he'd winced because he'd thought I was turning him down. "It'll be dark. You sure?"

"I'll be fine."

"Great. It'll be my way of apologizing for scaring you before. How's eight o'clock?"

What was I doing? I couldn't have dinner with him. What would I do with Molly? Angela couldn't sit at night—and I wouldn't ask her, not with so many nannies missing. No, I couldn't go.

"Fine," I heard myself say. "Eight o'clock's fine." My voice had answered on its own.

"Great. See you there."

I stayed in the conference room, jumbled, as if awakening from a nonsensical dream that I had to sort out. Why was Stiles asking me—a civilian—to get involved in a police investigation? And why had I agreed? No matter how much I wanted to help, I had Molly to think about. For her sake, I had no business putting myself at risk. I'd been impulsive. Maybe I should back out. Even as I had that thought, I knew it was wrong. I wouldn't back out.

Molly, Angela, our home and neighborhood—they were being threatened, and I had a chance to help protect them. No way would I turn it down.

For the rest of the day, my eyes wandered to the clock, counting hours until dinner. I couldn't wait. I was going to assist the police, however slightly. To be on the inside of this case. To help catch the damn kidnapper.

But there was something else on my mind as evening approached. I was intrigued by Detective Stiles, how his mind worked, how he approached a case. And, aside from all that, I liked the way he smelled.

ELEVEN

IT WAS DARK WHEN I GOT HOME. ANGELA REFUSED TO LISTEN.

"I'll pay for the cab."

"No way."

"Why are you being so stubborn?"

"I'm not. Nobody's going to mess with me, not in my neighborhood."

"But it's several blocks to your neighborhood."

"Anybody tries to mess with me, I know what to do. I got a good pair of lungs, and I didn't grow up with four older brothers without knowing how to defend myself."

She pulled on green wool gloves dotted with little red and white Christmas trees and headed for the door. "Bye, Molly," she called.

Molly looked up from her coloring book long enough to say good-bye. I walked outside with Angela. At least I could watch her to the corner. But across the street, carrying a large crate down the walk from Charlie's house, was a better solution.

"Yo, Jake," I called. "How's it going?"

He started, surprised, then popped the crate onto the back of his pickup, looked over, and waved. "Yo—how'd that salt work out?"

"Good," I shouted. "Real good. Thanks."

"Who's that?" Angela whispered.

"Jake," I whispered back. "You know him—"

"No, I don't."

"Yes, you do. He helped us move out Molly's crib."

"That was him? He looks different."

"His hair's longer."

"'Sup?" Jake approached our front steps, smiling broadly. His eyes, deep set and too close together, seemed sunken in the dusk. He was unshaven, shoulders bulging through a zippered hoodie.

"You busy right now, Jake?"

"Why? Something I can do for you, ladies?"

Angela covered her mouth. "Zoe, don't—"

I squeezed her arm. "Angela, you remember Jake. Jake, Angela."

He grinned broadly, teeth sparkling, chest out. "Sure. How's it going?"

"Yeah, okay." Angela gave him a disapproving once-over.

"Angela insists on walking home, Jake, and I don't think it's safe."

"No way. It's not. You want a lift, Angela? Where you headed?"

"I don't need a lift. I'm fine."

"No trouble. You gotta be careful these days. I just gotta run into that rehab for a second, then I'm headin' out anyway. I'll be right back. Stay put." He took off down the street and turned in to a half-renovated townhouse.

"I'm not speaking to you no more," Angela announced. "You got no sense of boundaries between us. What's my business is not the same as what's your business."

"I just want you to be safe."

"It's not your business if I'm safe. Besides, I'm not talking to you."

"Fine."

I walked her down the stairs to Jake's pickup. We stood there, not talking, breath steaming, waiting in the cold. A minute later, Jake came running back carrying a lunch box and a paint-stained tarp. He tossed them into the back.

"Hop in." He opened the door and reached gallantly for Angela's hand.

"Get her home safe, Jake."

"You got it. No problem. Glad to help out. Any time." He preened like a shining knight. Or a horny rooster.

Angela fried me with her eyes but climbed into the truck. Jake closed the door after her and ran around to the driver's side. "She couldn't be safer, don't you worry."

The engine roared and they drove off, Angela glaring at me through the window. Watching them, I realized how cute a couple they made. Except that Angela planned to marry Joe, her high school sweetheart. Otherwise, I might have played Cupid.

TWELVE

"Dinner?" Susan squawked in disbelief. She was in her manic mood again. "You're going out with the police detective?"

"No, I'm not going out with him."

While Molly lolled in her bath, I went through my closet, trying to find something to wear to dinner. "It's a meeting. He wants me to help him out, as sort of a consultant." "Consultant" sounded better than "snitch."

"I'm sure he does." Her tone was sarcastic. "The question is, how closely will you have to work?"

"I'm serious, Susan." I tried to sound calm.

"What? You think this is legitimate? You think Homicide normally consults art therapists?"

"I wouldn't know." I pulled out a gray dress and held it up in front of the mirror. Too frumpy and shapeless. And the navy was too daytime.

"About what, precisely, will you consult? Teaching watercolors at the Police Academy? Offering decoupage therapy to the Highway Patrol?"

"He wants my help with a case."

"A case of what? The hots?"

"Very funny." How did she know I was attracted to him? Had she heard it in my voice? Was it that obvious? "He wants to talk about the neighborhood. He thinks the nanny guy is local."

"Yeah, so do I. But why is he talking to you? Why not, say, to

Leslie? Or me—I live around here, too. I'll tell you why. Because Leslie and I happen to be dowdy and married, and you happen to be stunning and single."

Stunning? Me? I glanced in the mirror, saw definite cheekbones, symmetrical features. But stunning? "Susan, you're not dowdy. Besides, I'm a therapist. He thinks I'll have insights about the psychological profile."

"Sure. That's it. He's taking you to a candlelit dinner because you're a therapist. Zoe, you can't be that naive."

"Susan, not everything's about sex." I looked at my long black wool skirt. It was comfy, went with everything, had a slit up the back.

"You can't mean that. Everything certainly is about sex. Unless it's about food—but even food is about sex, really."

I shifted the topic. "So you're sure it's all right to bring Molly over?"

"Of course. Molly's always welcome."

"And you really feel better?" She sounded better. Probably she was. It was a pattern with her, swinging from emotional pits to soaring heights.

"Much better. Zoe, I don't know what happened, except that I was completely blown away by Tamara's disappearance. But somehow I've got it together again."

"Did you sleep last night?" I rifled through my sweaters. Purple? Mauve? Red?

"No, but I rested this afternoon. Tim surprised me and came back to town on the red-eye. We had . . . a long lunch." Her voice was a satisfied purr.

I smiled. "Good. I'm glad Tim's around." Maybe she'd feel safer now. "Maybe more 'long lunches' will stop the nightmares."

"I doubt it. But they have a definite therapeutic effect. I'm much less tense. My body's relaxed and my complexion's cleared up. At least for now—Tim leaves again Sunday."

"Damn. Think you'll go crazy again?"

"I might, but not as bad. I promise. Meantime, we decorated our tree and I've started the baking. I'm back on track."

"You scared me, you know. I thought you were in trouble. This didn't seem like your normal mood swing."

"I know. But I'm fine." She sounded happy. Too happy. She sounded idiotic. "I'm over my crisis. I'm upset and angry like everyone. But I'm not over the edge anymore."

"So basically, orgasms cured your breakdown?"

"Maybe. At least, they didn't hurt."

"What a staggering concept. Think of the implications for patients at the Institute. Instead of group therapy, we'll hold orgies. Instead of drugs, we'll prescribe sex."

She laughed. "It's worth a try. But I don't know if it's a cure. I still get nightmares; I just don't react the same way. I had this dream last night where I'm in court and next to me is a blonde. Just the blonde part—her head, on the chair, staring at me. She's got blood around her neck, and it's oozing into a puddle on the chair."

"Okay."

"I'm defending the guy who decapitated her, so she's angry. She wants me to feel sorry for her so I'll slip up and let him hang. But, instead, I start making all sorts of puns. To the jury. Stupid puns. About not losing our heads, remaining detached when considering the body of evidence, not getting ahead of ourselves, and minding the rules of law. The closing is uproariously funny to me, hilarious. The jury, the judge, and the defendant are all in hysterics. I win the case. And I wake up laughing out loud."

A chapped spot on my lips throbbed. I chewed it, tasted blood. "Hell of a dream," I said. "Think it was about the nannies? You're worried you'll have to defend the creep?"

"I just think it means I'm feeling confident again, not intimidated by doubts."

The dream sounded grisly, but Susan was obviously amused by it. Even motivated. She sounded almost like herself again. I took out a charcoal cashmere, a black patterned handknit, and the purple cowlneck. Why couldn't I decide?

"God, the gymnastics moms must think I'm a lunatic," Susan went on. "I think I scared them."

"I'd say so, yes. But you woke them up."

"Think they all ran out to buy guns today?"

"More likely, they're all at South Street Karate."

She laughed at the thought. "Leslie the Black Belt." Leslie was bone thin and barely five feet tall. "Seriously, though, we should follow up. Organize. Form a town watch. Set up that buddy system. And quickly."

Susan did sound better. I smirked, imagining Tim healing her with his potency. Superstud wasn't Tim's image. Paunchy, flat-butted, and bald on the back of his head, Tim seemed like a big stuffed animal, more stuffed than animal. Unexpectedly, Nick Stiles came to mind. He wasn't wearing a shirt.

"So bring Molly over. Meantime, I'll ask my guys at the Roundhouse what's up with Stiles." The Roundhouse was police headquarters.

"No, Susan. Don't—really—"

"I want to know his situation. Is he married? Divorced? Is he a player?"

I swallowed. "Susan, this is not a date."

"Of course it's not. And Molly can stay as late as you want. She can even sleep over."

"Susan—"

"Just in case your meeting lasts later than expected. She's welcome to stay."

It was no use arguing. Susan would think what she wanted. I knew the truth. My dinner date wasn't a step toward romance or seduction. It was a step in the pursuit of a serial kidnapper and probable murderer. When we hung up, I started for the bathtub to get Molly but stopped at the bedroom mirror.

Was I stunning? Strands of stark gray streaked the brown of my hair. My skin was pretty smooth, eyes clear. Brows dark and arched. Forehead high, facial bones defined. Lips full. The face was symmetrical. But stunning? I looked closer, trying to see my face as if it were unfamiliar. A stranger's. What would I think of it? Was it a face I'd even notice if it weren't on my own neck? What did stunning mean, anyway? I stared, trying to decide. I posed, changed expressions. Decided it wasn't possible for me to decide; the answer would be found by other eyes. Besides, I had to get moving.

I took a fresh towel into the bathroom for Molly, wrapped her up, brushed her hair, and tried to ignore the persistent image of Stiles, turning around, the muscles rippling in his back.

THIRTEEN

As I finished Molly's hair, the phone rang again. He's canceling, I thought. Stiles is going to cancel. I didn't want him to, considered not answering. After all, if he couldn't reach me, he couldn't cancel.

Molly came out of the bathroom, wrapped in a towel. She cocked her head, watching me as I stood motionless, staring at the jangling phone. "Mom—pick up the phone!"

I took a deep breath. What was wrong with me? Even without dinner, I'd still work on the case. I'd just pick up a copy of the profile in the morning instead of at dinner. Who needed his damned dinner, anyhow? I answered, prepared for his excuse, whatever it would be.

"Zoe? What's wrong?"

Phew. It wasn't Stiles. Our meeting was still on.

"Hi, Michael."

"I was beginning to think you weren't there. I was getting worried."

"Worried? Why?"

"Why? You can't be serious. You're a single woman. Single women are disappearing almost daily in your neighborhood. And it's getting dark, so I knew you wouldn't be out with your kid—"

"Wait. You think I never go out after dark?"

"Mom, I have tangles." Molly hopped up next to me on the bed, her brush caught in her hair.

"Are you saying that you do? With everything that's been going on down there?"

I ground my teeth and gently untangled Molly's knots, refusing to be baited. "As a matter of fact, I'm about to head out now. But thanks for your concern. What can I do for you?"

"Head out? Now? I was hoping to stop by. Bring you some Chinese."

"Some Chinese."

"Yeah. I'm in the area. I thought you'd enjoy it. Still like Peking duck?"

Oh Lord. What did he want?

The knots were out. "Who's on the phone?" Molly whispered.

"Go get dressed," I whispered back. "It's nobody." She nodded as if my answer made sense and scampered away, dragging her towel. "So, what's the deal, Michael? You trying to bribe me?"

Leave it to Michael to offer a couple of egg rolls in exchange for a flawless diamond.

"Bribe you? Damn, Zoe. Why do you always suspect the worst? I was just thinking of you, all alone there with your kid, nobody to check on you, trapped in that tiny house while all around you, every five minutes, single women are getting snatched—"

"Thanks, Michael." Was he trying to scare me? "I'm fine. No need to worry. Take it easy." I started to hang up.

"Wait—Zoe? Well. As long as I've got you on the phone, I might as well ask you. Have you given any thought to the engagement ring situation?"

Good old Michael. "That's what you really called about, isn't it?"

"No. Not at all. I told you why I called. I was worried about you. Have you decided yet?"

I sighed. I didn't want to give him another thing, no matter what it was, but the ring really belonged with his family. Still, I didn't want to be pressured. "Actually, no."

"No?"

"No."

He considered it. "No as in you haven't thought about it yet? Or no as in you won't give it back?"

"Pick one." The man would never give up. Molly ran back in, dressed in her underwear, carrying an armload of clothes.

"What should I wear, Mom?"

"How about the green sweatsuit?"

"The green sweatsuit?" Michael didn't understand.

"Molly's going to Susan's. She's deciding what to wear."

"I can't. I wore that last time I was there."

I sighed. She wasn't even six yet. I wondered what she'd be like as a teenager. "Then wear the gray or the navy."

"Okay, the gray. No. The navy. Wait—" She ran off again, leaving three outfits scattered on my bedroom floor.

"Look, Michael, I don't have an answer for you, and I have to get going."

He wouldn't give up. "Okay. How about we talk later? I'll bring dinner when you get back from Susan's."

"I'm not going to Susan's. Molly is. I'm going out to dinner."

He hesitated, letting the information sink in. "You have a date?" Like that was inconceivable. "A dinner date?"

"I've gotta go."

"Who is he?"

"You don't know him."

"So. Some guy's taking you out for a classy meal. Careful, Zoe. Sounds like he's trying to get in your pants." I thought I heard a hint of jealousy in his voice.

"Not everyone schemes the way you do, Michael."

"Why would I scheme? I've already been in your pants."

Lord. "Thanks for reminding me."

"No problem. Tell you what, though. This guy's pretty lame if he thinks he can buy in with just a pricey meal." There was definitely something indignant in his voice.

"Look—I gotta go."

"Me, too. But, Zoe, do me a favor—"

"Don't worry. I'll be careful."

"Just think about the ring?" He tried to cover up. "Well, of course, be careful. That goes without saying."

"Bye, Michael."

"I'll call you tomorrow—to make sure you're okay."

I hung up before he could mention the ring again. Gathering clothing along the way, I went to find Molly before she could pull every one of her outfits out of her drawers. I had to hurry, still had to pick out an outfit and get myself dressed. I told myself to quiet the flutter in my stomach. Despite what Susan and Michael might think, my dinner with Detective Stiles was about business; it was not a date. Still, maybe I'd go with the black sweater, black skirt.

FOURTEEN

Susan's hair was wrapped in a huge white turban of towel. Her eyes twinkled, her skin glowed, and she smelled like magnolia soap. She took Molly's hand at the front door and led us into the house. I wasn't ready to let Molly go; I hadn't spent time with her all day. But Susan whisked her away, removing her pink woolly mittens and matching parka, and Emily ran out, and the two of them scampered off together.

"Zoe—it's great you finally hit it off with someone, even if he is a cop."

"I told you. We didn't 'hit it off '—"

"You didn't have to say it. It's obvious. It's in your voice and on your face. You're wearing it."

I was? Damn.

The aroma of something deliciously garlicky drifted in from the kitchen. I looked around. The tree glittered in the living room, presents scattered underneath; stockings were hung by the chimney with care. In the sunroom, Lisa was reading and Mozart was playing; Julie was doing needlepoint.

Grinning, Susan pounded her chest as she walked to the kitchen. "Zoe, guess what—I've been planning my trial strategy. And I'm going to win. My guys are going to get off." She was practically squealing, floating above the floor, waltzing lightly along the hall, leading me to the kitchen.

I followed, unbuttoning my coat, noticing how uncluttered

the house was. There were no boots or bookbags to stumble over, no half-eaten snacks or scattered clothes. In her internal life, Susan rode a roller coaster, but somehow, in her external roles and relationships, she remained a rock.

"I thought you thought they were guilty."

"Defendants aren't guilty until the jury says they are. And my clients will be judged not guilty by juries of their peers, thank you very much." She curtsied, grinning, and called, "Molly, you like spaghetti, don't you?"

"With meatballs?"

She nodded. "Of course, with meatballs. And you and Emily can make the garlic bread. Come on, I'll get you started."

I stared at Susan, wondering what drug she was on. Or should be on. "Judged not guilty?" I brought her back to our topic. "But how?"

She took out butter, garlic, a garlic press. "What do you mean, how? They have a good lawyer. Criminal defense work isn't about what clients have or have not done. It's about their right to a zealous defense, a fair trial, and the presumption of innocence."

I knew better than to comment. Susan would argue legal ethics all night, would spin defensively in emotional somersaults. I thought it best to keep my mouth shut while she showed the girls how to make garlic bread. She fluttered from topic to topic, happily bantering about the joys of fresh garlic in the same breath as the art of jury selection and the luster-building capabilities of her new shampoo.

"You really ought to use some—wash your hair with it before you go out with Stiles." She opened a cupboard and pulled out a breadbasket.

"Mom, what did Susan say? Who are you going out with?" Molly had an uncanny knack for selective hearing.

"I told you. I have a meeting."

"Make yourself look good, Zoe. He's a hunk."

"A hunk? Who, Mom?" Molly looked at Emily and they both began to giggle.

"Does your mom have a boyfriend?"

Molly's eyes widened, "Mom, do you have a boyfriend?"

"Come on, Molly. You'd know if I did."

Susan smiled. "Your mom's got a business meeting tonight. Candlelight, soft music, wine, and business." She took the melted garlic butter off the stove and put it on the table in front of the girls, along with brushes and bread. Immediately, they got to work.

"Speaking of your business meeting," Susan whispered, "what about the jogger?"

"What jogger?"

Susan turned away so the girls wouldn't hear. "Some jogger found another finger in Washington Square. They think it's one of the nannies'."

I went cold.

"And you'll appreciate this—according to the news, this is the first body part that's been found."

"What about my finger?"

"What finger? Apparently, that never happened. This just shows you that the news doesn't mean anything. Reporters read whatever gets put in front of them. They don't know what's really going on. The cops aren't releasing all the facts on this one. And guess who's in charge of the cops? Your boyfriend."

I didn't take the bait. "Maybe," I breathed, "they held off telling about my finger so people wouldn't panic."

"Maybe. But the cops aren't telling us everything. We're having a moms' meeting Thursday night. At gymnastics."

"What are you whispering about, Mommy? Your boyfriend? Come on, tell me. Who is he?"

"Molly, I don't have a boyfriend."

"Is he that guy who always stares at you?"

What was she talking about? "What guy who stares at me?"

"You know who. That guy—on our street."

"On our street? You mean Victor? Or the new guy with the Santa Claus—Mr. Woods? Or Charlie?"

"Charlie? Charlie's your boyfriend!" She reeled with laughter.

I leaned over and kissed her. It was time to go. "See you later. Be good. I love you."

"Zoe, wait—take that shampoo." Susan rushed out of the room.

"No, thanks."

"Yes. Try it. I'll be right down."

The girls painted bread with garlic butter. The house was unusually calm. No television, no bickering kids. Where was the chaos, the conflict, the general tumult that typically surrounded Susan? Mozart floated through the house. Dinner was simmering, and the children were happy and organized. There was no trace of turmoil, no sense of danger here. Even grisly news of vanished women, of a finger found in the park, couldn't shake the pervasive warmth.

I suddenly felt very alone. I went to Molly and stood beside her at the table. A dish towel was tucked into her sweatshirt for protection, but she concentrated, trying not to drip. I smoothed her hair, and she squirmed.

"Stop, Mom. You'll make me spill."

"Sorry."

I took my hand away.

"I won't be late," I said. "Have fun. I love you, Mollybear."

"Have fun, too. I love you, too." Her words were distracted, automatic.

"Remember, she can spend the night, if you want." Susan was back, handing me a bottle of shampoo.

"I can? Can I sleep over, Mom?" Molly asked, carelessly dripping butter all over the counter. Emily chimed in, begging.

"Please? Please?" They were a duet, a chorus of begging. "Can we have a sleepover?"

Susan's skin glowed, her house gleamed clean, her children were radiant, and her husband was around somewhere, upstairs. Her home was warm and alive. "It's fine with us," she said.

I looked at my daughter. She was happy here, blending in, entirely at home. "Not tonight," I said. "Another time."

"Why? Why not tonight? Please?"

They continued pleading as I buttoned my coat, and I left quickly, selfishly, before I could be swayed.

FIFTEEN

OUTSIDE, THE WEATHER HAD CHANGED FOR THE WORSE. The temperature had dropped suddenly, refreezing the latest melt and the new rain, creating a world sheathed in glass. Trees along Pine Street sparkled like crystal under a darkening sky; branches glistened, heavy and stiff. Sidewalks and steps—even the stone bears in Three Bears Park—were treacherously glazed. The stretch of blocks between my house and Susan's seemed endless as I stepped carefully, trying not to slip; my face stung, assailed by bits of jagged ice. Raw wind sliced through my jacket, and each breath pulled precious heat out of my body. The streets were empty; I walked home on feet that had lost all feeling, darkness grabbing at my back, a chain of icy air circling my throat.

When I reached my house, I turned away from the wind, fumbling to take my keys out of my pocket with numbed gloved hands. Frustrated, pulling off a glove to try again, I saw something move in the backseat of an old, ice-coated Pontiac parked at the curb. Gradually, I realized that the something was a hand, waving to me. I took another look. Somebody was definitely in there. Waving. Or—tapping?

All the childhood warnings about strangers in cars flooded my mind. I hurried to put my key in the lock, but someone called my name. "Miss Zoe!"

Charlie peeked through the now open Pontiac window. His

voice was hoarse and guttural. My teeth were chattering, but I descended the steps, careful not to slip.

"No!" Charlie whispered. "Don't come any closer! You'll be seen!"

I continued toward the car, squinting in the sleet, leaning on the rear of Jake's frozen pickup truck so I wouldn't slip. Inside the Pontiac, I saw rumpled blankets and a pillow. A box of Ritz crackers. Cans of Dr. Pepper, Budweiser. Was Charlie living in this old car?

"What are you doing out here?" I asked.

"I had to get out of the house, miss."

"You'll freeze, Charlie. What happened? Do you need rent money?"

"Oh no. I'm the handyman, miss. I work for the owner; I got no rent. I just had to get out of there. Things are much worse." He crouched back into the seat and whispered through the window. "The evil's growing, gaining power. Now, see, my dreams have been taken over. My thoughts are being monitored. I'm under constant surveillance, see. Because I know what's going on."

He was absolutely crazy. And I was quaking with the cold. I wanted to run inside, to sip hot peppermint tea and take a bath in jasmine-scented bubbles. I had to hurry and get ready for dinner with Detective Stiles. But how could I leave poor Charlie out in the car?

"Charlie. You can't stay out in this weather. Go inside. Nobody's going to bother you."

"Miss, I told you I'd watch over you. There's danger coming your way. Soon, any day now. I'm warning you, there will be terrible consequences. We may be being watched, even now."

I was shivering so much that I had trouble hearing. My face was raw and my toes were frozen. Charlie turned away, staring into the street. His face glowed red, then green, reflecting the lights of Phillip Woods's blinking Santa.

". . . I know what's really going on. It's about revenge. Revenge and immortality. But it doesn't matter why he does it, see, because it's evil, pure and simple. Evil butchery."

He must have heard the news about the finger. He was rambling, tying together loose random thoughts, reminding me of my Institute patients. Maybe Charlie belonged there. A car drove slowly by. Charlie ducked. "See, people think I'm just a handyman. They think I'm old and slow. Well, I'm old, but not so slow. And I can tell he's used my tools. Downstairs. Takes my lockboxes. My tables. The space under the floor, below. He comes and goes, moves my things. And now that he listens to my thoughts— he'll find out that I know. He'll find out everything. Not only that I'm onto him but that I'm standing against him. That I'm warning you. I'm protecting you. He'll come after me now, for sure."

Charlie stopped for a long, scraping cough. He'd lost it completely, gone over the edge. He was raving. Delusional. He needed help. I wondered if I could get someone to see him at the Institute. Of course, by law, if he wanted treatment there, he'd have to admit himself. But beyond his mental state, Charlie was physically ill. His face glowed, damp with sweat. Red, green. Red. Green.

"You're sick, Charlie. You must have a fever. Please go in and have something hot. I can get you to a hospital—"

"No, miss. No hospitals. I'm staying right here where I need to be. But if I disappear, you'll know what's happened. See, he probes my mind. I feel him in my head like a hot wire. It's his telepathy. In the day, I can fend him off, see. But when I sleep, I can't be vigilant. So nights, see, I stay out here, where there's engines and sirens and radio interference, and he can't probe."

"Charlie," I shivered, "go inside. I'll bring you some hot tea or coffee. Or how about some cocoa?"

"No, miss. You go inside. Don't worry. I'm still protecting you and the child. Because otherwise, see, you'd end up in the paper. Or on the posters and milk cartons. 'Missing.' They're not missing. See, they've been taken. He takes them. I know. He works there, inside. He takes what he wants and leaves the rest. The coroners and judges, the police—they know, but they won't say. They don't dare. He has them under his control, holds their minds. Reads their thoughts, too. It's part of his plan. Returning the children to the hands of the original Mother, the Virgin—"

His words were lost in another fit of coughing so violent that he bent over, holding his abdomen.

Ice had caked my eyelashes. My jaw was numb now, not just my feet and fingers, and my cheeks burned from the cold. Wind ripped through my coat, slashing my skin.

"Charlie. You might have pneumonia. You have to call your doctor. Or tell me the number and I'll call."

I reached for the car door to open it and help him out.

"No!" he shouted. His eyes moved rapidly from side to side, searching the street. "Don't touch the car. Just go into your house, miss. Go in and pretend you don't see me."

He coughed into a rumpled handkerchief.

I was frustrated. "Listen, Charlie. If you want me to go inside, then you have to go, too. I'm not going unless you do." It was a bluff, but what else could I do? I couldn't let him freeze.

He thought for a moment. "Okay, miss. I think I can. For a little while, at least until he tunes in to my head again."

"Will you call a doctor?"

"A doctor? No, ma'am. No doctor—" A hacking cough stopped him.

"Charlie, you need a doctor. You're sick."

"No, miss! A doctor could be in disguise. Might make me sick." His eyes beamed feverishly.

"What if I knew the doctor? What if I took you to a friend—"

"No doctors, miss. I told you." He was vehement.

I bit my lip. "Let's go, Charlie."

"You go first."

"I'm not leaving until I see you get out of this car."

"Okay, okay. But don't you worry, miss. I'm on the job. Just watch the little girl." He looked around, suddenly alarmed. "Where is she?"

"She's visiting a friend, Charlie. She's fine. Now, come on out."

Slowly, bent and stiff, Charlie climbed out of the car. I took his arm, and together we shuffled across the ice to the steps of his house. His stooped body was sturdier than I'd expected, and he supported me as much as I did him. At the top of the steps, he wheezed, "Remember, Miss Zoe. People aren't who they seem. They can disguise themselves and fool you. Don't trust anyone."

I backed away. "Charlie, are you going to drink something hot now?"

"I'll have some soup, miss."

"If you're not better by tomorrow, either you call your doctor or I will."

He nodded and waved, then went inside. I watched his door close, then, assuring myself that he'd be better by morning, I slid back to my house, fumbled with my key, and finally made it safely inside. I stood at the door for a moment thawing out, savoring the glorious warmth of my cozy home. Then, still shivering, fingers and toes swollen and burning from the frost, I put up the kettle and turned on the TV. The StairMaster beckoned from the corner, offering to warm me with exercise while I watched the news; I threw my coat over it. The news was just starting. Rubbing my frozen hands together, I waited to hear the latest about the missing nannies, but the smiling anchorwoman talked about the ice storm. For the first time all week, something had preempted the story of the vanished women.

Taking out a teabag, worrying about Charlie, I looked out the kitchen window at the empty Pontiac. The lights came on in Charlie's living room. Poor Charlie was sick, and he sounded raving mad. But at least he wouldn't freeze to death. Not tonight.

SIXTEEN

THE WIND HAD DIED DOWN, BUT THE WALK TO THE RESTAURANT was lined with ice and shadows. Why was I walking alone at night? Why hadn't I accepted the offer of a ride in a nice heated police car? I told myself that I was fine, that this was my turf, that I would not allow somebody to terrorize me so much that I wouldn't walk a few short blocks. But the night seemed darker than usual. And Charlie had alarmed me. I stepped over glassy patches of ice, telling myself to stay calm. Between streetlights, I anticipated cold hands grabbing my shoulders and shadowy figures lurking just outside my gaze. I looked behind me, listened for the crunch of footsteps other than my own. By the time the lights of the restaurant came into view, despite the slippery sidewalk, I'd almost broken into a run.

A steep flight of stairs separated the street entrance from the dimly lit cavern that was Ristorante La Buca. I stood at the bottom of the steps, looking through the doorway to the restaurant, exhaling, collecting myself. Detective Stiles sat alone at the bar, sipping a drink. He was tall and lean, striking in a dark suit. A man waiting for someone.

Christmas lights blinked soft reds and greens along holly-draped walls; tiers of bottles glowed amber and silver, and pyramids of glasses stood like an altar to an alcoholic god.

Something—the chilled air? my gaze?—drew his attention. He swiveled toward me on his stool, rose, and stepped forward to greet me; one arm took my hand, the other circled around to my coat collar. He smiled a lopsided greeting, emanating warmth and a musky scent. Aftershave, or maybe tired cologne. A man at the end of a day.

"Have you been waiting long?" My question hung awkwardly unanswered as he guided me inside and handed my coat to the hostess.

"Not long," he finally said, "But I was worried about you. In fact, I called to see if you'd changed your mind about a ride, but you'd already left. I guess you made it here okay."

"It wasn't easy. Walking took longer than I expected, with all the ice."

He turned to assess me, still wearing his half smile. Oh dear. Maybe I should have worn the gray sweater instead. Or the cowlneck. Maybe the black was too dramatic, especially with the thigh-high slit in my skirt. The bones in my cheeks itched. "You look lovely, Ms. Hayes."

I looked lovely? "Thank you," I blushed. My face felt as red as the Christmas lights. The maître d' appeared with Stiles's half-finished Manhattan. "Your table is ready, sir."

He led the way. As we walked through the restaurant, Detective Stiles held my arm. My elbow tingled. I told it to settle down. This was a police detective, not a prom date. We were here to work. The maître d' seated me and handed us menus.

"One of these for the lady, please."

"Yes, sir."

I looked up, surprised. What made him think that I'd have a cocktail? Let alone what he was drinking, whatever it was. A Manhattan? But he greeted my eyes with a sheepish half smile.

"Is a Manhattan all right? If you don't want it, I'll have it. Order what you want."

I shrugged. Red wine was what I would have chosen, but I didn't want to make an issue out of it.

"A Manhattan's fine." I'd never had one, didn't even know what was in it.

He leaned forward, resting on his elbows. I was still on edge from my walk, still getting oriented. Relax, I told myself. Make small talk and get acquainted. "Do you always wear black?" he asked.

"What?" I thought I'd heard him wrong. He couldn't be talking about my clothes.

"Both times I've seen you, you've been in black."

I bit my lip. He remembered what I'd worn? Even I didn't remember what I'd worn. Well, I shouldn't be surprised; he was a cop. An observer of details. "It's comfortable. Hides the flaws."

"Come on, Ms. Hayes. You don't have to worry about flaws. You're a stunning woman."

Stunning again? Twice in one day? First Susan, now Stiles. But wait; I shouldn't be so easily flattered. Maybe this was a test. Cops did that, tested people, said stuff to see how you'd react. Was he watching? Assessing my character? I hid behind the menu, avoiding his eyes. The waiter's hands appeared, placing a Manhattan in front of me. I cleared my throat and waited for the hands to leave, ready to steer the conversation to more comfortable ground.

"Detective Stiles—"

"Call me Nick."

Nick?

"Then call me Zoe."

It's okay, I told myself. There's nothing wrong with first names between consenting adults.

Half his mouth grinned, pleased. My eyes darted away.

"Look, it was nice of you to ask me to dinner—"

"I'm glad you were able to join me. I usually grab a burger or a slice of pizza on the run. Alone. I'm still new around here, and my place is all the way out in Chester County. It's beautiful, but isolated. So I don't have much social life. Or much time for one, the way we're working."

He did look tired. Maybe even lonely. "Well, I appreciate your invitation. I don't go out to dinner much, either." I hadn't planned to say that. "I mean, because of my little girl." Or that.

"How old is she?"

"Almost six."

"Six. First grade?"

"Kindergarten."

He nodded. "You must be a great mom."

Lord, I hated small talk. "She makes it easy; she's a great kid."

He tilted his head thoughtfully, pausing. Thank God, he was changing the subject. "So," he began, "have you thought about what we discussed?"

I hesitated; he continued before I could answer.

"I understand if you're worried about repercussions. Hey, I work in a bureaucracy, too; I know all about in-house politics. But don't worry about that. Beverly and I have discussed your involvement."

Dr. Gardener was "Beverly" now?

"She admires you quite a bit."

"Really?" I hadn't been aware that Beverly Gardener even knew who I was.

"Oh yes. She praised your work, said you were bright and talented. She went on about you at some length."

I was uncomfortable, didn't know what to say. I'd never exchanged as much as "Good morning" with the woman. When we'd passed at the Institute, she'd been intent on her own thoughts, never even made eye contact. How was it that she'd been able to go on about me at length?

"Beverly agrees that your input might prove valuable. So don't worry about bureaucracy. You won't be overstepping."

Overstepping? What was he talking about? Politics? Professional protocol? Would it be a problem for an Institute art therapist to help police unofficially on a case in which a hotshot Institute psychiatrist/profiler was officially consulting? Actually, I'd never considered the repercussions of that. I wasn't sure I'd care about them, even if I had.

I swallowed some Manhattan. It wasn't a bad drink, once you got past the initial sweetness. The cherry in my glass peered back at me like a bloodshot eyeball. Detective Stiles sat silently in the maddening manner of a detective waiting for a suspect to spill his guts. Finally, I began.

"Actually, Detective—"

"Nick," he corrected.

"Nick. I'm not concerned about what Dr. Gardener or anyone at the Institute thinks about what I do. I make my own choices."

"Good. Still, it's better not to step on bureaucratic toes. Trust me."

Trust him? Was he crazy? With those eyes? They looked at me but took in everything, the whole room, even the part behind his back. How could anyone trust a man with eyes like that? Or that crooked half smirk that somehow made him look both tough and vulnerable at the same time? I sipped my drink, unable to recall what I'd started to say—what was it again?

Nick continued. "Look, all I ask is that you review the profile Beverly's created. She's very insightful; I think you'll be impressed. And her thoughts might stimulate yours. Just see what it brings to mind."

I nodded. My lips had begun to ache, an effect of the cocktail. It was stronger than I'd expected. I shouldn't be drinking while working, even unofficially. I bit on them to stop the throbbing.

"Are you nervous?"

"No. Why?"

"You're biting your lip."

"So?"

"So, it's normal to be nervous. Getting involved in something like this can be tough. Even scary."

I looked up. Was I 'getting involved'? Had he intended a double meaning? Or was he still testing my reactions? Or was I drinking too much? "I'm not nervous. Actually, I can't wait to read the profile."

His half smile appeared again.

"So, when can you talk to Beverly?" He watched me, waiting for my response.

Talk to Beverly? "I didn't realize I had to—"

"Well, it would be best if she went over it with you personally. Filled you in. And you should dialogue. You're colleagues, after all."

Beverly Gardener was hardly a colleague. She was a phenomenon. A presence, a supposed genius endowed with perfect legs and startling green eyes. "Any time. First thing Monday morning?"

And with that, we were done with business. Not even past cocktails, and done. I searched for casual conversation unrelated to the missing women, but the cocktail was having an effect. My mind drifted, distracted by Stiles's shoulders, his thick neck. I began comparing his Adam's apple to the cherry in my drink, which was magically full again. I frowned, searching for a topic.

"Well," I began. Good start. Keep going. "How do you like living in Philadel—"

"You look upset."

"I do?"

"What's on your mind?"

His bare chest, to be honest. Stop it, I scolded myself. There's more at stake here than your starving libido. I thought of Tamara and felt ashamed of myself. "What's on anyone's mind, these days? The nannies. Everyone's upset."

He uncrossed his legs and straightened his back. "Of course."

"One of the missing girls," I went on. "I know her."

He sighed. "A disappearance can be tougher to deal with than a death."

I pictured Tamara's shining eyes, recalled her musical laughter. I took another sip, felt the liquor slide, sear my throat.

"But—damn, there's no easy way to say this. Zoe, you need to be prepared for the worst, here. Chances are slim to nothing that your missing friend—or any of those women—is still alive."

Tamara's eyes lost their shine; her laughter choked to a stop. I felt the stab of my teeth jabbing my lip.

Stiles leaned forward, his voice almost a whisper. "If it's any consolation, I think we'll solve this one. Soon."

"Why do you say that?"

His eyes darkened. "Because he wants us to solve it." He took a drink. "Sonofabitch might not know it, but he wants us to."

"He wants to be caught?"

"I think so. At least, part of him does. He's getting bolder. More brazen. Leaving evidence. Daring us to find him." He paused. "Do you think that finger was left on your walk by accident?"

"What?" I gripped my glass, needing something to hold on to. What was he saying? That the finger had been dropped in front of my house on purpose? "You mean it wasn't?"

"Let me ask you." He leaned forward so his face was close, his voice low. "You're a therapist. You know Freud's theory that there is no such thing as an accident."

"I'm not following you."

"Okay. Let's back up. The abductions began several weeks ago. Since then, they've occurred more frequently, in increasingly open and more public settings. And the kidnapper's leaving evidence now, whereas he didn't at first. Consciously? Maybe, maybe not. At some level, he may be sabotaging himself because he wants to stop but can't. Or he might just be carried away by his sense of invincibility. Either way, he's accelerating, losing control. Getting sloppy. Making mistakes."

"But to make more mistakes, won't he have to take more women?"

Half his mouth twisted fleetingly. "He'll definitely try. We've got a serial killer here, and as you know, those guys are pretty consistent."

As I knew? What did I know? I'd taken a college course years ago on criminal psychology and read the textbook chapter about serials, but mostly what I knew about serial killers I'd learned from television. Detective shows. I knew, for example, that serial killers followed patterns in their crimes. I knew that some thought they were obeying a higher power who ordered them to kill; others believed their murders were altruistic, that they were eliminating "sinners" to cleanse the world. A third group simply got off on power. They got high, often sexually aroused, by having the power of life or death over their victims, terrorizing them, taking their lives.

"So what do you know about this one?"

He winked. Winked. "Read the report."

I stared at the red orb in my glass. Now it resembled a blood clot.

"Look, for now, let's just say he wants to be somebody. Someone famous. In the headlines. His ego's been fed by the news coverage. He's begun to think he can get away with anything. He's getting arrogant. Soon, he'll go too far and give himself away. Question is, how many more women will he kill first?"

It was a somber thought. "And the finger? You said it might not have been left accidentally."

"Accidentally or deliberately—either way, where it was found still means something. At the very least, it means the guy was in the area. He didn't just find his victim there; he also left a piece of her there after he killed her. Which indicates he's got a place there. Locally."

He paused, letting that thought sink in.

A guy in the area. Who had a place there. Did he know me? Had he chosen to leave the finger at my front curb instead of, say, the one next door? Why? And the other finger—the one found on Washington Square—had he left that deliberately, too? According to Stiles, he might have. But who could it be? Neighborhood faces raced through my mind. Victor, Charlie. The new neighbor, Phillip Woods. There were a lot more I didn't know by name, people I passed every day. People who came and went at different hours than I did. Night people. And what about Coach Gene? Or the mailman? Or the guys in Jake's construction crews—hadn't Angela said one of them had been bothering her?

"Look, can we talk about something else for a while? Behave like normal people?" He half-smiled. "I've been living with this case 24/7. I need to take a break. To pretend to be a civilian. How about we enjoy the ambience? Try to have a civilized meal. Is that okay? I think it'll be good for both of us."

"Of course. I understand." But I didn't, not entirely. Were we supposed to suddenly pretend that we were just two people out to dinner, that local women weren't being killed? That I might even know the guy killing them? Besides, what were we supposed to talk about? I clutched my drink, eyeing a nearby painting of a gondolier steering his boat along a Venice canal.

"Tell me about yourself. Who is Zoe Hayes?"

I blinked. Zoe Hayes? It was simple dinner conversation, but it seemed that I, not the murderer, was now the person to be profiled. My lips felt thick and boozy, too heavy to form answers, reluctant to give away information. I stalled, sipping my

Manhattan, wanting to jump into the gondola and be rowed away.

"Tell me. Where did Zoe grow up? Where did she go to school? Why did she become an art therapist?"

Loosen up, I told myself. Relax. Give the guy a break. "Baltimore, Cornell, because she doesn't paint well enough to survive as an artist."

Half his face laughed.

"And you? Who's Detective Nick Stiles?" Tit for tat.

"He's this." He shrugged, pointing to himself. "Just what you see."

"Not fair. I answered you."

"Okay. Fair enough. Be more specific. What do you want to know?"

I should have thought before I spoke, but I didn't. I just blurted out a question, without gentleness or tact. "What happened to your face?"

SEVENTEEN

INSTANTLY, I REGRETTED MY QUESTION. "SORRY—IT'S NOT my—"

"Took a bullet," he said. "No need to apologize. Took a bullet in the jaw, hit a nerve. Actually, before that, I used to be good-looking." He smiled.

I smiled back. "Is that a fact?"

"No, I guess not." Again, a shy glance down at his drink. Shyness didn't suit him; it was like a jacket that was too small. But there he was, wearing a tight, bashful half grin.

"Who shot you?"

"That's your second question. It's my turn again—"

"No, you asked three at once—"

Our eyes met. His were twinkling. Then not. The twinkle hardened, sharpened to a gleam. "A woman."

I didn't know what to say.

"It was a domestic thing. Woman found out her husband was leaving her," he answered.

"So she shot a cop?"

"So she started shooting. Shooting him, me, herself. Killed herself."

"Damn."

"Yeah, well." He gazed past me, into air.

I didn't know what to say.

"It's a long time ago. People get pissed and make bad decisions.

They don't think things through. Anyhow. That's what happened."

"What about the husband? Did she kill him, too?"

"No, actually, the sonofabitch survived. She was a lousy shot. He was lucky."

"So were you."

His eyes shifted. Obviously, the subject made him uncomfortable.

We were both quiet.

"I'm sorry." Damn. Why had I asked that question?

"No need."

"Well, no matter how it happened," I said, "I like it."

His attention returned to me. "Like what?"

"Your face. The way you smile. It's kind of sexy." Lord, had I really said that?

"You think?" Nick's half grin opened slowly, gladly. Too genuine to belong to a cop. "Well, good." He crossed his arms and gave a half smile. "And now, it's my turn again." He waited, coplike, for me to squirm. To anticipate what was coming.

My glass was still full. Or full again. How much had I had to drink? My hand held the stem, ready for the next round. Nick fired his next question, and I fired mine, each answer exposing more, peeling away more layers, revealing more of ourselves.

I learned that he was the eldest of four brothers, half Italian, half Jewish, parents both dead, a dozen nieces and nephews. He was a graduate of Columbia, had a master's in psychology, played football in high school, and rowed crew in college, liked to ski and snorkel, wore a size thirteen shoe. His marriage had ended badly, without children.

I'm not sure what I told him. I was aware of caution, careful not to tell him everything. I said I was an only child but didn't mention my parents' divorce or my mother's early death. I told him about marrying Michael but glossed over the mess of our divorce. I described the euphoria of adopting Molly, not the anxiety of parenting on my own. I said that my father was still living but skipped the detail that we hadn't talked in years.

I was aware that we'd become, somehow, more than coworkers, but I didn't know what. As we talked, at one point, strong fingers covered my hand. Large, warm fingers. I chewed my lip, took a breath. "Santa Lucia" drifted over white-linen-covered tables. I cleared my throat, trying to decide what to do, but couldn't. I held still until my hand began to throb. Was I supposed to leave it there and let him hold it? Or take it away? What did it mean, his hand on mine? Was he just making casual contact, or was it something else? My neck felt hot, and my sweater began to itch. Stiles—Nick—was talking, but his words swept past me, phrases without meaning.

". . . new . . . stranger . . . job . . . you . . . glad . . . comfortable . . ."

Oh my. The hand lifted, releasing mine. I grabbed my Manhattan glass, which, incredibly, was full.

"What? Did I scare you? It's okay. Don't be frightened. As you get to know me, you'll see that I don't have time for games. I size people up pretty fast; it's my job. Observing. Figuring people out. And at the moment, I'm observing you. Want to know what I see, so far?"

I nodded, feeling a little like a lab animal.

"Beyond the superficial sparkling eyes and jolly laugh, I mean. In Zoe Hayes, I see somebody real. Don't get me wrong—she isn't easy to get close to. She's guarded. But once she puts the guard down, she's real. No pretenses or hidden agenda. She's good-looking, smart, funny, and—hell, I gotta tell you, Zoe Hayes is good company. A miracle happened tonight. I actually relaxed. Believe me, that doesn't happen often. Certainly not since I started working on this case. I needed an evening like this, Zoe. Thank you." He smiled briefly, then looked away, into his glass.

I took another sip; liquor eased into my blood, numbing my aching lips. Who was this guy? Why didn't that little speech seem corny? Was he a player, adept at handing out lines? Or just a lonely cop, honestly enjoying his evening?

He reached for the relish tray, the seams of his jacket bulging at the shoulders, his hand toying with a carrot stick. His finger stroked it; I expected that it might purr.

I'd had much too much to drink.

He looked at me, head cocked, waiting.

I shifted in my chair, stalling. What was I supposed to say? That my hand tingled where he'd touched it? That I found him tremendously attractive? Or something bland and risk-free, like that I was enjoying his company, too? I didn't know. I studied the texture of the stucco wall. A thousand tiny plaster splashes, solidified agitation. A mirror.

When I looked at him again, he was still watching me. For a while, neither of us spoke. We just looked at each other. His eyes beamed blue light. Outside, women were dead or in danger. Here, for the moment, that seemed unreal and far away. Here, golden candles flickered. Aromas wafted by of roasting garlic, of sweet basil. An accordion played "O Sole Mio" for a couple in the corner. A dusty gondola floated down a painted canal, followed by a cart of fresh fish, swimming on ice. And I swam, too, into pools of pale blue.

"Would you like to hear the specials?" A voice slipped in and out of Italian, serenading us with menu items.

Even with the benefit of hindsight, it's difficult to identify the precise point where our relationship began, but by the end of the evening, something had been decided. Dining on lemon sole almondine and spinach gnocchi, sipping Soave, even without a gondola, I was swept into a river by currents too swift, too strong to resist.

EIGHTEEN

TIM ANSWERED THE DOOR, LOOKING HAGGARD. "C'MON IN."
He kissed my cheek.

I hugged him. "Hi, Tim. Welcome home."

"Thanks. It's only for the weekend. Then I'm off to L.A. again." He rubbed his eyes. "So, how was your date? Who's the new man?"

"It wasn't a date. There isn't any new man."

"But Susan said—"

Susan rushed to the door, brushing Tim aside with arms full of freshly folded towels. "Well?" she clucked like a perturbed hen.

"Thanks for watching Molly. Is she ready?" I peeked through the drapes at Nick's car. Tim peeked out, too.

"Guy drives an old Volvo?" he winced.

"What are you looking at?" Susan peeked. "Is he out there?"

"He's giving us a ride home." I looked at Tim. "What's wrong with an old Volvo?"

"Nothing. It's just not what I'd have imagined you out with."

"What's that supposed to mean?"

"Tim—be quiet. You're talking nonsense. Zoe, tell me. How'd it go?"

"I didn't go out with a car, Tim."

"A man's car says a lot about his character."

"Oh, come on."

"It's a fact. Somebody did a study. Volvo and Saab owners are educated liberals, Fords are steady Eddies, BMWs are upwardly mobile yuppie types—"

"Tim, will you be quiet? I'm trying to talk to Zoe."

"She asked. I'm just answering."

"Zoe, why's he out there in the cold? Tell him to come in. It's ridiculous, him sitting there—"

"No, it's fine. I just came in to grab Molly. It's late."

"What do you mean? It's only midnight. Your dinner took only about four hours." Susan was dying to hear details.

"Sorry, I didn't mean to keep you guys up. We started talking and lost track of—"

"Come on, Zoe. You're over twenty-one. You don't need to explain to us—" Tim caught Susan's glare and slunk off toward the den, leaving us alone.

"Well?" she asked.

"What?"

She tightened her lips, exasperated. She stomped off into the kitchen. I followed. A heap of fresh laundry waited on the table.

"Susan, I can't go into stuff now. He's waiting. I gotta grab Molly and go. Is she upstairs?"

"Damn, Zoe," she complained. "You mean you aren't going to tell me anything?"

"There's nothing to tell. Where's Molly?"

"In the den. Asleep. What do you mean, there's nothing? Did you at least read the profile?"

"Not yet. I don't have it yet." I started toward the den.

Susan was at my heels. "Why not? When'll you get it?"

"Probably Monday."

"You know, Beverly Gardener was on the news tonight, talking about the nannies." She seemed resentful.

"She was?" I stopped walking.

"She's getting a ton of publicity out of this case. She's on the news more than the cops. What do you think of her?"

"I don't really know her—"

"Tim thinks she's hot." Susan was miffed.

"Really?" I swallowed. Did Nick Stiles think so, too? Stop it, I told myself. Don't even think about that.

"Do you think she's good-looking?" Susan persisted.

I blinked, picturing Beverly Gardener. Yes, in a tall green-eyed brunette in her mid-thirties intensely ambitious energetic intelligent sort of way, she was good-looking. "Come on, Susan. Who cares? Tim saw her on the news. He made a stupid comment."

"But I don't get it. Tim never notices anything. I mean, a busload of naked belly dancers couldn't get his attention. But this woman—I swear, he was ogling."

Again, Nick Stiles flashed to mind, ogling Beverly Gardener. I blinked, steering the conversation in another direction.

"So what did she say?"

"Oh, she's come up with a nickname for the guy. She calls him"—Susan mimicked Beverly Gardener's delivery, mouthing each syllable—"'the Nannynapper.' Cute, huh?"

The Nannynapper? "It's catchy."

"Yep. Very Hollywood."

"What else?"

"Nothing much. Just standard stuffy, like the suspect is probably male, white, between twenty and forty. Mostly she posed and played authority figure. Personally, I think the cops just want to look like they've got an expert on the case because the guy hasn't given them much to work with, in terms of evidence."

"Well, we'll know more on Monday after I read her report."

Susan nodded. "And what about Stiles?"

"I'll probably see him Monday, too. Meantime, he's waiting to take us home." I turned to go into the den.

Susan took my arm and stopped me, frowning. "So it's strictly business? Nothing else?"

"You expected what? We had dinner. To talk about the

nannies," I went into the den. Molly was in her pajamas, snoring on the sofa.

Susan sighed. "Too bad. Because, from what I hear, the man's the genuine article, Zoe. A gem. You might want to reconsider your goals here and nab him."

Nab him? I pictured Stiles in handcuffs.

"I asked around," she continued. "Stiles is smart—Ivy League education. Forty-six. His father was a big attorney in New York. Mother was a society girl. And he's single."

"Susan—"

"Not single as in bachelor-with-a-fear-of-commitment or possible-closet-gay. Single as in widower. No kids."

"A widower? His wife died?" How dreadful. I felt awful for him. He'd said his marriage had "ended badly," not that it had ended with his wife's death. Probably it was too painful to talk about.

"It's been eight years, though. He's got to be over it—"

"Maybe not." If he were over it, he'd have mentioned it. "What happened? An accident? Was she sick?"

"What's the difference? She's dead." Her eyes dodged mine, and she paused in her search for the partner to a pink sock. "Oh, what the hell, you might as well know. She shot herself."

She what? Oh Lord. In a flash, I understood. It made perfect sense. He'd been talking about his own marriage—his own wife. It was a domestic thing, he'd said. A woman found out her husband was going to leave her and got pissed off.

"She shot him? His wife shot him in the face?"

"You knew? He told you about it? Wow. I was told he never talks about it. Ever."

And the husband, I'd asked. Did she kill him, too? No, he'd replied, the sonofabitch lived. He hadn't lied. But he hadn't told me the whole truth, either. Why would he? We barely knew each other; it wasn't the kind of thing you told a casual acquaintance.

"I can't believe he told you. Zoe, the man must be seriously interested in you."

"It's not like he gave me a detailed report. He just referred to it."

"Huh?"

"He was explaining what happened to his face."

"Which means he wants you to know about his past. It wasn't all business tonight. Zoe, tell me you're going to give this guy a shot."

"His wife already did that."

"Funny."

"Not funny. Look where she ended up."

Susan folded her arms. "It's where you're going to end up that concerns me."

I picked up Molly's jacket, lifted a limp arm, and gently stuffed it into a sleeve. She stirred, eyes fluttering. I kissed her. "Hi, Molly."

Susan kept talking. "Zoe. Give yourself a chance, will you? You haven't looked at a man since Michael left."

"I have, too."

"Like who? That amateur magician?"

I winced, remembering. His best trick had been vanishing. "I've been out lots of times—Dom, that insurance underwriter. And what's his name—the one with the airplanes—he wore all that jewelry?"

"As I was saying . . . You haven't looked at a man since Michael left. Everyone you've gone out with has given you yet another excuse for staying in your safe, controlled little world, all on your own. Okay, you've proved that you can manage on your own. That you're strong and don't need a man to survive. You're a great mom and a marvelous success at teaching schizophrenics how to do macramé. We get it: Zoe Hayes can do it alone. Now, move on before it's too late. Unless, of course, you want to be alone forever. Do you?"

As usual, Susan had hit a nerve. "Okay. I see your point."

"Good. So give him a chance."

"I don't know that he wants a. chance. The man has other things on his mind than his love life. Like, for example, catching a psycho."

"But that's just my point. Life is a dangerous and full of predators. No one knows what's coming, one minute to the next. That's exactly why we all need somebody we can trust, depend on, and cuddle up with at night. People aren't meant to be all alone, Zoe."

What could I say? Susan cared. I was touched. Meantime, while we were talking, Stiles had probably frozen to death. "Thanks, Susan. I mean it. I hear you. But I gotta go."

Molly floated zombie-like and semiconscious down the hall. I guided her to the front door, where Susan waited, three spare socks hanging over her shoulder.

"Call me," she commanded.

"Yes, Mom." I brushed cheeks with her, smelled magnolia.

Susan tousled Molly's hair and gave her a hug. Molly returned the hug and mumbled, "Thank you for having me," like a polite sleepwalker. Frigid winds burst through the open door. The night howled, holding a murderer.

I lifted Molly and carried her to the car, waving good-bye as Susan closed her door. Molly snuggled, dazed, against me as Stiles, half-smiling at her, pulled away and headed into darkness.

NINETEEN

OF COURSE, I COULDN'T SLEEP. I LAY IN BED, TOSSING, FRAG-mented thoughts popping in my mind. The missing nannies' faces, old Charlie's hacking cough, the serial killer's patterns. Snippets of conversations replayed themselves. Nick, saying the killer was local. Charlie, saying evil was close by. Susan, saying people weren't meant to be alone, that I should "nab" Stiles.

My head was overloaded; images splashed around in a pool of whatever liquor Manhattans are made of. Bourbon? Sweet vermouth? I didn't know, didn't care. If the killer was local, did I know him? Did he know me? Who could he be? Faces paraded by, too many too fast, making me dizzy. Stop it, I told myself. Calm down. The scent of Nick's aftershave drifted in, drenching the parade.

I closed my eyes, trying to let go and sink into sleep. Sleep, I told myself. Think tomorrow. But as I lay back, the room began to swim again, and I sat up waiting for the night to fade.

I thought about Nick. As he'd walked Molly and me to our door, he'd squeezed my hand good night. His touch had been warm, gentle. Warmer and gentler, I thought, than necessary. Certainly more than a compulsory thanks-for-agreeing-to-work-on-the-case squeeze.

This was crazy. What was I thinking about? This was a mur-der investigation, not a courtship. I wasn't even his type. Was I? What was his type? I imagined a deranged woman holding a gun. What had she looked like, his wife? I cleared my throat, thinking about a dead wife, a man's scar. And jealousy.

Not the dead wife's. Mine. I was, I admit it, suddenly very jealous. It was irrational, but I was jealous anyway. A woman had loved Nick Stiles desperately enough to kill him, enough to die rather than lose him. I was jealous of that kind of all-consuming, desperate, soul-searing love.

By comparison, when my own marriage had fallen apart, I hadn't felt anything. I hadn't wanted to kill Michael. I'd simply wanted him to go away. Now, of course, when he'd told me he was remarrying, I'd been stunned. But that was because some woman would put up with him, not because I was jealous.

But Nick Stiles's wife had loved him enough to kill him and herself. She'd failed, but she'd marked him for life. He'd think of her every time he looked in the mirror. Every time someone noticed his scar. He'd never be free of her or her love. Not ever.

And I'd managed to raise the topic of that love in our very first conversation. I'd asked him about his scar and brought his wife to mind. Hell, I'd invited her to our table.

Hold it, I told myself—the shooting was eight years ago. He must have learned to live with it by now. Must have dated women. Might even have a girlfriend. I wondered what type she was. Great, I sounded like Tim. Which was worse, judging men by their cars or their women? My mind teased me, showing me Nick with various women, searching. And there she was: a self-possessed, leggy brunette, about thirty-five years old, intense, focused. Draped on Nick's arm, as if she belonged there, balancing his rugged, damaged features with her confident charisma. Yup, she was his type. And she did not in the slightest resemble me. Actually, she was a dead ringer for Beverly Gardener.

Ridiculous, I told myself. I was letting Susan's comments get to me. Not all men would swoon over Beverly Gardener. Some would regard her merely as a single-minded, ambitious professional. A profiler. Certainly Nick would.

Okay, then. I could forget about Beverly Gardener. The real question wasn't about her; it was about me. Was I Nick's type? I got up and, for the second time that day, stood at the mirror analyzing my features. How would I look paired with Stiles? My hair was dark, striped with gray strands. My face was almost, but not quite, exotic. The cheekbones were prominent, the nose definite. The eyes more almond-shaped than round. Looking closer, around the eyes, I saw the unmistakable engravings of time. Not just of time. Of experience. Of humor. Of wisdom. Clearly, this woman had more to offer than some ambitious, brainy brunette. Any man worth being with could see that.

But if I had so much wisdom, why was I standing by the mirror examining myself? Nick Stiles and I had had one pleasant, personable, and mostly professional evening. That was all. True, there was good chemistry, but we were a long way from "nabbing" each other. We were still virtual strangers. More important, there was a killer to catch. Someone local. Someone I might know. Who might know me.

I plopped back on my bed and pulled up the covers. When I closed my eyes, the leggy, confident brunette leaned against Nick Stiles and twined her arms around his neck. My face itched. I scratched my cheeks and tossed but finally gave up and went downstairs, wishing I had someone to talk to. Susan was right about one point: People weren't meant to be alone, especially at night. I flipped on the television. A car blew up in some old detective show. I changed the channel. A televangelist made an appeal for money. I changed again. A woman ran out of a house, chased by a man with a gun. I clicked the set off, and the house was silent. The StairMaster, ever persevering, offered its companionship.

"Forget it," I said out loud. Great. I was talking to a machine. I sat down, glaring at it. It glared back, daring me to climb on, silently listing all the reasons I should, including Beverly Gardener's legs. That did it. I flung an afghan over it and went into the kitchen.

Dawn was still far off. Molly wouldn't be up for hours. I yearned for morning. The newspaper, coffee, my daily routine. Traffic on the street. Grinding decaf, I gazed out the window. Victor's house was completely dark, a shadow in the night. Construction vehicles partly blocked my view, but there was a light in Charlie's basement. I could see his shadow moving around down there, tinkering. Awake, like me.

Phillip Woods's Santa blinked on and off, beating at the darkness. I turned on the coffeemaker and waited, sniffing the rich aroma. It was strong and familiar, reassuring. I poured a mug and felt its steam on my face. Then, letting my mind wander toward exhaustion, I stared out the window at the frigid night. Crystalline ice still coated the trees, and the glazed streets were bleak and deserted. In the black intervals between flashes of the Santa, I watched the glow of Charlie's window and sipped warm liquid through aching lips, until finally, sometime after three, I was able to drift off. I lingered, though, wavering between wakefulness and sleep, bothered by images of seduction and murder, while faces of missing women peppered my dreams.

TWENTY

THE NOISE WAS LOUD AND JANGLING, AND IT TOOK A WHILE for me to realize it was the phone.

"Okay, I've relapsed. I'm crazy again. Make me a reservation at the Happy Home." Susan sounded frantic.

Damn, I thought. Here she goes again. Maybe I should refer her to someone, get her some medication.

"Zoe, you won't believe what happened—"

Molly ran in and jumped onto my bed, giggling. "Mommy, are you ever going to get up?"

"What?" I pulled Molly onto my bed and rolled her over for a hug.

"Did I wake you up?"

"Of course not."

"Yes, I did. I can hear it in your voice. Get the hell up—it's almost ten o'clock. I've already purchased a gun for Bonita, worked, come back, and had a nervous breakdown."

"I'm up. You got the gun?"

"Not yet. It takes a few days. This isn't about the gun."

"So what happened?" Molly lay on her stomach beside me, watching me talk.

"I was in the Roundhouse this morning about that Drews case—you know, that robbery-homicide—and who do I bump into? My buddies Pete and Ed. And some new guy named Stiles."

"You're kidding."

"No. For real. I met him."

"Did he know who you were?"

"He said sort of cryptically that he'd heard of me, so I guess he made the connection."

"And?"

"And he's very . . . intriguing. Too bad about that scar. Imagine what he looked like before he got shot."

I couldn't. Didn't want to. "So what happened? Please tell me you didn't—"

"Don't worry, I didn't say anything that would embarrass you."

"You swear?"

"Nothing. I didn't even directly mention you, except—"

"Except?"

"Except I asked if there was any news about your finger—"

"Oh, great. Now he'll think—"

"Wait a second—hear me out. Stiles looks me over like I'm nuts and says, 'You must mean the finger found in Washington Square.' I said no, I meant the first finger. The one Zoe Hayes found. And he said he knew nothing about anyone finding another finger."

"Wait—he said what?"

She repeated herself, doing a not bad impression of Nick. "Believe me, I was tempted to show him another finger—"

"But why would he say that? He knows you know about it."

"Dunno. Maybe he didn't want to discuss it. He doesn't really know me, after all."

"But he knows who you are—he sat in front of your house last night. And what about Ed and Pete—they know you—"

Molly whispered, "Get off the phone, Mommy. Please? I'm bored." She played with her loose tooth.

"Yeah, that's what I thought, too. I'm one of the guys down there. Cops don't like my clients, but they like me. And they need me. I'm part of the network—it's give and take in that asylum.

But the message Stiles gave me is that your finger is not public knowledge, not to be discussed with 'civilians,' even me. It's a full-blown, official nonevent."

"Come on, Mommy," Molly whined. "You've been in bed all day."

I squeezed her and whispered, "In a minute."

"So I backed off. Not five minutes later, guess what? I overheard Stiles and a couple of the guys talking, so I pretended to be on the phone, but really it was a busy signal—"

Molly sat up and pouted.

"And," Susan's voice descended an octave, almost to a whisper, "I heard him talking about trying to contain the press, not to release everything."

"Why would they do that?"

"The cops? Mostly to sort out false confessions—"

"You mean someone's confessed?"

"Not just someone. Probably a busload of people have confessed already. Crimes like this generally bring out wackos who want to be in the spotlight. So the cops usually hold back some of the evidence, to see who knows about it. That's standard procedure. But listen to what they're holding back. A body. An actual body."

"What? They found someone?"

"I heard Stiles say they think they've found one. Right near you, on Lombard."

I sat up. "Wait. 'Think' they've found? What does that mean? That she's dead but not identified?"

"Who's dead, Mommy?"

"Shh, Molly. I'm on the phone."

"Who's dead?" she repeated. "Is it Tamara?"

"Don't worry—I don't know who it is," I whispered. Molly sighed.

Susan was still talking. ". . . means that the police weren't sure yet exactly what they'd found. The press hasn't even been told yet—it's hush-hush. But they can't keep it quiet for long. It's bound to hit the news any minute—"

"Wait, what?" I wasn't following, must have missed part of what she'd said.

Molly tugged at the comforter. "What are we going to do today, Mommy? Can we go somewhere fun?"

Again, her voice drowned out the beginning of Susan's, but I heard, ". . . by a garbage man on Lombard Street. The bag stank. It was full of body parts. Small pieces. They have to assemble them."

"Get off, Mommy. Puh-leeeeze."

I heard the thud of flesh landing in a plastic bag. Susan was still talking, her words blending into a buzz as I envisioned Tamara, her bloodless face and matted hair, her eyes disappointed in death. I closed my eyes. It made no sense. A finger in the park. Body parts in a trash bag. Why? And why nannies? Why babysitters?

Chilled, I glanced out the bedroom window. Charlie was nowhere in sight. But he'd been right. Evil was prowling the city, wearing a disguise. Mailman, fireman, taxi driver, cop. The killer could be anyone, anywhere. He had been here, leaving a memento on our walk.

"Ow, Mommy—let go!" Molly squirmed, detaching my hand from her arm. Until then, I hadn't realized that I'd been squeezing it. The phone call left me jangled. I didn't want to be jangled. Didn't want to think about dismembered bodies or secret fingers or missing nannies or men who lied. I wanted peace. I wanted calm. I wanted explanations from Nick.

Who was Nick, anyway? Could I trust him? I could understand him not telling me about his wife; he hardly knew me, and those memories were painful and private. But what about the finger? Why, especially when she knew about it already, had he pretended to Susan that no finger had been found at my door?

Even if he didn't want the press to jump on the story, why hadn't he told me—someone supposedly helping him—the truth about something so significant as finding a body? Deliberate omission was the same as lying, wasn't it?

I told myself not to jump to conclusions. I'd ask him about the finger and the body; I'd hear him out before reacting. He'd have perfectly reasonable explanations. Probably.

Meantime, I wouldn't dwell on it. I'd go about my business. Molly and I made a pot of chicken soup. Well, we didn't actually make it. We started with canned broth and added carrots, celery, noodles, onion, and chunks of cooked chicken. When it tasted like soup, we poured it into containers and delivered it across the street in time for lunch. First, we left one at Victor's, ringing the bell to make sure he'd find it. Then we took one to Charlie's. He opened his door, exhausted and bleary-eyed.

"I sweated all night, miss," he said. "I saw a demon come through the wall, heard hell banging and buzzing, but I finally got the spell out of me. It was a spell, too, inside my head—"

"I'm glad you're feeling better, Charlie. Careful, the container's real full."

"Thank you, miss. I appreciate this." He took hold of the jar. "Remember what I said, though. Evil's all around—you be careful. I know what I'm saying—I've seen things—"

"Don't worry, Charlie. Get some rest and feel better." I took Molly by the hand and escaped before he could launch a diatribe.

"What was Charlie talking about?" she asked.

"I don't know," I told her. "Sometimes high fever makes people imagine things. It's like having a bad dream that seems real."

She nodded knowingly. "I've had those."

I squeezed her hand. So had I.

Saturday passed without news of further disappearances, but the nannies were still on everyone's minds. For the first time in days, I watched the early news on television. While the anchorwoman talked about the nanny case, a tips hotline phone number rolled along the bottom of the screen. The anchor said that so far over two hundred people had called in with tips and that the police were sorting through them, one by one. The screen showed a crisis center on South Street that had been opened to help locals deal with the stress caused by the case. Then the anchor discussed the ongoing investigation, mentioning the profile by an expert forensic psychologist. In the next shot, Beverly Gardener was standing close beside Nick Stiles, surrounded by a ring of handheld microphones.

"Dr. Gardener's profile has been invaluable. It's catapulted our investigation forward," Nick said.

Someone asked, "Detective Stiles, is it true that several people have confessed to being the Nannynapper?"

The camera zoomed in close; Nick's eyes penetrated the screen. "We have nothing credible at this point. False confessions are not uncommon in cases like this. But regardless, we intend to close this case soon."

The anchorwoman came back, remarking that, despite an experienced police investigating team, an expert profiler, and hundreds of tipsters, there still were no concrete leads to the identity of the Nannynapper.

I shut off the television and tried to do normal things. I made phone calls. I called Leslie to see how she and Billy were doing; no one answered. I reached Karen and set up a playdate for Molly and Nicholas. We talked about the nannies. Susan's gun. What we mothers were going to do. How we'd organize a buddy system, an e-mail list and phone chain.

Michael called twice; both times, I put him off. Mostly, I spent the afternoon doing the usual weekend chores: shopping, answering e-mail—mostly from Michael—scrubbing floors, straightening up, doing laundry. Molly and I worked as a team; while I cleaned one mess, she made another.

Around six, just as I was about to order Chinese, the phone rang.

"Hi. You busy?"

"Nick?"

"Bad time? Am I interrupting?"

"No—it's fine. What's up?" Ask him about the body, I thought. Find out why he didn't tell you.

"I remembered you said you hardly ever went out to dinner, so I took a chance, hoping you'd be free. Are you?"

Was I? "I guess so, but—"

"Good. I'm outside. At the door."

At the door? Now? Oh my. I was a mess. My hair tangled, hanging half out of a tired ponytail. Dressed in torn baggy jeans and an old gray sweatshirt, no makeup at all. Still holding the phone, I went to the door and peeked out the peephole. Yep, Stiles was there, his forehead round as my fishbowl peephole, a cell phone at his ear. I smoothed my hair with my free hand and opened the door. We stood face-to-face, still talking on the phone.

He was holding a big pizza box and a bottle of wine.

"What kind of pizza is it?"

He gave his half grin and disconnected his phone. "Can I come in?"

He looked so boyish, standing there, I had to smile. The pizza was white, covered with garlic, artichoke hearts, and shrimp. I was glad to see him but not certain why he'd come. Were we actual "friends" now? Were we going to hang out and watch a TV movie? Or was he here to talk more about the case—maybe to tell me about the bag of body parts? Molly had joined us. She stood beside me, gaping at him. It wasn't the time to ask.

"Molly, this is Nick Stiles. Nick, this is Molly."

"Mommy, 'sthis your boyfriend?" Her whisper was loud.

"Nick's my friend," I answered, my face warming.

Molly had never tasted artichokes, but she seemed to want to impress Nick and gobbled down two slices. After dinner, we played board games. Chutes and Ladders, then Perfection. Molly, an expert, beat us at both. Then, as I was hoping to take her up to bed, she and Nick began a jungle jigsaw puzzle, spilling pieces all over the floor.

"Start with the corners," she advised. "It's easier that way."

"Like this?" Nick held up a piece.

"Yes. Very good. Now, find all the pieces with a flat side and connect them. Those are the sides."

"Help us, Zoe," Nick invited me.

"Mom hates puzzles," Molly explained. "Don't bother asking her. It's hopeless."

Chatting and laughing, sifting through the pile, they isolated all four corners and separated pieces with flat sides. I sat beside them on the floor, sipping cocoa, watching them play, wondering if we looked like a family. If this easy comfort was how it felt to be part of one. We floated through the evening, and when I finally managed to get Molly to bed and tucked her in, Nick was waiting in the hall. At last I'd be able talk to him privately. I'd ask about the body parts, about Susan and the finger. But as I started to speak, he took my hand and gently put it against his lips. His eyes, when I looked up, seemed to see through mine, into my head. His arms wrapped around me, and I leaned against him, feeling safe and protected, letting my questions float away.

That night the moon was full, casting its rays, spreading its dust. As wolves howled, tides shifted, and lunatics raved, I, too, must have been swayed by moonbeams; I have no other explanation or excuse. Before I knew it, Nick's lips were on mine, melting my mouth. That night, Nick's face was what I saw last in the moonlight. And it was what I saw first when I awoke, a little after dawn.

TWENTY-ONE

THE BED WAS RUMPLED FROM THE NIGHT. SO WAS MY MIND.
Images and memories lingered, heavy like smoke. Maybe it had
been the wine or the full moon, maybe my weakness after several long years of sleeping alone, but somehow I'd stopped
thinking and allowed myself simply to let go.

Michael's pillow was smashed; it wasn't Michael's anymore.
Nick had claimed it along with Michael's place in my bed and in
my body. I'd kissed a chest less hairy than Michael's, tangled
with longer legs, sucked on fuller lips for the first time in over a
decade. And now, after just one evening, Michael seemed vague,
limited, and long ago. In the most primitive way, I belonged to a
new man. An invader who'd conquered me, inch by inch. I'd
been alone for so long that I'd forgotten about the details of sex,
the anticipation of each progressive step, the artichoke process,
the peeling away of clothes, boundaries, inhibitions. And all the
firsts. First ear nibble, first breast squeeze, first grinding of hips.
Had I ever been that excited with Michael? Had I ever let go entirely, trusted him completely, cried out without caring that he'd
hear? I didn't think so. Sex with Michael had been comfortable,
cozy, predictable. With Nick, it felt reckless, dangerous. Un-
leashed. I'd had no precautions, nothing in the medicine cabinet
to ward off pregnancy or disease. But Nick had taken care of
everything, to the tiniest detail.

Now, the morning after, I heard him downstairs, moving dishes and pots around the kitchen. His presence was everywhere, permeating everything. My possessions were no longer quite my own. The dresser, the bathtub, the bed had been touched, altered. They'd all acquired a new master; they sang out Nick's name. The kitchen, at that moment, was under his command.

And what about Molly? Oh my God. What had she thought when she'd seen him making breakfast? I hadn't thought this through at all. Hadn't considered her feelings. How selfish and impulsive I'd been. How insensitive. What kind of mother was I?

Quickly, I splashed water onto my face at the mirror where he'd shaved. Folding the towel he'd used for his shower, I was guilt-ridden and wary. I smelled coffee and breakfast and braced myself to reclaim territory. I came downstairs as he was showing Molly how to flip pancakes as if they made breakfast together every day.

I waited, observing, struggling with what I saw. Ever since the social worker had handed her to me and I'd carried her home, Molly had been mine. We'd been a family unto ourselves, our own universe. Now, Nick had cut in on the waltz that I'd danced alone so long with Molly. Tapping my shoulder, he was taking her for a whirl across the floor. And while I admired their easy grace, I mourned the private pace of mother and daughter.

"This one looks ready—see the bubble holes?"

"Should I flip it?"

"Yup."

"Oops—"

Even so, I wasn't eager to return to that isolation. Nick seemed to belong with us, as if he were right at home. So why wasn't I entirely happy about it? I told myself that my ambivalence was normal. Nick was sudden and new. I shouldn't have let Molly meet him yet. Should never have let him spend the night. It was a delicate matter, introducing a lover to a child. I should have taken time to prepare her, or at least to prepare myself.

I watched them, Molly in pajamas and Nick, barefoot, in jeans and a T-shirt. A man beside a child who was standing on a chair to reach the stove in a cluttered kitchen. A photograph. A greeting card. I came in slowly, cautiously. Molly turned suddenly and grinned.

"Mommy, look, we're cooking."

"Hi, guys." I kissed one head, then another. Nick smelled like soap.

"Morning. We've been busy. Molly did about a quarter of the puzzle and I climbed the Himalayas."

"You what?"

"On your StairMaster."

He'd used my StairMaster? The StairMaster had been my gift to myself. It was private territory, my own personal nemesis. I hadn't even broken it in yet. But I smiled, covering my feelings. I told myself it was no big deal; at least somebody had used the damned thing. Keeping my worries to myself, I ate pancakes and drank coffee. I smelled Nick's aftershave and felt his easy touch on my hand. I almost relaxed. But when Molly scampered off to get dressed, I had my moment, and I took it. This was my turf, my home. I had to make the rules. Had to.

"Nick. About Molly—"

"She's a great kid. Fun. You know what she said—"

"No. Wait. I have something to say."

"Uh-oh. Sounds serious. What did I do?"

"Nothing. No, not nothing. But you didn't do it. We both did. Look, what happened last night was, well, amazing. At least it was for me."

"It was amazing for both of us—"

I avoided his eyes. "Good. That's good. But it shouldn't have involved Molly. It isn't fair to her."

He blinked rapidly a few times. Was something in his eye?

"Exactly what are you saying? That you don't want her to know I was here all night? You don't want her to know about us?"

"She's a kid without a father, Nick. She craves a daddy. She used to ask me where her daddy was. Why he didn't live with us. I explained about her adoption the best way I could, and she doesn't ask anymore, but I know she longs for a man she can call Daddy."

"You're saying she wants me to be her dad?"

"I'm saying I don't want to risk her getting attached to anyone until I'm sure he's part of our lives—"

"So what's the bottom line here? Are you saying she shouldn't see you with a man until the wedding?"

"You know that's not what I mean—"

"What *do* you mean?" His eyes were piercing. Cold.

What was wrong with him? Why couldn't he understand? "What I mean isn't about you and me. It's about Molly. That I need to protect her."

He folded his arms. Protecting himself? Or belligerent? I thought of his dead wife. Had Nick wanted children with her?

"Okay. So you're saying you don't want me around Molly?"

"No. I don't know. I just want you to understand. I want us to be careful of her."

He nodded. Arms still folded. Distancing. "Okay. I understand. Anything else?"

Damn. I'd hurt his feelings. Half of me wanted to unfold his arms and climb inside them, but the other half made me go on.

"Actually, there is. As long as we're talking."

"Shoot."

Shoot? His wife popped to mind again, holding a revolver.

"It's not about Molly. It's about the case. There's a rumor going around that a body was found. A nanny body, in a trash bag."

He didn't flinch. He looked me right in the eye, didn't even blink. "Where'd you hear that?

I didn't implicate Susan. "Neighbors. People. Is it true?"

"It's bullshit. Who's spreading crap like that?"

"You haven't heard anything about this?"

"Not a word."

Why was he lying? "But if it were true, would you tell me?"

Aha. He blinked. "Zoe, don't believe everything you hear. People are on the verge of panic, and rumors are going to fly. Don't pay attention. Leave the investigation to the police and the FBI."

First a blink, then an evasion. Nick knew about the bag; Susan had heard him talking about it. He was lying, but I couldn't tell him that I knew. Was I as bad as he was, testing him? Setting him up?

"Nick, if we're going to have any kind of relationship, I have to be able to trust you. I have to know you'll tell me the truth. Not twist it for your convenience or omit it altogether."

He swallowed some coffee. "The truth? That's a pretty complex topic, isn't it? There are a lot of sides to the truth; it isn't solid and fixed like concrete. It's more like Jell-O—fluid, changing with the circumstance, the moment, the point of view. Most people can't grasp that."

"That's a sociopath's definition. Truth is truth, not something you can shape to suit your purpose."

"Okay. Is this about the nanny case? Or about life in general?"

"How can you separate the two?"

"Okay, then. If that's how you want it, here's the truth: I'll tell you everything you need to know about the nanny case. But the whole picture? That's for the police. Leave it to us. You're a civilian."

"So if a woman's body was found down the street, you wouldn't tell me."

Half his mouth curled. It looked almost sinister. "I wouldn't divulge information that could endanger a case. Not to you or anyone else. Please. Give this up, will you?"

"Give it up? You just said you wouldn't tell me—"

"So?"

"So you lied to me about the body, Nick. Didn't you? And, if you'd lie about that, what else will you lie about? What are the rules? What can I trust?"

"Oh, man." Nick's hand brushed his hair, and he sat forward, elbows on his knees. "Look. Let's get clear on this right away. You're a smart, talented, pretty lady. And I'm a cop. A cop. That's where the line is drawn. Understand?"

No. I didn't. But I understood that we were fighting. I was mad, and so was he.

"I decide what you or the press or the public or anyone else knows about this or any other investigation. I don't need people spreading rumors and making things worse than they already are."

"You decide what others are allowed to know? Is that just on police matters? Or on personal ones, too?"

He hesitated only a moment. "It's how it is. Period. Hey—you can be pissed if you want. You can tell me to get lost. But I am who I am, and I deal with things my way. Fact is, Zoe, I like you. I'd like to spend time with you. But that's not going to happen if you're going to interfere in the way I work. Or the way I am."

I was seething. "Fine." The words came through clenched jaws. "Then I guess that's that. Because I can't be with a man who isn't honest with me."

He didn't answer. For a moment, we sat deadlocked in silence. In a normal situation, he would have left then. I expected him to, wanted him to. But just then, Molly came back into the kitchen, eyeing us warily. Instantly, Nick and I slapped stiff smiles on our faces, masking our hostilities. I wondered, once again, if this was what it was like to be part of a family. Protecting children from being hurt by the affairs of the adults around them. Molly sat beside me and I put my arm around her.

"Still hungry, Mollybear?" I would ignore Nick. I would punish him by shutting him out.

She shrugged, looked from me to Nick. "Are you guys in a fight?" she whispered.

Nick answered in a calm voice. "No, your mom and I aren't fighting. Not really. Even good friends have disagreements sometimes. We're having one, and we're talking about it so we can work it out." His eyes watched me while he spoke, and I saw in them the almost painful tenderness of the night before.

Molly nodded. "Don't worry," she assured him. "Two people can't always agree every time." Where had she heard that? How had she arrived at that wisdom?

Nick smiled his half smile. "You're a smart girl, Molly. Smarter than a lot of grown-ups."

He reached across the table for my hand and held on to it, but I held mine in a firm fist, not relenting. Still, despite our unresolved issues, for a while longer, we remained calm and friendly for Molly's sake. We'd had our first argument, and as far as I was concerned it would be our last. What an idiot I'd been. How had I so casually—and so suddenly—let this man into our lives? And gone to bed with him? So soon? And introduced him to Molly? What had I been thinking? I glanced across the table, avoiding Nick's eyes, glimpsing his strong jawline, his shoulders, his meaty hands. My body reacted, even now. Obviously, I hadn't been thinking; that was the problem.

Well, no real harm was done. Molly hadn't invested emotionally yet, and although my feelings were bruised, I'd survive. I'd been stupid, but I'd learned some important facts: Even with his evasions, I knew that the bag with the body was real. And I knew that I was needier than I'd realized. That I had to be on guard and not fall so easily for a man like Nick Stiles.

That morning, sitting across from him, I marveled at how relaxed he seemed, how easily he played word games with Molly.

I couldn't help thinking about the woman who'd shot him. Had he been dishonest with her, too? Had she agonized over his deceit? Had it been merely omissions or actual lies? I pictured her, unsteadily aiming her gun at Nick, and I imagined him diving, struggling for the gun, getting shot in the face, and, in a bloody rage, grabbing the weapon and shooting her dead. Stop it, I told myself. That was absurd. Just because he'd hidden some facts about the nanny case didn't mean he'd lied about his wife's death. He hadn't killed her; she'd shot herself. Her death had been by her own hand. Hadn't it? If I asked him about it, all these years later, he'd certainly tell me the truth. Wouldn't he?

TWENTY-TWO

As if on cue, Susan called seconds later, just as I was getting into the shower. "I gotta be quick," she blurted. "We're late for piano lessons. Here's the deal: Leslie and I made preliminary plans for organizing the moms. We all have crazy schedules, so we're meeting Thursday during gym. Leslie is bringing about fifty whistles to distribute to nannies. Heather's got colored string—we're going to make necklaces to hang the whistles on. We've got oodles of ideas. Anyhow, you know the routine: I call you; you call Karen; she calls Gretchen, and so on down the phone chain just like for snow days."

"Great. You did good."

Her breathing slowed. "Okay. What's wrong?"

Dammit, I couldn't hide anything from her.

"Zoe, I don't have time to pull it out of you. What happened?"

"It's not important. The whistle necklaces are a great idea."

"I'll worry until I know."

"It's no big deal. Just that Stiles came over last night."

"About the case?"

"No. It was a social call."

"Really?" She was quiet for a minute, chewing on that. I could hear her mind whirring. "And?"

Good question, I thought. "And it got complicated. It went south."

"So fast? What the hell happened?"

"We don't share priorities. We have different values—"

"Zoe, what are you talking about? What does that mean? Who gives a damn about sharing values? Tim and I've been married seventeen years, and I don't have a clue what he 'values.' Hell, we don't agree on anything. We cancel out each other's votes every election."

I didn't say anything.

"Why not give it some time? Leave the door open for a while?"

My sheets were still rumpled. My face was sore from whisker burn. "I don't think so, no. Look, he lied about finding the bag of body parts. He denied to my face that it even exists. And he lied to you about the finger. Susan, the man lies."

"So? He might have reasons."

"You're saying that lying's okay if you have reasons?"

"I didn't say lying was okay. It probably isn't. But I don't see what the big deal is. People lie. We all do. Haven't you ever lied? Told someone you loved her runny soufflé? Swore you had a great time at a dull party? Faked an orgasm?"

"That's not the same—"

"Look, we can debate this all day, but the girls are waiting in the car. Remember, Zoe, the truth isn't all it's cracked up to be. We all need a good lie now and then."

"So. Do you lie?"

"I'm a lawyer."

"Okay. Do you lie to me?"

"I might bend the truth now and then. Depends on about what or why."

"Ouch."

"See? The truth hurts. I should have lied and said, 'No, I never lie to you.' You'd have felt better."

"Okay. I see your point. You're right. I'll give him another chance."

"You're lying, aren't you?"

"So what? You'll feel better."

"Okay. Look, I know you're pissed at him. I was pissed off when he pretended there was no finger. But remember, Stiles is working a sensitive case. He's not at liberty to reveal what he knows. It's not fair to ask him to."

Maybe she was right, but I didn't think so. I couldn't trust Nick professionally or personally. And if I were going to let a man get close to me, I had to trust him to tell me the truth, even if it was that my soufflé was runny, that my party was a bore, or that a bagful of body parts had been found a block from my front door.

TWENTY-THREE

"I LIKE YOUR BOYFRIEND, MOM." WE WERE ON THE WAY TO Karen's for the playdate.

"He's not my boyfriend." I never should have let Nick meet Molly. I had no right to involve her.

"Mom. He's a boy, isn't he? And he's your friend. So he's your boyfriend. Right?"

"If you put it that way. I guess he is."

We were quiet for a few steps. "Is Nick coming back tonight?"

"No. Not tonight, Mollybear. Why? Do you want him to?"

She shook her head as if I were missing the point. "Mom. He's your boyfriend, not mine. The thing is, do you want him to?"

She looked so serious, so like a tiny therapist, that even in my somber mood I had to laugh. She laughed, too. How was this almost six-year-old so smart? And how, with all the fear and alarm raging in our neighborhood, with me having just ended the shortest relationship of my life, were we able to laugh out loud half the way to Karen and Nicholas's? I didn't know. But we were and it felt good. A reprieve. A release of tensions.

Then, with half a block to go, she said, "Is it true about that killer, Mommy?"

The giggling stopped, shattering like a fallen icicle.

"What killer?"

"The man killing all the babysitters."

"No. It's not true." It wasn't technically a lie; he wasn't killing all of them.

She shrugged. "Everybody says it is."

"Well, it's not." Okay, so I was lying. But I had reasons. Besides, truth was like Jell-O.

"Will he kill Angela?"

"Of course not."

"But what if he does?"

"He won't."

She was quiet for a few steps. "Mommy. Just pretend. If he does kill Angela, who'll stay with me while you work? Will Nick?"

Nick again. She liked him. I remembered the pressure of his chest against mine. Damn. I shouldn't have let him come into the house, much less stay the night. "Nothing's going to happen to Angela."

"But I've seen him watching her."

"Who? Nick?" I slowed. A cloud of breath hung in front of her mouth.

"No. The killer."

"How have you seen him?" Was she having nightmares? Fantasies? What was she talking about?

"Just . . . I've seen him."

No way. "Where?"

"Um." She thought awhile. "All over."

I stopped walking and stooped to meet her eyes. "Molly, are you having bad dreams?"

"Tsk. I know the difference, Mommy. I'm not a baby."

She seemed certain. I stood and we started walking again. "Well, tell me about him. How do you know it's him?"

"I just know."

"Okay. What does he look like?"

She shrugged. "I dunno. Big. He has a baseball hat."

Okay. The killer had been seen "all over," he looked "big," and he wore "a baseball hat." That's what I got for interviewing a kindergartner. Her imagination was running amok; she was scared and had reason to be. I hadn't paid enough attention to what she'd heard and overheard. She must be terrified. It was time to reassure her.

"Listen, Molly. You're safe. Nobody's going to hurt you. I won't let them. And Nick's a policeman. He and the other police are going to catch the bad guy."

She looked convinced—but small and cold, shivering inside her hooded pink down jacket. I hugged her, and we held hands as we continued our walk. It must be wonderful to be six and still believe that there was order in the world, that grown-ups loved you and could pick you up in their arms and keep you safe, that they really had control over what happened in life.

Karen and Nicholas greeted us at the door, and the children ran off to play. It wasn't until later, when Molly and Nicholas were decorating holiday cookies, that I understood the effectiveness of my reassurances.

"You know Angela?" she asked Nicholas.

"Course." He smeared blue icing on a Santa cookie.

"She might be killed." Molly spread colored sprinkles over a pink snowman.

"How do you know?" He took the sprinkles from her.

Karen put down her spatula and touched my arm, eavesdropping along with me. She still hoped Tamara was alive. She didn't know about the finger I'd found or the bag of limbs that had been discovered a few blocks away.

"I've seen him. He sneaks around and watches her." Molly knocked over the bottle of cinnamon candies. "Oops—uh-oh." They began stuffing the spilled pieces into their mouths, giggling.

Karen whispered, "What's she saying?"

"It's anxiety," I whispered back. "She's imagining stuff." She had to be. There was no other explanation.

Karen nodded and went back to taking cookies from the tray.

"I love these." Nicholas's mouth was stuffed with candy.

"Me, too."

Karen's eyes began to relax. "I guess it's her way of coping," she whispered. But we continued to eavesdrop on the children.

"Where'd you see him?"

"By my house."

"For real?"

"Uh-huh."

"Then what's he look like?"

"Like—just—scary."

"You're making it up—"

"I am not—I've seen him—"

"Nicholas," Karen interrupted. Her eyes were disapproving. Alarmed. "Here's a batch of stars. You haven't done any stars yet."

The conversation was halted, the topic changed. The rest of the afternoon, nobody mentioned Angela or a scary man or any of the missing nannies. But when we said good-bye and left with arms loaded with cookie tins, I knew what would linger there, so I avoided Karen's eyes.

TWENTY-FOUR

MONDAY MORNING, ANGELA ARRIVED WITH AN ATTITUDE. SHE was miffed, wouldn't talk to me, wouldn't even look at me.

I tried to deal with her. "You got your nails done," I said. They were about three inches of crimson acrylic, a pattern of rhinestones glittering on her ring fingers. Molly craned her neck over the kitchen counter to see.

"Yeah." Her word pierced the air like a shot.

"Your hair looks nice, too." It had a few extra layers of spray, tough to break through.

She didn't answer.

"Can we paint my nails, too, Mom? Can we?"

"Sure. If Angela wants to. Go get the nail kit." The nail kit was an old shoe box where we kept polish and clippers; Molly scampered off to get it. As soon as she was out of the room, I asked, "Okay. You want to tell me what's up?"

"Nothing's up."

"Angela. Either tell me or don't, but either way, deal with it."

She turned to me, hand on hip. "Okay, you wanna know? You got no business setting me up with that guy."

It took me a second to figure out what she was talking about. Then I remembered: Jake. The ride home.

"I got you a ride home so you wouldn't have to walk alone—"

Angela wheeled around. "Look, there's just somethin' about that guy."

THE NANNY MURDERS 143

"He was probably flirting. Don't take it so seriously."

"No, no. I don't like him and I don't want his damn rides. I can take care of myself." Her fingers flew, nails carving the air. "I don't need no personal bodyguard. I take kickboxing. Don't worry about me. I know what to do, anybody messes with me."

"You take kickboxing?"

"I do. I'll teach you, too, if you want. I'm teaching Molly."

"You're teaching Molly?"

"Sure. Why not? She's gotta know how to defend herself, same as the rest of us."

"Angela, look. Those classes are great, but a real killer might not approach you the way the instructor demonstrates—"

"What do you know about it? They show us all kinds of ways. They come at us from every direction." Then she softened a little. "Look, Joe'd have a fit, me getting rides home from work with some guy. I know you got my interests at heart, Zoe. But I got it covered. Nobody's gonna bother me."

She took two eggs out of the fridge and cracked them into a bowl for Molly's breakfast. She beat the eggs a little too enthusiastically.

I understood about Joe, though. Her longtime boyfriend, a car mechanic with perpetually dirty fingernails, was known for his fragile ego and a hot temper. He was possessive and shifty-eyed, and I'd often wondered what Angela saw in him. "You know, with all those nannies missing, Joe should be glad someone drove you home and kept his eye on you."

"Yeah? Well, anybody keeps his eye on me, Joe's gonna punch it out."

"I don't think he'll mess with Jake."

"What's that supposed to mean? You think Joe's not as buffed as Jake? He lifts every day. Joe can lift one-sixty."

"I didn't mean that." Well, I did, actually. Joe was probably six inches shorter than Jake; he'd get clobbered. "I meant he had too much sense to mess with a guy who's only trying to help us out. If there were more people like Jake in the neighborhood, maybe some of those women would still be around."

"What? Are you inferring that it's Joe's fault that women are disappearing?"

"Implying," I said. "Not inferring."

She sputtered, defending her boyfriend, and I considered what she'd just said. Even if Angela didn't consciously suspect him, did she sense that Joe had something to do with the missing nannies? Joe wasn't local, but he was in and out of the neighborhood because of Angela. Besides, he had a nasty temper, insecurities about women. Should I mention him to Nick? What was happening to me? Because of Nick and his damned profile, I was beginning to suspect everyone. Joe wasn't capable of kidnapping and murder. He couldn't be.

Something out the window caught Angela's attention. She stopped scolding and stood on her tiptoes to see better.

Beyond the passing cars, Phillip Woods stood on his porch, buttoning his coat. A construction crew huddled with thermoses of coffee.

"There's Jake now." Angela's long nails arranged her hair. "I gotta go deal with this."

"Are you sure? With the whole crew around, you might not want to—"

But she was already out the door, a petite, busty woman without a coat, in skin-tight jeans, high-heeled boots, and fancy fingernails, headed smack into a cluster of bulky construction workers. I expected hoots and fireworks, but as she strutted up to them, they nodded cordially or tipped their hats. She and Jake stepped aside. Talking, gesturing. If her body language meant anything, it wasn't a fight.

"Here—I got it." Molly returned with the nail kit. "Where's Angela?"

Angela was standing in front of Jake, pointing her finger into his chest. Was she threatening him or flirting? Her clawlike nail rested on his jacket, provocative, either way.

"She'll be right back," I said. "Let's pick a color. I have to go to work soon."

"I want the same as Angela."

"Red, then."

"I know. Which red?" She searched the bottles, lining reds along the counter.

"Molly," I said, "has Angela taught you kickboxing?"

She grinned. "Yeah. It's like karate. Wanna see? Somebody comes at you from the front, you smash their nose like this and kick like that." She demonstrated on the air. "Or you go like this behind their knee and they fall."

She jabbed her foot into empty space, buckling an imaginary leg, an unfamiliar viciousness in her eyes. Who was this child? "I think this is the red Angela has."

She came running over to look.

Outside, Angela tossed her head and sashayed back to our house. Jake stood watching her, head tilted, bemused. If she'd wanted him to leave her alone, she might not have made her point.

TWENTY-FIVE

As ARRANGED WITH NICK, WHEN I GOT TO THE INSTITUTE, I
set out to find Dr. Beverly Gardener's office to pick up the profile.
Her office was listed in the lobby as Room 37, in the basement,
where most staff psychiatrists had their offices. My work almost
never took me down there; in fact, I'd been in the basement only
twice and hadn't enjoyed either visit. The air there was tomblike
and musty, the halls intricate and poorly lit. A catacomb.

But I was supposed to meet her there at nine to pick up a
copy of her report. So, bracing myself, I walked past Agnes to
the elevator at the end of the corridor and pushed the down
button. Tired metal rattled and creaked, and slowly the dial indicated that the car was groaning its way to the first floor.

Finally, the elevator doors slid open. I was uneasy about the
meeting. Dr. Gardener might think I wasn't qualified to work
with her—after all, I wasn't headline material. But I didn't have
to justify my role was here at the request of the police. Nick had
said he'd discussed my involvement with her.

The doors opened, and I entered the dimly lit labyrinth of
marble floors and drafty corridors. A maze of gray walls lined
with frosted glass doors. What was behind all those doors? Private offices? Patients' rooms? Closets? Passing an open one, I
peeked in. A huge expanse of white tiles surrounded a four-
legged bathtub in the center of the floor. Nothing else was in

there. Not a sink. Not a cabinet. Not a towel rack. Creepy. I kept walking.

I saw nobody, heard only my own footsteps echoing along the walls. I followed the numbers. 77, 75. At 59, I encountered a pungent smell. Pipe tobacco? At 53, shrill laughter rolled under the door. When I got to 47, a door slammed behind me; I looked around. No one was there. The click of high-heeled shoes echoed from an intersecting corridor. Somewhere a door opened and closed. Then silence. Just the padding of my own shoes. I looked behind me. The hallway extended emptily back to the elevator. I walked on. Now the door said 92. Damn. I was lost. I turned back and retraced my steps. At 84, harsh laughing erupted, then abruptly ended, emphasizing the silence that followed. At 43, the hallway veered left. 42. 41. I was back on track.

From somewhere came a dull, rhythmic thumping. Maybe from an alcove up ahead, a waiting area. Was it footsteps? Yes, maybe someone pacing. Maybe in the alcove. I slowed, listening, watching. A lone shadow emerged from the alcove and slid along the hallway floor. Back and forth. Then it stopped, lay still, a dark stripe among shadows. Had it heard my footsteps? Why was it so still? Who was there?

A clammy draft tickled my neck; I wheeled around, saw no one. The hallway was deserted, except for me and the shadow in the alcove. No stalkers. No ghosts. No reason to be nervous. Besides, Dr. Gardener's office was just a few doors ahead, within easy reach. I pictured myself breathlessly bursting through her door, panicking. No. I wasn't going to do that. The shadow began to pace again.

Okay, I told myself. Enough. The hall is dim and creepy, and every sound makes eerie echoes, but that doesn't mean that there's a serial killer in the alcove. Just keep walking and mind your own business. I made myself continue, step by step. I was fine. Even so, the hairs on my neck stiffened as I approached the waiting area. Passing the opening, I braced myself, ready to bolt.

I didn't bolt, though. I did a double take, not registering the face at first. I recognized it but needed a minute to place it; the face didn't belong at the Institute. Gradually, though, I recognized the spectacles, the pale face, the cashmere coat. The man in the alcove was my neighbor Phillip Woods.

Phillip Woods? I was so relieved, I almost hugged him and laughed out loud. But we were in a psychiatric hospital. I wasn't sure he'd want to be recognized, let alone to be embraced with laughter by his neighbor. What was he doing here? Was he a patient? Or visiting one? He gaped at me, wide-eyed, apparently as nervous as I'd been. I nodded and kept walking, trying to be discreet, trying to absorb the oddity of finding Phillip Woods pacing the bowels of the Institute's basement.

Finally, number 37 was just across the hall. The door featured large block letters announcing the doctor's name. I knocked but got no answer. Knocked again. Finally, I tried the doorknob. The door was locked, the office dark. What was going on? Beverly Gardener knew I was coming; Nick had set up our appointment. I didn't notice the envelope until I stepped back to leave. It was taped inconspicuously to the wood below the knob, and my name was on it.

"Zoe," I read. We'd never formally met, but she used my first name. Establishing her dominance? "Urgent police consult called me away. Call to reschedule." It was signed "BG." Not "Beverly."

Damp breath tickled my ear. "Are you—I beg your pardon, Ms. Hayes." I wheeled around and found myself nose to nose with Phillip Woods. I hadn't heard him approach. "Is that note perhaps—so sorry to intrude—but is that possibly a message from Dr. Gardener?"

I tried to back away but bumped into the door.

"Oh, excuse me," he exclaimed without moving away. "I didn't mean to startle you. I mean to say, I didn't realize you were acquainted with Beverly—oh my. Small world, isn't it?" He stopped to clear his throat, as if realizing the awkwardness of our situation. His eyes shifted, flitting to the wall, back to me. "Well. I didn't expect to see you. Certainly not here. Where's your little girl?"

I swallowed. "She's home. I work here, Mr. Woods. I'm an art therapist."

"Oh? Oh my. How fascinating. Yes. Well, then. You and Beverly must be colleagues." Mr. Woods peered at me through thick lenses, blinking rapidly. I tried to smile, but my mouth twisted, must have resembled a grimace. "So, your little daughter's at home. I don't have children myself, of course. Not yet. Although I may finally have found the right woman." He giggled briefly. "Well, maybe. Time will tell. But you seem a devoted mother. Lucky for your child. I was sent away to school when I was just a boy. To Europe. Switzerland, actually. You see, Mother traveled with Father. Diplomatic service. But it wasn't all bad. I met Charles, Andrew. Stephanie. All sorts of royals."

"Interesting," I said. "How many of you were there?"

"How many?"

"Children."

"Oh, well. Just myself. Just the one." He cleared his throat, eyes darting away. Changing topics. "I'm puzzled about Beverly— Dr. Gardener. I don't understand where she can be. She should have known I was coming by. I called the station first, of course. But they, well, they put me on hold. Can you imagine?"

"You called her radio show?" I'd often wondered what kind of people called in and aired their problems for others' entertainment. How could they seek serious help in three minutes between commercial breaks? But here was cashmere-coasted Phillip Woods, admitting that he'd made a call.

"Yes, I called. I told them I was a close friend of Beverly's, but they still didn't put me through."

"Dr. Gardener's your friend?" Prominent Beverly Gardener and mousy Phillip Woods? It was hard to imagine them in a room together, much less in a personal relationship.

"Oh yes. Of course. We're very close. Believe me, heads will roll when she finds out they put me on hold. I waited a half hour, and then they disconnected me—can you believe it? I called again, and the line was busy. So I called here and found out she was expected, and I left the message that I'd be dropping by. I should have done that to begin with. But I thought I'd give her a kick, you know, a dear friend popping up on the air."

"I see." His story seemed far-fetched. Probably he was making it up, creating a cover story, embarrassed to be found seeing a shrink. I began to move away, but he stepped into my path.

"The receptionist confirmed that Beverly was expected in her office today. I can't imagine where she is." Had Agnes sent him down here? She should have known better.

"Well, Dr. Gardener's a busy woman; you'd probably be wise to make an appointment."

"An appointment? Me? Oh, I don't think so. She'll make the time."

"Like I said, she's very busy." I looked him in the eye.

"Besides, she owes me half an hour. After all, I waited on hold all that time." He chuckled, as if at a joke. If there was one, I didn't get it.

"I don't know what to tell you. I don't know when she'll be in." I took a sideways step and began to walk away.

He nodded, staring at the floor. "Yes, all right."

"But I doubt it'll be soon." I walked a few steps and turned back.

He stood still, bereft. A lost man in need of help.

"Maybe Agnes, the receptionist in the lobby, can phone her beeper for you."

"No, no. I don't want to alarm her. It's no real emergency."

His gaze remained on the floor. His eye kept twitching and he bit his lip. I was afraid he was going to cry. I hoped he wouldn't; I didn't know how to react if he did. But his eyes remained dry, darting to the ceiling and back down again. "Very well, then. She's not coming," he sighed. "Well. Another time, then. Thank you, Ms. Hayes. Very sorry to have bothered you."

He turned back to the waiting area and resumed his troubled pacing. I saw a small suitcase on the sofa. Was he just here to see Dr. Gardener, or had he been planning to check in?

"But if you want," I offered, "someone else on staff could probably see you now. Dr. Gardener's not the only—"

"Why would I want to see someone else? I thought I made myself clear, Ms. Hayes. I'm here as Dr. Gardener's friend. We have a close, rather personal relationship."

"Oh, of course."

"Maybe I'll wait just a bit longer." He shifted from foot to foot, glancing up and down the hallway, and resumed his pacing. I left him there and quickly retraced my steps to the elevator. I'd ask Beverly Gardener about him. Maybe they were friends. But, if they were, why didn't he just call her cell phone or her home if he wanted to talk? What was the big deal about surprising her? Oh, well. Not my business. What an odd little man. And what a street I lived on. Charlie, the delusional paranoid. Victor, the phobic recluse. And Phillip Woods apparently had a few personal quirks himself. Then, of course, there was me . . .

The note was still in my hand. Dr. Gardener was off assisting the police. Assisting Nick. Was she with him now? I pictured them together. Intense, energetic Beverly Gardener and rugged, big-bicepped Nick Stiles. Maybe she was helping him sort body

parts. Maybe he was studying her profile. Maybe I should stop
thinking about what they were doing. Whatever it was, why did
I care? Dammit, why had I gone to bed with him? And why
couldn't I stop thinking about him? I had patients to see, a
group session to run. A killer to watch out for. I didn't need to
spend time wandering a chilly basement, feeling jealous and
suspicious, imagining the romantic escapades of a woman I
didn't know and a man I didn't trust.

I hurried into the elevator, pushed the button, and didn't
look up again until the doors opened, delivering me from the
bowels of the Institute to the gray light of the lobby.

TWENTY-SIX

THAT DAY AND THE NEXT, I CALLED BEVERLY GARDENER'S OF-
fice several times, only to get Agnes. I left messages about
rescheduling but got no reply. I thought of calling Nick about it
but didn't want to, except as a last resort. Besides, I was busy. I
had a new patient, Celia Dukell. Celia was fifteen years old and
had been carving herself with razor blades off and on for three
years. Our first sessions went well enough, but I suspected she
was saying and doing what she thought she was supposed to say
and do. Her family portrait showed her as a bland and hollow
figure amid relatives of substance and color. A polite, controlled, only slightly revealing sketch.

My other cases were demanding, as well. Amanda, almost
completely bald now, drew her family without including any
image of herself. Hank wouldn't paint at all until the bristles on
his brush were perfectly aligned, which was never. Sydney, having adapted to his medications, began a still life of a vase, but
the vase in his sketch, unlike the model, was severely chipped
and cracked.

Evie Kraus finally painted something other than her literal
surroundings. She did a self-portrait, examining her features
closely in a mirror while she worked. I looked over her shoulder
to see what she'd drawn; like the tattoos covering her arms, it
was a coiled, thick snake, devouring a cat.

I finally heard from Dr. Gardener on Wednesday morning. I'd

begun to think that I'd never see the profile, that Nick might have reconsidered having my input on the case. Then, Wednesday morning, I smelled flowers, heard the quick clack of heels against tile, and looked up to see Dr. Beverly Gardener herself bursting like floodwaters into the arts and crafts room.

"You must be Zoe." Her eyes focused on me, drenching me with their intensity. She wore a cranberry tweed suit with a knee-length skirt that showed off her incredible calves, and she examined me from head to toe and back to head again, as if measuring me for curtains. "I'm Beverly Gardener. Nick Stiles's friend."

His friend? Not colleague? Not consultant? His friend. Okay. I got it. Her makeup was simple, accenting her green eyes, and her dark hair was done up in a neat chignon. I stood to greet her. In her low heels, she was taller than I in my flats; I had to look up at her when we spoke.

"Nice to meet you." I extended my hand to shake; she cupped it in hers like a wounded bird, watching me. Studying my. reaction?

"Nick said to pass this along to you." She handed me a large white envelope, her eyes not leaving mine.

"Thank you."

"You live right in the middle of it, then? You found the finger?"

"Yes."

"How awful for you, dumpling."

Dumpling? I remembered now; on her radio show, she used epithets all the time. Callers were "honey" or "peach." It was her shtick to talk in food.

"Well, not as awful as it was for the woman who lost it."

"I imagine not." Her eyes probed mine, studying me. I felt them, hot like spotlights. "But cupcake, have you talked it out with anyone?"

Oh, please. Was she going to play sixty-second shrink with me? "Thanks for your concern, Dr. Gardener. I'm fine—"

"Really? Because Nick says you've been upset about the nanny case. He said one of the missing women is your friend."

"Did he?" Sonofabitch discussed me with her? What else had he said? That I was easy? That I'd hopped into bed after just two slices of pizza? "He must have caught me at a bad moment." Damned if I was going to let on that I was upset.

"Look, sugar, you don't need to impress me with your strength. This case is brutal. Horrible. You'd be nuts not to be upset." Her eyes were jade green. "Professionals like us don't like to admit that we can have problems, too. We're supposed to be invulnerable and help everybody else. But guess what? We're only human. Sometimes we need a shoulder to lean on just like everyone else. So if there's anything I can do for you—anything at all—just call. You hear?" She seemed sincere. Despite the food nicknames and the fact that she hadn't answered my calls for three days, I found myself oddly drawn to her. Warmed by her energy, flattered by her attention. Almost believing her sincerity. Almost wanting to.

"Thanks," I said. "I'm really fine, though."

"I hope so." Her voice was husky, like smoke. Her eyes glowed like green embers. "We're on the same team, after all."

We were a team? I pictured us in football uniforms, huddled around Nick. Not a good image. I blinked it away.

She was leaving. Heels clacking on my floor, reviving me. I remembered the message I had for her.

"Oh, Dr. Gardener?" Damn, why hadn't I said "Beverly"? "There was a man at your office, Phillip Woods. He was waiting to see you—"

"Woods?" Her eyes widened. "He was? Oh, Christ. When?"

"Monday morning. He said he was your friend."

"I'm sure he did. Actually, he's more like my devotee. He's a groupie. An infatuated fan. He writes letters and e-mails, sends me flowers, hangs around the radio station hoping to catch sight of me. I guess it was only a matter of time until he showed up here."

Were we talking about the same Phillip Woods? "Really? He didn't seem the kind of person who'd intrude that way."

"Actually, he's not that unusual. I've come to expect that sort of thing—it comes with celebrity. When you're in the public eye, people begin to think they actually know you, even that they're in love with you. Like Phillip Woods. He has a crush on me. It's a nuisance, but no big surprise." She shrugged. "Thanks for telling me. I'll take care of it."

When she waved good-bye, the air shimmered around her; after she'd left, the room seemed empty and deprived. Except for the lingering scent of her perfume, I was alone with her profile.

TWENTY-SEVEN

IT WAS IN A PLAIN WHITE ENVELOPE WITH NO COVER LETTER, no return address, no instruction as to what I should do when I'd finished reading it.

The report itself was surprisingly short and contained few surprises. It said that the likely perpetrator was male, probably under forty, probably a loner, probably with low self-esteem. He probably lived, worked, or had lived or worked in the neighborhood where the crimes were committed. He likely had some sort of sexual dysfunction as well as a history of violence and/or abuse in his childhood. He hated young women or nannies, might have been a chronic bed wetter, might have started fires, might have been cruel to small animals.

The wording was general, the findings broad enough to apply to many serial killers, not just this one. Most of the second paragraph was blacked out; what remained suggested that the suspect would have to be familiar with a variety of tools and adept at using them. He would be neat, intelligent, and organized; a stickler for detail; a patient, persistent person who might have a background in medicine, anatomy, hunting, fishing, engineering, carpentry, or design.

I held the paper up to the light but couldn't read the blacked-out section. I assumed, though, that it referred to specifics of the recovered victim's dismemberment, details of which Nick wasn't ready to reveal to a "civilian," even if she'd personally found one of the dismembered parts.

I read on. The suspect was probably but not necessarily white; his victims had no consistent racial makeup, and victims usually matched the race of their killer. He was precise and planned carefully. He believed he was empowered to kill because of his own innate superiority, the value of his mission, or the power of a superior being who directed him. He might or might not be torturing his victims. His father might have been an alcoholic or drug abuser; his mother might have abused him, possibly sexually. Also, he might or might not have had a nanny or babysitter who'd abused him. The increasingly bold and open nature of his kidnappings implied that he was confident, even taunting authorities, growing bolder with each crime.

The report so far seemed general and indefinite. Nothing particularly insightful or striking. Was this vague garble the kind of work that had earned Beverly Gardener world renown as a forensic psychologist?

The next paragraph was highlighted in yellow. It said that the killer might insert himself somehow into or close to the investigation, possibly pretending to protect potential victims or to help solve the crime. The fact that significant evidence had been left out in the open indicated that he intended to keep on killing. He might, in fact, leave significant clues in significant places where they would be found by significant parties. An arrow was drawn to a handwritten comment in the margin. It said, "E.g., finger? Z. Hayes? Significance?"

A chilled ripple slid down my back. With equally cold certainty, I understood why Nick had asked for my help.

TWENTY-EIGHT

FOR SEVERAL MINUTES, I SAT AT MY DESK, SHAKEN BY DR. GAR-dener's notation. Had the finger been dropped in front of my house deliberately? Was my doorstep a "significant" location to the killer? If so, why? Who was he?

The faces of local men stampeded through my mind. Victor. Charlie. Joe. Gene. Stop it, I told myself. Calm down. Think. I closed my eyes and took a deep breath, made the faces stand in an orderly line. Victor was first. He was the right age, some-where in his thirties. I didn't know much else about him, be-yond rumors. Supposedly, he'd lived with his mother all his life, until her death. Maybe something unnatural had been going on. Had he been abused? Victor was a loner, dysfunctional at every-thing, probably at sex, too. But Victor was so afraid of violence that he holed up in his house. Unless that was just an act. Maybe Victor wasn't phobic at all. Maybe he actually snuck out his back door, grabbed nannies, and chopped their fingers off in his spare room. Who would know? Agoraphobia would be a great cover.

What about Charlie? He insisted that he knew all about the evil around us. He said the evil guy was "in his head," control-ling, monitoring his thoughts; that sounded like a "superior power." Oh Lord. Was the dangerous person Charlie'd warned me about none other than Charlie himself? Had Charlie left the grisly clue at our door as a warning? He had a carpentry background. And skill with tools. And he'd inserted himself into the investigation, promising to protect me. He fit the profile in many ways. But that was ridiculous. Charlie had bad knees. He was no killer. Was he?

Then there was Phillip Woods. He'd seemed almost obsessed with Dr. Gardener. Here was a thought: He'd followed Dr. Gardener's career and read her books; he knew she was a forensic consultant for the police. Could he have killed women just to get her attention? To be the subject of one of her chapters? How infatuated was he? He was almost forty, a little old for the profile, but he fit it in other ways. He was a loner. A planner. Precise with details. Able to wire an electronic Santa—maybe he'd studied engineering.

There were others, too. Coach Gene, for example. Rejected by both Tamara and Claudia, maybe by others. He was physically strong. Lived alone.

Damn, the profile fit both nobody and everybody I knew in the neighborhood. Of course, there were a lot more men I didn't know. And hundreds of pedestrians who passed by each day. And friends or relatives of people in the neighborhood. The deliveryman who brought Victor his food. Joe, Angela's jealous boyfriend. Jake and his construction crews—a dozen guys, all strong and young and good with tools. Who knew if any of them had been bed wetters or abused as kids? And if they had, what would that mean? Nothing by itself. The report, as far as I was concerned, had been useless.

If someone had singled out my doorstep as a place to drop a finger, I had no idea who he was or why he'd picked my house. Besides, Beverly Gardener might be mistaken; the finger might not have been left there deliberately. Another, after all, had been found in Washington Square. The killer might have dropped them accidentally, might just have been passing by.

Within half an hour, I'd decided that my insights were

useless, that I didn't know the killer. I'd finished "consulting." It hadn't been worth my anxiety over it, hadn't required any risk or even much time. I would write Nick a brief, professionally worded note, offering my thoughts. I'd even be generous and praise the work of his "friend" Beverly Gardener.

And then, I'd be done.

TWENTY-NINE

SOME DAYS, NOTHING HAPPENS. OTHER DAYS, EVENTS ASSAULT relentlessly from all sides, nonstop. Thursday was one of those days. It began in the dark, before dawn. Susan called at six, hysterical for a change.

"She misses work for months, and then she gives me two weeks' notice? I've got a trial next week. What am I going to do?"

"Bonita quit?" I yawned, trying to wake up.

"I can't blame her, in a way. She's scared. A lot of them are quitting, even some of the live-ins. I gave her the whistle and a can of Mace. I told her I'd bought the gun and was getting her a permit. But she won't have any of it. She quit."

"Damn. I mean, I can understand—"

"Of course. But what am I going to do? Tell the judge I can't defend my client because the babysitter quit?"

"The girls can come to my house. Angela's still on the job."

"How are they going to get there?"

"It's only about a mile. Walk?"

My doorbell rang. I checked the clock again. It was barely six-fifteen. Who the hell was ringing the bell? It was too early, couldn't be Angela; besides, she had a key. Maybe Charlie? Was he feverish again?

"Mom? Somebody's at the door." Molly's feet thumped down the hallway. "I'll get it!" I heard her bounding down the steps.

"Molly, no! Wait—you know the rule. Susan, can you believe somebody's at my door?"

"At this hour?" She was appalled. Calling me at this hour, however, had been acceptable.

"I'll call you back."

"No, don't. I gotta get to work. It's round the clock for me these days. And thanks for your offer. But, fact is, with all their music lessons and swim team and all, it wouldn't work. I might have to ask Tim's mother to stay with us. Can you imagine? It could come to that. Dear Lord—look, I'll see you tonight, the moms' meeting, right?"

"Right."

The bell rang again. Molly called, "Mommy. Hurry up!"

I dashed down the steps to the door and peered out the peephole.

"Who is it, Mom?"

"Nobody," I said. "Go ahead, you can open it."

Carefully, she undid the bolt and turned the handle.

"Greetings."

Good Lord, he was growing a mustache. The thing looked alive, as if it had crawled onto his face.

"Jeez, Michael. What are you doing here? Do you know what time it is?"

"No, no, Zoe. You're supposed to say, 'Michael—how nice to see you! Michael—what a nice surprise. How sweet of you to bring doughnuts. Won't you come in?'" He stepped around me, carrying a bakery box.

Molly stood by my side, blinking coyly.

"And who's this pretty young lady?" Michael stooped to her level. "I'm Uncle Mike. What's your name?"

"Molly," she muttered.

He shook her hand. "Nice to meet you, Molly. How are—"

"Listen, Uncle Mike," I cut him off, "we have to get ourselves dressed here, so—"

"You have time. I came early so we'd have time to talk. Aren't you going to offer me a cup of coffee? Decaf if you have it." He was already helping himself, taking a mug out of the cabinet, reaching for the coffee grinder. "You know, this thing's the best investment we ever made. Nothing like waking up to fresh brew."

"So you came to visit the coffee grinder?"

"I came to see you, Zoe. Here. Let me fix us a cup."

"What's in that box?" Molly was clearly baffled. She hadn't processed my night with Nick yet, and now Michael'd shown up, bearing gifts.

"A surprise." He opened it, revealing assorted doughnuts. "Ask your mom if you can have one."

"Can I?"

Before I could answer, Uncle Mike had poured Molly a glass of milk and given her a wad of pink-iced dough, and the two of them were sitting together, chattering and laughing like a pair of happy old hens. What was going on? I'd barely opened my eyes, and already events had sped past me. I couldn't catch up, much less rein them in. When had I lost control? And how was I going to get rid of Michael? How many times in one lifetime did I have to throw the man out?

Calm down, I told myself. The coffee was brewing and smelled warm and toasty. And I was hungry. What difference would it make if I ate a doughnut. I could exercise away the calories. On my StairMaster. Besides, doughnuts were a basic food group, weren't they? Like gnocchi. Again, without wanting to, I thought of Nick. How his hand had felt on mine. Oh, the hell with Nick. I bit into chocolate icing and, in a few bites, devoured the whole doughnut. Then, unable to contain myself, I burst into their happy conversation.

"Molly," I told her, "Uncle Mike and I have to talk."

She was unimpressed. "I'm not done with my doughnut," she said.

"Molly," I handed her a napkin, "go watch television. Please."

Scowling, she gulped the last of her milk and took off.

"What's going on, Michael?"

"She's a nice kid, Zoe."

"Cut the crap."

"I stopped by to see you. To catch up. And find out if you'd de-cided to give back my nana's ring. Christmas is getting close—"

"Dammit, Michael. You've got balls—"

"As I recall, you once liked my balls—"

"I have a life here. You can't harass me like this, dropping in at all hours as if you're some long-lost relative—"

"But that's what I am. A lost relative. A relative who lost everything—even the coffee grinder."

"You can't keep doing this, Michael. Every few months, you want something else. The bonds. The silver. The sofa. Now my ring. I guess you'll want the coffee grinder, too, right? Enough. The divorce is over, and you agreed to the settlement—"

"And that's my point. I agreed. I made everything easy for you. Now, I'm asking you for something, and so far I'm asking nicely—"

"What's that supposed to mean?"

"Just what I said. I've asked you nicely for property that should have been mine to begin with. The only reason my nana wanted you to have that ring was because you were my wife—"

"Enough is enough, Michael. The ring's been mine for years. For decades."

"Yours? How can you say that?" His eyes bulged.

"How can you ask that? You gave it to me yourself."

"Because you were my fiancée. My wife."

"That's right."

"But you aren't now."

"Amazing. You do grasp the situation."

"Why do you want it? You don't wear it."

"Not now. I might someday, though, if I have it reset."

"You wouldn't—that setting's antique. It's exquisite—look. What if I buy it from you? How much?"

Why was I being so stubborn? The ring meant more to him than to me. Much more. But I had to draw the line somewhere. If I wanted him to back off and stop wangling, I'd have to be firm. "Michael. You have to go. I have to get dressed."

He stood still, fuming. Refusing to leave, "Dammit, Zoe," he growled. "I've been civil. I even brought you fucking doughnuts. That's it. I'm done with the nice guy bit."

Was that a threat? From Michael? I heard Charlie whisper, "Trust nobody. Evil is all around." But surely he didn't mean Michael. Michael was selfish, superficial, egotistical, two–faced, immature, and asinine, but he wasn't evil. Was he?

"I thought you'd do this one little thing for me, for old times' sake. We had some good times, didn't we?"

Did we? What was he talking about? As usual, Michael and I were on different planets. I closed my eyes, saw Charlie gesturing from his car, Tamara's hands reaching for help, a finger lying in the street.

When I didn't answer, he stuck out his lower lip, a protrusion of wet flesh under a wad of wiry hair. Michael was pouting.

"Please, Zoe?" He made his little-boy face. A mistake. It didn't work with the mustache.

"I told you I'd think about it, and I will. I promise. G'bye, Michael." I moved toward the door, telling myself not to feel guilty.

"When, exactly?"

"I don't know. When I get a chance." When hell freezes over. "Soon."

"Nothing's on TV, Mommy." Molly was back. Probably she'd never left. Probably she'd been listening in the hall.

"Uncle Mike has to go," I said. "He's just saying good-bye."

She stared at him, her fingers in her mouth. "Are you really my uncle?"

Michael said, "Sure," and I said, "No," at the same time. Our eyes met, sparkling with animosity.

"I want it by Christmas, Zoe," Michael's tone had become nasty. "I've promised it to Margaret, and she'll get it. One way or another."

How dare he bully me? Or promise her my ring before I'd agreed to return it? I went to the door and opened it.

"G'bye, Michael." I held the door for him, just as I had five years ago.

"I'll be in touch," he promised. "Bye, Molly." He winked and shot her with his finger. Then, finally, he was gone.

I stood at the window, watching him negotiate the icy sidewalk to get to his car. I turned off the coffeemaker and rinsed out Michael's cup, my hands recalling the hundreds of times they'd done that. The dozens of simple tasks they'd performed as part of a marriage. Lord. Why had I let Molly open the door? Michael was part of the past. We were over, finished, done. Trying to deal with him now was an anachronism. It was like raising the dead. I went to the door and bolted it, making the house mine again. Locked and secure, I was still standing there, leaning against the door, when the doorbell rang again.

THIRTY

MAYBE HE'D FORGOTTEN HIS GLOVES. I BRACED MYSELF AND opened the door. "What?" I asked.

But it wasn't Michael.

Nick, his back to me, was gazing down the steps, watching Michael's car pull away. Had he seen him leave? What would he think, seeing a man leave my house at not even 7:00 A.M.? Nick's Volvo was parked behind Jake's pickup. Jake stared up at my door. What must he think, seeing all this male traffic? That I ran a brothel? Did he want to get in line? Who else was going to stop by?

"Nick!" Molly ran out the door barefoot and gleefully jumped into his arms. I felt a pang of guilt for letting her form an attachment. Or maybe of jealousy. Watching them, I remembered having those strong arms around me. The comfort of being wrapped against his chest. Damn.

"I knew you'd come back," Molly was saying. "When I woke up, I thought it was you. But it was Uncle Mike. Look how loose my tooth is—maybe it'll come out today—"

"Molly, you have no shoes on. Come inside." My God. She couldn't stop talking. She made it sound like Michael had been there all night. But I owed Nick no explanation, wasn't going to offer any.

I hadn't even greeted him. I didn't know how to. I was still reeling from Michael, and now there was Nick, taking me by surprise, smelling of fresh soap or shaving cream or whatever that stuff was. What was he doing here?

"Okay if I come in, too?"

"Of course." I didn't look at him. Didn't dare. What was the matter with me? I was a mature woman, not some impression-able schoolgirl. And he was just a man like any other. He got holes in his socks, clipped his nose hairs like the rest of them. But seeing him was definitely knocking me off balance, and if I looked at him, my eyes might speak for themselves and give me away. So I aimed them elsewhere. At Molly.

"Sweetie, what are you going to wear today?"

"You already know, Mom. We laid it out last night."

"Then go put it on."

"But I want breakfast."

"You just had a doughnut."

"I want real breakfast."

Nick stood at the door, watching us. Listening. I felt my face get hot, revealing too much. Damn. And the heat of his eyes on me. The man is not for you, I reminded myself. You can't trust him. I repeated that mentally a few times, but when he walked into the kitchen and stood beside me, my legs began to melt. Why was he doing this to me? What did he want? To apologize? To talk? Fine. When would he tell me?

"Why don't you let me help? I can make breakfast."

Get out, I thought. Don't touch my pots. I've only just re-claimed them from the last time you were here. "That's okay," I started. "I can do it—"

"Pancakes? With nuts like last time?" Molly was in heaven.

"If your mom says so."

Molly's eyes pleaded. What could I do? Fine. Okay. Let Michael bring doughnuts and Nick make pancakes. Let's stuff ourselves till we all pass out. What the hell. I had a StairMaster.

So Nick took over the kitchen. Once again, events had taken

a turn, leaving me on my own without control. But I wasn't going to stay there and watch Nick and Molly play house. I went up to shower and dress while they made pancakes, Molly flipping them herself, just as he'd taught her.

Upstairs, alone, I began to think more clearly, and I realized that Nick probably hadn't come to see me or talk about us. He'd come about the profile, Dr. Gardener's report. Of course. She'd given it to me the day before; he wanted to know if I'd read it and what I thought. He was there legitimately, about the case.

Of course. This wasn't personal; it was business. I dressed for work in a loose long black skirt and sweater, prepared to go over my list of neighbors and compare them to the profile. To keep my feelings—like the rest of me—under wraps and focus on the case. Then I saw the table so carefully set and the two of them standing so proudly waiting for me, and I realized that, for all my preparation, I had not steeled myself against two pairs of eager shining eyes.

Once again, we sat like a little imitation family, eating breakfast, chatting, being pleasant and seeming to care. Halfway through my pancakes, acting my role, I wondered. Was it for Molly's sake I went along with this charade? Or for my own?

THIRTY-ONE

AFTER BREAKFAST, NICK AND I TALKED ABOUT THE PROFILE. BY then, our technique for conversation had been well established. One of us spoke; the other listened and replied. Everything was polite, proper in rhythm and tone. No one who saw or heard us would think anything was wrong, except me. And him. After all, he knew as well as I did that we'd once talked in other rhythms using different tones; we'd used postures less stiff, made contact more physical, held gazes less veiled. Not this time. This time was an official consultation. A report. A presentation of information. He even took notes when I talked. I watched his hands as they wrote. I knew the texture of those hands. Hell, I knew the circumference of each finger and what they tasted like. But that was useless knowledge, distracting knowledge that I didn't want.

"So. This handyman. Charlie. You say he's delusional. Do you think he's dangerous?"

Charlie? Dangerous? "Not that I can see."

"But possibly?" His eyes searched mine; I felt them probing. He's looking for facts, I reminded myself. It's not personal.

"Dangerous to whom? Himself? Yes, maybe. Others? Not likely. He says someone's controlling his thoughts. And that there's a conspiracy among the police, mailmen, and taxi drivers—no, among people disguised as police, mailmen, and taxi drivers."

Nick scrawled some notes on his pad. "Has he threatened you in any way?"

"No. But he says we're in danger, so he's appointed himself our guardian. He watches over us, day and night."

"In other words, he's stalking you."

"No. Protecting. He says he's my only ally, the only one we can trust. Look, Charlie's old and he's got bad knees. He's not your guy."

"You're sure."

I heard the thump of a finger landing inside a plastic bag and blinked it away. "Yes."

"All right." He crossed his leg, rested an ankle on a knee. Why did my gut react to every little move his body made? "What about Phillip Woods?"

"Come on, Nick, I've told you all this. Ask Dr. Gardener, about him. She must know more about him than I do."

"When you saw him at the Institute, he said nothing about why he wanted to see her?"

"Nick, you asked me that same question two minutes ago." He waited. His eyes took in everything, not just me. The entire room, the house, the street. "He just said that they were friends. He was dropping by to see her since he hadn't been able to reach her at her radio show."

"Just a casual visit to see a friend. He didn't seem, say, infatuated? Obsessed?"

"Obsessed? I don't know. Maybe infatuated. She told me he has a crush on her. To me, he mostly seemed distressed that she wasn't there."

"Distressed."

Oh Lord. How long was he going to drag this out? "Look, Nick, it's almost nine. I've got to get to work."

"Just another minute." He squinted at his notepad, looking over his scribbles, turning pages. "Gene O'Malley," he mumbled.

"Gymnastics coach, rejected by at least two of the missing nannies. Joe Molinari, boyfriend with a bad temper. Okay." He scanned a page. "Tell me about the phobic guy again. Victor. You said he's a loner, thirty-something. And a musician?"

"He plays cello. In the summer, when the windows are open, you can hear him playing it."

"Anything else? Do you see anyone in particular visiting him? Any women?"

"All I've seen are deliverymen."

"And he never goes outside. Are you sure?"

Why was he repeating his questions again and again? I didn't appreciate being interrogated, as if I were withholding some significant information. "Look, I've told you everything. As far as I know, Victor's been in there for years. I see his silhouette behind the shades at night. Sometimes he peeks through the blinds during the day. But the man doesn't go out. He doesn't even step onto the porch. We had to leave his Christmas cookies inside the storm door." I stood, indicating that the discussion was over. "If you want, I can give you a written report tomorrow, but I've got to get to work."

He opened his mouth as if to say something, closed it again, and stood. Say it, I thought. Go on. Tell me there's something else you want to talk about. Tell me you want to see me again. To start over.

He opened his mouth again, then hesitated. "Okay," he said. "Then I guess we're done."

"I guess." I didn't flounder, didn't give a hint that my body ached to tackle him right there. If he felt nothing, then I would feel nothing, too. Except that I didn't feel nothing. I felt like screaming. Like balling up my fists and throttling him, or knocking him down, pouncing on him, and mashing my lips against his mouth. Instead, when he thanked me for my help, I walked him demurely to the door.

He called Molly to say good-bye. She hugged him again and asked when he'd be back. Soon, he said, and, nodding briefly in my direction, he went out the door into the freezing rain.

Don't go, I thought. Please. Stop. Turn around.

He stopped. And turned around. "Zoe?"

Oh my God. It was happening. Now he'd say he was sorry. He'd ask if we could talk things out. I'd pretend to be reluctant, but then I'd rush outside and fall into his arms. I opened the door, ready to sprint. "Yes?" I breathed, a little too eagerly.

"If you think of anything else, give a call, okay?"

The sleet stung my face. "Of course," I said, closing the door.

Nick hurried to his car. Molly waved good-bye from the kitchen window. I stood against the wall, kicking myself for wanting what was not to be.

THIRTY-TWO

ANGELA ARRIVED AT NINE O'CLOCK. JOE DROPPED HER OFF IN the tow truck from his job at Torelli's Auto Repair, yelling that she should quit her goddam babysitting job until the fucking murderer was caught—she could work at his aunt's bakery or get a job doing manicures. Angela made a nasty gesture and shouted that he was not in charge of her and should shut his ugly face. He got out of the truck and met her, nose to nose. Gesticulating, shouting simultaneously, neither was listening to the other. I watched from the kitchen window, more aware than ever that I was putting Angela at risk by employing her. Even though he was a flaming hothead, for once I agreed with Joe. I'd ask Angela to take time off until the crimes were solved. I'd take Molly to work with me after school, or shorten my hours.

Outside, Angela ended the argument by turning her back to Joe and stomping up the front steps. I opened the door for her.

"Go," she huffed. "You're late."

"Joe has a point."

"Don't you start. Nobody's gonna mess with me. Not some psycho. Not Joe. And not you."

"Maybe just take off a week or two."

"And you'll do what? Who's gonna watch Molly?"

"I can manage for a few weeks."

"Zoe. Tell me. Would you leave your job if some kook was going after art therapists?"

"I might. For a while anyway."

"Yeah? Well, see? That's how we're different. This is my job. My business. No one stops me from doing it."

A horn honked. My taxi was outside. I had to go.

"What if I fire you? For your own safety."

Her hands flew to her hips. "Fine. Go ahead. For your information, Miss Bosslady, sitters and nannies are quitting by the busload around here. Those cute little au pairs? They're running back to Iowa or France or wherever the hell they come from, leaving families in need of experienced childcare professionals like me. So fire me. Fine. I'll get another job in like four seconds. I bet they'll pay more, too, with the shortage. I'm in demand."

"Okay, stop," I smiled, hugging her. She allowed the hug but didn't return it—Angela was in her spitfire mode. "Believe me, I don't want to fire you, Angela. What would we do without you?"

The taxi honked again.

"You'd be lost, that's what."

"We would. But I don't want you to be in danger. And neither does Joe."

"Screw Joe. He gets his way, I'll never leave the block."

"He wants you to be safe." Why was I defending Joe? He was controlling, possessive. Basically, a bully.

"Too bad. I gotta live my life."

"You're being stubborn."

"I'm being how I am."

"Just think about taking off a few days. Will you?"

She crossed her arms, impatient. "Your cab's waiting."

Angela had made her mind up. There was no point arguing. I hurried to say good-bye to Molly and ran out the door. Joe had gotten back into the truck but was still parked in front of the house, fuming, dark eyes intensely focused up the street. Was he on a stakeout watching for the kidnapper? A vigil guarding Angela? I followed his gaze, and it led to Jake, who was unloading supplies from his truck. Uh-oh. Did Joe know that Jake had driven Angela home? Lord, I hoped Joe wasn't going to start something. He sat at the wheel jumpy, about to explode. Short and wiry, he'd be no match for a meaty guy like Jake. I made a point of distracting Joe, waving to him, smiling a warm hello. When he saw me, he cursed, gunned his engine, and sped out of the parking spot, tires screeching.

Up the street, Jake stopped unloading and watched the truck careen past. Then, head bent into the wind, he began carrying his supplies inside.

The sleet was turning to snow. Flurries dusted fresh ice on the walk, and more storms were predicted through the weekend. I struggled across the slippery walk to the curb where the taxi waited with closed doors.

Just as I got there, Charlie raced out onto his front porch, waving his arms.

"Miss Zoe! Wait! Stop! Miss Zoe!"

I opened the taxi door, tossed in my briefcase, and hung on to the cab for balance. Sharp flakes stung my face like tiny needles. Damn. What now?

Charlie was coatless, his belt unbuckled. He waved frantically, yelling. "Don't go out today, miss! Stay home!"

He hurried across the street in his slippers.

The taxi driver drummed his fingers on the back of his seat, waiting for me to get in. "Ma'am? Are we going someplace today?"

"Yes, of course—"

Breathless and unshaven, Charlie grabbed my arm. He was unbalanced, sliding, and he almost pulled me off my feet.

"Stay inside today, Miss Zoe!" He bent over and looked inside the cab, whispered in my ear. "It's too dangerous!"

"Charlie, please stop saying things like that."

He held my arm. "Listen." He gestured for me to turn away and covered his mouth so the driver couldn't hear. "Miss Zoe.

Time is short. I've seen, I know. I look at things I'm not supposed to look at. But I know. I see where he keeps them, how he sneaks them in. And it's just the start. See now, now conditions are right. He's close. Today might be the day." Spit flew from Charlie's lips. He spoke in a guttural hush; his eyes were glazed again, delusional.

"Lady, you know I got the meter running, right?" The taxi driver was covering himself.

"Charlie. Listen to me. You need help." My words weren't sinking in; his face remained frantic, his grip on my arm tight. "Look. I'm sorry, Charlie. I have to go to work. Please don't worry. I'm fine." I started to get into the cab, but he wouldn't release me. If I were to move, I'd have to drag him with me.

"Listen, miss!" he whispered. "I deciphered the code—when my fever broke, I reversed the spell, changed the current from my brain to his. I've read his waves. I know his thoughts. Believe me, you must listen. Today, all day, you must stay put. Stay home. Lie low. Don't let go of your child. Evil is close—it's disguised, not as it seems—"

"Ma'am?" The taxi driver was getting impatient. "I'm missing calls here—"

"One minute, please." I glared at him, then looked poor Charlie full in the face. "Charlie," I spoke slowly. "You need help."

"No, Miss Zoe—it's you who needs help—"

"No. No more. Listen carefully." I looked into his eyes. "You're ill, Charlie. The illness is affecting your thoughts. You need to see a doctor. Do you understand?"

"No, miss, you must listen," he began. Wet snow was clinging to his hair.

"No more, Charlie." I had to go. "Please, call your doctor. Or call the Family Center for a referral. Tell them I said you need to be seen today."

I removed his hand from my arm and fumbled in my bag for a card and a pen. "That's the Center number. And that's my office number. Call me if you can't get a doctor's appointment. I'll make sure somebody sees you."

I put the card in his hand, but he didn't budge. "I told you, miss. I warned you not to go." He shook his head sadly and stood at the curb, arms by his side. And he stayed there, watching as I got into the cab and rode away. I had no idea how much I would later regret not heeding his advice.

THIRTY-THREE

WHEN I GOT TO WORK, BEVERLY GARDENER WAS WAITING OUT-side the art room, a vision in cherry red. To what, I wondered, did I owe this celebrity visit?

"Zoe, sugarplum," she cooed. Her eyes beamed green lasers. "How are you coping? Are you managing all right?"

"I'm fine, thanks." Why wouldn't I be? "How are you?"

I unlocked the door, and she followed me inside, her presence filling the studio.

"Oh, I'm peachy. Got a second to chat?"

I assumed it was about her profile report. "Sure. In fact, I wanted to ask you about a note you wrote on the report."

"The report?" She seemed baffled.

"The profile."

"Oh—not now, creampuff. I have television interviews in a minute—all morning long about the Nannynapper. The media love my name for him. I bet he loves it, too. All the attention it's getting him."

"You think he watches TV news?"

"His coverage? Of course. He's glued to his set. Probably jerks off to it, or would if he could get it up. He loves the fame, basks in the feeling of being a star."

Well, you'd know all about that, I thought.

"Believe me, I know all about that." She smiled, as if reading my mind. "There's nothing like being a complete nobody and suddenly being discovered and seeing yourself all over the media. It's an incredible ego trip. It happened to me ten years ago with my radio show, and it's happening to the Nannynapper now."

She sidled up next to me, her voice husky and confidential. "But, see, fame can be tricky. It's an illusion. It can make you forget who you really are and set you up for a fall."

I met her eyes, and for the briefest moment Beverly Gardener looked vulnerable. Then she looked away. Suddenly, for the second time in as many meetings, I found myself flattered, basking in her attention and apparent candor. There was a reason the woman captivated audiences. When she focused on you, somehow you felt important. As if you, not she, were the star. Still, I didn't quite trust her or her confidential tone. The woman who for years had never bothered to greet me in the hallway now spoke to me in confidence, as if we were dear friends, united by time-tested sisterly bonds. What was she up to? What did Beverly Gardener want?

"So, do you think fame will bring the Nannynapper down?" I asked, following her lead.

"We can only hope so. It might embolden him so he gets careless." She toyed with her collar, fingers skittering across her lapel, then glanced at her watch. "Look, pumpkin, he's not the reason I wanted to talk to you. Actually, I came by for personal reasons." She paused, as if not sure how to proceed. "It's about Nick. I want to make sure we understand each other."

Understand each other? "Sorry?"

"See, Nick told me—I mean, you do understand about Nick and me—our . . . deal?"

Nick and her? I stammered, unsure how to respond. "Your deal?" What was she telling me? And why?

"We've been spending a lot of time together, and he's told me how much he thinks of you. So I wanted to be sure you got it straight. For Nick's sake. And yours. Under the circumstances, I wanted us to be clear."

Clear? "I see." I didn't, but I wasn't going to admit it.

"Good. I didn't want anyone to be hurt. Look, Nick's a peach. Funny. He's not my type, not at all. At first, I didn't think we'd get along—he seemed so coarse and macho. But actually, he's quite cultured, and sensitive when you get below the surface." Exactly how far below the surface had she gotten? I swallowed, picturing her long fingers slipping beneath Nick's shirt.

"So." I cleared my throat, squared my shoulders. "What's your point?"

She leaned back, eyeing me. "Just—I want us to be open with each other. It's not like I intended to get between you. But, the way things are going, Nick and I are going to be pretty much inseparable. You need to know that."

My head was spinning. Was Beverly Gardener, famed bestselling author, profiler, problem solver, and internationally renowned star of radio, television, and the courtroom, threatened by me, innocuous unknown Zoe Hayes? Was she warning me to stay away from her man? Was Nick her man? Had he been all along?

Possibly. Why not? If he could hide the truth about a bag of body parts and a lost finger, why would he reveal the relatively minor detail that he had a girlfriend? Was there anything Nick hadn't misled me about?

Suddenly, I was tired of Dr. Beverly Gardener. Undaunted by her poise or confidence or even her hypnotic green eyes. "Fact is," I said, "where Detective Stiles is concerned, there's not much for me to talk about. I'm done with my report." I smiled as carelessly as I was able. Nick wasn't the only one who could lie.

She frowned. "Really? Then I must have gotten the wrong impression. From what he said, I thought you were personally involved." Her eyes probed mine. Warmly, as if she cared. "But, either way, at least we're cool with each other, you and I. And that's important. Truth is, I don't have many female friends. Most women feel threatened by me and keep their distance. But you aren't intimidated. I can see why Nick likes you."

What was going on? Was she asking me to be her girlfriend? Or warning me to keep away from Nick? Or both? Was she being deliberately obtuse, or was I simply slow?

Turning to go, she touched my arm and smiled, tiger eyes glowing. "Well, time to go. The TV crew's waiting."

"Yeah," I nodded. "Go get 'em. Fame calls."

A shadow darted through her eyes, but she didn't reply. With a fluttery wave, she hurried away, leaving me rattled and confused.

THIRTY-FOUR

BEFORE I HAD TIME TO DIGEST THE CONVERSATION, THE OR-
derly arrived with Celia Dukell. I tried to shift my thoughts
away from Beverly Gardener and Nick Stiles, to focus on work,
but Beverly's throaty voice kept taunting me, whispering
phrases in my mind. "Nick and I are going to be inseparable . . .
He's sensitive . . . under the surface . . . It's not like I intended
to get between you . . ."

"So? What do you think?" Celia's voice brought me back. "My
sleeves. I rolled them up today."

She had, indeed, exposing a patchwork of assorted scabs and
scars. A jagged cut here and a razor slice there. Normally, Celia
hid her wounds under clothing; today, she displayed her self-
inflicted carnage openly, almost proudly. Seeing the damaged
skin, I forced an encouraging smile.

"Wow, Celia," I congratulated her. "That's a big step. How
does it feel, baring your arms?"

"Embarrassing," she shrugged. "Naked."

I tried to concentrate on her eyes, not her ravaged flesh, but
when I closed my eyes, my mind recalled other grisly wounds. A
lopped-off finger. A gory bag of sliced skin and brittle bone. A
brunette profiler and a rugged cop. Stop it, I scolded myself.
This is Celia's time. Focus on Celia.

I gave her some soft modeling clay, hoping it would give her a
physical focus. Some patients found it soothing to make pinch

pots or animal figures. Working and molding the clay, Celia talked freely about herself. "You know, for the longest time, nobody knew I was cutting," she bragged. "The only reason they found out is that I got carried away and went a little too deep into my thigh."

In fact, she'd almost bled to death, having dug a razor into her femoral artery. Celia's stream of consciousness continued for the entire session, revealing how sly she'd thought she'd been, how carefully she'd hidden her secret, how long she'd been doing it. She talked calmly and matter-of-factly about slashing herself as her fingers worked and squeezed. When the orderly came to get her, she released her clay onto the table in a twisted, strangled wad.

The day sped on, a staff meeting and private sessions in close succession. My final patient was the silent schizophrenic, Evie Kraus. Evie's chart indicated some dramatic changes had been made. Her medications had been reduced, and she'd become more alert and responsive. And although she hadn't actually spoken, she'd begun expressing herself vocally. Evie had begun to sing. In fact, she'd been singing all week. Even as I greeted her, she was crooning a tune.

"Somebody's knockin'. Somebody's knockin'." I recognized the song. An oldie, recorded by Terri Gibbs. It was about the devil. About choices, giving in or resisting sin. I made a note on her chart, even wrote down the words as she sang them.

"Lord, it's the devil. Would you look at him? I've heard about him . . . But I never dreamed . . . he'd have blue eyes and blue jeans."

Evie's voice was clear and, in contrast to her imposing size and tattooed limbs, surprisingly sweet. I was thrilled to hear it and told her so. She looked my way but didn't respond. She just kept singing. "He must have tapped my telephone line. He must have known I'm spendin' my time alone."

Working with pastel oil sticks, she drew a pink door, just the door, no house or building attached. The door was locked, pad-locked in vivid purple. She sang and hummed as she worked, the same song. Over and over. "Somebody's knockin'. Should I let him in? Lord, it's the devil. Would you look at him?" On and on. Over and over. When her session ended, she was still singing. After she was gone, for the rest of the day and well into the night, her song remained in my head, an endless loop of melody and words.

Finally, it was time to go home. I grabbed a taxi, puzzling over Beverly Gardener's morning visit. The more I thought about it, the angrier I got. Who'd given Beverly Gardener the right to claim Nick as her personal property? And what made her think she could order me off? Thinking about her made my head throb. Evie's devil song didn't help, beating over and over in my mind. The cab headed across town through a drizzling, ominous dusk, and I rubbed my temples, eager to get home, lock the door, and settle in for the night.

But—oh damn—it was Thursday. Gymnastics night—the mothers' meeting. Susan was bringing whistles; we were going to organize and plan ways to protect our nannies and our neigh-borhoods. Like starting a town watch, a buddy system. Arming the nannies with cell phones and maybe Mace. Discussing An-gela's kickboxing classes, the possibility that her instructor could start a nanny program. Maybe I'd alert the others to the details of Beverly Gardener's profile. Damn, there she was again, Beverly Gardener, brazenly intruding into my thoughts. Claim-ing her turf, clinging to Nick's arm. I closed my eyes, erasing the image, and kept humming Evie's song.

By the time the cab pulled up to the house, the sky was dark and the drizzle had turned to glassy sleet. Even so, I sprinted up to the door without slipping. Thanks to Jake's guys, my steps had been freshly salted.

THIRTY-FIVE

"DON'T HANG UP."

I was changing, getting ready for gymnastics, when Michael called.

"I can't talk now, Michael." Or ever, for that matter.

"Look, that stuff about no more Mr. Nice Guy? I got pissed. You frustrated me and I lost my temper. But you know it was all smoke."

"It doesn't matter, Michael. Stop pushing."

"Pushing? Oh, you think I'm calling about Nana's ring? No, Zoe, I'm calling because I'm worried about you."

"Really."

"Christ," he sighed. "You bet I am, with you and your kid all alone right where all those single women are disappearing."

"Don't worry. I'm not single; I'm divorced."

"You think some lunatic's going to make the distinction? You're an unattached woman, that's all that matters."

"They were all nannies or babysitters, Michael. Not moms."

He paused; I was sure he was thinking, "Well, you're not really Molly's mom—she's adopted." But he didn't say it. Didn't dare. "The latest one disappeared right around the corner from you. On Lombard."

"I heard." I pulled on a pair of loose corduroy pants.

"How can you be so nonchalant?"

"I'm not. But it's not like I can do anything about it." Why was he trying to upset me? "Look, I really can't talk now."

"I'm serious, Zoe. Nobody knows if this maniac does strictly babysitters. How big a leap is it from a babysitter to an unmarried woman caring for a kid?"

"Thanks, Michael. That makes me feel real safe."

"I don't mean to alarm you. I'm just concerned."

"That's sweet. But you don't need to be. And, like I said, I've got to go."

"What, you got a hot date or somethin'?" His tone was sarcastic, as if the idea were absurd. There was a tiny, awkward pause while he realized that, oh, maybe it wasn't so absurd; maybe Zoe actually did have a hot date. "Oh, hey. Do you? Is it the same guy? From the other night?" He couldn't help it, had to ask, and I couldn't help responding with silence, even though I had nobody to go out with. Nick appeared on the bed, his head on Michael's pillow. I blinked him from my mind.

"Well, good for you. So. Is he as good-looking as I am?"

"Don't even start, Michael." I fluffed the pillow, smoothed the comforter.

Molly wandered in, dressed for gymnastics. "I'm ready, Mommy," she announced.

"Michael, chatting with you is grand, but I really have to go."

"Okay, then—oh, by the way, have you thought any more about the ring?" He strained to sound casual.

"Actually, no."

"Because I'll give you five thousand for it. You can buy yourself a great new ring for that."

Was he serious? He sounded desperate, and I felt sorry for him. But I wasn't going to let him pressure or manipulate me. Not again.

"Or—have it appraised. I'll pay whatever they say. How about it?"

Women were disappearing, and all Michael could think about was getting a diamond ring. I looked at the clock; it was time to leave. "Let's talk later, Michael."

"It's a fair deal, Zoe. I'm not cheating you."

"I'll think about it."

"Promise?"

"Yes. Michael, I'm late."

"Okay, okay. But—Zoe?"

"What?" If he mentioned the ring again, I was going to slam the phone down.

"Just . . . be careful, okay?"

I was touched. Michael was genuinely concerned about me. "Thanks. I will."

"And think about the ring? Like I said, I'll go as high as the appraiser says."

Before he could say another word, I hung up, breaking the connection, wishing it could be that simple.

THIRTY-SIX

EVEN WITH THE BAD WEATHER, GYMNASTICS CLASS WAS packed. All the moms showed up, even Leslie. Pale and thin, she seemed to have lost weight in just days. She hadn't answered her phone or returned calls all week. But she'd shown up for the meeting. And I was glad to see her.

"Are you managing okay?" I asked her.

"You should go to your mother-in-law's place in Florida," Karen advised. "Get some sun for a few days. Thaw out."

"I can't. It'd probably rain and I'd be stuck inside with Billy and my mother-in-law."

There were sympathetic chuckles. "Well, we're glad you're here."

"Besides, Florida wouldn't be an escape. Tamara'd still be gone no matter where I went."

"But you'd get a change of scene."

Leslie shook her head. "You don't leave your head behind. Trouble travels with you."

Charlie whispered for me to go home and stay there. I shrugged him away, but he was in my head. Like trouble.

"Leslie, you should get some pills—Zoloft or Paxil. Ask your doctor. You don't have to feel so bad, even with all that's happened." Davinder was the local expert on prescription drugs.

"Yeah, I know," Leslie sighed. "But pills won't change the

truth. Those poor girls. And Tamara—I really miss her. I really, really do."

"Oh, come on," Gretchen piped up. "Let's stop concentrating on the bleak side. Life could be a whole lot worse." She smiled, pleased, as if she thought she'd said something helpful.

With that, Susan cleared her throat and stood to begin the meeting. "Well, it looks like most everyone's here, so let's get started. Why don't we begin by brainstorming? List everything we've thought of to do, and then form a committee to follow up on each? I'll read my list to start with, and then we can add other ideas."

The discussion took off, women sharing ideas, uniting their efforts, combining their strengths. We formed six committees. I'd volunteered as a block captain for town watch and as cochair with Gretchen to set up a buddy program, so young women wouldn't travel the neighborhood alone. Finally, with committees defined, deadlines set up and sign-up sheets posted, Susan handed out whistles and we began stringing them on necklaces.

"Is there any more news about Tamara?" Karen asked.

Leslie shook her head. "The police don't tell us anything. To them, she's just one of the missing nannies."

"They weren't all nannies, you know. That fourth one was actually the mother, not a sitter. She'd adopted a baby from China."

I tensed, listening.

"Really? Well, that breaks the pattern, doesn't it?"

"Not necessarily. The mom was blonde and fair. The baby was Chinese, so she didn't look like her mother. Plus, the mom was young, in her twenties. The killer probably thought she was a nanny."

"Killer? Why'd you say 'killer'? Do we actually know that they're dead? I mean, they haven't found any bodies, have they?"

"Who knows what they've found?" Susan said, her eyes meeting mine. "They're probably withholding a lot of what they know, so they don't tip the guy off."

I couldn't speak. Couldn't move. Not just nannies were victims. Adoptive mothers might be targets, too. I wasn't going to mention the garbage bag or fingers. Neither, apparently, was Susan.

On the other side of the glass, Coach Gene cheerfully demonstrated a cartwheel on the balance beam. Kids in leotards bounced on trampolines, did flips on uneven parallel bars. I envied their innocence, their glee.

Gretchen opened a box of homemade Christmas cookies. "Okay, we have our plan. Now let's cut the glumness. Help yourselves." She took a star coated with green sugar. We passed the rest around, and for a while we munched and talked, trying to be normal. A cheery tape of "Jingle Bells" drifted in from the gym, the music, the conversation as weightless as snowflakes. But, instead of mistletoe and holly on the walls, we hung alarm whistles on string.

"Peas?" I heard Davinder ask. "Your kids eat peas?"

"They love peas. Frozen, straight from the box, like candy. Or in tuna, or with rotini and cheese."

I wandered off and sat by the observation window, watching the children practice, listening to the lulling rhythm, the gentle flow of women's chatter. After a while, Leslie drifted over and sat beside me, staring quietly at her knees. She was deeply depressed about Tamara. I thought about suggesting help, offering her a referral, but then Karen joined us.

"Is Billy okay, Leslie?" she asked.

The voice startled her, bringing her back. "Huh?"

"I wondered if he's changed. You know, his sleeping or eating. Sometimes with kids, that's the only way to tell if something's wrong. Emotionally. I mean. He must be a mess with Tamara being gone and you and his dad being so upset—"

Karen stopped midsentence. The interruption wasn't a noise or even a gasp; it was a sudden, pervasive silence. Leslie spun around to face the door. Everyone froze as the stranger entered and scanned the room. I looked up and, in the instant before he saw me, I had just enough time to recognize Charlie—and the fact that he was carrying a gun.

THIRTY-SEVEN

UNSHAVEN, UNKEMPT, HIS FRAYED JACKET HANGING LOOSELY over grease-stained pants, Charlie shuffled in. Dark circles ringed his red, strained eyes, and he spoke slowly, as if no one were in the room but the two of us.

"Don't you worry, miss," he said. "I told you I'd protect you."

Susan stepped directly in front of him. She was accustomed to guns and criminals. "What do you think you're doing, sir?" she stared at him, ignoring the gun.

Charlie stepped back and closed the observation room door, shoving a chair under the doorknob. "Step back, ma'am. Don't interfere. I'm here to help."

Susan spoke calmly, as if men wandered in carrying guns all the time. "Well, you have to put the gun away. There are children—"

Charlie scowled as he aimed the gun right at her. "Who are you? Mind your business. I've got to talk to Miss Zoe."

I ran over and stood between them. "Charlie, what are you doing? You can't just point a gun at people. These are my friends."

He waved the gun toward the window. "Let's go over there and talk, Miss Zoe." Charlie limped along, guiding me back across the room, wheezing as he stepped around chairs. Women huddled close, wide-eyed and silent.

"What the hell is this, Charlie?" I asked. "What's the gun for?"

"Protection, miss. I told you. You're in danger. But don't worry. I'm here for you and the little girl."

Behind him, Susan pointed and waved, trying to send me some message I couldn't decode.

"You'll scare the children, Charlie. Put the gun away."

"I can't do that, miss. I followed you all the way over here. I believe you're next, see. It could happen any time. Just sit down and listen to what I have to say."

The gun pointed at my belly. No one had ever pointed a gun at me before. The muzzle looked cold and indifferent. I watched it warily and sat.

Coughing and hacking, Charlie peered through the glass at the children. Then he perched on the windowsill, facing me. I looked past him, searching for Molly, locating her in line for the vaulting horse, her back to us.

"The rest of you just go about your normal business," Charlie commanded. "And nobody open that door."

Nobody moved. Women whispered, the tape of "Jingle Bells" repeated automatically, my heart pounded, and Charlie wheezed. But nobody moved.

"Please don't be afraid of me, miss," Charlie instructed. "The gun's for your protection. I can't sit by and watch anymore. I told you I'd protect you, and I will."

Behind Charlie, Gretchen and Davinder formed a wall around Susan, who was making hand signals at the observation window. She pointed at Charlie, miming that he had a gun. I prayed that if any of the instructors could see her, they'd get the message and get help.

"Miss, you haven't been careful. You've let evil get too close. I warned you—I told you he disguises himself. Why didn't you listen? He isn't sure how much I know, or I wouldn't be here. But I've seen things, his comings and goings. I'm the handyman. I have all the keys, see. And I have his brainwaves, see. I fixed the wiring. Reversed it, so I could read his thoughts, find out his plans."

I tried to make my voice sound calm. As long as he kept talking, he wouldn't hurt anyone. "You know his plans?"

He wheezed, then coughed deeply. Fire burned deep in his eyes. Sweat droplets swelled on his forehead. He leaned forward and enunciated more carefully, as if that would help me understand.

"I've told you. He won't stop. He's killed all those girls and he needs more. A fresh supply for his work."

Sitting behind Charlie, Leslie began to twitch. Her eyebrow flicked spasmodically. Her knee bounced involuntarily. I wondered if she was having a seizure. I looked at Karen. Her lips mouthed a silent question. "Who is he?"

"All those young women. Dead. So much waste—"

"Who's dead? What young women are dead?" Leslie cut in. "What's he saying?"

Charlie didn't respond. He went on, "See, the women weren't blood. They had false bonds, no true connections. That's why they had to die."

Leslie asked again, "Who? Who had to die? Answer me—"

I shook my head, trying to quiet her. Karen touched her arm. Behind them, blocked by Davinder, Susan continued miming that we'd been visited by a man with a gun.

Charlie continued. "But the work's not done yet. Life and death, love and hate, Satan and the Lord God. Everything's the same to him. He spits at it all, pastes it all together as a circle. His work is evil, Miss Zoe. And evil feeds on itself, begets more evil. It's an endless cycle. He'll go on killing until somebody stops him."

Leslie panted, "He means Tamara? The nannies? They're dead? How does he know that?"

Charlie gazed through the window. I looked out and saw Molly take a running jump and leap over the horse, clearing it by inches. Landing, she turned to see if I was watching.

Amazingly, I was. I even smiled and gave her a thumbs-up, just as if nothing were wrong. She grinned proudly and was moving on to the parallel bars when, beside me, Karen suddenly stiffened. Somebody shrieked. And Leslie tackled Charlie from behind, grabbing for the gun.

"You sonofafuckingbitch! You killed them—"

Fearless, maddened, she clawed at him. When the gun went off, the bang was deafening.

THIRTY-EIGHT

CHUNKS OF DRYWALL FLEW THROUGH THE AIR, AND A HOLLOW ringing muffled all other sounds. Leslie stopped in midair, her face distorted in disbelief. Then she sank to her knees on the floor. Children turned to face the window; women shrieked. Karen and Ileana ran over to Leslie and held her, looking for wounds. Leslie hadn't been hit, but she gulped air, yelping like a wounded dog. In the gym, children froze, staring at the observation room window, large eyes searching for their mothers.

Charlie got to his feet, holding the gun in the air. "Everybody calm down, now." He wheezed through the ringing sound. "I don't want anybody hurt." His voice broke into a fit of coughing. "Sit down, please," he continued. "I'm here for Miss Zoe. But I'll take care of all of you, all of you."

Coach Gene pounded on the door. "Everything okay in there? Open the door."

Shaking, I got up and crossed the room.

"Don't open it, miss."

I didn't answer. Charlie wouldn't shoot me. With trembling hands, I moved the chair; Coach Gene flew into the room, gaping at the hole in the wall. "What the heck's going on in here?"

"Just a little accident," I said. "But everything's okay." I looked at my terrified friends. Susan was beside me, smiling stiffly, indicating that Gene should play along.

"We're fine," she said, drawing his attention to Leslie, who was still yelping on the carpet. Women clustered, hugging each other. Gretchen, Davinder, and Ileana huddled together, bug-eyed. Karen had moved to the doorway and now sheltered Nicholas in her arms. All eyes were riveted on Charlie. "Jingle Bells" continued its maddening endless loop.

"Who's that?" Nicholas pointed to Charlie.

I remembered then that nobody knew. Crossing the room, I stood beside him. "Everybody. This is my neighbor Charlie." I could barely hear my own voice. It came from far away. "He wants to keep us safe, so let's all stay calm and let him help us."

Gene, pretending nothing was wrong, gave a nod and backed away. "All right, then. Okay. I see. Everything's under control, then. Nice to meet you, Charlie. Come on, Nicholas. Mom, why don't we take Nicholas back to class? In fact, why don't all the moms come watch in the gym?"

"The women better stay with me," Charlie told him. "They're safer here."

Coach Gene's eyes darted from Charlie to the exit door. I thought he might run for it, leaving the rest of us to fend for ourselves. Finally, though, he led Karen and Nicholas back to the gym: Karen glanced back at us as Gene reached for his cell phone. Help would come soon.

"Charlie thinks somebody may be trying to hurt me," I kept talking, trying to hold Charlie's attention.

"Dammit," Charlie gasped. "What's wrong with you? There's no maybe. He's about to do it. She knows." He pointed at Leslie, still whimpering on the floor. "She already knows what I'm talk-ing about. Don't you read the newspapers? Don't you see the TV? I'm not making this up."

"We know that, sir. We all know." Susan's voice came from across the room. "And we appreciate your courage in trying to protect Zoe. And the rest of us, too."

She was going along with him, trying to calm him. But Leslie didn't get it. "What the hell, Susan? He's not protecting any—"

"Shh." Susan squeezed Leslie's arm, shutting her up.

"Don't be afraid." Charlie ignored them, speaking softly to me. "As long as I'm with you, you'll be safe."

We sat for a few moments in silence. Waiting. Listening to Charlie's labored wheezing, wondering what to do. Then, over Charlie's shoulder, through the observation window, I saw Gene gather the children into a circle at the far side of the room by the pit. Uniformed policemen crept into the gym, taking cover behind stacks of mats, sneaking along the walls, leading the children out the back door.

"Charlie," I begged him. "Please, give me the gun."

"No, miss. Can't."

His forehead dripped sweat. His pupils were dilated, his breath short. He grabbed my arm. When he leaned close, I smelled sour wine and stale sweat. White globs foamed in the corners of his mouth.

"Charlie, please," I interrupted. "Put the gun away before someone gets hurt."

"You still don't get it?" Charlie coughed, holding up the gun. "Don't you realize what I've done? Coming here? I've signed my own death warrant."

"Charlie, please." Behind him, police had their guns drawn, aimed at the window. Susan waved at me, signaling that I should move away from Charlie, but I stayed put.

"No. He'll never let me live, not after this. Look. He's not alone. There are others like him all over the country. Where do you think all those missing young people are? All the kids who go to the mall and never come back, who hitch rides and disappear? They've been taken—just like the women—"

Susan couldn't be silent anymore. "Charlie, sir? The police are here. Put down your weapon or they'll take it from you by force."

He wasn't listening, didn't seem to hear her voice. "Remember, miss. Evil wears disguises, and as long as those like him live and breathe, caution's your only hope."

"Charlie, listen," I repeated Susan's message. "The police are here. They want you to put down your gun. Give it to me. Please." I held my hand out. His eyes widened, but he shook his head. No.

Cops were everywhere now. I could see five of them. If Charlie turned around, he'd see them scattered through the gym, guns raised. Any second, they'd rush the room.

Charlie slumped against the window and wiped sweat off his forehead with the sleeve of his overcoat. The gun hung loosely in his hand. I sat beside him. Would he shoot me if I grabbed it?

"Sorry, miss." He looked at Leslie. "I wish I'd stopped him sooner. But at least I'm stopping him now." Charlie looked at me with glazed and somber eyes.

A voice called over the loudspeaker. "You, in the observation room. Charlie. This is Sergeant Bennings of the Philadelphia Police Department. You are surrounded by police officers. You have no way out. Put down your gun now and come out with your hands on your head."

Charlie turned and gazed out the window, gun raised. "I told you—he's closing in, miss. I'll stay by your side and hold him off as long as I'm able, but you have to be on guard, too. Mind my words. Trust nobody."

"Charlie, you have sixty seconds to release your hostages and come out of there peacefully."

"Please, Charlie," I said.

Leslie wailed. Susan gestured for me to move away. The rest of the mothers sat silent and still.

"Charlie, do what the man says," I begged. "I'll go out there with you. Please. We'll go together."

Susan came over and grabbed my arm. "Zoe. For godsakes move away from him."

"No—it's okay. Charlie and I are going to go out there to-gether, right, Charlie?"

"They mean business, Zoe."

"Charlie? Let's go, okay?" I touched his shoulder and stood.

"Zoe, I'm serious—move away—"

"Just a second—"

"Dammit," Susan scowled. She stood glaring at me while Charlie leaned forward, peering through the glass. He looked exhausted, pensive. Seconds passed, each one leaden, adding weight to the next. Thirty, forty. The room was silent. Motion-less. The air too heavy to breathe.

When a minute had passed, Sergeant Bennings began to speak again, but Charlie shouted over him. "Okay—zero hour—here we go! Get down!" He raised the gun and fired at the window. Glass shattered, shards soaring.

"No!" I screamed. "Charlie—the children!" Susan pulled at my arm; I yanked it away and pulled at Charlie, trying to stop him. With surprising strength, he shoved me away. Behind me, women shrieked and dropped to the floor. Susan ducked; someone ran for the door. Charlie shouted obscenities and kept firing, popping two shots, three, until suddenly what remained of the window exploded in a glittering shower. A gush of red burst from Char-lie's hand and his gun flew through the air onto the floor. He turned to me with a look of surprise. His mouth opened, forming words I couldn't hear, and his skull exploded. Brains, bone, blood, bits of Charlie flew all over the room. Warm, sticky spray splattered my clothes, my face, my eyes. I couldn't see, squinted to find Molly through a warm, crimson veil.

On the floor, the mass that had been Charlie twitched awhile before it lay still. Susan led me to a chair. Then she was gone. Coach Gene stared from the doorway, his mouth moving, no sound coming out. Police in white jumpsuits shoved past him, clearing the room. Sometime, out of nowhere, Nick appeared, wrapped me in his arms, and carried me out. I saw events as a silent movie, heard no voices, no commotion, no cries. Long seconds passed before I realized that I'd been deafened by the gunfire, so I couldn't hear any sounds at all, even my own screams.

THIRTY-NINE

POLICE CARS BLOCKED OFF OUR STREET, THEIR STROBES LIGHT-
ing Charlie's porch. Blue and white flashes pierced the night,
outshining the Santa's red and green. Police swarmed all around
and inside Charlie's house. Neighbors and passers-by gathered
on the sidewalks. Jake must have been working late again; he
lingered at the curb, talking with a policeman. Phillip Woods
stood on his porch. Victor peered through his blinds; I actually
saw his hands. I sat on my steps, watching, breathing on my fingers for warmth.

Inside, Karen, Davinder, and Gretchen watched the children.
Ileana and Susan had left their kids with us while they went to
the emergency room with Leslie and Coach Gene, who'd become hysterical after the shooting. The rest of us stayed together
simply because we weren't able to separate. We didn't know,
couldn't imagine, how to return to the lives we'd left just that
evening. Though nothing was said about it, each of us suspected
that those lives had been, with Charlie's, blown away.

An ambulance had arrived at the Center to remove Charlie,
and someone had given me a clean sweatsuit to change into. I
had no idea where my old clothes were, the ones coated with
clumps of Charlie. Nick had taken Molly to be with Susan and
Emily, minimizing her contact with the frightful sight of her
mother. Then he'd taken me to the locker room, where he'd
helped me peel off my gore-soaked clothes and wash away the

carnage that covered me. Under a steaming shower that had splashed his pant legs and shoes, Nick had washed my face and shampooed my hair. Then he'd stayed while I'd given the officers my statement. I'd begun trembling, shivering so badly that Nick had wanted to take me to the hospital. But I'd declined. I'd wanted to go home. To take Molly inside and lock the door.

Nick had driven us. My ears rang: I had trouble hearing. But I understood that Molly was asking questions and that Nick was answering. I heard him say that Charlie had been very sick. That Charlie had imagined things. That it was very sad, and Charlie was gone, but everyone was safe now. Everything would be okay. I wondered what she'd seen and heard, what she understood, but I didn't have the energy to talk to her about it yet. Even Molly was beyond my reach.

At home, Nick held me, kissed me, and promised to return in a few hours. I accepted the touches, the kisses, didn't question the fact that our relationship had somehow instantly resurrected itself. I watched Nick talk to Molly and hug her, then cross the street and talk with police before hurrying to his Volvo and driving off.

Women from gymnastics gathered with their children in my living room. I wasn't comfortable. I didn't want company yet couldn't bear to be alone. I knew I should talk to Molly but had no idea what to say. I stroked her cheek and hugged her, whispering trite reassurances. But I couldn't sit, couldn't stay inside, paced from the kitchen to the office, the office to the living room. I couldn't stay away from the windows where I could look out at Charlie's house, as if somehow the house would explain things to me, set me straight. Finally, I wandered out the front door and sat on the dark icy steps, watching, waiting, realizing that what I was waiting for would never happen. Charlie would never again appear.

The police milled about. A couple of them protectively urged me to go inside. But I couldn't budge. Charlie's blood had spattered all over me. His life had spilled onto my skin, soaked into my pores. And it was my fault. I should have stopped it, should have been more forceful, grabbed his gun, protected him. I'd never believe that he'd intended to shoot anyone, but he'd shot first, and with children around the police had had no choice. What had happened to Charlie? Had there been a turning point, a precise moment when he'd lost it? Did he have some chemical imbalance? A brain tumor? A split personality? In a way, it didn't matter, now that he was gone. But I'd miss his pipe glowing in the dark, the warm aroma of his tobacco, his watchful concern, even his overprotective warnings. Tears stung my cheeks in the cold. Mourning Charlie, the irreversibility of death.

Suddenly, a policeman ran out of Charlie's house. Before he reached his van, he dropped to the curb, puking. I went down the steps, but a strong arm restrained me. "Stay back, ma'am."

Another officer yelled from the doorway, and radios began barking. Uniforms scurried into Charlie's door as a guy strung more yellow tape around the property. Men in overcoats arrived. An ambulance drove through the blockade, lights flashing. Heavy men in navy parkas carried a stretcher into the house.

"What's going on?" Karen stood beside me. She looked haggard.

"Dunno."

"A stretcher? Is somebody else inside?"

"He lived alone."

Karen shrugged. "Hot tea?" She handed me a mug.

"Thanks." My hands were trembling. Tea slopped onto the steps, melting the thin coating of ice.

"You better come inside, Zoe. It's really cold out here."

"I'll be in. I just need to see this."

"Are you all right?" She looked me over. "You're not, are you?" Her eyes were sad, her voice gentle.

"No," I said. "Are you? Is anyone?"

She put her arm around my shoulders. "Maybe you should get checked out at the hospital. You might be in shock or something. I can watch Molly."

"No, I'm okay. Thanks."

Men shouted back and forth, and we looked across the street. The men in parkas stumbled out Charlie's door carrying the stretcher. They moved slowly, as if straining under its weight.

"What's that?" Karen asked. "His garbage?"

"Oh my God," I breathed. Karen looked bewildered. Across the street, Jake and his men stood at the curb among pedestrians, staring. Phillip Woods stepped over to the yellow ribbon edging his railing and watched. Victor's blinds lifted; he actually pressed his forehead against the windowpane, straining to see. The ambulance crew yelled for police to help them carry the stretcher down the steps. It was apparently very heavy, loaded with lumpy green bags of trash.

FORTY

Susan arrived as the phone rang. I answered the door with the phone in my hand, greeting Susan's person and Nick's voice simultaneously, hearing fragments of their conversations through ears still ringing with silence.

"I'll be there as soon as I can—"

"What's with the ambulance? Did someone else get shot?"

"—developments I have to look into—"

"We heard sirens on the way—"

"—we have to talk when I get there—"

"Coach Gene was so pale—he was ice cold and couldn't stop shaking—"

Susan stopped talking midsentence and gaped at me. Karen called down the steps, "Are you okay, Zoe?" Nick harmonized the question in baritone.

By their reactions, I understood that I'd done something inappropriate. Had I screamed EVERYBODY JUST SHUT UP or only thought it? I couldn't remember, wasn't sure, but I apologized, and they seemed appeased. My ears were ringing, head throbbing, and Nick began talking again.

"Zoe, I don't want you there alone after what's happened . . ." The words buzzed like mosquitoes. I wanted to slap them away.

As Emily ran off to join the other children, Susan rifled through my cabinets, searching for something edible to relieve her stress. She found a bag of Cheese Doodles, frowned at them, gobbled a few, and sucked cheese scum off her fingers. Red nails disappeared inside moist lips, slid out and returned to the open bag. As she stuffed her mouth, it occurred to me that Molly hadn't had dinner. Were the children hungry?

". . . somewhere for a few days," Nick buzzed on.

Out the kitchen window, another ambulance pulled away. Only one remained now, being loaded with the last of the garbage bags. Police cars still blocked off the street, and a bunch of uniformed men hovered on Charlie's front porch.

"Dammit—they're calling me, but I'll be over as soon as I can. Who's there with you?"

"A couple of people." Gretchen had taken Hannah home a while ago, and Davinder had just left with Hari. "Susan, Karen—"

"Can I talk to somebody? Susan?"

I pressed my tongue against the spot where my lips had cracked, felt the thin, sharp pain. Susan chewed an oatmeal cookie. I handed her the phone without wondering why he wanted to talk to her. Upstairs a child—Nicholas?—was angry, yelling that something wasn't fair; Karen's gentle voice hushed him.

Susan's head bobbed up and down as she listened. Mouth full of cookie, she made sounds of agreement, one syllable each. When she hung up, she said that Nick wanted me to stay at his place for the weekend. "It's in Chester County. Go—it'll be good for you."

Good for me? Chester County? What was she talking about? Nick and I weren't a couple. Were we? We'd called it off, hadn't we? And what about his "deal" with Beverly Gardener? Still, I remembered his protective embrace, how naturally he'd gathered me up and cleaned me off. How safe it felt to be beside him as he'd taken us home. But Chester County? I'd had no idea where Nick lived. What kind of place was it? A condo? A farm? Was it clean? Child friendly?

"Zoe, you look—well, I love you dearly, but frankly I've seen murder victims who look better. Go with him. You need R and R." I was too tired to discuss it, but I wasn't going anywhere. I didn't have the energy, didn't want to bother, even if I were sure about me and Nick. And what about Molly? How would she feel, suddenly whisked away to Nick's? She needed normal structure and familiar settings—stability after the traumatic events of the night.

"Go. Molly'll be fine." Had Susan read my mind? Or had I said my thoughts out loud again? I didn't know. Did it matter? Did I care? I rubbed my temples and leaned back against the kitchen counter. My legs didn't seem able to support me.

Upstairs, overtired children were slamming doors, running, jumping, an extension of gymnastics class. Molly's soprano giggles flittered down the steps. For the moment, incredibly, she was fine.

Susan stared raptly out the window, biting into another cookie. "What about that? Trash bags full of nannies, just like the one I told you about. It's their bodies. Gotta be. That's why the ambulances. Otherwise, why not take trash bags away in, like, a trash truck?"

Her teeth tore off another cookie chunk. I was tired, floating. I closed my eyes and savored the burn. Outside, in the street, the ambulance doors closed, and I felt the pulse of flashing lights as the vehicle drove away.

FORTY-ONE

"WELL, THAT'S THAT." SUSAN FOLDED HER ARMS ACROSS HER chest.

"What's what?"

"No more serial killer. No need for a trial, either, since the dude's dead. Just the coroner's hearing to determine the facts." A crumb stuck to the corner of her mouth. "It's a shame, in a way. I might have got him off, if I'd had a chance." She chuckled and suddenly stopped. "Oh, what am I saying? I'm such an ass, trying to make light of it. I'm still shaking, see? Look at my hands. I can't imagine how you must feel. You were right next to him."

"I'm okay." She looked me squarely in the eye and licked away the crumb.

"No. You are not. But hey, thank God they stopped him before he hurt anyone else."

I looked toward the stairs. "I should go check and see how Molly is."

"She's fine. Let her be with the other kids. There are moms around if she needs one. Who else's here?"

"Karen." I didn't remember who else. "Maybe just her."

"Karen's enough. Relax. You look ghastly."

"So do you."

"Do I? Damn. Time for a dose of medicine." She took a bottle of Scotch from my liquor cabinet. "Here." She poured. "Drink."

"Susan."

"Drink." It was an order.

I drank. She made a toast in what sounded like Italian and gulped.

"Look. At least we know they got him. We don't have to worry about a loose psycho anymore. Maybe Bonita will come back to work."

I looked at Susan as the Scotch slid down my throat, golden and warm. She held up her glass again.

"Here's to the sharpshooters. And our luck that they shot straight."

I nodded. "That thought occurred to me."

"Shit. If somebody'd sneezed, if a guy's finger trembled, you'd have splattered the walls instead of Charlie. Believe me, the cops haven't heard the end of this. I intend to—"

Something beeped.

"Damn." Susan reached for her bulky embroidered bag and took out a phone. I swallowed more Scotch while she spoke efficiently, rapidly, with few syllables, and stuffed the phone back into her handbag.

"Well, that was interesting." She wrestled with a date book and a cosmetics case, jammed them together, and zipped the bag, fraying the edges of a manila envelope. "That was Ed. I guess he saw me at the shooting, so he thinks I'm an insider again."

"What did he want?"

"To keep me informed." She gazed out the window. "Guess what they've found in Charlie's basement?"

I closed my eyes and drained my glass. "Don't tell me," I said. "I don't want to know."

But Susan had already started to tell me. With a trembling hand, I reached for the Scotch and poured myself another shot.

FORTY-TWO

"CUTTING TOOLS. ALL KINDS. SAWS, AXES, CHISELS, KNIVES—"

"What a surprise, Susan. Charlie was a handyman. He worked with tools."

"He had everything he'd need to dispose of the bodies. Even a big worktable. But that's not all." Her eyes widened. "Here's the corker. He had their stuff. Claudia's handbag, Tamara's locket. Shoes. Earrings. Keys. Mementos. Something from each victim."

I pictured Charlie's bad legs hobbling down shadowy stairs to visit some gruesome shrine and shivered. Susan shoved a lock of hair behind her ear and frowned.

"It doesn't make sense," I said.

"What?"

"Charlie. I just can't believe it. He didn't seem like a murderer."

"He was stark raving nuts, Zoe. He cut up women's bodies in his basement."

"But if he was a killer, why didn't he kill me the way he killed the nannies? Why would he insist that he was protecting me? And why did he start shooting? Who did he think the killer was?"

"Whoa." Susan put her hand on my arm. "Slow down. Don't upset yourself more by trying to get inside a maniac's mind. Stop applying reason to behavior based on insanity."

She was right. I wasn't thinking clearly.

"Meantime"—she glanced at her watch—"I'm starving. We missed dinner, and the kids have to eat. I ordered pizzas."

"You did?"

"They said half an hour. If they don't get here soon, somebody's head's gonna roll."

"Somebody's already did." I didn't intend to joke.

"Really funny, Zoe. Bag it."

"Now, there's an advertising concept. For extra-heavy-duty trash bags?" I wasn't smiling. I could see television commercials showing cleanup crews carrying green plastic bags from the guillotine, Jeffrey Dahmer stuffing them into his fridge, Ted Bundy storing them in his car.

I ripped skin off my lip with my teeth, tasted blood. Saltier, not as sweet as Charlie's. Tamara's head rolled across a shelf in Charlie's basement, scowling.

Susan looked me over. "You really look awful."

"You already said that."

"Well, you do. You worry me."

"I'm okay. Are you?"

"No, not even close. So how can you be?"

"Well, I am. Or I will be."

She picked at a cuticle. Her hands were trembling. "I wish Tim were here. Or Nick."

I squinted, wondering why. What good could Tim or Nick or anyone do? Bags of body parts, weapons, and the personal effects of each missing nanny had been found in Charlie's basement. Charlie'd been protecting me, but apparently it had been from himself, his own secret depravity. It was difficult to believe that old Charlie had been capable of such despicable acts, but the evidence was clear. Nothing could change that. Just as nothing could remove the warmth of his wet brains from my skin, or his surprised dying face from my memory.

From upstairs, a small voice called, "Where are you, Mommy?"

"Down here, Molly." I felt wobbly.

"Can we have those whistles? Mommy?" Oh God. I hoped they wouldn't start blowing those damned necklaces.

"Not now." I started to stand.

Susan put her hand up to stop me. "Karen'll take care of Molly. Sit."

Against my will, I sat. Actually, I sank. My legs were liquid, and I was groggy. The room tipped slightly, probably from Scotch on a shocked and empty stomach. Susan hefted her hip onto the table and leaned over me.

"Zoe," she scolded. "You know what? Go to Nick's. Get out of here for a while. You need a rest."

"So? So do you."

"But my lips aren't bleeding."

My lips were bleeding? I tasted them. They were.

"You're biting them nonstop."

"I'll stop."

"Go with Nick. Get pampered."

"I don't think so."

"Why not?"

"Why not? You know why not. I can't just leave—"

"Don't give me that crap, Zoe. Of course you can. Molly can stay with us—"

"Oh no. Uh-uh. I'm not leaving Molly, no way."

Upstairs, Molly shrieked triumphantly. "Never mind, Mommy!"

"Okay, Mollybear," I called.

Susan wouldn't stop. "Fine. Then take her along. But go. It's only a goddam weekend. Get out of this house and off this street for a couple of days. Don't think, don't cook, don't worry about work or patients or Charlie or anyone but yourself and your little girl. Do it. Go. Lord knows I would if I could."

"I don't know."

"Go. Spend some time with the guy. Zoe, Nick cares about you—I could see it today. He was right there for you. I mean, the man washed somebody's brains out of your hair."

Susan's phone rang again. She fumbled it out of her bag and spoke with a raw voice. "It's okay, Lisa honey. I told you before, we're fine, don't worry. Did you eat? And do your homework? Well, you have to do it, even so. Turn off the television. I don't know—as soon as I can." The frown line etched its way back between her eyebrows, and she turned away, whispering, explaining.

Upstairs, children's feet thumped the floors. Shouts and sounds of movement drifted down. Molly was fine; so were all the other kids. I didn't remember going there, but somehow I'd landed on my purple living room sofa. As Susan tried to convince her oldest daughter that the crisis was over and she was okay, a chorus of raucous laughter bounced down the stairs, and I huddled under an afghan, sipping Scotch through torn and bloody lips.

FORTY-THREE

By the time pizzas came, everyone except Susan and Emily had gone home. I kept telling Susan to leave, but she wouldn't.

"I'm not leaving you alone."

"I'm not alone. Molly's here. Besides, Lisa and Julie saw the news. They must be freaked—"

"They're fine for now. What'll you have, sausage or pepperoni?"

She refused to leave, even though the weather was rapidly worsening. Big snowflakes fell heavily, the beginning of a storm expected to continue all weekend. She and the girls ate pizza, but I had no appetite. The sauce, the sausage—it all looked like pieces of Charlie.

The girls were exhausted and sat, eyes glazed, watching television, but Susan wouldn't leave until Nick arrived. When he did, at around nine-thirty, she still didn't leave. Nick looked worn-out, so Susan fixed him a Scotch, dealing with her stress by becoming hostess, rifling through my cupboards for some hearty late-night snack.

"You okay?" he asked me. His clothes were rumpled and stubble shadowed his face, but his gaze was warm, concerned.

"Are you?" I avoided answering.

"We need to talk." He seemed urgent, harassed.

"Okay." I couldn't imagine focusing long enough to discuss anything, but we went to the sofa and sank onto velvet cushions.

"I was an asshole—"

"Really, Nick. It doesn't—"

"Please just listen, Zoe. I guess I blew it with you, so I'm not surprised you don't want to hear what I have to say. But I'm responsible for what happened tonight, so I—"

"Wait—what? How are you responsible—"

He interrupted. "You told me about this guy, how nuts he was. You gave me the information, and I should have taken care of it. I should have prevented the whole damned thing. It was my responsibility. I screwed up. I let you and those other people down. And I'm sorry." He took my hand. "Man, you're like ice." He moved closer and began warming me, rubbing my hands. "You want a blanket? A sweater?"

I shook my head. I didn't object to the contact, but I didn't say anything. I didn't know what to say. I hadn't yet absorbed the idea that Charlie was the killer. And, if fault for what had happened were to be assigned, I'd get my share. After all, if I'd listened to Charlie that day and not gone out—if I'd only stayed home in my own house with my little girl, everything would have been different. Charlie wouldn't have followed me. Molly would be upstairs, tucked in her bed. No trash bags or keepsakes would have been found in Charlie's basement. And Charlie would still be alive.

"Give me a minute," Nick said. He took off his jacket and hung it on my shoulders. When he went into the kitchen, I wandered over to Molly and Emily. They were sprawled in front of the television.

"You okay, girls?" I joined them on the floor.

Molly looked my way. "Charlie's killed, right, Mom?"

I took her hand. "He's dead, yes."

"Told you," she said to Emily.

"No, I told you," Emily insisted. "You said he'd get better."

"Uh-uh—you said that—"

"Well, he's gone," I said. "He was sick and he couldn't think straight, and he made a bad mistake."

Molly spoke with authority. "He had bad dreams that seemed real, Em. It was like—he couldn't wake up from them. Right, Mom?"

"That's right." Once again, it surprised me how much she understood.

"But if he was sick, why'd the police shoot at him?" Emily asked.

"'Cause he shot at them."

"But why'd he shoot at them?"

Molly rolled her eyes as if the answer were obvious. "'Cause he didn't know they'd shoot back at him." The explanation baffled me but seemed to satisfy both of them.

"Well, it was very sad. And scary. But it's over and we're all safe." I put an arm around each of them, almost melting from their hugs.

"Mommy?" Molly's voice was urgent. "Do you think my tooth will come out tonight?" She wiggled it for me. It was still tethered securely.

"Not tonight. Maybe tomorrow." I stroked her head.

Emily grinned. "Yes!"

"Yes?" I asked. Clearly, they'd discussed it.

"If it won't come out tonight, then the Tooth Fairy won't have to find me. So maybe—can I sleep over at Emily's? Pleeeeze?"

FORTY-FOUR

MOLLY SLEPT AT HOME THAT NIGHT. I WOULDN'T LET HER GO anywhere, even to Susan's. I couldn't. But somehow, by the time Susan and Emily left, I'd agreed that Molly and I would spend the weekend at Nick's place in the country. Nick and Susan seemed convinced that I should get away, have a view of something other than Charlie's empty house. A break from responsibilities. Nick insisted that I was to do nothing, not cook, not clean, not plan, not think. I was to pack a minimum and allow Nick to take care of everything.

I went along with the scheme, aware of my uncharacteristic passivity. I didn't see what difference it made where we were, but I didn't argue. My body was limp and drained. I was weak, nonverbal, slow to react. I found it difficult to form clear thoughts. I couldn't imagine standing up, let alone fixing dinners and breakfasts, doing daily chores for Molly or myself. I'd sunk into a kind of exhaustion I'd never imagined, too tired to swim through it or even to try.

Finally, Susan went home, and Molly was asleep. When I crawled into bed, it felt like almost morning, but the clock said just twelve-thirty. I remember falling onto my soft, cool pillow, the fluffy comforter folding over me, Nick tucking me in. Nick? Why was he still there? And why was I so glad to see him? He talked about his home in the country, about escaping. About fireplaces. About pine trees and fresh air. It seemed natural, as if he belonged.

I remember thinking, falling into sleep, that before I left I'd have to call someone to say where I was going. Michael? No, Michael and I were divorced. Weren't we? Then who? No name, no face came to mind. But it was somebody. There was, had to be, someone I had to call. But, drifting, I couldn't think, couldn't remember who it was.

FORTY-FIVE

THE FIRE POPPED. I JUMPED. NICK GRABBED MY HAND.

"Sorry." It had sounded like a shot.

"Relax," he said. "Let me fix you a drink."

The day had passed in a haze. My headache pills must have relaxed me into unconsciousness. Or maybe not. Maybe I'd simply "gone away" for a while, too numb to participate.

At any rate, my recollection of getting to Nick's was, at best, hazy. I had little memory of getting into his car or of making what must have been a forty-five-minute drive to his house in Chester County. I wasn't sure if we'd left in the morning or afternoon. Waking, dressing, eating breakfast, getting Molly ready—I'd done it all in a fog. Worst of all was Molly. Shortly after we'd arrived, I'd seen her scamper off to play in the snow, but I couldn't remember her coming back inside. And that troubled me. How could I forget to watch my child? Why didn't I know if she'd made a snowman or worn her mittens or had hot cocoa when she'd come in? Was it possible that I hadn't noticed, hadn't made certain that she'd been safe?

Nick rearranged me on the pillows. What a wimp I was. My arms were leaden. My eyes burned. My head weighed tons. Each thought, each image was heavy and hard to hold on to. I wanted to snap out of it, but whenever I closed my eyes, Charlie's blood splattered the walls, covered my face. His hand held mine, even when his skull shattered, even when his brains flew across the room. His voice implored me to be careful.

No, I told myself. Get rid of Charlie. He was nuts. Don't let his delusions seep deeper. Don't worry about Molly. She's fine. She's resilient and wise. But no matter how I reassured myself, I felt Charlie squeeze my hand as his head popped open, splashing my face.

The fire popped. No need to jump, nothing to scream about. Nick went to the kitchen, and I heard water running, paper rustling, glass clattering. Molly's voice asking, "Like this?" Nick's voice muffled, offering an answer. Then giggling. Molly was helping him cook again, I guessed. They were fine. I lay back and watched the fire wrap itself around the logs. Fingers of flame held the wood, reaching into cracks, sucking out everything but ash. There was no escape; the fire consumed until there was nothing left.

Nick offered me a glass mug of something hot and steamy. The liquid matched the fire, glowed with golden light. My arms wouldn't move to take it. What the hell was wrong with me? Nick held the mug to my lips and told me to take a sip. I smelled cloves and looked up at him, grateful to be taken care of. Charlie whispered, "Don't trust anybody," and reptilian eyes squinted at me, sharp as knives. I blinked, and Nick's blue eyes blinked back, taking me in.

"Mommy, we made hot cider." Molly cuddled beside me, careful not to spill her drink.

"Have some," Nick urged. "It'll soothe you."

Lifting a leaden hand to take the drink, I put Charlie's warnings aside. Nick was a cop, a detective. He had flaws, but he was decent and generous, trying to make up for what had happened. Taking us into his home. Charlie's paranoid suggestions and the trauma of his death had warped my thinking. If I weren't careful, even in death Charlie might take over my thoughts and distort my judgment.

Spicy, steamy liquid glowed, tickling my lips. I sipped, tasted tart apples, cloves, cinnamon, and a shot of rum.

"Do you like it, Mom?" Molly sipped hers. "I love it. But yours is spiked."

Nick laughed with half his mouth. "Molly learned a new word."

"It's delicious," I said.

"The cider's authentic. From local apples. There's an orchard out back."

I drank, felt the rum relax me.

"What's an orchard?"

Nick explained, inviting Molly back to pick apples in the summer when they were ripe. Their chatter tickled my ears, and I leaned back against down-stuffed pillows. The fire toasted my skin. In a while, Molly leaned against me and I wrapped her in my arms. Safe, together, we stared at the crackling fire as the flames blurred through my tears.

"What's wrong, Mommy?" Molly reached up and wiped my cheek, a reversal of roles.

"I'm fine, Mollybear," I said. "Sometimes you just have to cry a little, right?"

"I bet you're crying about Charlie. He made me cry, too. I was scared."

"You were?" Why hadn't I known that? Why hadn't I been there to comfort her? "I'm sorry. I didn't know you cried. Where was I?"

"In the locker room with Nick, getting calmed down. It's okay. I was with Susan."

Nick moved closer, stroked my hair. "You're recovering from shock, Zoe. Give yourself time. You'll be fine. We all will be."

He sounded so sure. Mesmerized by the flames, tired from playing in fresh snow, Molly dozed off with her head on my shoulder. Beside the crackling, popping fire, Nick sat with me, sipping cider, and I drifted, wondering, as if from a distance, what we were doing there. And why we'd ever want to leave.

FORTY-SIX

NICK DOZED. MOLLY ROLLED OFF ME ONTO A CUSHION. I reached for my mug and sat up, swallowing lukewarm cider, finally alert enough to get my bearings.

The house was a simple A-frame with a cedar ceiling. The kitchen was at the rear of the main room; a bathroom and two guest rooms were off to the left. The master bedroom was a loft space above the guest rooms, overlooking the main room. The furniture was sparse and practical. An oak dining table, a cushy sofa. A large fireplace was surrounded with rugs and pillows. Late afternoon light poured in through large windows and snow-covered skylights.

I liked Nick's house. It was simple, uncluttered. Open.

Odd, I thought. One's home was supposed to reflect one's personality. Incongruous that a man who didn't value truth or honesty would create such an open space in his home. Stop it, I told myself. Let go of the past. Besides, the truth issue was irrelevant. Nick wasn't trying to restart a romance. Hadn't Beverly Gardener made it clear that he wasn't available?

Still, as I watched him nap, the relaxed line of his jaw, the slow and easy rise and fall of his chest, I wanted to curl up beside him and wrap myself in his arms. What would he think of that? How would he respond? Would he hold me there? Would he want me to stay?

Well, I wasn't going to find out. I wouldn't risk it. I was vulnerable and needy; that was why I was drawn to Nick. Besides, I didn't know what was going on with him. In the duration of a gunshot, Nick had gone from barely speaking to me to carrying me off to his cabin in Chester County. So far, he'd given no indication that he was interested in renewing a personal relationship. He'd made no innuendos, no passes, no references to either our disastrous one-night stand or the future. Maybe the truth was just what he'd said, that he wanted to give Molly and me a weekend of relaxation in the country. I'd accept it as that and keep my thoughts out of his arms and away from his body. Still, I remembered lying against him, fitting snugly, feeling safe, and the memory made me ache.

Nick's snores harmonized with Molly's. Bass and soprano, in stereo with complementary rhythm. I listened, watching them sleep until my eyes burned, letting go of memories and possibilities. Then, lulled by their snores and the flicker of hungry flames, I sank back into a warm, rum-coated sleep.

FORTY-SEVEN

I AWOKE IN SHADOWS, NOT RECOGNIZING WHERE I WAS. THE air was cold, smelled foreign. Like ashes. And cedar. And pine. I tried to sit up; my head felt like a sack of sand. Dim light seeped through the window blinds. Dusk. A dying fire. I blinked, orienting myself.

"Molly? Nick?"

No answer. I got up, searching.

"Nick? Molly?"

My voice hung forlornly, drifting through the empty room. I went to the window. Tall pines ringed the farmhouse like frozen sentries, rigid at attention. But no Nick. No Molly. I crossed, weightless, to the kitchen.

Yes, there they were, out back. Trekking through the glowing snow toward a woodpile. Behind them, through the open doors of a shed, I saw a pair of yellow snowmobiles, ski equipment, snowshoes hanging on the walls. A snowplow hunkered beside the shed like an oversized dog. Nick's toys.

I wandered into the bathroom and splashed my face with water, waking up. The mirror shocked me. Dark semicircles underlined my eyes. My skin was pasty, my lips chapped and rough. I looked hollow, but I felt better, more alert. Slapping some color into my cheeks, smoothing my hair back, I went for my jacket and joined them outside.

"Mommy's up!" Molly squealed. "We're getting firewood."

Cheeks glowing, she climbed through thigh-high snow, hand in hand with Nick.

"Feeling better?" Nick half-smiled, welcoming me, and we walked the snowy countryside around his house. The cold, fresh air revitalized me, and when Nick stopped to tighten a bootlace, I couldn't help it. I creamed him with a snowball. Right between the eyes. A battle ensued, a flurry of dusty white ammunition, flying arms and legs, and laughter. Molly ambushed us both by pretending to be hurt, then blasting us with two fierce chunks of snow when we came to her aid. We all froze our fingers, noses, and toes. We tumbled. We played. The horrors of the day before—of the past month—got lost in a frosty flurry. For the first time in years, I felt mischievous, silly, goofy. As the sun set, I rolled with Molly down hills of frozen white down, hung upside down over Nick's shoulder, landed in pillows of soft snow. By the time it got dark and we came inside, a lost part of my life had been restored. Partly because of Molly. Mostly because of Nick.

FORTY-EIGHT

I WASHED MOLLY'S HAIR AND LET HER SOAK IN A WARM, BUBBLY tub. When I came out, Nick was putting water up for pasta. I offered to help cook, got turned down. He handed me a glass of wine and told me to sit. I sat and leaned against the island, relaxed and a little dreamy.

"Can we talk about what happened with Charlie?" Nick gulped some wine.

The question startled me. At the mention of Charlie, my chest tightened, banishing whatever relaxation I'd felt. I didn't want to talk about Charlie, didn't want to remember why we'd come to the cabin or what had happened back home. "You saw my statement to the police. What else is there to say?"

"Details. Like what he talked about just before he died. Was he rational?" Nick sounded like a cop now. His shoulders rolled as he turned a pan, spreading olive oil.

My head began to throb. "He said he was there to protect us."

The shoulders stopped rolling, held stock still. "Protect you. From what?"

Near the pantry, Charlie raised a finger to his lips, hushing me, but I went on. "From evil. I assumed he meant the nanny killer."

"And Charlie was going to keep you safe." His shoulders relaxed. He reached for a paring knife. "By stalking you."

"By watching us. Guarding us. He said he knew the killer and that I'd let him get too close, but he'd keep Molly and me safe."

Nick lifted an eyebrow. "But he never said who the killer was?"

"No."

Nick gathered vegetables from the refrigerator and set them on the counter. Releasing a long sigh, he swallowed more wine and stared intensely at an eggplant. Neither of us spoke. The conversation felt strained and uneven. I felt awkward and self-conscious, not clear on our ground rules. Were we cop and witness? Detective and consultant? Former jilter and jiltee? What? I wanted to change the subject, re-create the lightness we'd shared outside. Nick had other ideas.

"I talked to Beverly about him."

Oh. I'd almost forgotten about Beverly. The captivating Dr. Gardener. As long as we were chatting, I should ask about their "deal." "And?"

"And she had some interesting comments."

He wanted me to ask. But I didn't. I wouldn't.

Nick leaned against the counter, crossing his arms in a casual, professorial pose, knife in hand. About to deliver a lecture? A knife as his pointer? "She said that paranoid delusions like Charlie's can be insidious—so detailed and vivid that even psychiatrists sometimes buy into them."

"So?"

"So you might find yourself believing what Charlie said. Even small parts of it. And if you do, you need to sort it out."

I didn't understand. He didn't make sense. Was he implying that by listening to Charlie I'd become delusional? That Charlie's madness was contagious? That I'd caught it?

"Beverly says Charlie's delusions must have begun way before the nannies began to disappear," he went on, "and that the person he was guarding you from was none other than himself—that is, part of himself."

"What?"

"Charlie divided himself into 'good' and 'bad' parts. His good part didn't like the bad, so he blocked it out and gave his bad self a separate identity. In other words, he created an evil alter ego out of his own dark side."

"And that's who was reading his thoughts? His alter ego?"

"Exactly. The evil murderer who wired his dreams and listened in on his thoughts was really himself. His own other half."

"Beverly Gardener said all this?"

"She's very smart."

"And she knew so much about Charlie because—"

"Because of the police investigation. And what you said in your response to her profile report." His words merged, became a steady flow of senseless syllables. Beverly Gardener was apparently Nick's ultimate authority on everything, but I wasn't sure she was as smart as he thought. How could she claim to know so much about a man she'd never met? Her explanation was all theory, a bunch of impressive psychological terms thrown together to sound good, nothing to do with the real Charlie. Nick spoke slowly, as if doubting that I could follow him. My fingers were ice. Coming close, he put his hands over them and squeezed, pressing warmth into my skin.

"The victims were ordinary women. But Beverly's convinced that to Charlie they were substitutes for another woman who's anything but ordinary. A woman who was very special to him. A woman he watched tirelessly from afar and was fascinated with to the point of obsession. Zoe Hayes."

Me? Charlie was obsessed with me? The idea was unfathomable. Behind Nick, in the shadows, Charlie harrumphed indignantly as Nick's voice sailed past me, full speed ahead, skimming the surface, not sinking in. I sat still, aware of the meaty warmth of his hands.

He kept talking. I heard him repeat Beverly Gardener's name,

recite her comments point by point. Did he memorize everything she said? Ask him, I thought. Go ahead. But I didn't ask,
didn't want to hear his answer.

"Nick, if it's okay—can we not talk about this anymore?"

"Sure. It's a lot to digest all at once." He released my hands
and went back to his vegetables. Chop, chop. Dice, slice. Another swig of wine. He lopped the florets off broccoli. I listened
to the blade hit the wood, heard the screaming of mushrooms,
the rending of veggie flesh. Veggie flesh? Oh please, I told myself. Not every situation is one of culprit and victim. I needed to
let go of my pervasive sense of danger.

"I can understand why you don't want to talk about him,"
Nick said. "But you're safe now. Charlie won't be bothering you
anymore."

Except that he was, even at that moment, bothering me. Making faces at Nick's knife, mocking his chopping motions. Nick's
knife twinkled, dripped tomato seeds onto the floor.

Finally, he stopped cutting. "Okay, enough. You're right. We
should put all of this aside."

Put it aside? Where? On the counter beside the bread?

"You look pensive. Is there something else, honey?"

Honey? I took a breath. Swallowed. Nick liked me. He wasn't
just being a cop; he'd called me "honey." It was odd, alien. Pa-
ternalistic? Maybe, but still nice, sort of. What was going
through honey's mind? Images, not words. Images of Nick's
buns as he prepared dinner. Did I want to talk about them? Uh-
uh. Images of Beverly Gardener with her glossed lips and
implant-enhanced breasts. Images of a lopped-off, polished
pinkie. And images of Charlie. Charlie on his porch, on my
steps, in his Pontiac. I could almost hear his hoarse cough.

Okay, I'd tell him. "Charlie was sick," I said, "but Charlie
didn't kill anyone. He couldn't have. He was harmless."

Nick hesitated, taking in the comment. "What makes you so sure?"

"I just know."

"Well, there's a lot of physical evidence that disagrees with you. Body parts were found in his damn basement, Zoe."

"I know."

"So how can you be sure that he's innocent?"

"Charlie wasn't a killer."

"Not the side of him he showed the world. That side didn't seem like a murderer. If it had, he'd never have gotten close to the victims. But who'd suspect an old handyman with arthritic knees? No one. That's exactly why the nannies didn't run off while they could."

I wasn't convinced. "Charlie didn't have the physical strength to overpower all those healthy young women."

"No, but he didn't need it. He was the handyman. When a babysitter let him in to do repairs, he'd pull a knife on her, or some other weapon, and she'd go with him without a struggle. Or he'd walk up to a sitter in the park and shove a weapon into her back. No one even noticed him. He was nonthreatening. Inconspicuous. An old man. What a perfect disguise."

What had Charlie said? "Looking normal would be the best disguise of all." Something like that. Had he been warning me against himself? The thought gave me goose bumps.

"Beverly agrees. She says that, as a paranoid schizophrenic, Charlie could fit the profile despite his age." Nick seemed sure.

"So. You're not looking for anyone else?"

"The case is closed, Zoe. Relax. It's done." He resumed cooking. Bits of garlic cloves, cherry peppers, and anchovies lined his butcher block. The windows had darkened; ice crusted their corners. We'd emptied our bottle of wine, opened another. Aromas of spices and warm bread swelled around us. We were almost getting comfortable being together, settling in, but I couldn't let go. I simply could not believe that the killer was Charlie. Did Nick really believe it? Or was he lying again, hiding the truth, withholding privileged information? Stop it, I told myself. Nick hadn't necessarily lied. Maybe I was wrong. Maybe Charlie had been a serial killer. But doubts still nagged at me.

"Charlie said the killer used his tools."

Nick pushed chopped veggies into bowls. "Zoe. Forget what Charlie told you. He'd divided himself into two, remember? He talked about the killer as if it was someone else."

"But why nannies? If, as Beverly said, the women represented me, why did he kill younger women? And why nannies? Why not mothers?"

I thought of answers as soon as I asked the questions. To Charlie, I was a young woman. And I wasn't a typical mother; I'd adopted Molly. Didn't that make me sort of a permanent nanny? One of the victims had been an adoptive mother like me. If I'd been the person he modeled victims after—no, that idea was absurd. Wasn't it?

Still, I expected Nick to give me a glib answer. Some easy explanation that would banish my doubts. But Nick didn't say a word. Instead, he lapsed into silence. He stood rapt, back rigid, legs apart, arms folded across his chest. Why? What was he thinking about? Charlie? Whether to reveal another secret? How long to simmer his sauce?

"What's going on?" I asked.

He shook his head. "Sorry. Just thinking."

About what? He didn't say. He stood silently, staring out the window at darkness.

"Smell my hair, Mommy." Molly joined us, wrapped in an oversized towel.

I did. It smelled clean and sweet, like vanilla. We went to the guest room to put on her pajamas, stopping every three seconds so she could wiggle her tooth.

"Do you think it'll come out tonight?"

"Maybe. Maybe a few more days."

"Because the Tooth Fairy doesn't know where we are."

"I told you. Don't worry. The Tooth Fairy knows. Finding kids is part of the job."

"It's you, isn't it?"

"How can you even think that?" I dodged, avoiding the truth. Avoiding a lie.

"Mommy, come on. Tell me—"

I kissed her vanilla head. "Let's go see Nick."

"Mommy—" She stuck to my side, asking.

In the kitchen, Nick was finishing a phone call. Hanging up, he forced a smile. "Hungry?" he asked.

"Thtarved," Molly answered while wiggling her tooth.

"Good. Spaghetti's my specialty."

I heard sizzling, smelled garlic frying. Nick's shirt rippled over his back as he sprinkled diced peppers, anchovies, and tomatoes over broccoli, peppers, capers, olives, mushrooms, and eggplant chunks in the skillet. Occasional odd pieces toppled off the butcher block onto the floor. I took note of the deftness of Nick's fingers, the decisiveness of his hands, the inability of onions to defend themselves. The force of his slices.

Molly chattered and Nick cooked. Eventually, fighting a headache, I left them at the stove to discuss herbs and spices. I sat by the fire, watching flames curl and lick their helpless prey.

FORTY-NINE

"COME AND EAT, MOMMY. DINNER'S READY."

Nick and Molly did all the work. They didn't let me fold a napkin or set a fork. Nick seated me at the table and set before me a plate of steaming linguini in a thick, chunky vegetable sauce. Molly brought a basket of fresh bread; Nick poured wine and milk. Then he lit the candles, spreading fire from match to wick, evenly, easily, until his skin and his eyes glowed with yellow flame.

And after dinner, ashamed and appreciative, lulled by wine and a full belly, I let myself fall again for Nick. I put aside old differences; they didn't matter anymore. For the last twenty-four hours, Nick had been entirely devoted to me and my daughter. He'd done his best to anticipate our reactions and address our needs. If his intentions were unclear, they were also irrelevant; for the moment, it was enough just to be there with him. To be away from the city. To dwell in Nick's space. Here, the air was crisp and fresh, the moon a bright half melon. No sirens blaring, no psychopaths looming. I was in a rustic farmhouse beside a strong man who not only cooked but even read bedtime stories to my daughter and helped me tuck her into bed.

But then, once Molly was in bed, Nick and I were alone. Without Molly around, I felt awkward, uncertain how to behave. Nick stoked the fire, added a log and turned to me with his crooked half smile.

"Thanks for today," I said.

"Are you tired?" he asked at the same moment.

We both stopped, waited a beat, and began again. Again, we both talked at once, both stopped, both apologized at the same moment. Finally, we both laughed.

"Seriously, Nick," I managed. "This day has been medicine."

"It's been good to have you here," he said.

We stood facing each other, grinning stupidly, as seconds ticked by. Say good night, I thought. Say good night, step into the guest room beside Molly's, and shut the door. But I didn't. I stood outside Molly's door, gawky and silent, wishing Nick would reach out for me. Wanting him to. Wondering if he wanted to. If he would.

Do something, I told myself. But I did nothing. I stood silent, idiotic.

Finally, Nick took a step, closing the space between us. He put an arm around me, and I reached out and touched his face. My fingers traced the scar his wife had left. He stiffened momentarily; a painful glint shot through his eyes.

"Sorry." I took my hand away. I hadn't wanted to hurt him, hadn't planned the touch.

"No, no need. I'm just numb in spots, can't feel anything. The bullet ripped through nerves that never healed."

He led me to the main room, to sit by the fire. Slowly, he took my hand and brought it back to his face. He held it there for a moment.

"I don't talk about that much." He forced a half smile.

"It's okay. You don't have to." I already knew what had happened. And that he didn't talk about it.

He let go of my hand. His eyes reflected the fire. "I told her a hundred times that I was leaving. A thousand. I guess I'd told her so often, she didn't believe I'd ever really go. So when she saw me packing my stuff, Annie—my wife—she . . . she made a bad decision. Didn't think it through." He paused, thinking. "When she shot herself, she must have thought I was dead. I damned near was."

"I'm sorry." It was all I could think of to say.

Nick nodded. "I don't remember the last time I talked about it. Fact is, I'm not sure why I'm talking about it now. I mean, it was a long time ago. Not something to dwell on anymore. At least, not now. Not tonight. Not while I'm with you."

Nick leaned my way, and his shoulders towered above me. His arms enclosed me and held on. And there, by the crackling fire, I looked into Nick's blue eyes and watched the tides rise, the moon fall, the blue skies open and swallow us whole. I felt myself spin, spiraling dizzily past nannies and body parts, past Charlie's Pontiac and his exploding head until, limbs interlocking, flesh melting, I landed in strong arms that reached out, caught me, and carried me up the stairs.

FIFTY

I KNEW THAT I WAS IN A DREAM, BUT I COULDN'T PULL MYSELF
out of it. I lacked the strength to open my eyes, let alone move a
leg or an arm. So, reluctantly, I surrendered, letting the phone
ring unanswered, allowing the dream to progress until I could
muster the energy to lift my eyelids.

First, I had to get the damned corpse off of me. I could
hardly breathe for the dead weight of the body lying on my
chest. I pushed, lifted its leaden arm, and felt it land with a
thud. I struggled to roll its torso and shimmy off to the side. Finally, the body slid off. Air rushed into my lungs. I sat up, pulled
away from the corpse, and looked at it.

Nick, not a corpse, lay beside me, soaked in blood. I tried to
scream, but no sound came out. I shook him. He didn't respond. The phone stopped ringing, shocked to silence.

Frantic, I looked around the room. I saw parallel bars, easels, a
fireplace with burning embers. Where were the nurses? The staff?
Once again, I tugged at Nick's arm. It flopped limp and cool.

"Nick!" I whispered. Nick's eyes remained closed, his body
motionless.

I was on my feet, running in circles. Still Nick didn't move. I
reached for a lamp, knocked it crashing to the floor. I tried to
find the light switch on the wall, couldn't. Of course I can't, I
told myself. This is a dream. There's not going to be a switch on

the wall. It's a nightmare. Not real, not real. Wake up, I told myself. But my eyes were stuck shut. I couldn't escape, not yet.

And Nick's bulk lay lifeless near the fireplace. His arm was
where it had been when I got up, his back drenched in blood. I
sank down beside him, trembling.

I heard myself howl and pounded his chest, trying to remember CPR, the xiphoid process. Something about the xiphoid process. I exhaled into his mouth. Again. But Nick lay stubbornly
lifeless. Dead. Gone. He wore a vacant expression, not emotional, not relaxed. Just blank. Discarded features with no one
inside them. I backed away, shivering. This is a dream, I
thought. A dream.

"Oh God," I mumbled, rubbing my eyes. Empty plates and
wineglasses sat unwashed on the table. My napkin lay on my
plate, just where I'd dropped it. Molly's damp socks and boots
lay by the door. This dream had too many details, was far too
vivid. The phone started to ring again.

It took all my energy, but I strained, tugged, squirmed,
twisted. Somehow, I pulled myself free of the nightmare. I
opened one eye. Finally, the other. The corpse disappeared, but
the phone kept ringing. I could barely lift my head; it weighed
tons. Groggy, I let it go. It fell back onto the pillow.

"Oh God," I repeated. The phone jangled on. I reached across
the bed to wake up Nick but couldn't find him. My hand groped
crumpled blankets, tangled sheets, scattered pillows. But no
Nick. I rolled over and blinked through the darkness, straining
to see his side of the bed. It was empty. Nick wasn't there.

Maybe I wasn't up yet. Maybe I was still dreaming. Maybe
that was why I was so groggy. Besides, Nick must be around
somewhere. In the bathroom. Or the kitchen getting a snack.

"Nick?" My voice sounded raw, shaky. "Nick?" This time I
called louder. No answer.

The phone rang on. Where the hell was it?

I tried to sit up. Too fast. A wave of dizziness rose suddenly, knocking me back down. I lay still, but the bed seemed to rock, a raft in a stormy sea.

Was I sick? Hungover? Maybe Nick was, too. Maybe that's why he hadn't answered the phone; maybe he was throwing up. In the bathroom. Or outside. Maybe he'd gone outside for fresh air. To clear his head.

Maybe.

I sat up, made myself wake up enough to stand. Cold and naked, I wrapped up in a flannel sheet, got out of bed, and headed toward the ringing. Was it downstairs? Maybe the main room. Or the kitchen. It might wake Molly, although nothing could wake Molly when she was tired. Unsteady, wobbling, at the end of the bed I bumped into a table, knocking the lamp onto the floor. Where was the damned phone? And who was calling in the middle of the night? Oh dear—was there a police emergency? Was Nick's department trying to reach him? I hurried, stumbling through darkness, searching for a light switch.

Still caught in the images of the nightmare, I felt my way along the wall, searching for a switch. Finally, I made it to the stairs and, trying not to trip on the sheet, went down carefully, step by step.

"Just find a light," I told myself. "Turn on some lights. There." I flicked on the kitchen switch. Light blasted the counter, the stove, the sink and spilled into the living room, blinding me, making me blink. I looked for Nick's cell, found it beside a salt shaker on the kitchen table. Of course, as in a nightmare, it stopped ringing before I could cross the room.

FIFTY-ONE

I STOOD BUTT NAKED IN NICK'S KITCHEN, DIZZY AND SHIVER-ing and dragging a flannel sheet. Where was Nick? Who'd been on the phone? I stared at it, trying to think, but I was cold, and my thoughts were fuzzy and hard to define. What time was it? Two? Three? Where was a clock? Slowly, holding on to the kitchen table, I scanned the walls, saw darkened pictures, wob-bly window frames. But no clock. The guest room where Molly slept was off the main room. I was on my way to check on her when the phone began to ring again.

I pivoted, hurrying back to the phone. Who was calling? Why so late? Maybe it was Nick, calling to tell me where he was. Why he was gone. When he'd be back. I took three giant steps and pounced on the phone.

My voice was still asleep, not working. Nothing but a hoarse gurgle came out when I tried to say hello, but before I could try again, someone was talking. Not Nick. A sultry voice, familiar. "Nick? Where the hell are you?"

I could almost smell her perfume. She went on, assuming Nick had answered.

"Pumpkin, you were supposed to be here an hour ago. I'm going nuts, waiting—look, the door's unlocked, so just come right in. How long till you get here?"

"Sorry. It's not Nick."

She stopped cold. "Who's this? Zoe?"

"Nick's not available right now."

She was silent, thinking. "Zoe, is that you?" Her voice was tentative, alarmed. "Are you there with Nick? Let me talk to him."

"Nick can't come to the phone."

"What? Why not?" She paused. "What happened? Why do you have his cell phone?"

Her breathing was rapid, urgent. I said nothing, didn't know the answers.

"Zoe? Where's Nick?"

Excellent question.

"Where are you? At his place? Has he left yet?"

"Why is any of that your business?"

"Damn it, Zoe. Why are you being so difficult? You know the situation. What's going on?"

Another good question. "You'll have to ask Nick."

"Trust me, when he gets here, I will." A loud click. Beverly had hung up.

I looked out the window, saw only my reflection. A still life: nude wrapped in a sheet, holding a cell phone. I slapped the switch, turning the light off so I could see outside. What I saw was snow. Pine trees. Nothing else. No Nick. Where the hell was he? And why the hell was Beverly so agitated? What had she said, that she was waiting for him?

But that wasn't possible—Nick was out in the country with me and Molly. Except that he couldn't be found. Oh Lord. Had Nick gone back to town to meet Beverly? In the middle of the night? She certainly seemed to be expecting him. But if Nick was involved with Beverly, why had he brought me here? And taken me to bed? What sick game was he playing?

I made my way through the dark, avoiding the table and the lamp. Shivering, I tied the sheet around me; then, holding on to the phone, I made it to Molly's room. I opened her door a crack and watched her sleep, bathed in moonlight, undisturbed. I crept in, pulled her covers up under her chin, and stroked her head.

Nothing made sense. We were in the middle of nowhere, cold, alone in inky darkness too dense for shadows. I was accustomed to the city, nights ringing with sirens, revved engines, shouting voices, blaring radios. Here, no one was around to disturb the night. While Molly slept, I hugged the sheet, clutched the phone, and listened to silence so loud it hurt my ears.

Think, I told myself, but my mind felt clouded and thick. My body ached to lie down and get warm. Maybe I should climb back upstairs, get back under the covers, and start over. Wake up again, this time to Nick's snores. Stop it, I told myself. Get a grip. Think. I closed my eyes, tried to form coherent thoughts.

Nick. The hairs on my neck tingled and stood at alert. Who was he, really? What did I really know about the man I'd just slept with, the man I'd allowed to dump me and my daughter in the middle of nowhere? Except that he was a cop who'd once been shot by his wife. I wandered back to the main room. It was sparsely furnished, gave little information. No photographs or personal items. I walked around, snooping, looking for clues. I opened Nick's closets, his dresser drawers. I found a woolly fleece robe that smelled like him. I put it on, wore it as I further invaded his privacy, rifling through sweaters and socks, pushing aside hangers, poking into jacket pockets, reaching up onto closet shelves, pulling down a tennis racket, an overnight bag, a box of bullets. In his linen closet, I found spare towels and sheets; in his kitchen cabinets, I found dishes, spices, cans of food. His desk held a drawer full of old cable and phone bills, menus for local pizza parlors, an L. L. Bean catalog, a bunch of brochures for small sailboats.

What I found, finally, was in a stationery box in the bottom drawer. A collection of articles and pictures of Nick and a woman. A woman who, I thought, looked very much like me.

FIFTY-TWO

THE HEADLINES READ, "MURDER/SUICIDE—REAL OR STAGED?" "'I Did Not Kill My Wife': Cop Claims Innocence." "Cop Suspended Pending Murder Investigation."

Shaking, I scanned the articles, gradually accepting the truth. Nick had been suspected of killing his wife, Anne. He'd denied it. He'd insisted that his wife had taken out the gun, that they'd struggled. It had fired, wounding him in the face. When he was down, he said, she shot herself.

But there was conflicting evidence. Such as the location of the wounds. Anne Stiles was left handed; Stiles was wounded on the left side of his face. If he'd been facing her in a struggle as he said, a gun fired by her left hand would have wounded him on the right. There were other reasons for doubt, as well. The residue on his hand . . . the trajectory of the bullets . . .

I stopped reading and sat, shivering, trying to understand. Had Nick, not his wife, been the shooter? No way. In the struggle, he might have turned his head. There could be a dozen reasons that the bullet struck where it had. And why there had been residue on his hand. He'd been exonerated, after all.

I stuffed the articles back into the box, not wanting to know more, but the face of the dead woman stared out at me from a page of yellowing newsprint. Our resemblance was clear. Was that why Nick noticed me? Why he'd made love to me? I shivered, beginning to understand. Oh my God. Nick had been interested in me because I looked like his dead wife.

Was it possible that Nick Stiles killed her? No, I told myself. No way. But my skin rose in goose bumps and my mouth went dry, insisting that yes, indeed he might have.

Agitated, I moved from window to window, searching the snow, the pine trees, wanting to find Nick. To ask him and find out, for better or worse. Outside, though, nothing moved. Nobody. Snow was beginning to fall, burying footprints from our hike, smoothing over our crumbled snowballs. Concealing all signs of our presence. From the front window, I could find not a single sign of human life.

Not even, it hit me, a car.

Nick's Volvo was definitely gone. And so was Nick. He'd gone to see Beverly. The sonofabitch had actually driven off to meet her and left us there.

My adrenaline surged. Clutching the sheet, shivering, breathing shallowly, I heard the hollow silence of frigid country air as questions ran through my mind. Why had Nick brought us out there only to leave us there alone? And why had he left us his cell phone?

I should call someone, I thought. I should let somebody know what was going on. But who? It was the middle of the night, after 2:00 A.M. If I called anyone, what would I say? That Nick Stiles had left Molly and me alone in his cabin? Or that, years ago, he'd not been found guilty of killing his wife?

Slow down, I told myself. Don't let your mind race. First of all, forget those old newspaper articles. They don't mean anything—they even say Nick was exonerated. No charges were filed against him; he'd even kept his job. The only thing the articles proved was that Nick still cared about what happened enough to keep the record of it in his closet.

And there was no proof that Nick had gone for a tryst with

Beverly Gardener. Maybe his car was gone because he'd gotten an important call. Police business. Maybe he intended to be back before I woke up, hadn't wanted to disturb my sleep. For all I knew, Beverly Gardener's call was beyond his control. Maybe Dr. Gardener was pursuing Nick, hounding him. Chasing him without encouragement, unwilling to accept rejection. Maybe Nick would explain everything shortly, when he got back. In a few minutes. Soon.

Time passed, though; minutes stretched into hours, and still Nick didn't return. Whatever explanations I tried to concoct became pathetically unconvincing. The night that just hours ago had blanketed us with passion and warmth had turned treacherous, hiding secrets, concealing lies. I wandered the house. Down the stairs, through the main room. Carrying the phone, wearing Nick's robe, I made the rounds from window to window, room to room, checking for what, I wasn't sure. For a while, I sat on the bed up in the loft, from which I had a view of the main room, the kitchen, Molly's room, the front door. Wrapped in Nick's blankets, I waited for a formerly suspected wife-killer to return from a night out with a self-absorbed, seductive brunette. Would he tiptoe in? Make a grand entrance without apology? Or would he clatter about and make a ruckus, pretending simply to have been downstairs making pancakes all the time?

Enough, I told myself. What's the matter with you? You've got him tried and convicted before you've even heard his case.

The phone rang in my hand. I jumped.

Don't even answer it, Charlie's voice urged. Just grab Molly and get out. But I didn't listen to him; I answered, hoping to hear Nick.

A long inhale. An exasperated exhale. Then the husky, insistent voice. "Where is he, sugarplum? For godsakes, tell me. Is he on his way?"

I made my voice sturdy. "What do you want, Beverly?"

"I think I've been clear, dumpling. I want Nick. Where is he? Tell me."

I didn't answer.

"Look, honeybun. This is serious. He was supposed to be here. A long time ago. He hasn't shown up, and I really can't wait much longer."

"And I should care about that because . . . ?"

"Because I'm worried. The roads are terrible. What time did he leave? He was supposed to be at my condo—"

"Do you two always get together in the middle of the night?"

"Amazing, isn't it? But often, yes. We're both available around the clock, and he's never kept me waiting before. Not like this, anyway. Look, cupcake, if he calls, tell him not to go to my condo. I can't wait here anymore. I'll be at the Institute. In my office. Got it?"

The Institute? I began to say that it was an odd place for a late-night rendezvous. But she'd already hung up.

FIFTY-THREE

THERE WAS NO DOUBT ANYMORE, IF THERE HAD EVER BEEN. Nick had definitely gone to meet Beverly Gardener. He'd snuck out of bed with me in the middle of the night and driven back to town to be with her. It was incredible, hard to absorb, and humiliating but apparently true.

What was I going to do about it? What could I do? I was stuck out in Chester County with Molly, who was sound asleep.

After the phone call, I was spitting mad. I sat listening to sounds of the night, fuming. Feeling like a chump. The more I sat, the angrier I got. The isolation didn't help. Was that the wind howling or the cry of a hungry wolf? Was it a tree branch scraping the window or the claw of some night creature?

Stop it, I told myself. No one's out there. It's just your nerves. Still, I walked around in the dark, checking doors and windows, making sure they were locked. I checked on Molly every few minutes, comforted by the steady sound of her breath. I went up to the loft and peered out the window, feeling trapped and frantic. Furious at Nick for bringing us there, at myself for having come. Up in the loft, I stared out at the night. I lay down, tried to sleep, pictured Nick with Beverly, sat up, and stared out at the night again. I paced, went down to the main room, back up to the loft. Despite myself, I could see what he saw in her; the woman had charisma. She was a celebrity. But I asked myself over and over why Nick had taken us there if he'd wanted to be with Beverly. I had no answers and eventually got sick of asking. All I knew was that I wanted out. I wanted to go home.

Finally, the sky began to lighten. It was almost dawn, and Nick was still gone. Downstairs again, I stopped pacing and stared at the front door. What was I supposed to do? Stay there all day and wait? The front door gave no reply.

But Charlie did. "Get out, Miss Zoe!" I heard him wheeze. "Hurry up. Leave before it's too late."

I didn't argue. I wanted to get the hell out of there, not wait around to hear excuses and lies. But how was I supposed to leave? Nick had taken the car. Should I call a cab? Did they even have cabs way out in Chester County? At the crack of dawn?

Finally, as the sun rose higher, I'd had enough. I wasn't helpless, didn't have to stay there waiting. I had options. The Volvo was gone, but Molly and I had legs. There were snowshoes in the shed. We could walk back to Philadelphia if we had to, or at least to a highway. I'd take the cell phone, and when we found a main road I'd call Susan and tell her where we were. She'd come and get us. Good. I felt better already; I wasn't trapped. I had a plan.

I gathered my clothing in a rush, but trembling, rushing, I had trouble putting it on. My feet kept missing, wouldn't go into the leg holes of my jeans, got stuck halfway. The harder I shoved my feet into them, the more the fabric resisted. Finally, I gathered the material at the bottom and held it open, aiming my toes through the holes as if I were threading a needle. Calm down, I told myself. Find your socks. Put on your boots. My skin stung as my sweater rubbed spots Nick's rough whiskers had scraped raw. Damn Nick. Cheating lying sonofabitch. Controlling manipulating two-faced bastard. Cursing him felt good. I straightened my sweater and smeared away angry tears with the back of my hand.

Finally, my clothes were on. I was ready to go. All I had to do was bundle up Molly and get the snowshoes. Then we'd hit the road.

FIFTY-FOUR

MOLLY'S FIRST THOUGHT UPON WAKING WAS ABOUT HER tooth. It was still there, hanging tentatively to a few strands of tissue. Her second thought was of Nick.

"He's not here."

"Why not? Where'd he go?"

"He went back to town. Here. Put your socks on."

"Why'd he go back to town?"

"He didn't say."

"But Mommy, he said we could make banana pancakes. He promised."

"I know. Something came up. Here, pull this over the turtleneck. It's cold out."

"Can we make pancakes, Mommy?"

"Maybe later. Not now. Now we're going outside. Put your arm in."

"But Nick said—"

"Mollybear, put your arm in the sleeve? Good."

"He said we could—"

"For now, let's fix just a snack, okay? We'll see about pancakes later."

Finally, she was dressed. I made cinnamon toast and filled a thermos with hot cocoa for the road. I'd never walked in snowshoes, had no idea if Molly would be able to. Maybe Nick had a sled. A sled would be much better, easier to negotiate.

I looked out the kitchen window, squinting at the shed, searching, hoping to see a sled. Snow was falling in large, heavy flakes. The woodpile was already buried, a tiny lump on a blanket-covered mountain. I couldn't see a sled, but there might be one out there. If there was no sled, we'd put on the snow-shoes and be on our way. I zipped Molly into her jacket and gazed outside, assessing the depth of the snow—and dimly, through the blizzard, I saw a bulky shape hunkering at the door of the shed. Forget the damned snowshoes, I thought. We had a better way to get home.

It was sitting right there by the shed, a big yellow plow hooked up to its front end. I could drive a stick shift, could probably manage a pickup truck.

I pulled on my jacket. Good. I had a new plan. First, we'd gather our bags and pack up our toast and cocoa. Then, we'd go out back, climb into that baby, start the engine, and roar the fuck out of there.

FIFTY-FIVE

GET THE KEYS, I TOLD MYSELF. BUT WHERE WERE THE KEYS? Were we never going to get out of there? Nick's bags were scattered near the door. Maybe the keys were in there. Unless they were outside in the truck. Damn. I hadn't seen keys when I'd looked through his stuff. Maybe they were hanging on a hook somewhere, or lying in a kitchen drawer.

"What are you doing?" Molly watched me ransack Nick's kitchen.

"Looking for keys to Nick's truck. We're going for a ride."

"But I want to make a snowman. And a fort. And Nick said—"

"Molly, sweetheart. We can do other stuff later. Help me find the keys."

I opened Nick's overnight bag, found a sweater, jeans, a book. A holster. No keys. For the second time that night, I scanned the shelves, rifled through drawer after drawer, even opened a cookie jar. It contained cookies. While Molly ate one, I found a flashlight, candles, and a kerosene lamp, but no keys. I looked in nightstands, behind doors. In the broom closet, I found a shotgun and some shells; inside his shaving kit, a razor, a toothbrush, condoms, deodorant. No keys.

Then, in the upstairs bathroom, the light revealed a piece of paper taped to the mirror. A note from Nick.

"Good morning, sleepyhead. I didn't want to wake you. I had

to run an errand, but I'll be back in time to make pancakes. I'll bring the bananas. See you soon. Nick."

Good morning? When he'd written the note, he was planning to be gone all night. He hadn't expected me to wake up and find him gone, hadn't counted on Beverly calling again and again, waking me up. Filling me in. No, Nick had thought himself very clever, leaving a note that he'd gone out only to do an errand. A note that had been deliberately, carefully written to deceive me. From a man who may have killed his wife. I shivered at the possibility. How sinister—how dangerous—was Nick? What kind of man was he? Damn him, anyway. I tore up the note, threw it into the toilet, and flushed, hoping it would stop up his plumbing. Flood the whole goddam place. But the note didn't go down. Its pieces sat sodden, floating on the water.

"Did you find them?" Molly called.

The keys, I remembered. "No, not yet."

"Let's face it, Mommy. They're not here. Let's just make a fort? Can we? Please?"

I came downstairs. "Mollybear, don't whine. Think. If we lived here, where would we keep the keys to our snowplow?"

"Somewhere easy to find them."

"Right—someplace we could get to them quickly if it snowed really hard."

"Somewhere in the shed?"

She was probably right. They must be in the shed. On a hook. Or in the truck itself.

"Molly, you're a genius." I looked out at large, dense snowflakes, falling heavily in the eerie morning glow.

Carrying the phone, our overnight bags, the thermos, and the flashlight, I took Molly by the hand and trudged outside. The sun hadn't quite made it above the pine trees; snow and sky blended seamlessly, fading from ominous to forbidding shades of gray. The pines seemed nearer than before, closing in like the snow, and though I knew no one was among them, I didn't look to the left or right, dreading what I might see. My eyes remained directly ahead, fixed on the swirling snow. We trekked through drifts, knee deep for me, hip high for Molly, grunting and panting through gusts of wind, tasting flakes that blew into our mouths, stopping several times for Molly to catch her breath or balance, for me to rearrange my load.

Finally, we slid to a stop at the door of the shed. I dropped the bags and scanned the walls with the flashlight. There were hooks holding showshoes and bicycles, shovels and rakes. Hooks holding saws and axes and drills and hammers. But no hooks holding keys. Damn.

"Where are they, Molly? Where would Nick keep his keys?"

"Maybe inside the truck. In the glove compartment? Can I look, Mom?" She ran to the door of the truck.

"Let me."

"Why can't I? I thought of it."

"Molly, please don't whine."

"But why can't I?" She stopped whining.

"Here, hold the thermos."

I climbed into the truck, leaned over the passenger seat, and reached inside. Maps. Headache pills. Kleenex. Candy bars. A yo-yo. Registration and insurance cards—a yo-yo?

A yo-yo. It was red and blue, made of wood. Blinking at it, I stuffed everything back into the glove compartment, slammed it shut, and yanked my hand away. There wasn't time to dwell on a yo-yo. The yo-yo didn't matter. All that mattered was the keys.

Still eyeing the glove compartment, I felt above the sun visor, under the driver's seat. That's where I found them, on the floor, under the seat. Next to the gun.

I pulled my hand back as if from a fire.

Of course, there was a gun under the driver's seat. Nick was a cop; cops had guns. He probably kept them all over the place, under cushions, in the bread box. No big deal. Not for Nick.

Just take the keys and go, I told myself. I reached under the seat and retrieved the keys.

"Got 'em," I said, holding up the key ring.

"Yeah, Mommy. You rule. Let's blow this pop stand."

"Let's what?" Where did she get those expressions?

She wiggled her tooth, shrugging. "Angela says that."

The ring held lots of keys. A dozen, at least. Lord. What were they all for? I climbed out, grabbed Molly, and hefted her up into the cab. As she climbed across to the passenger seat, I tossed in our bags and hopped up behind the wheel. I slid the driver's seat forward so my feet could reach the pedals, aimed a key at the ignition, tried another and another until I found one that fit. Then I pushed down on the clutch, held down the brake, felt for a hand brake—was there a hand brake?—released what I thought was a hand brake, stepped on the gas, and turned the key. The engine sputtered and coughed. Then it died. Damn.

"What's wrong with the truck?" Molly wanted to know.

Good question. Was the battery dead? Was it frozen? Was there any gas? "I don't know."

"Do you even know how to drive a truck?"

"Yes, of course I do."

"Then why isn't it going?"

"Molly. Give me a second, okay?"

Try it again, I told myself. I turned the key. The engine gurgled. I stayed on the gas. It complained and it groaned, but it finally came to life. Molly gave it a round of applause.

"I never rode in a truck before, Mommy."

"Me either."

"Then how do you know how to drive one?"

Oops, she'd caught me. "It's not that different from a car."

She pondered that.

"Don't worry, Mollybear. We're fine."

She looked unconvinced but stopped chattering for a while.

The truck forged slowly through the snow, grumbling loudly. Time to shift, I told myself. Shift. Remember how? I found the clutch, pushed down, pulled the stick—and cringed at the piercing screams of grinding metal. The truck lurched to a halt. Oops, I thought. The gears.

"Mommy, what was that?" Molly cried.

"It's fine." We weren't even off of Nick's driveway, and I'd already stalled. There was a lever in the car—connected to the plow? I pulled it, and the plow lowered into plowing position. Amazing. Something actually was working. Molly kept talking, giving me advice on how to drive.

Start over, I told myself. Get the timing. Push down on the clutch. Now shift. Now accelerate. Now—slowly—release the clutch. Better. A bit of a jolt, but no screeches or stalls.

For endless minutes, the truck snorted and chugged. At first, Molly reacted to each bump. She asked questions about how the plow worked, about Nick. She criticized my driving, cited Angela's expert advice, and updated me on the status of her teeth, showing that another one was loose. As we chortled around curves, through hills, along walls of silent pines, she eventually leaned back in her seat and dozed. For miles, I drove randomly, with no idea where we were or how to get to a main road. My eyes darted around, checking the rearview mirror as if someone might be following, knowing that no one was. Finally, the winding side road reached an intersection. Not a major artery, but big enough to merit a stop sign. I turned onto it, heading east toward the rising glow in the sky. Chester County was west of the city. So I was headed in the right direction. Soon the sun was higher; shadows evolved into shapes. And the road led to Route 30. A familiar number. I took it. Snow coated the pavement, and the truck felt clumsy, drove heavily, sluggish with the weight of the plow, but when we hit 202 I knew my way. Even with the snow, we could make town in under an hour. We were on our way home. Whatever awful memories awaited me there, they were mine, and I'd deal with them in my way, on my own. I would face Charlie's empty house and the truth about what had happened there. And if I had my way, I'd never hear of Nick Stiles or Beverly Gardener again.

FIFTY-SIX

THE ROAD WAS SLICK WITH SLUSH AND ICE. I SPED THROUGH A
frigid landscape of hilly suburbs and industrial parks onto the
Schuylkill Expressway. Molly slept while Nick's truck roared
like a beast, too loud for me to hear my own mind. I floored the
pedal, surging ahead, slowing down for no one.

Time hung suspended; distance was its only measure.
Snowflakes swirled against the windshield, dissolving into
droplets, getting wiped away. Wheels spun furiously under us
while Molly and I sat motionless, waiting for the monotonous,
interchangeable scenes out the window to pass, replaced by
images of our destination. Of home. From now on, I'd rely on
nobody, let no one too close. It would be just me and Molly.
Molly and me. We were our whole family, didn't need anyone
else.

At last, the Vine Street Expressway. At Sixth, I turned off and
plowed south, literally. Not much traffic, due to the snow. A few
pedestrians, up to their knees. Arch, JFK, Market, Chestnut,
Walnut. I pressed on steadily, unstoppably, toward our street,
inch by inch, block by block.

Finally, we approached our street. Everything was quiet,
coated with white. Construction vehicles, cars, and vans lay
buried, lifeless under mounds of snow. Behind Mr. Woods's
snow-blocked window, Santa throbbed like a painful wound; in

Victor's upstairs window, the blinds were shut tight but oddly askew. Charlie's house looked mournful, drooping yellow tape separating it from the street, snow hanging heavily on its roof. The street seemed off balance and bruised, but even so, I was glad to be there. We were home.

I hadn't thought of parking when I'd taken the truck. Finding a spot wouldn't be easy. Except that I was driving a damn snowplow. No one would argue with a double-parked snowplow. Not today. I parked alongside one of Jake's trucks and woke up Molly.

"Mollybear, we're home."

She opened her eyes, blinked, and looked around. I gathered our bags and went around the truck to help her out. When I came around and opened her door, she was busy with her tooth.

"Hop out," I said.

"Huh-uh." She shook her head, still wiggling.

"Come on, Molly, let's—"

"Aach!" Eyes wide, Molly held out a tiny, blood-coated kernel. "Your tooth!"

She grinned, revealing a blank space in her ravaged gums. Blood trickled along her fingers and over her teeth. As she noticed, her chin began to wobble; her eyes filled with alarm.

"It's okay—you'll be fine." I kissed her, then searched for some white snow and packed a snowball. "Try this. Press it onto your gum."

"Bite it?"

"Yup."

"It'll get all bloody."

"It'll stop the bleeding." We traded. She took the snowball, and I took her first lost tooth and placed it safely in a tissue in my pocket. Then I reached out to lift her out of the cab. Just then, Phillip Woods's door swung open. I expected to see him emerge with a shovel or a snow blower, prepared to clear his front walk.

Instead, dressed in knee-high boots and a red sheared-beaver coat, her long brunette hair loose and blowing in the wind, Beverly Gardener stepped onto the porch and marched up the street, cutting her way through the snow.

FIFTY-SEVEN

WE FOLLOWED HER.

"Get back in," I told Molly and closed the door before she could take the snowball out of her mouth to ask a question. I went around to the driver's side and climbed into the cab. Without thinking. Without quite knowing why.

"Why aren't we getting out?" Molly asked. The snowball was melting, dripping in her hands.

"Here, open the window. Throw that out. It stopped bleeding, I think." I started the engine.

"Where are we going?"

"I'm not sure—I want to see where that lady's going."

She cranked down her window and threw out the mushy snow. "Why? Who is she?"

"Someone from work. I want to know what she was doing at Mr. Woods's house."

"But I want to go home—"

"We will. Soon."

That seemed to satisfy her.

"And can we make pancakes?"

"We'll see." When Beverly was a few houses up the block, certain that she hadn't seen me, I started driving, staying half a block behind.

What would I do if she saw us? Confront her? Demand to know the truth about her relationship with Woods? With Nick?

If she didn't see us, how long would I follow her? Would I lurk with Molly indefinitely outside her condo? Or in front of a store if she went shopping? And what if she was meeting Nick?

I didn't know. I didn't care. I was ready to take both Nick and Beverly on and make a fool of myself, even in front of Molly. I kept going. At Sixth Street, she walked north. Damn. Sixth was one-way south. I couldn't follow. I pulled over and watched her. And saw her get into the driver's seat of Nick's old Volvo, parked halfway up the block.

FIFTY-EIGHT

I WATCHED FROM THE INTERSECTION AS THE VOLVO STRUGGLED out of its parking spot. It pushed through snow and made its way right past us. I waited until the car was a few houses down, then lowered the plow and followed, shoving snow aside, blocking driveways and walling in cars as I went. Where was she heading? At Bainbridge, she turned left, progressing at a slow but steady pace to Fifth, where she turned left again and went north, crossing Lombard, Pine, Spruce, Walnut. When she got to Market, she made another left. Gradually, as she crossed Broad Street and continued west toward Thirtieth Street Station, I recognized the route. We were on the way to work.

The Institute parking lot was only half plowed and nearly empty; it was the weekend, and undoubtedly the blizzard had kept everyone but essential staff away. Weekend visiting hours wouldn't begin until three, not for hours. Beverly Gardener pulled into a spot in the plowed part of the lot and headed inside. Was Nick waiting in her office? Sleeping on her lush leather sofa? I envisioned his bare chest. Stop it, I told myself. Think about what you're doing.

I knew what I was doing. I was setting myself up for a full-blown emotional catastrophe by confronting Nick and Beverly together, at my place of employment, with my daughter by my side. I was about to humiliate myself beyond my wildest imaginings, but I didn't care. I felt good. Righteous. Ready for high drama. Catharsis. It would be cleansing, better than throwing up.

Even so, I thought better of subjecting Molly to the spectacle. She'd stay with the security guard in the foyer for a few minutes. I wouldn't be gone long.

After Beverly went in, I waited a few seconds to give her time to clear the foyer. I didn't want her to see me, not yet. When I thought she'd made it to the hall, I pulled up to the front door, took Molly out of the truck, and led her into the Institute.

But the foyer was empty. Where was the security guard— what was his name—Reginald? Something like that. He was on duty during the quiet shifts on weekends, covering Agnes's reception desk until afternoon visiting hours. Why wasn't he there? What was I going to do with Molly?

We walked toward the desk, past the monstrous, glittering tree. Rufus—was that his name? Rufus must have gone on a coffee break. Probably he'd be right back. We kept walking, passing his desk. The nameplate read RUPERT SIMPSON. That was it: Rupert. Well, Rupert still wasn't there. I'd have to take Molly with me. Maybe it would be better that way; with Molly along, I'd have to behave myself.

"Where are we going, Mommy?"

"I'm not sure."

I looked up the main corridors, past empty offices, bulletin boards, water fountains. Which way had Beverly gone? Where was she? I looked, listened for footsteps. Heard, saw nothing.

"I want to go home."

"I know. Soon."

"I don't like it here."

"Why not?"

"I just don't. Where's your art studio?"

"Over that way."

Molly kept chattering, and I answered her automatically,

without thought, trying to figure out what to do. Up the middle corridor, the empty elevator opened, then closed; someone had pressed the button. Beverly? We followed the sound, heading toward the elevator, and Molly finally stopped talking. We passed locked office doors, heard and saw no one. Not one nurse or an orderly. Not a single staff member. I stopped and listened, heard only the echo of our own steps.

Of course, I reasoned, it was too early for visitors. And the blizzard had probably reduced the staff. A few doctors on call would straggle in later. Silence was not necessarily an indication of trouble. Still, the quiet was unsettling. Unnerving. Then I saw Rupert, sitting on a bench across the hall. What was he doing? Waiting for the elevator?

I nodded at him. He didn't respond. He sat slouched, staring at his lap. "Rupert?" I asked. "You all right?"

No answer. Amazing. The man was dozing, napping on the job. Should I wake him up? Embarrass him? Molly let go of my hand and pushed the elevator button. "Are we going up, Mommy?"

Were we? Suddenly I thought we should leave. I'd followed Beverly on impulse, but I'd been exhausted and bitter, not making good decisions. "No. I don't think so."

"Down?"

"No."

"Then where?"

Being there felt stupid, foolish. Not worth the effort. And Molly shouldn't have to watch me confronting Beverly. We needed to leave. To go home before I caused a disaster.

The elevator rattled somewhere in the shaft. The bell dinged, doors rolled opened and shut. Who'd gotten in? Nick? Beverly? I didn't know. But it wasn't my business. I was getting overheated in my jacket; sweat rolled down my midriff. Time to go.

"Come on, Molly." I took her hand and crossed the hall, eyeing

Rupert. A ding announced the arriving elevator car. I glanced back. The door slid open, revealing Beverly Gardener. She'd removed her fur jacket. Taking her time, she smoothed her hair, adjusted her glasses.

"Mommy, there's the lady!" Molly announced.

"That's okay—"

Too late. Beverly looked up, pausing and squinting at us through tortoiseshell frames. Our eyes met, locked, and froze. And suddenly I remembered: Beverly Gardener didn't wear glasses.

Phillip Woods did, though. And he fit snugly into Beverly Gardener's clothes. His mouth opened. He froze, surprised. I grabbed Molly's hand and called to Rupert, but Rupert didn't wake up, didn't even stir. I hurried over to him, noticing only now the blood smeared on the wall behind him, the dark stain on the shoulder of his uniform. Molly was saying something, but I didn't hear what. I was pulling her across the hall, dragging her into the staircase. As the stairway door swung shut behind us, I looked back and saw Phillip Woods sneering at us while the elevator snapped shut on his high-heeled leather boot.

FIFTY-NINE

Woods? Phillip Woods? dressed as Beverly Gardener. Suddenly I understood. Beverly Gardener hadn't been visiting Woods; Woods himself had left his house, dressed as Beverly Gardener. And Rupert, the security guard, was dead. Murdered. Rupert must have noticed something odd about Dr. Gardener. Maybe he'd confronted her. Was that why Woods killed him? I thought of Charlie, his warning that the killer wore disguises. I could almost hear his hoarse whisper, "Trust nobody," as I tugged on Molly's hand.

"Mommy," Molly huffed. "Why are we running? Where are we going?"

Where were we going? Good question. What was I doing? I stopped dragging her. We stood panting on the landing below the third floor.

"Why are we running away from that lady? You said we were trying to find her."

I could hear the elevator rising in the shaft. Was Woods in there, riding up ahead of us? We shouldn't go up, had to go down.

"Molly, I can't explain everything now, okay? I'm sorry. I goofed up. Just come with me. We're going back downstairs."

Pivoting, reversing our steps, we went down, down, around. A few times I stopped, leaned over the railing, and looked up, half expecting to see spectacles and a lipsticked smirk looking down at us. But no one was there. We made it to the first floor and headed for the door. But I stopped, my hand on the knob. Was Woods out there? Maybe he hadn't gone up in the elevator but had waited in the hall, outside the door. I turned away. Molly and I kept going down.

The door to the basement opened to shadows, doorways, corridors branching off in all directions. The Institute maze, silent and empty. No Woods. Nobody at all.

The door squeaked; the sound ricocheted off the walls. I pressed on, clutching Molly's hand.

"Where are we going, Mommy?"

"Shh," I whispered. "We have to be quiet."

"Why? I don't want to be quiet. I want to go home." She stamped her foot.

"Molly." I stopped walking and knelt, meeting her eyes. "It's important that we keep our voices down. Try not to talk. I'll explain later, okay?"

"Now—tell me now. I don't like it here. Let's go." Her whisper was louder than her voice had been.

"Soon, I promise. But first, I need you to help by being quiet. Like a mouse."

She nodded, but she was running out of patience. I kissed her forehead and stood, wondering how long it would be before Woods figured out where we were. Then it hit me: If the person I'd been following was Woods, where was Beverly? On the phone, she'd said she'd be here, at the Institute. She might be here still. We'd go to her office, find her, and call for help. Great. Good plan. But I had to remember where her office was. What was the number? 35? No—37. I remembered finding her note there. And Phillip Woods, pacing in the waiting area, frantic to find her. Claiming to be her friend. Damn. Was he going to her office now? Or already there? I could feel him hunting, waiting in ambush. Oh, where was number 37? The door beside us was 12. Not too far from 37. But we had to get out of the main corridor, out of sight of the elevator and the stairway. We ducked into a side passageway and waited. Molly began a question, but I cut her off, pressing a finger to my lips, reminding her to be quiet. I listened, peering into the hall behind me. Seeing nobody.

"Are we hiding from the lady?" Molly whispered.

When I nodded, her eyes widened, and her grip tightened on my hand.

Somewhere behind us, a door closed. Footsteps clacked along the floor. We hurried away from the sound, turning into a dead end. I tried a doorknob. Locked. Of course it was locked. We turned back, and I peeked around the corner. The footsteps continued, softly, steadily. I led Molly around the corner, down the hall, and turned again to keep out of sight.

"Mommy, I'm scared." Molly's whisper was hushed, frightened.

I stopped and leaned down. Her eyes were wide, doelike. How had I gotten us into this mess?

"Don't be scared, Mollybear. Help me find room number thirty-seven. We might get help there."

Her chin wobbled, but she nodded, looking at doors. Backed against the wall, I stood still and listened. The footsteps persisted, muffled and distant. The office across from me was number 49. Damn. We had to go back. Toward the footsteps.

I told myself to be calm. Breathing deeply, I recalled Rupert's back bathed in blood. Oh God. Where was Nick? Had Woods found him with Beverly? Who was coming down the hall?

A lone lightbulb glowed dully in the ceiling as we cowered and crept through the dingy basement. Shadows flickered in the dim light; footsteps echoed from all directions, or maybe from none at all.

I thought of what would happen to Molly if Woods caught up with us, and told myself to stay focused. Molly reminded me that 53 was higher than 51. That we should turn around, go the other way. Yes—49, 47. Fabulous. Another division, a fork in the hall. Which way to go, left or right? Somewhere behind or off to the left of us, footsteps paused. Was Woods listening? Deciding which way to go? We went left. And, bingo! 37. The door announced, with boldface block letters, DR. BEVERLY GARDENER. We'd made it. I looked across the hall, checking the waiting area. Woods wasn't there. He wasn't in the alcove, waiting. Not this time. No. But oh my God. This time, Nick was.

SIXTY

THE WAIL WAS UNEXPECTED. DEEP, WRENCHING, IT ERUPTED from my belly. I stood frozen, staring at Nick's unmoving form. Eventually I managed to take a breath, then another. But I still couldn't move. Maybe it was Nick's stillness, his unnatural position. Or maybe the crimson liquid clotting on his head.

Then I remembered—Molly—Molly was there with me, her small hand still in mine. I looked at her, saw the mirror of my own scream frozen on her face.

"Molly," I heard my voice urge. Other than her name, I couldn't manage to make words. She was trembling, swallowing air.

I stroked Molly's face, telling her to breathe. Nick's face was in my hands, a bad shade of gray, lips apart, head slumped and bloody. So very bloody. Then my hand was under Nick's jacket, where he was still warm, still familiar. My fingers, lingering, trying to smooth and caress death away. But Nick didn't stir.

The office, a voice in my head said, go into the office. But my legs were numb and useless. I knelt beside him, holding my breath, listening to his chest for a heartbeat, but hearing only the whisper of passing time. Molly's face was covered with tears, and I wiped them away, smearing blood across her cheeks. Blood? Oh God. Nick's blood, from my fingers. What was I doing? I had to take Molly away, not let her see this.

"Get up, Nick," I heard myself say, and Molly echoed, "Get

up, Nick." I grabbed him under the arms, reached around him, and pulled. Molly helped, tugging at him. His torso came up, but his head flopped backward. We couldn't move him. He was dead weight. Suddenly, from somewhere, leather soles clacked on linoleum. Someone walking. A guard? Or Woods? How long had we been there, tugging on Nick?

Molly looked at me, alarmed. I took her hand, reassuring her.

"Mommy, let's go." Molly pulled at me, whimpering.

The footsteps were coming our way. I let go of Nick's hand and hurried Molly across the hall. We'd get into Beverly's office and call for help. The police. An ambulance.

The door should have been locked, but it wasn't. The footsteps came nearer, became more distinct. Any second, Woods would pop around the corner. Show up down the hall.

We ducked into the office. Close the door, a voice whispered. Lock it and call the police.

But before I did, in the alcove, someone moved. Woods? I quickly closed the door, just glimpsing Nick as he slid sideways, keeled over, and crumpled onto the floor.

SIXTY-ONE

I LOCKED THE DOOR AND HUGGED MOLLY, AND SHE HELD ON to my sleeve as I made my way across the office to find the phone. An outdoor security light cast dim beams through the window; even so, I stumbled on loose papers, tripped on the back of a chair. An overturned chair. Righting it, I told Molly to sit down, but she wouldn't let go of me, hung on for her life. Together, we inched our way past the leather sofa and made it to the desk. My hand found Beverly's big desk chair and swung it around. I reached for the phone and sat down—and jumped right back up. Molly leaped onto me, clutching me so that I couldn't see or move. Finally, holding her, I turned around slowly, dreading what I'd see. Sure enough. I hadn't sat on a leather chair. I'd sat on Beverly Gardener.

SIXTY-TWO

I SET MOLLY DOWN AND TRIED TO COMFORT HER. "MOLLY." I
hugged her, whispered in her ear. "I'm going to call for help."
She nodded, speechless, and stood beside me, clinging, her
head buried in my side, her entire body shaking. I trembled,
too, cemented to the floor.

"Beverly?" I managed. She didn't answer. I stuck out a finger
and touched her arm. Her skin was cold. Well, it was December.
She wore only a bra and panties; of course she'd be cold. That
didn't mean she was dead. I poked her again, harder. Her head
lolled off to the side, and with a sense of dread I noticed a stock-
ing hanging around her neck. Pulse, I thought. Check her pulse.
My hands were unsteady; I couldn't feel anything but Molly's
trembling. Was Beverly breathing? I put my finger under her
nose, thought I felt the slightest tickle of warm air.

I followed my instincts and gently lowered her off the chair
onto the floor. It wasn't easy, with Molly hanging around my
waist, but I managed. Beverly didn't make a sound. I listened at
her chest, felt her breasts against my head. Was that my heartbeat or hers? I covered her with my jacket, got up. I had to use
the phone. Quickly.

Beverly's desk was a mess. Drawers hung open, and files lay all
over the floor. Move, I told myself. Just call the police. I guided
Molly, stepping around Beverly, and picked up the phone.

9-1-1. Nothing happened. No ringing. Then I remembered:

the outside line. To get an outside line, I'd need to dial 9; all I'd actually dialed was 1-1. I started over, pushed the button: 9. Good. A dial tone.

Now another 9. Now a 1.

Footsteps. Very close, approaching the door. Then they stopped. A silhouette with shoulder-length hair darkened the frosted glass window near the top of the door. I pulled Molly down and we crouched, huddling under the desk. Where was the damned 1 button? In the dark under the desk, my arms around Molly, I felt the phone buttons, pushed what I thought was the right one.

He was trying keys. How did he have Beverly's keys? I heard a jangle, then the thrust of metal. He was turning the knob, jig-gling, twisting it. Trying another key. Then another. In a second, he'd be in. Another key. Another. Then a violent metallic slam. Under the desk, I curled over Molly, felt her terror, and tried to fade into mahogany.

Silence. Had Woods given up? Thrown the key ring against the door?

Why hadn't any of the keys worked? If they weren't Beverly's, whose keys did Woods have? Who would have keys? In the darkness, I remembered the key ring dangling from Rupert's belt. Of course. Woods had taken Rupert's keys.

Suddenly there was an ear-shattering bang. Molly flew against me. The door shook. Woods was ramming, shoving, slamming his body against the door. Someone was talking, repeating him-self, offering help. Not Charlie, not the guard. A real voice. Where? Who was it? I looked around, then remembered. The phone. The voice was on the phone. I snapped to attention, breathless. My voice scraped raw, trembled, tasted like acid. But I heard it gasp what needed to be said. Even that the guard in the downstairs hall was dead.

SIXTY-THREE

HE'D STOPPED BATTERING. I HEARD NOTHING BUT MOLLY'S rapid breathing. No footsteps, no sound at all. Had he given up? Gone to get an ax? Where was he? Sitting outside the door?

The operator told us to stay where we were. Good advice, since there was no way out except past Woods. The police could not possibly come in time, not nearly in time. Nick lay lifeless in the alcove, Beverly beside us on the floor. There was only one door. Beverly's desk sat somber and morose, offering nothing. No pens or pencils. No letter openers. No scissors. Just a Tiffany lamp, a briefcase, and a vase of wilting lilies.

But the briefcase—maybe Beverly kept Mace in there. Or a small jewel-handled revolver? I picked up the case and clicked it open. The light was dim, but I knew right away that nothing in the briefcase could help us. Just files. Radio scripts. And a folder labeled in big block letters: PHILLIP WOODS 302.

Now, I was only an art therapist, but, working at the Institute, I'd often heard the term. A 302 was the provision that gave the state permission to commit a person without his consent if he was a danger to himself or others. The Institute housed a number of people who'd come there through 302s. And it seemed Beverly Gardener had prepared the documents for Phillip Woods to join them.

"I'm just getting a light," I told Molly. Then, quickly, I reached up and pulled the lamp down under the desk. I turned it on and saw the fear on Molly's face subside a little with the light. Holding her against me, I scanned the papers in the file. Copies of police reports, of a restraining order—and a lengthy harassment complaint Beverly had filed with the police. Nick's name was at the top. Had he taken her complaint? Why was a homicide detective involved in a harassment case? Obviously, because he had a special relationship with the complainant. And that was why they'd met last night—to fill out the 302, stating that Phillip Woods had become a danger to himself or others. I looked out at Beverly's bare, outstretched legs. An immediate, imminent danger.

I skimmed the complaint. The incidents started with fan letters and e-mails. Then phone calls, physical visits, stalking. Then threats. Beverly obtained a restraining order, but Woods ignored it. An attachment indicated that restraining orders had been placed against Phillip Woods in the past decade by others: author Susan Erstine, violinist Erica Olsen, and local newscaster Deirdre Bogarth. When Beverly Gardener had confronted Woods and insisted he leave her alone, Woods said that she had no authority to insist on anything, that she was obviously an impostor, not actually Beverly Gardener at all. He threatened to expose her, said that he'd dealt with impostors like her before and that she could easily "meet the same fate as the others." She took this to mean that Woods was irrational and intending her grave harm.

Attached to this last page was a Post-it. "Nick: Impostors = those who act as others. Woods has problem with impostors. 'Deals' with them. Nannies = impostor mothers ⇒ Could Nanny-napper be Woods?"

SIXTY-FOUR

"COULD NANNYNAPPER BE WOODS?"

Beverly thought Phillip Woods was the Nannynapper. Phillip Woods. Not Charlie. I thought back to the profile. What had she said? The killer might believe he was doing something good by killing, maybe righting a wrong? Had Woods seen his victims as impostors? Fakes? Mother impersonators who, in his mind, needed to be eliminated? But why? It made no sense.

I huddled under the desk, trying to put pieces together that didn't seem to fit. All I knew for sure was that Beverly Gardener had been stalked and threatened by Woods. She'd gone to Nick for help, and they'd arranged to go for a 302. Woods was out of control; it couldn't wait. Nick hadn't wanted Molly or me in the neighborhood in case things got out of hand, so he'd left us at his place where we'd be safe. But why the secrecy? Why not just explain? Of course, I knew why. Nick was why. Nick would reveal only what he needed to, nothing else, not one fact more. Never the whole picture. Never one more detail than he absolutely had to. Dammit, Nick, I thought. Why couldn't you trust me?

Furniture scraped the floor out in the waiting area. Woods was back. I held Molly, warned her to be quiet, and snapped off the lamp. Any minute, any second, he'd come bursting through the door, breaking the frame or throwing a chair through the glass at the top. No more time to think or read. I had to find a weapon, something to defend us with. Beverly lay limp, offering no suggestions, no advice.

I chewed my lip, clung to Molly, and looked from the door to the coat closet to the file cabinet to the window. The window. It was level with the top of my head. The kind that pushes open. If I could get us up there, we might be able to slither through. It was a chance.

Something was scraping, scratching at the door. Was he trying to file away the lock? The scratching stopped, and for the moment everything was quiet again.

"Molly," I whispered and pointed to the window. I gestured, showing her what I was going to do. She nodded, eyes wide, and let go of me. I moved the desk chair, climbed up on it, and pulled at the window. It resisted, wouldn't give. I found the clasp, which was old and rusted and promised that it hadn't been unlocked in decades, but I pushed and turned anyway, trying to unlock it. Damn. My fingers slipped, and I saw flashes of white as pain slashed my fingertips. I'd torn a nail, and blood seeped under it, pulsing. But there was no time for cursing. I tried again, grabbing the clasp firmly, tugging at it slowly, steadily, with all the weight of my shoulders and torso. Finally, in slow motion, it gave. I turned the handle, pushed, and the window opened outward. Frigid wind slapped my face.

There was a crash at the door. The sound of something large butting the solid wood. Molly jumped up and ran to me.

I pulled her up onto the chair with me. The window looked very tiny. The door shook. I reached up, lifting Molly up to the windowsill. I pushed; she scooted and was out. I tried to follow. I grabbed the frame and tugged. No way. I was too bulky, too big to fit through. Another crash at the door. And another. I ripped off my sweatshirt and threw it out into the snow. I was thinner now, but not much. Woods rammed the door again and again. The top hinge burst. A few seconds and he'd be in. I had no time.

SIXTY-FIVE

GRASPING THE FRAME, I PULLED MYSELF UP. THE WINDOWSILL scraped my breasts, then my belly as I squeezed over it, barely fitting through. Molly grabbed my head and pulled. The palms of my hands stuck to frozen metal and my fingers burned, then throbbed. But I slid, slithered, and kicked, bruising my knees and my shins, clawing ice until finally, with Molly's help, I landed on my face in the snow.

As I reached back to close the window, I heard the shattering of glass. An arm in a pink mohair sweater reached down through a jagged hole in the glazed pane where Beverly's name had been, feeling for the bolt. I pulled Molly away from the window and we hunkered against the wall, shivering in merciless cold. I put on my sweatshirt and tried to get my bearings.

The fence closed us in. We were boxed in by three walls of brick and one of wire, barbed at the top, and higher than we could hope to climb.

Behind us, I heard Woods rummaging around in Beverly's office. I thought he'd see my jacket on Beverly, notice the chair beneath the open window, and come charging after us. But he didn't. The shattering and crashing were followed by sounds of papers shuffling. And wind blowing. I crouched beside the window, holding on to Molly, afraid to move. From where I sat, I was able to see only a few square feet of the office, the small part of the floor between the desk and the window. What was he doing? I didn't dare lean over to see more, couldn't risk being discovered. But I pictured Woods at the desk, looking around. Was it possible that he hadn't noticed my jacket? Or the open window?

I released a breath and looked at Molly, who was bug-eyed and silent, her teeth chattering. Inside the office, drawers slammed. Papers and manila folders flew across the slice of desk I could see. Files and patient records landed on the floor. What was he looking for? Then I knew: the 302. Woods was searching for the documents Beverly had prepared for his commitment. Even if he'd silenced Nick and Beverly, the paperwork could still speak. It would incriminate him. Unless he destroyed it.

I hugged Molly and the wall, listening, waiting for Woods to find the open briefcase under the desk. Then there was an audible pause. A silence. Then footsteps clacked beside the desk. The desk near the window. The open window. Beside which we huddled, shivering in the snow.

SIXTY-SIX

I DIDN'T DARE LOOK. I HELD MY BREATH, SQUEEZING MOLLY. Had Woods seen the window? Noticed the chair beneath it? I waited, expecting him to pop out after us. But he didn't. Maybe he was so intent on finding the papers that he couldn't notice anything else. Or maybe not.

I looked around the courtyard, up at the windows. Maybe someone would look out, see us, and get help. Or maybe the police would come to the rescue and find us before we froze to death.

Maybe. But neither was likely. I had to get us out of there myself. Fast.

The fence offered no advice. Its barbs snarled. The brown brick walls yawned, old and indifferent. Molly's whole body was shaking. I rubbed her legs and arms with icy hands.

"Here. Stand here," I whispered, pressing her against the wall, sheltering her from the wind with my body. Distraught, desperate, I leaned my head back, closed my eyes, and tried to think. No luck. No inspiration. When I opened my eyes, I saw a window just above us, on the first or second floor. It was half open, smiling a half smile. Mocking? Or inviting? It didn't matter. Either way, it was too high. I stood on my toes and reached up. The open window was about two feet beyond my grasp. Not quite close enough.

"Molly, help me. Make a hill."

She didn't say a word. Didn't ask a question. Jaw rattling, she knelt beside me, depositing snow in a pile. Quietly, quickly, we used our arms to plow snow into a mound against the wall. My hands were frozen, burning, numb; Molly's must be, too. Frozen or not, we shoved piles of snow against the building, packing it down into a solid hill. I raced, afraid Woods would turn and look outside, alarmed by the commotion of snow or the huffing of breath.

In seconds, we'd built a small mountain of snow, adding the two feet I needed to reach the open window. I stepped onto it and looked up. Molly watched, silent and pale. The only sound was the wind. On my toes again, I reached numb fingers up and touched the windowsill. If I could lift Molly up, she could slide inside.

"Molly," I whispered, "I'll lift you. Then boost yourself up through the window. As if you're at gym, swinging up onto the high bar. Got it?"

She nodded.

"Ready?"

She nodded again. Nick's blood had crusted on her cheeks, and her skin was fading, becoming colorless. I grabbed her, hefted her up over my head. Too fast. Too much momentum. Something—maybe her head—thunked the wall.

"Oh God. Sorry—Molly? You okay?"

She made no sound, didn't cry out, said nothing. I could feel her regaining her balance, though. She didn't weigh even fifty pounds, but holding her up over my head with numb hands wasn't easy. "Can you reach it?" I whispered.

She didn't answer, but suddenly her legs kicked my shoulders, pushing off, and her weight lifted as she sprang upward, knocking me backward into the snow. Looking up, I saw her hips disappear over the windowsill, feet flying behind her through the opening. Just like in gymnastics. She was in.

My turn. I got up, brushed myself off, stood against the wall, reached up, puffed and cursed. I could reach the windowsill, even grab it, but hanging there, I couldn't get leverage to lift myself. I'd need to build up the snow, make the hill higher. I let go and dropped to the ground, banging the drainpipe as I fell. Damn. Had Woods heard?

I stood still, listening, hearing footsteps. The scraping of a chair. A dark wig appeared at the window. A hand, a pink sleeve reached out. Woods had heard, yes. And he was climbing out.

SIXTY-SEVEN

I DIDN'T DARE LOOK AT HIM. TERRIFIED, I LOOKED AROUND, searching for an escape. But there was none. Only brick walls. Desperately, I eyed the drainpipe, the wall, the window above, and knew what I had to do.

Thrusting my foot up, I secured my boot between the drainpipe and the bricks, then grabbed a hunk of metal and lifted myself. My already frozen skin stuck to the pipe and tore as I reached higher, grabbing another handful of icy steel. Hands ripped and bleeding, I boosted my way up, hand over hand. I dug one boot, then the other between wall and pipe, pushing with my thighs, sliding higher, climbing brick by brick. I didn't dare look back, certain that Woods would grab me. Then, finally, my raw fingers slid across the windowsill, and my hips thrust upward, lifting with astonishing ease. My arms extended outward, grabbed the inside ledge, pulled, and smoothly, weightlessly, my body followed upward, slithered inward. Serpentlike, I slipped to the floor. Snow-blind, I felt Molly crouching beside me, watching, not saying a word.

For a moment, I lay next to her, curled on linoleum, catching my breath, letting the air warm me. We'd made it. We were inside. When I could move, I took Molly's face in my bleeding hands, kissed her, asked if she was okay. She nodded, but even snow-blind I could see that she looked awful. Above the smears of blood and tears, a purple bump was rising on her forehead where she'd hit the bricks. She needed ice. And a warm bath. And home. I had to get us out of there.

Helping her up, I got to my feet. With bleeding hands, I slammed the window shut and locked it, looking out into the courtyard.

Woods was nowhere in sight.

SIXTY-EIGHT

AS MY EYES ADJUSTED TO THE DIM LIGHT, I SQUINTED AND SAW, among dancing dots and flashing sparks, a dresser, a hospital bed, and a metal nightstand with a vase of wilting black-eyed Susans. To the left was an easy chair, occupied by a plump, gray-haired woman in a yellow terrycloth robe and matching fake fur mules. She was eating breakfast.

We were in a patient's room, somewhere in the back of the first floor.

"Oh my. Excuse us," I breathed.

"The food's not bad," she answered. "Except on Mondays."

"Do you have a phone?" I knew, as I asked it, that she didn't. Of course she didn't. This was a mental hospital. "Or a way to call for a nurse? A button?"

"Help yourself," she nodded agreeably. "Take all you want."

My arms and shoulders ached, hands stung, thawing. I wiped away blood with tissues from the woman's nightstand and led Molly to the door. But I didn't open it; Woods might be out there, waiting. The man was slight, but he'd overpowered Nick and Beverly, had killed a burly guard and maybe five women younger and stronger than I was. I stood with my hand on the doorknob, listening. It was only a matter of time, maybe seconds, until he'd find us. There was no choice.

"Molly," I told her. "That lady with the long dark hair? She's dangerous. The police are coming soon, and they'll find her. But until then, we have to keep away from her. So if anything happens—if she gets close to you, run fast and get away. Understand?"

Another nod. Another silent, alarming nod.

I squeezed her one more time, then turned the knob and inched the door open, looking up and down the hall. As we stepped out, before the door closed, the woman stated, "Monday's hash. Everything from the whole week, all mashed together."

SIXTY-NINE

HER ROOM WAS ON THE FIRST FLOOR. I WORKED ON THAT floor, knew it well. It had wider, brighter halls than the basement, and a less intricate layout. Woods would probably take the closest, most accessible stairway, the one nearest the foyer. He'd wait there for us to try for the front door. I rushed Molly to a smaller staircase at the far end of the corridor. There would be a fire exit there. We could get out. I hurried my daughter down the hall, pulled the heavy door open, crossed to the exit, and threw myself against it. It didn't budge. It was locked.

But we couldn't go back out the stairwell door; we'd run into Woods in the hall. Unless he was still downstairs. I stood still, holding Molly's hand, debating which way to go. Out? Down? Finally, I decided. We'd cross the building upstairs. We went up to the second-floor landing, stopped, and listened at the door. No footsteps, no voices. No Woods. Why was it so quiet? Where was everybody? A pipe clanked somewhere, maybe a heater. Nothing else. No sounds of patients or staff, no meal trays, no music. Maybe this was normal after a blizzard. Maybe weekends were always sluggish and dull. Or maybe something had happened to quiet everyone. I couldn't figure it out, didn't have time to. We had to keep moving.

Holding my breath, I led Molly out of the stairway and oriented myself. We were down the hall from the locked partition that separated the violent patients in Section 5 from the rest of the Institute. Surely there would be help in Section 5. We hurried along to the partition door where someone would buzz me in. But no one had to. The steel partition door hung wide open. Unlocked.

Woods. He had been there. Or might be there now. He must have used the guard's keys and unlocked the high-security area.

But why would he unlock the door? Didn't he know that these patients were dangerous? If they wandered out, who knew what might happen? A voice in my head whispered, "That's just the point."

Of course. Woods wanted the violent patients to escape. He wanted them to scatter all over the place—in every alcove, conference room and corridor—so it would look like they had stolen the keys, attacked Nick and Beverly, killed the guard, rifled through papers, vandalized offices. With chaos like that, no one would ask questions or look further for explanations.

Unless there happened to be witnesses.

I held on to Molly, not sure whether to go forward or back. The nursing station was close, a hundred feet away. There were phones there. And, with any luck, nurses. And staff.

Warily, we stepped through the security door into the territory of violent patients. Patients with dangerous, unpredictable behavior. Like Evie Kraus. I listened, hoping to hear her singing. But I heard nothing. Nobody seemed to be around. Where was everyone? The staff? Had the patients already gotten out? We headed toward the nursing station. The floor gleamed, reflecting hazy light. But nothing moved. We passed patient rooms, a kitchenette, a shower, a linen closet. We were approaching the nursing station when a wiry brunette rushed out at us. Her stride was swift and confident; I recognized her spectacles, her high, glossy boots. I yanked Molly's hand and veered across the hall an arm's length ahead, barely glimpsing the thin, shiny object slipping from the brunette's pink sleeve. I sprinted forward, dragging Molly, glancing behind us. The brunette swung her arms out and pounced, catlike. Pain ripped through my back; I let go of Molly's hand and heard myself tell her to run out to the hall. The way we'd come.

I whirled around to show her, trying to go with her. But the hallway lost definition. The brunette, the walls, the doorways—everything blurred and darkened. Hot pain hissed, slid under my ribs to my lungs. Charlie shouted something as my legs buckled and stuck to the floor, and pain opened its fangs and swallowed me. I sank, thudding beside the black boots, fading. I thought of Molly, heard a sweet voice call, "Mommy!" and, looking up, saw small feet scampering away, disappearing through an open door.

SEVENTY

THE BLACK HIGH-HEELED BOOTS DIDN'T MOVE RIGHT AWAY. I lay on the floor, looking at them, trying to focus. Woods's spectacled face emerged, painted with red lipstick. The dark brown wig was now askew, sitting like a nesting bird atop his head. He adjusted it and peered down at me. I tried to speak, but, unable to find any part of my body that made words, I decided that I must be dying, if not already dead. Apparently, Woods shared that opinion; he walked off, checking his sweater for something, probably blood.

The corridor was silent. I lay there, unable to move, watching the walls wobble and sway. Molly was my only thought, my only care. I couldn't let Woods catch her, had to stop him. I listened for her voice, heard nothing. Not a sound. Why? My thoughts blurred. Move, I told myself. My body didn't know how. Nerves had shut down, disconnected from muscles; muscles couldn't respond. Had Woods severed my spinal cord? Was I paralyzed? Warm liquid pooled under me, and breathing was difficult. Inhaling was excruciating, took all my energy. But I was still breathing. That meant I was alive. And if I felt pain, some of my nerves must be alive, too. In that case, I should be able to move. To find help.

Slowly, with monumental effort, I managed to turn my neck, move my head to see the hallway better. Images pulsed unsteadily, but I strained my neck so I could see ahead. I pressed my shoulders against the floor and repositioned my head. I'd never been very aware of the floor, never paid attention to it. Now the floor seemed fascinating. Solid. Dependable. And very strong. I lay against it, letting it support me, realizing that it was my friend. It would help me. If I pressed one arm against it and rocked the opposite way, I'd be able to push off against it and roll onto my stomach. If I had the strength. I thought of Woods and Molly, closed my eyes, and pushed. Pressing and rocking, I began moving slightly from side to side.

I rocked from side to side until I had momentum. Then I pushed, gasped, gave a wrenching shove, and rolled over onto my stomach. Pain blinded me. Were the lights dimming, or was I passing out? I couldn't pass out, had to stay awake. Get help. Find Molly. I waited for the pain to ease, heard only my own panting, no footsteps, no screams, no struggles. Grimacing, I bent my knees one at a time, lifted my hips, hoisted myself up with my elbows, and pushed forward, inching my way ahead. Finally the steel door was within a few steps. I pushed myself up, slipped, hit my head. Landed on my face. I lay there, face on cold linoleum, and knew I couldn't make it. I wouldn't be able to get help. I'd just about given up, accepting the fact that I would die, when I reached my arm out and touched cool steel. The security door. I'd made it this far, couldn't stop now. I pushed ahead again, reached out another time—and froze, afraid to look at what my hand had found. I lay there, gathering the strength to raise my head and find out whose arm I'd grabbed. Finally, drawing a breath, I craned my neck.

Evie Kraus was wearing a bright blue sweatsuit. Crouched against the wall, she'd begun to sing, rocking back and forth in rhythm, cradling a bloody knife.

SEVENTY-ONE

I SWALLOWED AIR AND BLINKED, STRUGGLING TO STAY CON-
scious. Evie huddled silently over her dripping knife. "Somebody's knockin'." I heard her clear, strong voice. "Lord, it's the
devil. Will you look at him?"

Where was Molly? Or Woods? I grunted and pushed to get
back up onto my elbows and look around, made it only halfway.
I tried to say Evie's name, to ask her to go get help, but couldn't
make a sound. Then I saw a figure in black boots, rumpled
skirt, and pink sweater, lying on the floor behind her.

I remember letting my head drop on to Evie's lap. Her face
was calm, almost pretty. "I've heard about him, but I never
dreamed," she sang, "he'd have blue eyes and blue jeans . . ."

When I reached for the knife, she surrendered it without re-
sistance. But it was heavy. I couldn't hold it and heard it clatter
to the floor.

"Mommy?"

Molly? Was that Molly? Where? I couldn't talk, could barely
breathe. Evie regarded me indifferently as she continued her
song. "He must have tapped my telephone line . . ." I felt myself
fading. Falling. Where was Molly? I opened my eyes and saw a
small angel beside me, holding my hand. With a final effort, I
took the small hand and reached for Evie's, connecting them,
but I couldn't hold my head up anymore, couldn't talk. My head

banged the floor as I fell back. "He must have known I'm spendin' my time alone . . . Somebody's knockin' . . ."

Dropping, letting go, I couldn't be certain whether Evie understood, whether she would take Molly and go for help or sit singing until someone wandered by.

SEVENTY-TWO

KEVIN FERGUSON WAS JUST BEGINNING TO COLLECT THE breakfast trays when a goose-bump-raising, ear-splitting, high-pitched howl zoomed past him and down the hall. It seemed to come through the wall, from the plaster.

Kevin saw the security door standing open and stepped war-ily through it toward the noise. As he rounded the corner, his jaw dropped. The big catatonic one was walking toward him in a bloodstained sweatsuit, carrying a child. A blood-covered child. Kevin called out for a nurse. "Hey—nurse? Anyone? I need help here!" Somehow, the huge psychotic woman had got-ten her hands on a kid. And Lord knew what she'd done to her. Kevin's knees turned soggy; his stomach flipped. The woman approached him, sleeves rolled up, cradling the child in her strong, tattooed arms.

Kevin reached into his pocket to beep for help, but the woman moved suddenly, kicking the beeper out of his hand, dislocating his thumb. He backed up to the security doors, but before he could step through and lock them, she kicked again. Kevin flew backward through the door into the stainless steel cart, knocking it over, sending trays and dishes and leftover food crashing to the floor.

The day shift had just begun, and two nurses in Unit 8 around the corner had just come on duty when they heard the racket and came running with an orderly. Kevin Ferguson saw them standing over him and heard them ask what had happened, what had caused all the mess and commotion. Dazed, he told them about the patient and the little girl. They called the security guard; getting no answer, they set off the emergency alarm and went off to search the area. Aching and bruised, thumb and belly throbbing, Kevin stumbled to his feet to help. But no one found any sign of the woman or the child. They were gone.

Down the hall, though, Kevin and the others did find some other people. Locked in a utility closet, they discovered a chloroformed orderly. Near the security door, they found the art therapist, stabbed in the back. And in the nursing station, the night nurse and an aide lay under the desk, gagged, their hands and legs bound together. As he limped along through the carnage, it dawned on Kevin that every single room was empty. The patients—the most violent psychotics in the Institute— were gone. What the hell had happened that morning? Had there been a damned revolution?

Mystified, Kevin reached the end of the hall and was about to give up his search when he got to the catatonic's room. Stepping inside, he let out an involuntary scream. It wasn't the blood-stained pink sweater beside the commode that spooked him; it was what lay on top of it. It turned out to be just a wig, but at first glance it looked like a giant dead brown rat.

SEVENTY-THREE

OF COURSE, I WAS AWARE OF NONE OF THAT. I HEARD ABOUT Kevin Ferguson later, when they told me that Phillip Woods had escaped. Wounded, his pink sweater sliced and blood-soaked, he'd left a trail of blood from Evie's room through the hall, down the back stairs, and out into the snow. There, like the man who'd spilled it, the trail had disappeared. So had Rupert's car, although it had been found hours later, empty, crashed into a telephone pole on South Street near the Schuylkill River. But I didn't know any of that. Not yet.

The first thing I really remembered was surprise at opening my eyes. Convinced that I'd died, I was amazed that pain still seared my ribs. And I was indignant that death should hurt.

Then, looking around, I realized that, unless heaven or hell was an emergency room, I hadn't died, at least not yet. There were tubes in my nostrils, and some green-masked person was leaning over behind me, hurting me. I protested, pulling away, emitting something between a yelp and a groan. More eyes, another green mask darted above my head. A voice muffled through the mask welcomed me back, apologizing because I'd felt that.

"Tell her I'm almost through," said a voice, and the second mask reported that the doctor was almost through. Another jab, stab, searing scrape, and tug. My nails dug into my palms, but I couldn't move. My arms, apparently, had been strapped down. I looked around. IV bottle, green masks, green walls. This was not hell, I told myself. I was in a hospital because I'd been stabbed by Woods, and because I'd survived. And Molly?

Where was Molly?

I struggled to turn over and sit up. Was she okay? I'd left her with Evie. I tried to speak, but no one was listening. Hands, and now one, two, a third green body held on to me. I squirmed to get their attention, tried to tell them to listen to me. I needed to find out where Molly was.

"Wait," I said. "Just a second—"

"Hold her still. Don't let her move."

The hands tightened, pressing me down. I struggled and shouted, but they seemed not to hear. The more I tried to talk, the more they resisted listening.

"Relax, Zoe," a mask said. It sounded female, soothing. "Everything's going to be okay." Why wouldn't she answer me? Had something happened to Molly?

Another stab, this time in my arm, and a moment later I decided to lie back and rest. Still, I fought to stay awake, my ears straining to hear Molly's voice. In seconds, though, the pain lifted and my thoughts muddled. My questions became less urgent. Fading, I couldn't manage to study the eyes above the masks, couldn't be sure none of them was Phillip Woods wearing a new disguise.

SEVENTY-FOUR

SUSAN? SUSAN WAS TALKING TO ME, OR, NO, NOT TO ME. TO other people. Talking about a man dressed as a woman. And something else, about Beverly Gardener. But I couldn't hear what. And she said no one could question Zoe Hayes; Zoe Hayes was far too weak.

I listened for Molly, strained to hear her, but couldn't. Her voice wasn't there. Why not? Where was she? My eyes wouldn't open, lips wouldn't budge. A few times, I heard a man. Nick? Wasn't he dead? I listened closely, aware that if I could hear a dead man speak, I must be dead, too. Or lingering in a place where voices echoed like dreams and dreams like voices. Drifting, I couldn't distinguish real from imagined, alive from dead.

Then there were more than just sounds. Hands touched me. Held my fingers. Rested on my arm. Whose hands? Too big, too heavy to be Molly's. But I couldn't hold on to my thoughts, couldn't connect them, so I let go of my questions and once more slipped away.

SEVENTY-FIVE

WHEN MY EYES OPENED AGAIN, BRIGHT LIGHT BLINDED THEM. Squinting, I saw a head silhouetted by brightness. The face was unfocused and the head swollen. Swollen? No, bandaged. And it was Nick's. Damn, I thought. I'm dead after all. He's come for me. The way people say that someone who's died comes to get you, to take you to the Light. I squinted harder. The bright light began to resemble a window, and sunshine peeked through curtains behind Nick's head. But Nick had been bludgeoned to death at the Institute. So he couldn't be here. I was dreaming again, must not have opened my eyes after all. I told the dream to go away. It didn't. So I told the face out loud, in muffled words from a dry mouth.

"Gwey." The face refused to obey. Instead, it smiled, leaned over, and kissed me on the mouth.

The kiss was warm, and I could smell Nick. And antiseptics. I could feel his breath on my face. Apparently, he wasn't dead, and neither was I. In fact, he whispered a thank-you, saying that I'd saved his life. The ambulance I'd ordered had arrived. The EMTs had gone to Beverly' office, just as I'd told the 911 operator. They'd found them both there. Nick and Beverly.

Nick talked slowly, mouthing words carefully, and I wondered if his brain had been damaged, but he didn't say. He told me that he had a nasty gash and a concussion, but he was recuperating. Beverly was also expected to survive. Woods had

beaten her badly; she'd be hospitalized for a while. All the patients were back in their rooms. Evie'd been found walking
along the train tracks, singing and barefoot, headed toward Center City. I'd been found at the entrance to Section 5, Evie's blanket draped over me.

And Molly? Where was Molly? Why didn't he tell me? Nick
told me I'd need a lot of rest; I'd bled a lot. He said the knife had
slashed long and deep, nearly puncturing my lung. He went on
about how sorry he was, how it was all his fault. I listened, waiting for him to mention Molly. But he didn't. Not one word.

"Whzzmllee?" I asked him. My tongue wouldn't move,
seemed glued to the floor of my mouth.

"Don't try to talk, darling." Darling? He touched my face. I
was furious. What was wrong with him? What had happened to
Molly? I had to see her. Who was watching her?

I mustered my strength to articulate another question. "Wehz-
mawlee?"

This time, I knew he understood me. His eyes lit. "Molly? At
Susan's. We thought it best if she didn't see you until you were
conscious."

I closed my eyes, warding off tears. Molly was at Susan's.

"Howshee?"

"She's a trouper. Worried about her mother. But a patient—
the one we found on the train tracks? She took Molly to the art
room. Get this—she even got paper and crayons out for her.
Molly was fine—"

"Evie," I breathed.

"What was that, honey?"

Tears spilled. I couldn't help it. Evie had rescued Molly, had
taken her to the art room, a place she thought of as safe. Thank
God. They were both okay. My skin ached to hug my daughter,
but I'd see her soon. And Nick was alive. And so was I. Slowly,
cautiously, I let this information sink in, feeling the glow of it

spread through my body. One by one, my muscles untensed, relaxed by the knowledge that Woods was gone. That Molly and I would soon be together, home again. Safe inside.

Nick sat beside me, coaxing me to sleep. Promising to stay with me. His voice was deep and rhythmic, like waves. I had lots of questions, but I was too tired to ask them. Instead, I stared at Nick's living face and the light behind his blue eyes until my own eyes burned. Then, when I trusted that if I shut them, they'd open again, I let them close.

SEVENTY-SIX

THE HOSPITAL RELEASED ME THE NEXT DAY. WE HAD CHRIST-
mas dinner with Nick and Susan's family. Susan outdid herself,
preparing a feast of duckling in cherry sauce and wild rice. Nick
played the jolly saint bearing gifts: a new robe, sweater, and diamond earrings for me; for Molly, a bicycle, a jigsaw puzzle, and
a stuffed ape larger than she was. He'd even bought gifts for Susan's family and signed both our names to the cards.

For me, Molly's smile was the best gift of all. I watched her
for signs of anxiety or trauma, but though she didn't want to
talk about what had happened at the Institute, she seemed to be
amazingly fine. Soon after the Tooth Fairy left a dollar under her
pillow, another tooth loosened. She ate well, played hard, and,
except for some nightmares, slept soundly.

Michael stopped by Christmas Eve, dripping concern and
prepared for a fight. I handed him the ring without comment.
Baffled, speechless, he wrote me a check. I accepted it, but the
fact was that I wanted him to have the ring. It mattered to him;
to me it was just an object, pretty to look at, nothing more. As
he left, Michael thanked me and asked, "You okay, Zoe? You
don't seem quite yourself." Of course, he was right. I wasn't
quite myself, at least not the self he'd known.

Over the holidays, Nick spent more and more time with us.
We talked about what had happened; he explained that after the
trauma of Charlie's death he'd wanted to protect us from the

corralling of Phillip Woods. He swore that whatever had passed between him and Beverly Gardener had been purely professional. I neither believed nor disbelieved him. And I never mentioned my resemblance to his wife, never asked if he'd killed her. Beverly Gardener and Nick's marriage were beyond my concern. I moved ahead tentatively, hour by hour, day by day, accepting that truth was elusive, indifferent to how it might be grasped, represented, or perceived.

When she could be moved, Beverly Gardener went off to a swank Palm Beach clinic to recover. From her hospital bed, she signed another book contract and had her agent arrange to syndicate her radio program nationwide. She was negotiating for a television show. When and if she came back to work, it would not be quietly.

Days passed into weeks. The pace of life picked up, began to feel almost normal. But not quite. There was still no sign of Phillip Woods, and I watched for him routinely, ready for him to spring out of a closet or from under the bed. Phillip Woods had become the bogeyman, haunting but elusive. Aside from that, loss weighed heavily—Charlie, all those poor women. Life was altered, would never be the same.

When Molly slept, I sometimes wandered the house, searching for signs, for some place or point to connect to. But I was unhinged. Not long ago, a woman had lived there with her daughter. A man had shared her bed. But that woman, like the nannies, had vanished. The child was still there, her books and flannel bunny. Even the man had returned. The furnishings remained—her paintings, her purple sofa, even her cursed StairMaster. But these were props. Illusions. The place was a house full of tricks that made it seem that a real woman with a real life lived there.

I knew better. I didn't feel real. Whatever defined me was external. From the outside, I was a friend, a mom, a neighbor, a therapist, an ex-wife, a lover. Inside, underneath, I was vacant. Blank. Who was I? Who was I to myself?

I had no idea. But whoever I was, I was my own companion as I walked in circles, centered in a homespun web. At times a howl, or something like it, swelled silently inside my belly, my chest. I didn't know why or what kind of howl it was, only that it was my howl, something I could release or keep. Something real and known only to me. Something, maybe the only thing, I owned.

For days and weeks, recuperating, I paced the floors, walked from room to room, looking for something I couldn't find. Nick was often there, sleeping on the sofa, resting in the chair, cooking forty different flavors of spaghetti. I made myself cups of decaf, felt the steam, inhaled it deeply. The howl was building, battling to burst from my lungs. No, I told myself. I would not let it go. Not yet. I would hold on to it and wait, letting it grow inside me. I swallowed cups of murky hot liquid, washed the howl back down, and looked out the window as if life were normal, as if I were calm.

Charlie's empty house returned my gaze. His worried eyes peered forlornly from basement windows. I met his eyes but couldn't comfort him. It would take time for Charlie's spirit to find peace.

Nor would peace come easily to me. I watched for Phillip Woods, always on alert, unable to relax. Peace, I realized, wouldn't knock at my door or ring the bell. No. If I were ever to get it, whoever I was, whatever I was made of, I'd have to go out and find it on my own.

SEVENTY-SEVEN

IT WAS TUESDAY MORNING, LATE IN JANUARY. I'D GONE BACK to work a few days before and was waiting at the door for Angela, who was late. As soon as she arrived, I'd have to rush off.

Molly was still in her pajamas on the sofa, reading *Amelia Bedelia* aloud to her dolls. Outside, the sun was trying to break through heavy blue clouds. Blackened crusts of snow lined the curbs, and someone was parking a big white van in front of Phillip Woods's house, obscuring my view of the FOR SALE sign.

Phillip Woods. The man had worn tortoiseshell glasses, a cashmere coat, and tasseled shoes. He'd claimed to know celebrities; his handshake had been soft. It still seemed impossible that he'd attacked Beverly, much less killed the security guard, several other women he'd become obsessed with, the nannies, and who knew how many others? Then again, maybe he hadn't killed the nannies. No one knew for sure who the Nannynapper was. Officially, the police still named Charlie. Unofficially, they suspected Woods. He'd had access to Charlie's tools and basement and to each of the victims, and he'd had that recurring problem with "impostors"—which gave him means, opportunity and a possible motive.

Not a lot of effort was spent looking for the truth, though, since both suspects were dead. For weeks now, no nannies had disappeared—well, one, but her ex-boyfriend was suspected in that. The neighborhood was quiet again, if not the same. Life went on.

Meantime, where was Angela? She was fifteen minutes late. Molly held her book up to show the pictures to her dolls before turning the page. I leaned out the front door, looked up and down the frosty street, saw passing cars, pedestrians hurrying on their way to work, Victor coming out his front door. No Angela. What could have happened? Why hadn't she called?

Wait a second. Victor? I looked again. Sure enough, across the street, Victor had opened his gate and was rushing down the street, disappearing behind a parked SUV. My mouth fell open. Victor? How was that possible? Victor was outside?

He reappeared at the other end of the SUV. I blinked, but he didn't disappear. I'd never actually had a good look at Victor before, only glimpses. He was taller than I'd have imagined, and lanky, but the man definitely looked like Victor. He had Victor's shaggy black hair, Victor's pasty white skin. As he came across the street, I could see his face. There was no question. The guy was definitely Victor. Except that it couldn't be; Victor never left his house. Never. Not in years. Victor was so phobic he couldn't take his trash to the curb; neighbors had to carry it from his door. Victor never went outside. Ever. But there he was. Why? What could possibly make him come out now?

"Molly?" I called. "I'm going out front to wait for Angela. I'll be right back."

" 'Kay." She didn't look up from her book.

I waited until he'd crossed the street. He kept looking over his shoulder, left, then right, then left again, as if making sure no one was following. Or watching? When he stepped out of the line of sight, I went outside and down the steps. Where was he? He'd been headed toward the pair of newly renovated

townhomes on my side of the street. But they were still unoccu-
pied, not even finished. Why would he be going there?

Maybe he wanted to buy one. To move. Or invest. But it
didn't matter why. After all, Victor had every right to cross the
street. It was none of my business. Still, I couldn't help but wonder. Why would Victor venture outdoors to go to an empty
house? From the bottom of my front steps, I saw him pass
through the front gate of one of the new houses. Casually, as if
out for a stroll, I wandered over. No one was around. No workers. No one. The place seemed abandoned.

It made no sense. Maybe Victor had recovered. Maybe he'd
overcome his agoraphobia. Maybe, as part of his recovery, he actually went outside and took walks every day—after all, I hadn't
been watching him. Even so, why would he go into an empty
house? I told myself to mind my own business, to stop staring at
the windows and the open gate. I was about to go home when
the front door burst open and out flew Jake. Jake? But what
about Victor? Was he still inside?

Jake hurried down the front walk so preoccupied that he
didn't look where he was heading. If I hadn't said hi to him,
he'd have barreled right into me.

"Christ," he exclaimed, hopping sideways.

I smiled. "Sorry—"

"My fault, no problem," he muttered, still moving.

"I haven't seen you lately," I went on. "How've you been?"

He glanced back at the house he'd just left, ahead at the
street, shifting from foot to foot as if running in place. "Busy.
Haven't been around much—I got some jobs in Jersey, so I'm
wrapping things up here."

Ask about Victor, I told myself. Ask if he's seen him. But Jake
had gone on his way, calling over his shoulder for me to take it
easy. "See ya," he yelled.

Strange, I thought. What was Victor doing in that house? Did

Jake even know he was there? And why had Jake been so un-friendly and unsettled? Something wasn't right.

Mind your own business, I told myself as I watched Jake hurry down the street and climb into his truck. Go home. But I didn't go home. I stood on the sidewalk, thinking. What was bothering me? Something about Jake was rattling me. What was it? Think, I told myself. Figure it out.

Angela disliked him; he made her uneasy. And what did I re-ally know about him? Nothing, really. Nothing at all.

I reminded myself that Molly was home alone—I had to get back. But I didn't go. I stood on the sidewalk, staring at the house. Maybe I'd just check inside. Pop in briefly, quietly, see what Victor was up to, and leave. I'd be back before Molly even knew I was gone.

I watched Jake start up his truck and drive away. When he'd rounded the corner, I swung the gate and stepped onto the property. Trespassing. But the front door was open—it wasn't like I was breaking in. I was just a neighbor, making sure an-other neighbor was okay.

I glanced around the interior. Unpainted drywall. A half-built fireplace. Exposed wiring. An unfinished stairway to the second floor. No Victor. Quickly, I went into what would become the kitchen. From there, a second stairway led down to the base-ment. There was a light on; maybe someone was down there, working. Or maybe it was Victor. I couldn't hear him and wasn't about to go look—I'd already gone too far, had no business be-ing there. I didn't want anyone to catch me snooping. I'd just leave. No harm done. Sneak out the way I'd snuck in.

I turned, stepping away from the staircase. That was when I noticed the hallway. The small scarlet puddle clotting on the hardwood floor.

SEVENTY-EIGHT

THE BLOOD WAS FRESH, STICKILY WET. THIN SCARLET SMEARS led to my feet; smudges and droplets continued down the stairs.

Oh my God—Victor! I ran down the steps, following a path of blood drops. At the bottom, though, the path abruptly ended. I scanned the empty basement, saw nobody. A toolbox at my feet. An empty worktable. An electric bulb hanging from ceiling wires. Exposed ceiling beams, concrete blocks, a wood-paneled wall. No Victor.

I stood still, not breathing, listening for moaning or panting or any signs of life. Nothing.

"Victor?" I called softly, knowing he wasn't there. I could see that he wasn't. "Victor?"

He had to be here. Unless I was mistaken. Maybe Victor had gone out the back door. Or up to the second floor. Maybe the blood wasn't even Victor's; maybe it was Jake's—he might have had an accident—that might be why he was hurrying away—

But if so, why was it smeared on the steps as if someone had been dragged into the basement?

I looked at the paneled wall where the path stopped. There was a patch of blood, not just drops, beside it. Why? I pictured Jake tugging a bloody Victor down the stairs, resting him against the wall at the bottom. That would explain the patch. But then what? What had Jake done with him? Where could Victor be?

I walked around the basement, looking again for a door, a

crawl space, a closet, a trunk. Nothing. Just an empty expanse of space with concrete walls. Except for one. The one at the bottom of the steps was wood. Why?

I didn't know much about construction. In fact, I knew nothing about it. But I tapped the paneled wall and heard a hollow sound. I tapped harder, above my head, down at my knees. I walked from one end of the wall to the other, knocking, hearing a reply of vacant space from the other side. And I knew. Victor was back there. Jake had put him there. And I had to get him out.

I shoved the wall. I pushed and banged it. It didn't budge. I called out Victor's name and got no answer. Go home, I told myself. Call Nick. Let the police take care of this.

"Victor," I told the wall, "I'm going to get help. I'll be back."

Turning to go, though, I saw the toolbox lying at my feet. I looked at the wall again, saw screws embedded in the wood. It took a few minutes to unscrew the center panel, but when I finished, surprisingly, almost effortlessly, I'd dislodged an entire segment of the wall. It moved easily to the side, opening to a secret room, releasing the odor of something foul.

SEVENTY-NINE

A DIM LIGHT INSIDE REVEALED A CUBICLE ABOUT THE SIZE OF my bathroom. The walls were covered with art—some kind of textured work. Collages? The floor was covered with Victor.

His legs were splayed; his head remained in shadows. I knelt beside him, vaguely noticing the garbage bags lining the floor. I felt his throat and found a pulse.

"Victor," I kept saying, "wake up. Please wake up."

He didn't stir. His face was masked with blood. Don't move him, I remembered. Go get help. I turned to go, but stopped. What was that form huddled in the shadows? Was someone lying there, not moving? I dreaded what I'd see, but I made myself look closer. Angela lay on a foam mattress, tied up, motionless, unconscious or dead.

EIGHTY

HER HEART WAS BEATING, BUT HER SKIN WAS COOL, THE TEM-
perature of basement air. Her neck slumped to the side, loose
like rubber. Jake. Jake had taken her, had taken all of them. Jake
was the Nannynapper. Not Charlie, not Phillip Woods. Jake had
watched the nannies on the street, selecting his victims. He'd
seen Angela on her way to work, had trapped her and taken her
here, just like the others. My God. Why hadn't I known? I
hadn't even suspected him. Nobody had. Jake had been around
the neighborhood so long, he'd become a fixture. As unnotice-
able as a streetlight. Camouflaged by his obvious presence.

I had to go call Nick. Get an ambulance. Find help. I spun
around, inhaling a rotten stench. Don't panic, I told myself.
Just go.

I took the steps two at a time and ran through the kitchen
into the hall. I headed for the front door, was almost there.

Maybe I heard a thump. Maybe I even felt a blow. But I had
no memory of either. In fact, I remembered nothing, not even
darkness.

EIGHTY-ONE

I WAS BLIND. I STARED AT BLACKNESS, TRYING TO FIND A CON-
trast, a shape, an outline of anything. Nothing. Not a shadow,
not a shade. My head throbbed, pulsing white pain. I tried to
call out, but something—a rag?—was stuffed into my mouth,
gagging me. I couldn't move my arms or legs, turned my head
slightly, felt a cloth draping my face—a blindfold? Maybe I
wasn't blind. I turned my head again and the cloth slipped
slightly, just enough to let in a sliver of yellow light—yes, thank
God—I wasn't blind. But why couldn't I move? What had
happened?

I tried again but couldn't lift my arms. My elbows were
caught—tied to my body. In fact, all of me was tied. I couldn't
lift my legs, couldn't sit up. Oh my God, I remembered. Jake.
The basement room. He must have found me.

Pain raged in my head. I turned it too quickly; waves of nausea
rocked me. Don't throw up, I thought. You'll choke on the gag.

I lay still, waiting for the nausea to pass. I nodded my head
carefully, working the blindfold up little by little, rubbing it
against the mattress. I slid the blindfold higher and higher until,
if I raised my chin, I could see a slice of the wall. I recognized
the paneling. I was in the basement of the empty house, in the
hidden room.

I turned my head slightly to the left, nausea again. Smelled something rotten. Slowly, I craned my neck all the way to the right. Angela was there, lying limply on the mattress. But where was Victor? I strained to lift my head and look around, but I didn't see him. It took a moment to realize why my mattress was so lumpy and narrow and why, at my waist, it divided in two.

EIGHTY-TWO

MY HEAD THROBBED. I MANAGED TO ROLL OFF VICTOR AND, leaning against him, survey the room. Green garbage bags coated the floor. The kind they'd found the nannies in. And the door was screwed back in place.

The gag made it hard to draw in enough air, and what I did get reeked. Breathe slowly, I told myself. Find a way to get rid of the damned gag. But how?

I twisted my arms, trying to get free. Exertion made breathing more difficult. Breathe, I told myself. Keep breathing. I worked my head against Victor's shoulder, inching the blindfold up over my eyes until they were both free.

Under the dim lightbulb, I wondered about the artwork on the wall, why Jake would hang it in a room only to wall it off, sealed up and tomblike. Oh my God. Was that Jake's plan? To wall us up until we died here? The walls edged in closer. I panted, pulled, pressed, and stretched, but got nowhere.

I thought of Molly and realized I had no sense of time. How long had I been gone? Had I left her minutes ago? Hours? Days? Oh God. Molly. I'd left her alone, not told her where I was going. Was she all right? Did she think I'd gone off to work without saying good-bye? Oh God. My mind raced, ricocheting from thought to thought. I pictured Molly alone, waiting with her dolls for Angela, for me, for somebody. Would she wait alone all day until Nick arrived for dinner?

Make a plan, I begged myself. But nothing, no plan came to mind.

Again I turned my hands and—twisting, rotating—pulled my wrists apart as far as I could. Which wasn't far, but there was some slack. I kept the pattern up, determined to get back to my daughter, tugging and rolling, twisting and pressing, trying to slide one hand down and away from the other. My wrists burned, scraped raw, and sweat or blood—something wet— made my skin slippery, until finally one thumb moved down through the plastic rope that tied me and got jammed. I couldn't move it up or down, and when I tried, pain shot up my hand and through my arm. But it didn't matter if I tore my damned hand off; I wasn't going to stop pulling until the rope was off. I turned, scraped, stretched, and ripped my skin. I told myself, you're made of water, ninety-some percent water. Just pour through the rope. Think slimy. Think thin. Think about Molly and getting home. And finally, miraculously, my jammed hand slid a bit over the knuckle of my thumb. I twisted and pulled and it moved a bit more. And then my whole hand came out. One, then both. My hands were free.

I pulled off the blindfold and undid the rag that was stuffed into and around my mouth. Plastic yellow rope still tied my elbows to my body and held my legs to the mattress. My vision was blurred and the light was dim, but I could see. My wrists were raw and oozing blood. Angela and Victor hadn't moved.

Victor didn't respond when I nudged him.

"Angela," I whispered. "Can you hear me?"

She didn't move. I noticed she'd done her nails again. Each was two-toned, a combination of light and dark shades. I wished my nails were that long, able to dig in, separate fibers and untie. But mine were short stubs, and I had to work the rope with blood-and-sweat-slippery hands, slowly, bending elbows and stretching fingers to reach knots that clung tight. Each knot took eons. But methodically, breathing evenly, I loosened the rope around my arms enough to reach the one around my legs. When that was loosened, I reached down under the rope and untied my ankles.

When I tried to stand, the walls tilted and spun. I sat and leaned back against the wall, not focusing, waiting for the room to hold still, the nausea to pass. Gradually, the whirling slowed. The room settled into a hover, ready to take off again if I jarred my head. Slowly, carefully, I raised myself in increments until I was standing. When I had my balance, I stepped over to Angela, untied her hands, touched her forehead, her throat, felt a weak pulse. Thank God.

"Angela?" I whispered. "Can you hear me? Angela—"

She quivered, stirring. I waited, held her hand, repeated her name. But Angela didn't seem to hear.

Listening for Jake, I put my head against the wall, beside the collage. The light was dim, so it took a while for me to realize what it was made of, why the air was reeking so. I saw what the textured pieces were; one still wore a shiny silver ring.

EIGHTY-THREE

T<small>EARS STREAKED MY FACE, BLURRED MY VISION.</small> I <small>WAS FRANTIC.</small>
I backed away, flailing.

Look for a weapon, I told myself. But what? Nothing was there but two unconscious people and a grotesque collage. Upstairs, I thought I heard movement. Footsteps. Was Jake still here? Had he heard me moving around? I listened but heard nothing. Had he gone away? Or was he outside the wall, listening? Think, I told myself. Maybe it's not even Jake. If it's not Jake, you'll get rescued. If it is, you can jump him, take him by surprise. You have nothing to lose. Knock the wall down. Ram it and kick it and run like hell. And so I did.

EIGHTY-FOUR

THE RAMMING AND KICKING MADE A RACKET, BUT JAKE DID NOT appear at the top of the stairs. I steadied myself, grabbing the banister along the unfinished steps, and pulled myself up toward daylight.

I expected to feel Jake's meaty hand on my shoulder or my throat any moment, to be pulled back down to his closet of horror. Finally I was at the top step, the door. I turned the handle and thrust myself through the open door.

The light through the window was blinding. I blinked, saw a bracelet of blood clotting on my wrists and hands, the unfinished kitchen. I slowed, seeing and hearing no one. Jake must have gone.

I remembered the Institute, running from Phillip Woods. I could do this. A piece of cake. I was as good as out the door. Molly'd be waiting at home. I'd be there in minutes, in seconds. I was already in the living room, rounding the corner to the hall. The front door was only a few steps away when it opened.

"Yo."

Jake. There was no sense running. His hand grabbed my wrist, yanking me to him. I cried out in pain.

"Hai-ya!"

The voice sounded childlike, not like my own. Jake was holding my wrist, twisting it.

"Hai-ya!" I heard again, certain this time that the voice was not mine. Molly? Jake's knee buckled and he went down, almost pulling me with him. Stumbling, he reached out to balance, releasing me, and his knife clattered to the floor. I managed to kick it away just as Jake reached for it.

"Fuck," he yelled. Molly was behind him, kicking Jake's ankle, the back of his knee.

"Mommy," she screamed. "Did you see me?"

I was stunned, trying to process what was happening. Molly kicked again. I saw the knife across the room, gleaming on the hardwood floor.

"You little shit," Jake growled, trying to get hold of Molly. "I'll kick your sorry ass."

"I don't think so." I leaped at him. No, I flew, fingers extended, aiming at Jake's eyes. He turned his head away, dodging, so I just poked one eye. Still, he bellowed, writhing with pain, while Molly kept kicking the hell out of the back of his leg. Jake turned in circles, half blinded, trying to catch me or her, and I had the image of a pig roasting on a spit but felt no pity. I slammed my boot into his privates. I kicked so hard my toes hurt. Jake curled into a whimpering ball on the floor, reaching, trying to crawl, even then, for the knife. I ran to pick it up and held it high, ready to strike.

"Molly?" I panted, reaching for her. "My God, sweetheart. Are you okay?"

She ran over and snuggled against me. "I got him. Just like Angela showed me." She repeated her move, kicking the air to show how she'd toppled Jake. Then, chin wobbling, she burst into tears.

EIGHTY-FIVE

WITH HINDSIGHT, WHAT HAD HAPPENED SEEMED OBVIOUS. VICtor had been watching the street from his window for years. He knew everyone by sight. He'd seen Jake drag Angela into a vacant house, and he'd come running, heroically, defying his phobia, to rescue her. Jake, of course, had overpowered him and hidden him in the basement. Which is where I'd come in.

Molly, meantime, had followed me down the street. When I'd gone up the block, she'd trailed behind, watching me go into the house, waiting on the stoop next door. When she'd seen Jake go inside holding a butcher knife, she'd followed. And saved our lives.

Her picture was in the newspaper, minus two front teeth. She practiced her reading by searching the article for familiar words in the stories, "Superkid Kickboxes Nanny Killer" and "Kindergartner Nabs Nannynapper." She was even interviewed on television; Molly had a whole week of fame. And the Nannynapper was finally history.

Phillip Woods, however, remained at large, at least for a while. Late in February, some boys made a grisly discovery in the snow near the South Street Bridge. Woods's frozen body, still in a nurse's uniform, lay beside an old coal dock, almost invisible in the ice and mass of tall weeds along the Schuylkill River. After he'd crashed the stolen car, he'd apparently stumbled, bleeding and disoriented, to the dock, where he'd frozen or bled to death.

With Woods gone, breathing seemed easier. Slowly, the rhythm of life began to resume. Time passed. Each day, I took note of the dusk, confirmed that the sun lingered for a few more moments, that darkness was waning.

Molly was growing almost visibly. New teeth appeared; more came loose. Bored with jigsaw puzzles, she played computer games and still loved any craft that involved beads. She continued to amaze me with her insights and ability to take in stride events that knocked others off their feet.

Once again, I broke my New Year's resolution to work out on the StairMaster half an hour each day. It continued to lurk in the corner, taunting my conscience, but I found plenty of excuses to avoid it. At work, my caseload grew, but I looked in on Evie Kraus even on days when we had no sessions. She still sang—often her devil song, but also others. And she'd begun to draw subjects outside her direct view. She sketched stone houses, hilly landscapes. A tattooed woman standing at a bus stop. I thought her face looked softer, more peaceful than before.

Beverly Gardener went on a six-month leave of absence to recover and write her book. Agnes announced her early retirement.

When Angela regained consciousness, Joe asked her to marry him. The wedding was planned for October.

Victor's daring trip across the street had ended in an emergency room, where he panicked and had to be sedated so he could be treated. He went back into seclusion as soon as he got home. Molly and I began regularly bringing him casseroles, cakes, or lasagnas, convinced that with a little urging he might again emerge one day.

Michael called to borrow our crystal punch bowl for a party—after all, he said, it had been a wedding gift to us both. I knew he'd never return it, but I didn't mind. I told him okay, fine.

Susan managed to keep one of her clients out of jail; two were convicted of lesser charges. For their anniversary in January, she and Tim went to Europe for a week, leaving the kids with Bonita.

And Nick. Nick stayed around. He was part of our lives. Instead of doubting or questioning him, I let go, didn't worry about where we were headed or dwell on his past. I neither needed nor minded having a man to take care of me; even in his presence, I rode the days solo, one at a time.

Days became weeks, putting a cushion between us and the nannies, Charlie, and Jake. At dusk, I watched darkness settle onto the street. A solitary lightbulb glowed in Victor's upstairs window. Woods's blinking Santa was long gone; the new neighbor had put up awnings, drooping eyelids veiling the view. In the middle, the skeleton of Charlie's house released a hollow sigh and settled down for the night.

I listened to the hum of the refrigerator and the whoosh of occasional passing cars. Sooner or later, I knew, there might be an aftershock, a surge of anger. Or fear, or grief. Or maybe self-pity. But so far, nothing. Nothing. No feelings boiled over. I waited, alert, but felt completely neutral. Not empty, exactly. More like an idling engine. My heart was weightless, for now. But I knew better than to trust that lightness; it was only a passing phase.

As for Molly, she seemed unscathed by everything she'd been through. I watched closely for signs—behaviors like withdrawal or aggressiveness, sleeplessness or nightmares. But after a pizza, a bubble bath, and a good night's sleep, Molly seemed to bounce right back to her normal almost six-year-old self. She gave no indication that she'd been traumatized.

One day around Valentine's Day, she barreled into the kitchen, her blanket flying behind her. "Mommy, can I have a hot dog?"

Hugging her, I smelled sunshine in her curls. I felt a flutter, an unfamiliar tickle in my chest. The new year had begun; spring couldn't be far away. In just a matter of weeks, the ice would thaw. If I listened closely, even at that moment, I might be able to hear the sighs of snow melting, the exultation of water bursting free. Maybe I'd paint tonight.

"Sure." I got out buns and pickles, savoring the ease of our ordinary routine. I'd learned to take pleasure in small moments.

Maybe there would be no aftershock. Maybe just this quiet change. Nothing earth-shattering, but still a change.

"Can we melt cheese on them?"

"Cheese?" I wondered if we had any. And how old it might be, and where. Yes, there were some slices of American in the door of the fridge. I didn't remember buying cheese, but there it was.

Someone knocked at the door. I almost didn't answer, didn't want to be disturbed. I was enjoying our quiet privacy.

"Mommy, someone's here." Molly ran to the door. "Can I get it?"

"No. You know the rule." She waited at the door, hand on the knob. I looked through the peephole and saw Nick's sky-colored eyes. He knocked again.

"Somebody's knockin'," Molly began to sing. "Should I let him in?"

"What?"

She didn't answer, just kept singing, swaying to the tune. "Lord, it's the devil. Would you look at him?"

Shivers ran down my back. She was singing Evie's song. "Where did you learn that?"

She shrugged, grinning, holding on to the doorknob. "Somebody's knockin'. Should I let him in?"

Of course. Evie had rescued her; Evie would have been singing her song. Molly had heard it then, and the knocking reminded her. She kept singing. "But I never dreamed . . . he'd have blue eyes and blue jeans . . ."

Nick knocked again.

For a moment, I watched him, his blue eyes magnified, distorted by the peephole. Then, taking Molly's hand from the knob, I opened the door.